W9-AHG-887

SF FLINT ERIC
Flint, Eric.
Pyramid power /
ALPA

0 1 NOV 2009

PYRAMID POWER

Baen Books by Eric Flint & Dave Freer
Rats, Bats & Vats
The Rats, The Bats & The Ugly

Pyramid Scheme
Pyramid Power

With Mercedes Lackey:
The Shadow of the Lion
This Rough Magic
also in this series:
A Mankind Witch by Dave Freer

Baen Books by Dave Freer
The Forlorn

Baen Books by Eric Flint
Ring of Fire series:
1632 by Eric Flint
1633 by Eric Flint & David Weber
1634: The Baltic War by Eric Flint & David Weber
Ring of Fire ed. by Eric Flint
1634: The Galileo Affair by Eric Flint & Andrew Dennis
1634: The Bavarian Crisis by Eric Flint & Virginia DeMarce (forthcoming)
1635: The Ram Rebellion by Eric Flint and Virginia DeMarce et al.
1635: The Cannon Law by Eric Flint & Andrew Dennis
Grantville Gazette ed. by Eric Flint
Grantville Gazette II ed. by Eric Flint
Grantville Gazette III ed. by Eric Flint
Ring of Fire II ed. by Eric Flint (forthcoming)

Joe's World series:
The Philosophical Strangler
Forward the Mage
(with Richard Roach)

Standalone titles:
Mother of Demons

Crown of Slaves
(with David Weber)

The Course of Empire
(with K.D. Wentworth)

Mountain Magic
(with Ryk E. Spoor, David Drake
& Henry Kuttner)

With David Drake:
The Tyrant

The Belisarius Series
with David Drake:
An Oblique Approach
In the Heart of Darkness
Destiny's Shield
Fortune's Stroke
The Tide of Victory
The Dance of Time

Edited by Eric Flint
The World Turned Upside Down
(with David Drake & Jim Baen)
The Best of Jim Baen's Universe

PYRAMID POWER

ERIC FLINT
DAVE FREER

Tulare County Library

PYRAMID POWER

This is a work of fiction. All the characters and events portrayed in this book are fictional, and any resemblance to real people or incidents is purely coincidental.

Copyright © 2007 by Eric Flint & Dave Freer

All rights reserved, including the right to reproduce this book or portions thereof in any form.

A Baen Books Original

Baen Publishing Enterprises
P.O. Box 1403
Riverdale, NY 10471
www.baen.com

ISBN 10: 1-4165-2130-5
ISBN 13: 978-1-4165-2130-3

Cover art by Bob Eggleton
Maps by Randy Asplund

First printing, August 2007

Distributed by Simon & Schuster
1230 Avenue of the Americas
New York, NY 10020

Library of Congress Cataloging-in-Publication Data

Flint, Eric.
    Pyramid power / by Eric Flint and Dave Freer.
        p. cm.
    "A Baen Books original"—T.p. verso.
    ISBN-10: 1-4165-2130-5
    ISBN-13: 978-1-4165-2130-3
    1. Life on other planets—Fiction. 2. Mythology, Norse—Fiction. I. Freer, Dave. II. Title.

    PS3556.L548P97 2007
    813'.54--dc22

                                                            2007015780

10 9 8 7 6 5 4 3 2 1

Pages by Joy Freeman (www.pagesbyjoy.com)
Printed in the United States of America

To Dorothy Hermine Bagnall
For whom we could not find Idun's apples

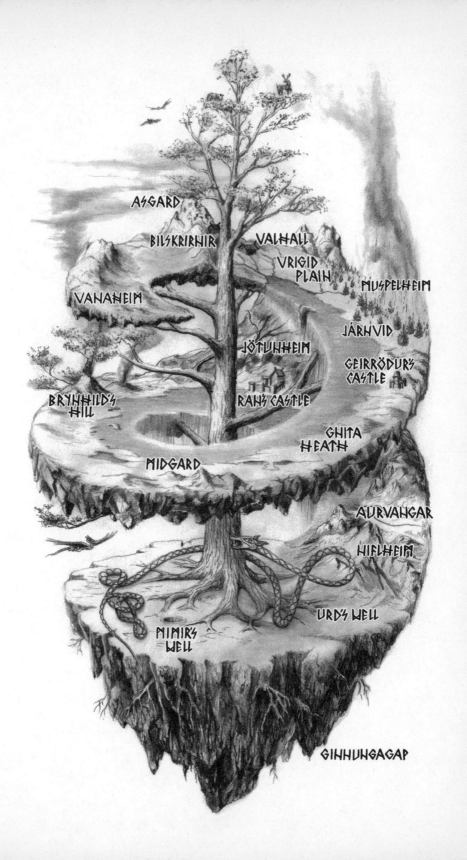

ASGARD

BILSKRIRNIR

VALHALL

VANAHEIM

VRIGID
PLAIN

MUSPELHEIM

JÁRNVID

JÖTUNHEIM

GEIRRÖDUR'S
CASTLE

BRYNHILD'S
HILL

RAN'S CASTLE

GHITA
HEATH

MIDGARD

AURVANGAR

HIFLHEIM

URD'S WELL

MIMIR'S
WELL

GINNUNGAGAP

PART 1

FOOLS RUSH IN

CHAPTER 1

ⓔⓔⓔⓔⓔ

Professor Miggy Tremelo, once a University of Chicago senior administrator and professor of High Energy Physics and now the head of the National Science Advisory Council, which was charged with investigating the alien Krim artifact, slammed the phone down. He'd always thought university bureaucracy and politics were tough, but he'd mastered them. He was well regarded in military research circles. His work at Nellis had him a security clearance from here to the middle of next week. It still hadn't prepared him for the new Pyramid Security Agency that the U.S. government had set up in the wake of the Krim pyramid crisis.

Alas—as had happened in times past—the administration had felt compelled to prove to the electorate that it was Doing Something, and Congress had fallen all over itself to comply with the President's proposals. Indeed, Congress had added any number of silly curlicues of its own.

The worst of it, from Miggy's viewpoint, had been the creation of a brand new Pyramid Security Agency to "oversee all national security issues involving the alien menace." The end result had been a ramshackle, hastily slapped-together new bureaucracy—just what the country *didn't* need. With, to make things perfect, a newly appointed director whose chief qualification for the post seemed to be nothing more than that Helen Garnett was more ambitious than Lucifer and had superb skills when it came to political infighting and backstabbing within the Beltway.

Needless to say, the existing security agencies had been exceedingly disgruntled by the situation. And, needless to say, had immediately retaliated when Garnett demanded they provide her with the required security personnel. No doubt some competent people had made the transfer, as well. But from what Miggy could see, the PSA had become a classic instance of what federal employees meant by the slang term "turkey farm." The CIA, the FBI and everyone up to and including the Coast Guard had found a great place to transfer every lackwit, goofball and loose screw in their ranks.

Without thinking, he turned his head and shouted: "Marie, help! I need coffee!"

But there was no clatter, no cheerful obscenity-laden reply from the outer office. Instead, rather timidly, a head peered around the door. Not Marie Jackson or Marie Jackson's style. "Sir?"

Miggy bit back his response. It was not Rachel Clements' fault that Marie wasn't in the front office. Rachel was just a temp with a great security clearance, who'd replaced Marie after she'd gone on sick leave. With no skills in the coffee-making department, unfortunately.

On the bright side, she was pleasant enough, unlike the troll out of Brothers Grimm the security establishment had thrust onto him last time, before he got Marie.

"Forget it, Rachel. Look, I'll need you to place two calls for me. Colonel Frank McNamara of the 101st, and Professor Jerry Lukacs. If you fail to get Jerry at his own number, try Dr. De Beer's apartment." He allowed himself a small smile. "It's just possible that he might be there."

She nodded. "Yes, sir. Mrs. Jackson called while you were on the other line to the PSA. She said she didn't want to waste her life on hold. She said to tell you that she and Lamont are coming in this morning. She said she needs to talk to you."

Miggy smiled. "Well, that's one piece of good news."

"She didn't sound too happy," said Clements doubtfully. "Not like herself at all."

Liz De Beer, Marine biologist, graduate of both Cape Town and Rhodes Universities (which had taught her a lot less than her time at sea as a scientific observer, especially about exple-tives), wondered just how she could deal with someone who was definitely not a morning person. She tended to wake up when it got light, and crash early. As long as she had the caffeine kick start, she was even reasonably good tempered in the morning. The man sleeping peacefully next to her, on the other hand, considered midday way too early and first light not a bad time to go to sleep.

Liz had to admit that was Jerry Lukacs' most serious fault, other than a major inability to speak anything but academese in public. Granted, he wasn't a beefcake—although he had built some impressive wiry muscle in the Mythworlds. Still, he was as solid as a rock when you needed him, and one of the few men she couldn't walk all over, mentally, physically, or in terms of courage. That had to be worth some tolerance of nocturnal behavior, she figured.

She decided she'd give him until 8:30. She was due another thrilling day with the U.S. Immigration and Naturalization Service. "*La migra*," as Sergeant Anibal Cruz called them.

The phone rang. That was possibly another call from the South African embassy. Funny, the South African government, who had been their usual unhelpful selves when she'd needed them, were falling over themselves to get her home when she didn't want to go. Jerry said that wasn't an African, but a worldwide phenomena. She wasn't sure that that was helpful information, but *la migra* were doing their best to prove him right.

Jerry hadn't even stirred, although the phone was an inch and a half from his ear. She reached over him and snagged it. "Hello. Liz De Beer speaking."

"I'm trying to reach Dr. Jerry Lukacs for Professor Tremelo," said the American midwest accent on the other end.

"Well, he's here," admitted Liz, "but actually speaking to him before he's had coffee is probably a lost cause. I can try, but you'd do better to call back in ten minutes." She knew that that was a little optimistic. "Ask Miggy if I can help."

There was a moment's silence. Then the woman said, "Please hold for Professor Tremelo."

"You'd think that by now I'd have managed to get it into my head that he's not an early riser," said Miggy Tremelo apologeti-cally. "Sorry. These Pyramid Security Agency idiots are turning my mind to cheese, to keep theirs company. I've already spent ten minutes getting nowhere fast this morning. The fact that we've been working in close proximity to the pyramid for the last two weeks, and we know what we're doing, is beyond that woman."

That woman had become Miggy Tremelo's all-purpose reference to Helen Garnett, the head of the PSA. "And without Marie," he said, almost whining, "I have to bull my own way to the top of the food chain."

"And here you stop part way up it again," said Liz cheerfully. "It's all right. I was going to wake him in the next ten minutes or so anyway. He just won't make much sense until the coffee has time to work on his speech centers. What can I do for you, or what can I have Jerry do for you, once I get him up?"

"I'm afraid I've got another battery of tests I need to have run on all the 'escapees.' And I wanted to see if Jerry could shed some more light on the inconsistencies in the myths that the Krim is creating."

"*Re*-creating is more like it," said Liz. "The Mythworlds seemed to derive their life from the myths in some way. But I'm sorry, I can't make it in to your office today. I need a visa extension, and I've got to spend the day in the offices of the INS. Why the Krim pyramid couldn't have landed on them instead of the University of Chicago's perfectly nice research library, I do not know."

"Because the Krim were using the location of the original atom bomb fission experiments as a target locator—and the INS had its meltdown sometime in the last century." She could practically hear Miggy grinding his teeth over the telephone.

"Damn it," he said. "Does nothing go smoothly? I had to do some serious straightening out with the officials from Fish and Wildlife about the dragons, and had to get someone to intervene with a petty official from the INS who wanted to have Bes arrested. I'm sorry, I didn't know you were having problems too. I'll see what can be arranged. A squad of paratroopers as an escort might work. Bes went in there with some of his new buddies from the WWF. I believe they found it easy to process his request. Look, if you just come in for an hour, I'll arrange some serious smoothing."

"It's a deal," said Liz, grinning at the thought of Bes confronting some petty official. He didn't really need WWF-size support, being, as he was, a dwarf-god from Egypt, Punt and Carthage.

He was his own army. "If I can wake the night owl we should be there in forty-five minutes."

"Good. I'm expecting Lamont and Marie too," said Tremelo.

Liz brightened at that. "Did he buy that stretch limo?"

A chuckle came down the line. "I know he used one to tender his resignation from the campus staff. So how is your arm, by the way?"

"Cast came off two days ago. I've kept it for the artwork," said Liz.

"It's probably the only serious attempt at Dali on a plaster cast I have ever seen," admitted Tremelo.

Two minutes later Liz set about the interesting task of waking Jerry. Like most non-morning people, he didn't believe that he was hard to wake.

"I'm afraid you don't have any choice about it, Sergeant," said the PSA senior agent. "You either come along or we take you along. Those are our instructions from the highest level. Ask your colonel." He jerked a rather scornful thumb at Sergeant Anibal Cruz's commanding officer. "But don't waste too much of my time. You've got five minutes to get your personal kit."

Anibal studied the man thoughtfully. "And you're threatening my wife and kids with *la migra*," he said, in a flat voice that would have worried someone less full of their own self-importance. The tone just bounced off the senior agent. It was a cool, overcast morning, and the jerk was wearing shades. He probably slept in them.

"I must strongly advise you against threatening dependents of U.S. service personnel," said Colonel McNamara, in a voice that could cut glass, and would have made it asses and elbows time with most of the men in his command. Cruz looked at the PSA agents. There were only seven of the Pissant suits. Three each, and they could argue about the remaining one. Out of respect for the Old Man's rank he'd let him kill the leftover.

Senior Agent Ledbetter gave McNamara a humorless smile. "Deportation of illegal aliens is not a threat, Colonel. It's our duty. There are serious discrepancies in their paperwork. We've got very little choice but to send them back to their country of origin."

"Unless I cooperate," said Cruz.

"No, Sergeant," said Ledbetter coolly. "You, and the Army, have very little choice but to cooperate. But if we have your fullest, most wholehearted cooperation, I'm sure that we can intervene. The PSA has been granted sweeping powers, as you know."

The colonel drew a deep breath. He was a dangerous color, for a man of his age. "I'm going to go and call General Brasno at the Pentagon. It seems I can't stop you 'requisitioning' my men. But I can damn well do something about this. We won't tolerate this blackmail. The Army looks after its dependents, Sergeant."

The PSA agent shrugged. "I have told you that the Alien Pyramid Security Act has been invoked for this project. Call your General, have him call Ms. Garnett—and then you might as well await your court-martial, Colonel."

"If you attempt to remove any women or children from this base I'll take my chances," said the colonel grimly. There was no back-down in that voice.

"Let me talk to my superiors," said the agent.

He walked off to use his cell phone. Two minutes later he came back. "They're to stay here, under PSA guard."

"You're placing them under house arrest," said McNamara flatly.

"Protective custody. Purely for their own safety, I assure you. I'll be leaving four of my men here now, to watch them in shifts. I suggest you quarter Corporal McKenna's wife here too."

Cruz looked at the colonel.

McNamara bit his lip. "Are you putting my men into a combat situation?"

"Isn't that what they get paid for?" asked the agent with just a hint of a sneer. "I'm not authorized to tell you what the PSA requires these men for, Colonel."

"Soldiers and their dependents are entitled certain allowances for combat zone deployment," said the colonel. "That provision is *not* superseded by anything in APSA. Sergeant Cruz now has a wife and two young children. A four-year-old and a seven-year-old. I need an answer. We do things by the book here, Agent Ledbetter, and there are certain legal formalities that have to be gone through. I don't personally care jack-shit if you've got an authorization from the head of your agency or not, and APSA does not override military payroll procedures. You and your men are not going anywhere, or calling anyone, until I establish that. And if I have to call the Pentagon and take whatever flak happens, so be it."

For the first time the agent looked a little less than sure of himself. He pursed his lips. "You'd better make sure that they get that allowance, Colonel. If you want to know any more you'd better talk to Ms. Garnett. Take my advice. Don't. You've already pushed things a bit far."

Medea had stood silent through all of this. Now she lifted her patrician nose and looked down it at Ledbetter. "Is this man a representative of your Uncle Sam, Anibal?" she asked.

"You'd better believe it, lady," said Agent Ledbetter.

"He has made a poor choice in you," she said disdainfully to the agent. "I think you must also be a relative, because only nepotism could have got you the job."

She turned to her children. "Your new father is a noble and an honorable fighter honored to serve his Uncle, Sam, in new conquests for the Islands of America. He does not have to be coerced by his wife and children being held hostage. I hope that we will get a suitable gift of lands for this, because this house is rather small, although the magic plumbing is wonderful."

Anibal Cruz put an arm around his wife, and enjoyed looking at the senior agent whose mouth was working, but with no words coming out of it. Even when he got into the black SUV, he was still grinning.

Mac wasn't, though. The red-haired Corporal McKenna looked very close to doing something stupid.

"Take it easy, Mac," murmured Cruz. "What's the worst they can do to us? Compared to the big-time ranger school we lived through in Myth-Greece? These suits aren't much of a threat. It's not like they could send us back there."

Jim McKenna said something obscene and physically improbable. Using his wife, Arachne of Colophon, as a hostage for his cooperation was possibly even stupider than using the Sorceress Medea for that purpose.

"Besides," Cruz added, "if there is any problem with *la migra*, I took steps. The colonel will have a word with someone who ... dwarfs the problem."

The corner of Mac's mouth twitched and the storm on his brow lifted. "I'm almost tempted to hope that these Pissants try to do something stupid."

The agent in front of them started to turn around, and began to say something, but then obviously changed his mind. It was probably a wise thing to do, under the circumstances, Cruz thought.

Like the two of them shutting up until they found out what this was all about. Probably training Pissants instead of paratroopers on how to deal with what they'd found in the Mythworlds. The best advice Cruz could give them was "stay away and stay out" and if you're snatched—which is not something you can plan on—make damn sure you've got Dr. Jerry Lukacs there with you.

Arachne of Colophon didn't mind sharing a house with Medea. She would even put up with the agents left there to guard them. What she really didn't like was Jim McKenna going out without her there to keep an eye on him. Medea might be infected with the Greek notion that nobles had to fight and conquer, and that any man under arms was a noble, but Arachne knew better. Colophon's people weren't so foolish. A man's purpose was to make money—as was hers—and not to waste their talents on hitting people with swords. Any idiot could do that.

Not only had they cut her off from Mac, but they'd cut her off from a Colophonian girl's best friend—especially one who used to be a spider-bodied woman: the World Wide Web in general, and electronic stock trading in specific. Oh, and the other thing was that Medea kept dusting for spiderwebs. It was a good thing that no one had trained the princess in the art of actually doing her own housekeeping. This morning she had given the vacuum cleaner a good beating for not doing a proper job.

Arachne couldn't help noticing that it was more conscientious and respectful afterward than her own vacuum cleaner had been.

But even cut off from telephones and her laptop, and even if she wasn't spider-bodied any more, Arachne could still pull strings. Her web weaving started with a cup of coffee for the hapless agent watching them. Medea had berated him for being in the way and Priones, the four-year-old, was practicing his lunges with a small wooden sword. Information is any girl's next best friend, after a few hundred cubits of spider-silk. Everyone with any intelligence knew that the more secret a thing is supposed to be, the more certain it is that the hired help knows altogether too much about it. And Arachne would bet that this Agent Schmitt was no exception.

"I'm sorry you have been put on this dull duty, while your fellow nobles are out raiding and warring," she said. "Priones. Stop that, or there will be trouble."

Priones looked at her darkly, and pointed at the agent. "Mummy doesn't like him here. I hope she chops him up and boils him in a pot."

"She probably will, dear," said Arachne urbanely. "Later. Now go and play with your toy soldiers, if any of them still have heads."

He showed no sign of moving, but just went back to, "Mummy doesn't like him here."

Arachne licked her lips. "I haven't eaten a little boy for weeks."

"You wouldn't dare," he said, but he backed off. Medea called from the bedroom, which provided him with the chance to stick out his tongue and run.

"He needs a good hiding," said the agent, taking a mouthful of coffee. He was lucky that Medea hadn't made it. Medea's coffee pot hadn't been any more obedient for being given less grounds, but the sorceress believed that she had to persevere with disciplining it.

"Probably," agreed Arachne, "but I wouldn't try it. Medea really did chop up her half brother. Anyway, Priones is as good as gold with Cruz. But you have sent his new daddy away, so he's cross. He doesn't want you here. He'll probably be a monster until our husbands get back. Will they be away long?"

"As long as it takes to find Harkness and—" said the agent, before suddenly breaking off. "As long as it takes, Miz. I can't and won't talk about it, so stop trying to pump me. And keep that kid away from me."

Arachne smiled sweetly. "I'll do my best." She wondered if it would be easier to bribe Priones to drive him mad or to sic Neoptolemeus onto him. Neoptolemeus had decided he liked her. A seven-year-old can be a very deadly weapon, or at least a pretty annoying one.

And now all she needed was to establish who this "Harkness" was, and why her husband and Cruz were needed to find him. She'd have to find a time to talk to Medea privately. Maybe she'd know. Mac had certainly never mentioned the name, and they'd talked about pretty much everything.

CHAPTER 2

⊚⊘⊚⊘⊚⊘

James Horton apparently enjoyed the august title of Assistant Director, Operations, of the Pyramid Security Agency. Jim McKenna hadn't been aware that the PSA even *had* an "operations directorate." Until the Pissants showed up at Fort Campbell, he'd been under the impression that the PSA was an information gathering outfit, like the National Security Agency. A pure intelligence agency, so to speak, not one that actually did rough-and-ready field work.

He wasn't sure, but Mac had a growing suspicion that this "Operations Directorate" was even more brand spanking new than the PSA itself. That would help to explain the bizarre combination of agents throwing their weight around even with army colonels on an army base—yet seeming to have not a clue about what they were supposedly doing.

If Horton here was their boss, Mac didn't have any trouble understanding the reason. Fortunately, being paratroopers and an elite unit, the 101st generally got good officers assigned to it. But Mac had been in the U.S. Army plenty long enough to know that some officers were pure and simple goofballs. And Horton reminded him of several such goofballs he'd known in times past. Especially a certain Captain Worthington—and how the hell the man had risen beyond second lieutenant remained a mystery to the sergeant—who'd combined incompetence with a "gung ho" attitude that would have been funny except for the misery it put the grunts through.

For starters, Mac was pretty sure that Horton was the origin of this silly habit of PSA agents wearing sunglasses. The screwball was wearing them *here*—inside a room with no windows and only fluorescent lighting. The other agents had at least had the sense to take them off when they came indoors. Did these guys know just how much they looked like cheap movie government agents? Did they *try* to look like them?

Most likely, Horton had been inspired by watching the *Men in Black* movies—and hadn't noticed that they were comedies. And wasn't that a scary thought?

The building they were in lent credence to that theory, now that Mac thought about it. He'd noticed on the way in that it looked like some sort of power plant, located in a rural area not too far from Clarksville.

"I hear you've been treating my operatives with some disrespect," Assistant Director Horton said to the two paratroopers, in a tone of voice he apparently thought was arctic but fell a good hundred and fifty degrees short of any competent drill sergeant.

So they'd been tattling to mommy, probably about being called Pissants. Mac flicked a glance at Cruz. The sergeant had his poker face on. Well, Cruz was a lot more experienced at dealing with trouble than he was, even if McKenna was better at getting into it.

"No, sir, not yet," said Cruz. His own tone of voice made it clear that serious disrespect could start very easily. "Your operatives have obviously not been taught military protocols, and they have disgraced both you and their organization. If you want to confirm that you could try asking my commanding officer. They treated him with disrespect, in the presence of his men and their dependents. We in the military don't like that. I'd like to you to censure them, sir. Then I'd feel that mutual respect could be established."

Mac had to restrain a grin.

Horton's eyes widened. "Do you know who I am, Sergeant Cruz?" He was now striving for a voice the temperature of liquid nitrogen. It was pretty pathetic. "I answer directly to Director Garnett herself."

He said that last the way a man might say "me and Moses consult daily on such matters as parting the Red Sea."

Cruz looked at him with a completely blank expression, as if he'd never heard her name at all. Which would be quite a feat, since Helen Garnett was nothing if not a public recognition addict. Ever since she'd been put in charge of the PSA, her face had been on enough screens for everyone to know it.

"No, sir. These men are from the PSA, so I'd guess that you are also from the PSA. I'd like to know why we've been brought here, and why our families are being held hostage."

Horton slithered away from a direct answer. "You'll be told presently what your mission is—and the term 'hostage' is ridiculous, Sergeant. Your people are simply under protective custody." He leaned forward a bit, apparently striving for a menacing aura. "I just want to clarify one thing before I send you off to be briefed. Even the lowest agent here outranks you. If I hear of any more problems, or disrespect, you could just be spending several years in the stockade at Fort Leavenworth. Do you understand me?"

Cruz didn't reply. His muscles just tensed. For the first time in his military career Mac decided that it was time to bail his senior buddy out. Deflect fire. "Yes, sir. Can we send a message to our families?"

"No. You're strictly incommunicado." He waved a hand at one of the suits. "Take them to Agent Supervisor Megane."

Agent Supervisor Megane looked like a dodgy used-car salesman. In a suit, rubbing his hands as he talked. Still, it was an improvement on being in the same room as Horton. At least Megane wasn't wearing sunglasses indoors.

"Our mission is one of utmost gravity and sensitivity," he said. "You're probably not aware of it, but a senior government man from the National Security Council was snatched in the early phase of the alien pyramid attack. A man by the name of Tom Harkness."

Mac remembered the name. That cop, Salinas, had wanted to tell Major Gervase about it. And Professor Tremelo had said he'd seen him get snatched. "Yeah, I heard it reported," he said.

"In the press?" demanded Megane. "That would be a serious breach of—"

"To my field commander. Major Gervase."

The agent looked taken aback. "Oh."

"We were there, remember?" said Cruz. "We were there just after it happened."

"Oh, yes," said the agent again. "I was told you that you would be our military advisors on . . . on matters inside the pyramid. Gentlemen, this is a Matter of National Security."

He looked like he'd been waiting to say that line for a long time, capital letters and all.

"Yeah?" said Mac, because Megane seemed to expect some sort of response.

Megane nodded gravely. "Mr. Harkness has not returned. He is too valuable a man to be left in enemy hands. Dead or alive, we need him back. He knows far too much to be left there to be interrogated."

Mac looked at Cruz. Cruz looked back at him. Cruz took a deep breath. "I don't want to rain on your parade, Mr. Megane. But the Krim never showed the least inclination to interrogate any of us. I don't think it cares."

"How the alien treats ordinary soldiers, and how it deals with a high-ranking official, is logically going to be different," said the agent condescendingly. "Your knowledge and importance in the scheme of things is pretty unimportant compared to a man like Tom Harkness."

Cruz shrugged. "I don't think that this is the sort of military-type problem you guys think it is. But I don't suppose you're listening."

"Anyway," said Mac, "I hate to break this to you, Agent Megane—"

"Agent *Supervisor* Megane," the PSA man said brusquely.

"Ah, right. Agent *Supervisor* Megane. But my point is that if your Harkness person is still inside there . . . well, that's just too bad. There is no way to get to him. He'll be spat out old and dead soon enough. Even if nothing in the Mythworlds kills him, time moves about five times as fast in there."

Megane blinked at him. "It just seemed that way to you, soldier. Anyway, the point is that we actually do have a way in to the pyramid. And we're arranging transport back. We need you to help us brief the snatch team, and then to guide us."

Mac looked down at his feet. The floor hadn't suddenly turned to quicksand and wasn't swallowing him up. But it felt like it.

Cruz spoke first. "With respect, Agent Supervisor Megane, I don't think you guys have done your homework. Time really does move at a different rate inside the Mythworlds, for starters. Ask the scientists."

It looked like with or without respect, this was the first time that Megane had been told that he hadn't done his homework. Mac fended off the explosion with a calming gesture. "If you read the debriefing reports, you'd know that we had to be guided around there ourselves. And if we hadn't had an expert and local help and lot more luck on our side, we'd have got ourselves killed, PDQ."

"Expert?" asked Megane.

"Dr. Lukacs," said Cruz. "He's an expert in mythology."

Megane raised his eyebrows. "He's also a civilian with a dubious security record."

Mac wondered how Jerry Lukacs had managed to get a "dubious" security record. He'd probably made a pun in the presence of an overly serious FBI agent. Or simply used too many multisyllable words in front of a PSA agent. "He's still the guy who kept us alive and beat the Krim."

"He hasn't been cleared by the PSA. He's also currently consorting with a citizen of a country that cannot be considered wholly friendly." If reading up on the technical reports was too much for this Megane fellow, checking out on people's private lives was apparently right up his alley. "You will have a team of skilled professionals to back you up this time, boys."

"Swordsmen and expert survivalists who can do magic?" rumbled Cruz. "The sort of people who can out-think gods by knowing a lot about them?"

Megane gave a lopsided smile, intended to tell them how tough he was. He slapped his chest. "Top agents. Profiled to be selected by the pyramid. I think we better go through and meet them. Then you can be properly briefed and equipped. Follow me."

He led them out of his office. Mac had a chance to say, quietly, "We're up shit-creek, Sarge."

Cruz hadn't needed Mac tell him that. It was more than obvious that these spooks had two things. The first was delusions and the second was no fricking idea what the hell they were heading for. Besides, if Cruz understood it right, then what they planned to do to get the Krim to take them, was to select the sort of guys that that Chicago police lieutenant Salinas had been. People who were credulous, among other things. Salinas himself was still somewhere in Mythological Greece, as happy as a pig in shit, because Circe had turned him into one.

But Cruz wasn't particularly worried. The trick was simply not to be in physical contact with these losers when it all happened.

He just had to get the word through to Mac. He wasn't keen on explaining to the spider-girl that he'd lost the kid.

When he met the "team" and saw their equipment, he began to realize that Mac hadn't even started to guess just how far up the creek they were.

Megane held up the horse-hair plumed helmets. "The radio units are hidden inside the helmet crest. They have a transmission radius of about eight miles and we've got you about sixty hours battery life. The breastplate is high-density Kevlar. Now, handguns. We're issuing you with .40 caliber pistols. The agents carry various other weapons, but there is no time to train you to proficiency in them."

"Like what?" said Cruz, who was curious about weapons of any description.

"Well, the spear disassembles into a hollow shaft—that's the rifle barrel—and the sword hilt covers and hides the trigger mechanism, revealed by twisting the pommel. It also holds the magazine. The block is the upper section of the blade. The stock is a folding one, fitted inside the shield as a brace. Fortunately, these Greek swords are chunky—apparently they had to be to stop them bending—but it still puts some limits on caliber. We're using the new .177 HM rounds. Ammunition is the biggest problem, of course. So we've settled on these authentic looking packs, which have the actual fabric lined with loose rounds."

Cruz snorted.

"You guys just don't really understand what you'll be dealing with, do you?" said Mac. The boy was still trying to get through to them. Maybe he just didn't want to wear that kilt-skirt thing that the PSA had decided was the right outfit for this lot.

Agent Bott just looked offended. Agent Sternal at least tried to explain. He looked like a lot of people had explained things to him. Mostly jokes. "We've had the best historical research teams working on this, and based on what you and others have reported, we should be nicely inconspicuous."

"Let's start with getting this clear to you," said Mac. "When you get over there, none of this gear is gonna work. Our M16s didn't. And all the modern stuff that did work had converted itself into Greek-era goods. Only things which would have worked then, worked. Our water bottles became leather. A lighter became mothball-stuff."

"Your gear was examined, microscopically, when you got back," said Agent Bott, with a sniff. "It was some kind of hallucination, or maybe a switch. But we should deceive the aliens with the correct gear."

Mac sighed. "Listen. To. Me. It isn't gonna work. This isn't some covert op where you have to sneak things past the locals. Things change. They. Actually. Change."

"And trust me," said Cruz, leaning against the wall. "None of us could pass for locals anyway."

That got their attention. "So the kit is not quite authentic? What's wrong with it?" asked Megane.

"You guys are," said Cruz. "However, if you like we can fix it." He smiled nastily.

"Talk. ETD is set for the day after tomorrow, at eleven hundred hours."

"Well, you better get yourselves hair jobs. And beards. And fleas. And you need at least a week of no baths, and local food, to smell right. Then you get rubbed with olive oil and scraped with, what was that thing called, Mac? Oh yeah, a strigil. You've got to smell of old sweat and rancid olive oil."

"You're kidding, right?" demanded Bott.

Cruz shrugged. "Check it out with your pet historians."

"Get onto Maritz," said Megane. "The hair and beards will have to be glued on."

Mac shook his head. "You guys won't pass anyway. You're all too tall. And too pale."

"Skin dye. Anything else?"

Cruz took a deep breath. "Good knives. Whetstones. Fire-making stuff. A good tent, a decent sleeping bag. Maybe some decent composite bows and the skill to use them. A sword that doesn't have a detachable handle and a shield that isn't made of aluminum. A crash course in how to speak Greek. Unless you end up like we did for a bit, in Egypt."

"Megane and Bott speak Greek. I speak Arabic," said Sternal.

Cruz shook his head. "That's not the same as ancient Egyptian, or, from what Jerry said, classical Greek."

Megane bit his lip. "Well, I guess our cover just can't be perfect then. This mission had to put together in a hurry. I gather that not all the locals are hostile."

"Nope," said Mac cheerfully. "What do you reckon, Sarge? Seventy-five percent hostile?"

"Yeah. And most of the other twenty-five will kill you for the loot you're carrying." Cruz sighed. If he and Mac ended up going, despite his best intentions, they might as well be kitted out as well as possible. "Look. If you can't look perfect, why not settle for camo? If you won't, and want to go along with all this stuff, well, we're paratroopers, not experts in covert ops. We don't know how to pass ourselves off as anything else. You guys do. Do you mind if the two of us choose our own gear? We'll pretend to be foreigners or something."

"Cruz and I could pretend to be prisoners, groaning under the weight of our stuff," put in Mac brightly. "It'd make you guys look really tough."

Cruz wished that Mac would ease off a bit. They weren't that dumb, surely.

"I'll ask," said Megane, proving, like the man said, that you can never overestimate the power of human stupidity.

"There is just one question I really have to ask," said Cruz, mentally compiling a list of things he'd love to have had with him the last time. "Just how do you plan to get back?"

"We've arranged to take along the mutant animal that you brought back with you. By all reports that's how you got home."

Mac gaped. "Throttler? The Greek sphinx?"

"I believe that's the term applied to it," said Megane. "We're arranging to bring the creature here from Las Vegas. That's what the delay is about."

Mac was about to say something when Cruz kicked him. Throttler could get them back, all right. If she wanted to, she could get them there too, without the dangers of going via the pyramid. But that wasn't something Cruz wanted to point out, or the fact that the Greek sphinx—with the head and breasts of a woman and the body of lion with huge eagle wings—was pretty bad tempered and very deadly. Someone—or probably all of them—were going to end up coming back from the Mythworlds a lot sooner than even Cruz anticipated. He and Mac were *definitely*, come hell or high water, going to masquerade as prisoners. And remember their riddles. If humans didn't get them right, Throttler would kill them.

Medea might not have brought her magical command of spirits and sprites with her from mythological Greece to modern America, but she had lost none of her skills at making potions.

Arachne didn't even have to fake looking unwell, and throwing up was easy. The PSA agent did accompany her to the base doctor, though.

At the door of the office, Arachne looked the agent straight in the eye. "There are certain things ... certain ... female problems, that I do not discuss in front of strange men. So you will wait out here."

He looked as if he might argue, but just at that point a very large corporal, with his arm in a sling, cleared his throat and got up. Arachne recognized him. His name was Dale Thompson and he was one of Anibal and Mac's friends. "I'd let the lady see the doctor in private, mister."

The PSA agent looked incredulously at him. "You want time in Leavenworth, boy?"

Thompson grinned. "I got a concussion. I have these blackouts when I don't remember anything. I'm feeling real faint right now, in fact."

Arachne took the opportunity to slip into the doctor's room. She'd been extremely embarrassed by the examination he had given her a few weeks before, and had no real intention of repeating the experience.

"I'm not sick," she said hastily. "I just need know something from the war-captain ... Colonel. Who is 'Harkness'? Mac and Cruz have been taken to fetch him. Ask him, and arrange to bring me a potion and tell me."

"Uh ..." said the doctor.

"Medea said if you do not do it she will bring Priones to visit you again," said Arachne.

The doctor's eyes bulged slightly. He nodded. "All right. You do look rather pale though, Ms. Arachne."

"You may bring me something to help with nausea. And to help me sleep," she said as a sudden afterthought. A sleeping potion could be useful, if Medea couldn't provide.

She went out into the doctor's waiting room to find her minder furiously trying to extricate himself from the embrace of a lolling Corporal Thompson, who, for a man who was struggling to stay upright, gave her a very nice wink before collapsing onto the floor—and dragging the agent down with him.

"Perhaps you should render some assistance," said Arachne, coolly, to the furious agent, after he extricated himself. "The doctor will bring my medication later, and I am feeling faint myself. I shall go out and take some air."

"He hasn't fainted. Wait until I get onto headquarters about this," he snarled. Arachne smiled at the rest of the waiting-room crowd, who all seemed very tense—and furious with the PSA agent. "I wouldn't do that," she said. "All these people saw the poor man faint." The roomful of people nodded like marionettes having their strings pulled. "I think one of you should call the doctor to look at him," she added, as she walked out, leaving the PSA agent to scurry after her.

Colonel McNamara had a serious problem on his hands. He was constrained by some of the more outlandish provisions of the Alien Pyramid Security Act. Like all security legislation passed by Congress in a fit of hysteria, APSA was riddled with idiotic clauses that gave a sufficiently ambitious and unscrupulous security official the ability to ride roughshod over common sense as well as other people. He was also constrained by a duty to his men, and a growing suspicion that this PSA action was at least a semi-rogue one. That would explain why the agent-in-charge had backed down when he'd finally gotten mad enough to risk his career.

The colonel had talked to Professor Tremelo, and he understood the implications of pyramid expansion with each human that it had snatched, and the increasing snatch radius. He also knew just who Tom Harkness was, and when he had disappeared. The only way to get him back was to ask his men to do what they'd been the only survivors of doing before—get snatched again, and go inside a world which shouldn't really be able to exist. An impossible world that spat out a lot of dead people.

There was a specific presidential directive forbidding anyone who was at risk of becoming a snatchee from entering the safety perimeter. Overriding that directive had to be approved by the Pyramid Scientific Research Group as well as the PSA. That meant that Tremelo must know about this. It was a pity. He'd seemed a sensible man, for a civilian and a scientist.

This all seemed more than enough reason to call General Brasno. Unofficially. And damn the PSA. It all smelled, and it wouldn't be the first time that secret service agencies had used secrecy to provide cover for their own agendas.

"I need advice, sir. And I didn't call you. Or rather I called you about different matter altogether."

While the colonel was officially not talking, the base medical officer was arming himself with a generous ration of candy in case he met up with a certain small boy again. Who would have thought one child could yell and bite so much?

In a remote corner of a wildlife reservation, some distance away, a winged dragon sighed gustily and licked his new white little teeth with a long red snaky tongue. They helped his speech as well as his chewing. "I feel as if my life is lacking something."

His sibling, Bitar, licked his chops too. "Something of the flavor of life."

"Could be ketchup?" said Smitar, after serious thought, and then concentrated on trying to reach an annoying itch between his shoulder blades.

"Or it could be hot sauce. Who would have thought that American maidens would be in such short supply that they'd have to be protected game?"

"Over hunted," said Smitar righteously. "Should have introduced a permit system. Or reservations. Or a minimum size limit."

Bitar shook his vast armored head at the iniquity. "A bag limit." He paused. "It wasn't you, was it?"

"Not unless I'm sleep-eating again," said Smitar. "If it wasn't me, was it you? And can you scratch this spot for me?"

"We need Cruz," said Bitar, obliging. "He can give a decent scratch with an oar. Do you think we're molting again?"

"Could be. It's this foreign food. Very greasy. Fattening." Smitar patted his midriff.

"You haven't been eating these foreigners again?" demanded Bitar accusingly. "You know Medea told us not to. Anyway, you could have shared!"

"Phttt," said Smitar. "He was barely a snack. And Cruz said that anyone from the INS was fair game. I still feel something's missing in my life. I've got this sort of inner itch too."

"Could be indigestion. But I have it as well. And I never even got a bite of the INS official." Bitar sniffed dolefully. "Could use a good scratch with a pole from Cruz."

Smitar wrinkled his scaly forehead in thought. "I think it is that time of life when a young dragon's thoughts turn to love."

"Could be. What time is that?" asked Bitar, tasting the idea.

"This century, I think."

"Hmm. In that case I think we need some male advice on how to draw chicks."

Smitar looked a bit puzzled. "I thought you just grabbed them and dragged?"

"Doesn't that lack finesse?"

"Probably. It could work though."

"We need to ask Cruz," said Bitar, rubbing his back against a rock and shattering it. "It's time he sat us down and gave us a little talk about the birds and the bees."

Smitar tasted a piece of the rock. Chewed it thoughtfully and then asked, "Why?"

"I think it's what you have to talk to girls about," said Bitar knowledgeably. "Cruz will know."

Smitar spat out rock fragments. "And he could give us a good scratch."

As they took off and began searching for thermals, Smitar asked, "So what's this finesse stuff? Some kind of sauce? Or a lubricant to help with the dragging?"

Bitar nodded. "Both. It's got chocolate in it, too."

Chapter 3

⊙⊙⊙⊙⊙⊙

Liz had to smile at Miggy Tremelo's ill-contained frustration. He'd had several minor fumes at various aspects of the PSA's new "system" ever since she and Jerry had arrived five minutes back. The PSA kept dragging its way into the conversation like some kind of pernicious disease. It was obviously driving him up the wall. She could identify with that. Minor bureaucrats who seemed to derive enormous satisfaction from making petty matters into insurmountable obstacles, and saying "no" whenever possible, had been a feature of her life, especially lately. Normally Miggy and Jerry would be feet deep in animated theoretical discussion by now. It was obviously preying on Tremelo's mind almost to the exclusion of everything else. She wished that Lamont would get there. Even a few puns would be welcome, although she could never admit that in public.

Then the Jacksons arrived. And it was immediately apparent that things with Marie were not improving. Even the kids were silent, which as Liz knew from their previous get-togethers, was straight *un*natural. Little Tyrone normally was the best reason she'd ever come across for having silencers fitted to all kids at birth. As they said back in South Africa, the kid had been born with the volume control stuck on full. And the twin girls had competed with his volume by doing it shrill and in stereo. Only the fifteen year-old live-in nephew, Emmitt, seemed to be the same as usual. He hadn't smiled much then and he wasn't smiling now. They all looked like they were heading for a funeral.

Which was accurate.

Marie's.

"He said I've got secondaries in my liver and my chest cavity already," said Marie calmly. "Too late for chemotherapy, too late for surgery. I've got about three months. It doesn't hurt much."

She was the only one who appeared to be calm, and talking about it. "I'm sorry, Miggy. I've come to give my notice. There's no point pretending I'm just on sick leave, anymore. Me and Lamont and the kids, we want to spend as much time as we can together now. While we can."

"At least money's not really an issue any more," said Lamont with a sigh. "I never thought I'd be able to say that."

"Ain't no use cryin', for heaven's sake. I thought we'd maybe go on a road trip. See places we've never seen."

Lamont nodded. "We wanted to fly to Greece. But it seems like I'm a national asset, not to be risked in a foreign country. It's an attitude I wish they'd had when they sent me to Vietnam."

Standing aside, talking to Jerry, Lamont looked like a skyscraper that just lost its foundations. "What the hell is the use of having all the money in the world if I haven't got Marie? I reckon my luck has deserted me, Jerry."

He bit his lip, his eyes downcast, voice shaking. "I'd swap anything in the world, just to make her well. That's the worst kind of luck that can happen to any man. I was the luckiest man in the world, thanks to Tyche. Now, I think I'm the unluckiest. Marie's . . . she's my life, I guess."

Jerry didn't quite know what to say. He just leaned over squeezed Lamont's shoulder.

The telephone rang.

"I'm not taking any calls right now," snapped Miggy.

"But, Professor, it's Ms. Garnett," said Rachel Clements, popping her head around the door. "And she is . . . well, insistent."

Marie rubbed her hands. "Shall I deal with her? For old times sake?"

Miggy Tremelo smiled for the first time since he'd heard her news. "I'm tempted. But I'd better handle it. As little as I like that woman, I'll have to deal with her, for the foreseeable future."

"And I won't have to cope with the aftershocks, I guess," said Marie.

Miggy picked up his phone. "Professor Tremelo speaking."

The person on the other end was shouting. Not quite loud enough for the rest of them to make out all the words. Just: *sphinx*.

"I am afraid that you're blaming the wrong person," said Miggy. "But I strongly advise you not take on the environmental lobby over . . ." He held the phone away from his ear, and then put it down on the cradle.

He looked at the phone as if it was an envenomed serpent. "I should have let you handle it after all, Marie. Still, I think that woman may have bitten off more than she can chew, this time."

"What's happened?" asked Liz, curious.

"It appears that certain PSA agents were observed loading Throttler on a cargo plane at McCarran Airport in Las Vegas. God only knows how they talked her into getting on it—without getting killed in the process."

Miggy smiled beatifically. "And, while PSA can ride roughshod over most things . . . Not the Endangered Species Act. Throttler and the dragons have been declared endangered species, if you recall, and now it appears that the two Greek dragons have disappeared too. It hasn't taken the wildlife authorities long to put the two together, and go public about it. It would appear that when their rare and endangered species are involved—especially crowd-pullers—Fish and Wildlife don't actually care if you're the head of the PSA. Especially since one of the loopholes in that screwball Swiss cheese legislation they call APSA exempts them from PSA authority."

Jerry's eyes widened. "It does? Why, in God's name?"

Miggy's grin was almost scary, now. "What do you think? The usual trading and swapping you get whenever Congress rushes through legislation too quickly. One of the key legislators involved—Montana's Senator Frank Larsen—saw a chance to do a favor for the U.S. Fish and Wildlife Service. He's very partial to them, partly because he's an avid outdoorsman himself, and partly because his nephew Mark O'Hare happens to be the agency's director."

Lamont chuckled. "So an agency nobody thinks has anything to do with 'alien pyramid security' gets a better deal from APSA than the CIA or the FBI, or even the military. What a laugh. It reminds me of something I read once. If a police car, a fire truck, and an ambulance—all answering emergencies with their lights flashing and their sirens blowing, mind you—come to an intersection at the same time as a Post Office van making routine deliveries, guess which vehicle legally has the right of way?"

"The Post Office vehicle," said Miggy. "Of course, in the real world, no postman would even think of not pulling over to let the emergency vehicles go past him first—but, legally, he could pull rank on them if he wanted to. Yup, and that's technically the situation here. Except that in this instance, Fish and Wildlife is hopping mad. Mad enough, even, to be willing to take on that woman publicly."

"What does Garnett want Throttler for, in the first place?" asked Liz. Militantly, she twitched the strap of her new shoulder bag. The bag wasn't yet as full of useful things as the old one had been. It still felt unnatural and quite emaciated, poor thing. It couldn't weigh more than five pounds. "They better not hurt her. She's biologically priceless."

"So, it would appear, Ms. Garnett has just been told by the Fish and Wildlife director. She somehow reached the conclusion that I had told the conservation authorities that the creatures were to be brought here. How I was supposed have done that when this is the first that I've heard about it, I don't know. But I suspect logic is not her best friend."

"I don't think logic even gets near her mind," said Jerry, shaking his head, "unless it involves political maneuvering. The PSA still hasn't allowed me back to the Oriental Institute to collect my papers, although I have absolutely zero chance of being snatched."

"Or let me back to the Department of Ecology and Evolution," said Liz with a grimace. "And quite a lot of my documentation is still sitting there. Documents Immigration and Naturalization want."

"I'll get some of my people onto that," promised Miggy Tremelo. "Still, I think its a good thing that we have nothing to do with her dragon-problem. It'll probably explode on her."

෧෧   ෧෧   ෧෧

"The thing to get into your head," said Cruz, patiently, "is that the people you're facing, as Doc explained to me, are the idealized warriors of their age. That means they've been fighting all their lives. They're more used to cold-blooded killing than any U.S. mass-murderer. And to them you are a barbarian. If you're not Greek, you're a barbarian. A Greek life isn't worth that much. A barbarian's life is worth a little less than that of a stray dog. They don't know what your human rights are, because you aren't human. Only Greeks are."

Agent Stephens blinked. "We're posing as Greeks."

Cruz shrugged. "At a distance, maybe." Greeks with hidden rifles, .50 caliber IDF Desert Eagles, abseil gear, night-vision goggles, laser sights, heat-seeking RPGs . . .

And not a clue. Some of that gear could be useful, maybe. Depending on what it turned into.

"Anyway, to be frank with you, Sergeant, they're not up to our level of training," said Bott, practicing assembling his rifle. He might be faster at that than a bastard like Odysseus would be at dismantling him before he was finished, but Cruz wouldn't bet on it.

CHAPTER 4

⊚⊚⊚⊚⊚⊚

Even if the dragons flew to a remote part of the wildlife reserve, to have a break from pesky tourists they weren't even allowed to eat, there were inevitably eager dragon watchers with binoculars somewhere in the park, tracking their upward flight.

Up, up, up . . . into the clouds.

"So, where to from here?" asked Bitar.

"Dunno. Thought you did."

"It's north."

"So which way is that?"

Bitar thought about it for a moment. "Let's ask someone."

Dragons have keen eyesight. It's useful for spotting prey from a great height. Good for spotting a really well camouflaged greenhouse in the woods, too.

Carl Frederick, cultivator of the fine green product known variously as purple haze, ganja, weed and, lately, thanks to his new English girlfriend, by the charming epithet "skunk," owed his skill in camouflage to time spent in the 101st, prior to his not-entirely-honorable discharge. He owed his survival over the next few minutes to being too stoned to care. He just sat there and smiled vacantly.

There was no other reasonable way to treat a seventy-five-foot dragon landing on your greenhouse. Especially when his brother dragon is investigating your ear with his tongue.

"We need to get to Fort Campbell. How do we get there?"

It was not exactly a destination Frederick thought he'd ever see again. Or had any desire to. "Hey man, that is not a cool place to go."

"Good. We like warm places," said the dragon happily. "Got any food?"

"Besides you, that is," said the other dragon. "You smell funny. Like those Lotophagi."

"Wouldn't want to eat him then," said the first one. "They made my tummy feel odd. Like it was flying without me."

"We could nibble a bit and see." One of the dragons licked his small but very sharp-looking teeth with his forked tongue. He took Carl's arm into his mouth and the grower of the green product felt the illusion's teeth. Carl shrieked and pulled his arm away. "Hey man, you can't eat me!"

One of the dragons looked at the other, wrinkling his forehead. The other looked equally puzzled. "Why not?" they asked in unison. It was, plainly, a serious question.

There is nothing like the blood trickling down one's arm from a number of razorlike teeth to focus even the most stoned of minds. Even if they were hallucinations, he'd still better humor them. "Because . . . because I won't be able to show you the way to Fort Campbell."

"Hmm, true. But I'm still hungry. Can't we just eat half?" said the first dragon.

His companion agreed eagerly. "I'll have the left half, you have the right."

"But two halves make a whole," protested Carl.

The dragon nodded. "I hope it'll fill the hole where my tummy used to be."

"But, but that's the whole of me," said Carl. "I'd be the whole that you ate."

"No you wouldn't. I'd only have eaten half," said the dragon with impeccable logic. "Half a whole would only half fill the hole."

"And if you were a whole," said the other dragon professorially, "there'll be no point in eating you because you can't fill a hole with hole."

"So you can't eat me. I'm whole," protested Carl.

The two dragons looked at each other. "We'll have to dismember him before we eat him," they said in unison.

Frederick clung to the only straw in this whirlpool. "But then I can't show you the way."

"Well, that's true," said the first dragon grumpily. "You carry him first, Smitar. We'll have to find something to eat along the way."

"Road-food always gives me gas," said the other dragon.

"Good. We'll need it," said his companion.

Carl found himself in the airborne again, despite the not-entirely-honorable discharge. Well, airborne again, anyway. Without the benefit of a parachute. "Take us to Fort Campbell," instructed the dragon.

This had to be the strangest weed he'd ever grown. "Man, it's more like you're taking me."

"Which way?" asked the dragon carrying him.

"Uh. Northwest," he answered.

"Northwest it is," said the dragon obligingly. "So which way is that?"

Swales was a small town. It wasn't entirely true to say that it was a one horse town. The horse had died some years before, but Beth Camero had some nice pictures of it. Now it briefly became a two dragon town instead. Well, the diner on the edge of town became a two dragon diner. A two hungry dragon diner.

"What's that?" asked Bitar, pointing to the billboard with a faded burger painted on it.

"It's a hamburger," said Camero, who had emerged from the diner with a shotgun for company.

"Can you eat it?" asked Bitar, tasting the edge of the billboard.

"I make ones you can eat. Cheeseburgers too." Beth swatted his nose away from her sign with the shotgun.

"What about maiden-burgers?" asked Smitar, keeping a coil around their guide-captive-half-meal.

"You big snake! Mind what you say to a lady." Camero was acting as if dragons landed in her diner's parking lot every day. "Now, what'll it be?"

"Food," said Bitar.

"Lots," said Smitar.

"With ketchup!" said Bitar licking his chops, studying Camero's bright red hair. "Now that you've reminded me."

"Lots," agreed Smitar. "Lots and lots of ketchup."

Beth leaned the shotgun against the wall and put her hands on her hips. "And who is paying for this 'lots'?"

"What's paying?" asked Bitar.

"You know," said Smitar. "Giving something in exchange for dinner instead of catching it. They use gold sometimes."

"Gold's not very tasty. No crunch to it," said Bitar, dismissively. "So you get captive dinner. We've got that."

"Turn him upside down and see if he has any gold," suggested Smitar.

Bitar did, and shook him. A wallet, a packet of cannabis and some keys clattered to the ground. "No gold," said the dragon, dolefully. "I like the way it shines, even if it has no crunch to it."

"Anyway, he's a captive already. No use paying for him," said Smitar.

"Never mind," said Camero, picking up the wallet and opening it. She smiled cheerfully after examining the contents. "Food and ketchup it is. I don't get that many customers dropping in that I can afford to turn two big eaters down, I reckon. You eating too, mister? Seeing as you're paying."

An hour and one hundred and fifty-four half-pound burgers with cheese and all the trimmings, twenty-four hot dogs and all the mustard and ketchup in the place—and an empty wallet—later, they rose, slowly, heading northwest.

"Say, what's your name, half-dinner?" said Smitar.

"Carl Frederick," answered the man.

The dragons peered at him suspiciously. "Have you been to Colchis?"

"Never heard of the place, honest."

"Ach. What did Mac say they called it these days? . . . ah! Georgia."

"Uh. Yeah," admitted the good-ole-boy from Georgia, USA, in cheerful ignorance of any other Georgia.

The dragon wrinkled his nose in distaste. "You keep those golden fleas to yourself, now."

"They got under my scales last time," agreed the other dragon.

☙☙   ☙☙   ☙☙

It was just after three that frantic wildlife officers got their first lead on the two missing rare and endangered animals. In response to their radio broadcasts and TV appeals, someone named Beth Camero from a small town forty miles from the Tennessee state line called in. A state trooper was dispatched immediately to the spot.

The state trooper looked at the wallet. "I'll be damned. Carl Frederick." He shook his head. "We've been trying to get our hands on that drug-dealing son of a bitch for a while now. So which way was he heading with those dragons, ma'am?"

Beth pointed. "And I'd offer you boys a burger and a cup of coffee, but they ate everything I had."

Back in the patrol car, the officer called in. "You can tell the Fish and Wildlife guys that it's not strayed dangerous animals any more. It's poaching. Frederick. The local weed king? Yeah, well, the bastard's decided to move from trafficking dope into trafficking wildlife."

Beth Camero went on painting her new sign. *Dragons' Rest Road House.*

"That's the perimeter fence. You just follow it and you'll come to the gate," said Carl. "Look, can't you let me go here? I'm . . . uh, not really welcome there." The thought of the base MP's reaction to his arrival, even on dragonback, was not a comfortable one. "You don't need me. And you've damaged my life enough. Couple of damn muggers, what you are."

The dragons were still full, and bulgingly good tempered. "I suppose we are here. And you have fed us," said one.

"But what have we done to you?" said the dragon, setting him down.

"You destroyed my livelihood. Landed on my crop," said Carl righteously. "Not to mention robbing me blind."

The dragons looked at each other. "It's only fair that we make it up to you."

Visions of dragonback bank raids flashed through Carl's mind. "That lot of skunk was worth easy . . . half a million bucks."

"That's a lot of buck," said a startled dragon. "A whole herd."

"You grew skunk?" asked the other.

"Yeah. The best," boasted Frederick.

Both dragons undulated off. "Back there," said one, sniffing.

Moments later he had two black and white—and frightened and angry—contributions from above. "A fresh start for you," said the dragon.

"Enjoy!" said the other, as the skunks lifted their tails.

Having fled through the bushes, Carl was running headlong down the road when the patrol car spotted him. Never had he been so grateful to see cops. They could shoot the skunks or the dragons.

"Carl Frederick, you're under arrest. You have the right to remain silent—"

"But I haven't done nothing!" He was as clean as a man could be. Not an ounce of skunk on him. Well, except for the bouquet that was making the deputy's eyes water.

"Illegal trafficking in endangered wildlife."

Carl sat down on the road and wept. So did the deputies who handcuffed him. But that was probably the smell . . . Or maybe the thought that he would be going in the back of their patrol car.

Of the dragons there was no sign. It was only a little later that a conservation officer put two and two together about the location, so close to the Fort Campbell perimeter fence. "They probably went looking for their former owner, once they got away from the dragon-napper!"

Someone was dispatched at once to Fort Campbell to see one Sergeant Cruz and his wife Medea. To be met with zero cooperation from two PSA agents. Who, under pressure, had to produce PSA IDs. It was just about the same time, 10:00 PM, as the story of Throttler's mysterious removal from Las Vegas—by PSA agents—hit the news channels.

America liked having the world's only living dragons. Until the story hit the wires, the politicians had been unaware of just how much the public fancied the idea.

Instructions came at 4:00 AM to move the detainees to a more secure secret location, while the dragons slept peacefully on the firing range. Not even the arrival of a cold front disturbed them.

CHAPTER 5

@@@@@@

"Harkness," explained Arachne, "is some prince of theirs. He was seized by the pyramid and has not come back. They plainly plan to try to rescue him. That means returning to our world, a world where the gods still rule."

"Albeit, under Typhoeus. We must stop this!" said Medea, between clenched teeth.

"Yes," said Arachne. "First, I'm not having Mac go there without me, and second, if he went *with* me, well, I might end up with great legs. Eight of them."

"And how will they get back? Without Throttler they have no way to return."

"True. We need to get there and stop this. But we don't even know where they've taken them."

"This Chicago place, I would guess. That is where the pyramid is. We were going to go there, remember, to see this Professor Tremelo, and Doc Jerry."

"Well, that is where we must go then. Is this isle far off? Where is it? I will call my dragons . . . I hope that the call still works."

"I hope it does. They could deal with these guards. It is a good sixty leagues if I have it aright. A fair distance. We can maybe catch them while they travel—but these Americans travel faster than the Greeks or my people did. Anyway, long journey or no, it must be done. I will poison the wakeful one, and you can cut the sleeper's throat," said Medea grimly. "We go, with or without dragons. I do not know if my powers to call them will work here."

Arachne held out the little vial that she'd gotten from the doctor. "With any luck you could just make all of them sleep. Or I can. They've tasted your coffee."

"I'll help you to cut their throats then."

"We probably should just bind them fast. We do not wish to start a blood feud if we can help it."

"Will taking them captive help? Have they value as hostages? I think they are lowly fighters. Mere slingers. And will that not be cause enough to send the soldiers of Cruz's Uncle Sam to seek bloody vengeance? Better to cut their throats and be done with it."

"They would have to admit they were bested by a pair of women and two small children," said Arachne, smiling seraphically. "I have noted that American warriors are no better than Greeks at that."

Medea nodded. "We had best dispose of their weapons, though. It will take them a little while to rearm. When do we do this? Tonight?"

"In the morning. They are all here at the dawn. The hour six, as these Arabian numerals show it."

Medea grimaced. "Priones has yet to learn to let me sleep past it. It will be easier than in the dark. Guards are more suspicious then. Very well, I shall call the dragons to me. Maybe they will come. Otherwise we will have to find charioteers and ships as need be."

Medea looked poisonously at the PSA agent. Medea was not someone you wanted to cross at the best of times, and waking her before dawn was a life-risk, no matter who you were. It was probably just as well that she was half-handicapped by a sleepy little boy in one arm nuzzling into her, and another holding onto her nightgown.

"Not without coffee," she said. There was a certain grim finality in that tone. "And over my dead body in my nightgown. If you try I shall scream. And my man's fellow warriors are not so far off, that they will not come. They will deal ill with someone who molests his wife."

"You can have a few minutes to pack up," said Agent Schmitt placatingly. "I'm sorry, ma'am, but these are orders from higher up. And I'll make coffee. I could use a cup myself."

She gave him a look that would have frozen a cockatrice. "I'm just instilling proper discipline into that coffee-pot. I won't have you spoiling it. Arachne is bad enough. She keeps giving it more grounds when it doesn't deserve them and hasn't tried hard enough with the old ones. *I'll* make any coffee in this house. You can sit here and drink it, while we take ours and pack our clothes."

Agent Schmitt decided it wasn't worth arguing about. When he tasted the coffee, he decided that that had been a bad decision. But it was hot and wet, and an extra spoon of sugar helped.

"See that they drink all of it, Neoptolemeus," said Medea, taking her cup.

So, under the unnervingly stern gaze of the seven-year-old-boy, the agents drank.

"The tall one is trouble," said Neoptolemeus righteously. "He did not drink all of the drink you made for him, Mama."

"Oh?" said Medea, calmly checking the edge on her dagger. That didn't worry the boy in the least, Arachne noted.

"Yes," said Neoptolemeus, nodding. "He fell over when there was still at least a quarter of it left. I tried to make him sit up and drink the rest, but most of it spilt down the front of his shirt."

"Those tablets must have been strong!" exclaimed Arachne, looking at her cup. She'd nearly reflexively taken a mouthful. And the doctor had said that they were mild!

"Well," said Medea, taking the cup from her hand. "I didn't know how fast they would work, so I used a potion of my own too."

"It's to be hoped that we haven't killed them," said Arachne.

Medea snorted. "Small loss. But it is not likely. And better that they fell asleep now rather than when they were driving those chariots of theirs. I think we must disarm them and bind them, just in case they do wake up before we leave."

"I wish I had some decent spider web," Arachne said as they walked out of Medea's bedroom to the lounge, where the agents sprawled.

"My new papa has rolls of it," Neoptolemeus informed her. "He calls it fishing line, though. I'll get it. I am not to play with it although he said he was going to show me how to use it, soon. I'm sure it'll be all right if you use it, though."

While he went off, the women searched through the pockets of the agents. Shortly they came upon shoulder holsters.

They looked at the firearms very warily. "Cruz has showed me," said Medea. "Within are small metal arrows. You release them thus." She removed the clip, and put it carefully aside.

"I found some more of those," said Arachne. "What shall we do with them, and the guns?"

Medea's eyes narrowed. "The vacuum cleaner," she said. "It has a bag which it refuses to apply itself to. It is full of dust and scraps. Let them look in there. Cruz told me that the weapons have to be kept clean to work."

A little while later the firearms were being put safely into the dust-bag of the vacuum cleaner, along with the car keys, both from the victims and Cruz's own vehicle. "Now, you see that you look after those. You can bite anyone if they try to take them away from you," said Medea sternly. The vacuum cleaner huddled in its cupboard and looked nasty. Arachne had to admit that she wouldn't try to take anything from it, not even the dust it hoarded.

"And the clips?"

"In among that fiendish Lego-stuff that Cruz bought for the boys," said Medea cheerfully. "You could search for a year and not find the pieces you need." It was a vast barrel of Lego. A few shakes had the clips well-buried, and they went back to the sleeping agents. Priones was sitting eating his breakfast Coco Pops with supreme unconcern, as he sat between them and watched the TV, while his mother and Aunt Arachne continued doing the mysterious things adults did.

Medea looked at the card she had taken from the sleeping agent's pocket. "It is a powerful magical talisman of some sort. I saw the other one threaten the warriors with it. But it has his image painted on it, so it would be of little use to us. I think we should dispose of it. Here, Priones, take it to your favorite toy. You may work the magic handle. But only once, mind."

"He'd better take the other ones too, then," said Arachne, tying more knots in the inferior spider-thread from the reels. "And their mobiles."

"And while you are there, you'd better go. I don't want to

have to stop the chariot for you," said Medea, practically. "Both of you."

The women went on tying. It was fairly feeble spider-thread, this "fishing line," but it was the best they had. They heard the sound of flushing and Priones' delighted giggle, as the agents' PSA IDs went to impress the sewers.

Soon Medea stood up, dusted off her hands and looked down on the sleeping cocoon arrayed in front of the Cartoon Network. "That will have to do," she said. "Stop being so prissy and precise about it, Arachne."

Arachne tied off a last knot, neatly. "It's a habit, I suppose."

"Do you want to bite them and save them to eat later too?" asked Medea. "I really could use that coffee now, but I suppose we'd better go."

"Maybe we should eat something first?"

"That's a good idea," said a voice from the window. A dragon-ish voice.

"Food is always a good idea, Smitar, so long as Arachne makes it," said Bitar. "So where is Cruz? We need to ask him about which birds and bees to eat."

"Trust me," said Medea. "I still have some powers. Bitar, spot a truck with a flat bed at the back. One of those with many wheels. Let me know when you see one."

"With pillows?" asked Bitar.

Medea was used to dragon logic. "Just with a flat back part. You have to provide your own pillows."

"I had a pillow once when I was little, but I ate it."

"That was a goose," said Smitar. "You complained about feathers for ages afterwards."

Bitar wrinkled his forehead. "That's right. Pillows have their feathers on the inside. I remember that now. Geese should be made like that too."

"Look out for the truck or you'll have feathers," said Medea grimly. "And I don't mean inside you. Neoptolemeus. Go up his neck, and keep a look out."

He nodded eagerly. He liked trucks. A few minutes later he called out, "Eighteen wheeler coming, Ma. A flatbed."

Medea nodded. "Time for us to do our magic, Arachne."

∾ ∾ ∾

Mike Convey hauled steel. He'd just delivered twenty tons to one of the big machine shops in Clarkson. He was on his way back to Pittsburgh, still swearing because the return load had fallen through, and the company needed his rig back to finalize part of a massive contract. Nice contract. Shitty late delivery clause. So here he was deadheading.

He did not pick up hitchhikers or hookers. Well . . . sometimes a guy needed a bit of company. When he saw two very good-looking women standing at the roadside sticking a leg out at him . . . Suddenly he was hit by a powerful and irresistible compulsion.

These "truck" things could move faster than a dragon could fly, at least over long distances, and once the trucker got over his initial wrong impression he was very cooperative. Especially when he figured that a dragon could take a look in the window. And the glass wasn't that thick.

While the Air Force scanned the skies, two dragons sped by road toward Chicago. Passing vehicles admired the realistic dragon models on the back of the flatbed. People always see what they expect to see.

"I can't take you to Chicago!" Convey protested. "My boss will have sixty fits."

"What if we paid for the hire of your vehicle?" Arachne came from Colophon, the timocracy of the ancient world where money ruled, and commerce was everything. "It cannot be financially lucrative for you to drive an empty motorized chariot."

Mike gave a quick glance at her, before turning his attention back to the road. It was obvious enough what he was thinking, though. Arachne had had people not take her seriously before, because she was a slight young woman. It was at times like this that still having a spider's body could have been useful.

"Come on, lady, it's a good joke, but this isn't a cab. It's . . ."

"A Peterbilt. A 379 Pete with a five and half Cat and an 18-speed transmission," put in Neoptolemeus.

That got a glance of surprise from Convey. "Bright kid!" he said admiringly.

"I am entirely serious," said Arachne calmly. "I never make jokes about money."

Something in her tone made Mike think twice. "Sure, lady. I

just don't think that you have any idea about how much money you're talking about. The company charges four dollars a mile for this rig."

Arachne picked up her laptop, opened it, and took a platinum credit card out of her purse. "Approximately how many miles are we talking about? If we can find a hot-spot, I can do a direct online transfer. Of course there will be a substantial gratuity to you for all the extra trouble. Shall we say one thousand dollars? Or what do you think, Medea?"

Medea sniffed disapprovingly. "I've never really understood the point in chaffering and trade. It's not something a princess has to do. Personally I think we should offer him a choice. This Chicago-place, or Bitar and Smitar can eat him."

"That's the advantage of trade over the aristocracy. Who would drive the horseless chariot then?"

"Me," said Neoptolemeus hopefully. "I want to."

The trucker saw a dragonish eye peering in at him from the side window.

Medea sighed. "I know that look. They're hungry again. They're always hungry. So, is it you for their dinner or do we get to go to Chicago?" There was no jest in that matter-of-fact tone.

Convey took a deep breath. "Look, there's a truck stop ahead. How about I call the boss, and you talk money to him?"

"Perhaps there will be food available," said Arachne.

"And I need to wee," piped little Priones. "Soon."

Neoptolemeus said nothing. He just concentrated on the gears and the physical operations of the vehicle, imitating the movements of the driver.

That was the most worrying thing of all, maybe.

"We're two blocks from the Pyramid Exclusion Zone," said Convey. "I can't take you any farther." There wasn't much traffic here. The road didn't go anywhere anymore.

"So you see," said Arachne, smiling devastatingly and handing over a wad of crisp $100 notes. "It wasn't that hard."

Medea nodded. "The seats are better padded in these chariots than in mine. Now, children, let's get going."

"Will you teach me to drive someday?" asked Neoptolemeus as he scrambled out. "I want to drive a chariot with so many horses under the hood."

"I just want to see how you fit them all in," piped Priones. "And I want to wee." It seemed like that was the kid's favorite statement.

One of the dragons sniffed. "Can smell Cruz," he said happily.

"Right," said Medea. "Let's go. Up you get, children."

Mike felt sorry for someone.

The dragons began to slowly rise, spiky and glittering above the roadway, and definitely headed toward the exclusion zone. Convey watched, shrugged, and decided that it was a good time to get into his truck and get the hell out of here.

CHAPTER 6

❧❧❧❧❧❧

Agent Schmitt bravely arrested Johnny Bravo for molesting the Cow, and shot the Chicken, while, Ed, Ed and Eddy cheered. But did they have to cheer so loudly?

He opened his eyes. Ed, Ed and Eddy were cheering . . . on the TV screen in front of him. They weren't, his confused mind realized, cheering for him. Maybe they were cheering Agent Erskine. They couldn't be cheering for that useless idiot Reno. But what had Erskine done to get cheered? He was snoring his head off, the side of his face covered in either some horrific scabrous disease, or dried Coco Pops. He hadn't shot the Cow and arrested the Chicken for molesting Johnny Bravo. . . .

Something was wrong! With a force of will, Agent Schmitt tried two things. First, to sit up. Second, to think clearly.

Schmitt failed entirely at the first task. He tried to use his hands and it appeared that they were tied together. His head did clear slightly, though. He remembered drinking part of a truly terrible cup of coffee, before taking the detainees . . .

Detainees. Now he woke properly. Enough to yell, at least. That woke Agent Reno. Reno said "Shurrup!" and rolled over, and fell off the couch. He landed with a thump, which must have done a better job of waking him, because he tried to get up.

"I'm tied up," Reno said.

45

He always did state the obvious, thought Schmitt, struggling to stand up himself. "I know, you moron," he snapped. "The coffee was drugged, and we're all tied up and the detainees have esca—*aaaaaah!*"

The last part of his "escaped" converted to a scream that was lost in the shattering of glass as he fell over Agent Erskine's feet and crashed over onto the glass-top coffee table.

It didn't cut him too badly. And it did wake Agent Erskine, who blinked and said, "Isn't there something on another channel?"

They tried yelling. Nobody came. Agent Reno thought he saw something at the window, but no one came in.

So, using a piece of broken coffee-table-top, Erskine managed to saw through some of the line on Schmitt. Agent Cangi slept happily on as they cut each other loose. As soon as his hands were free, Schmitt felt for his mobile and his gun. Neither were where they should be. He stumbled on numbed legs over to the telephone, only to realize, as it echoed hollowly in his ear, that they'd ordered it cut off at the base switchboard.

The other two were trying to shake Agent Cangi into wakefulness, having cut him free.

"Leave him. We need to get in touch with the duty officer as soon as possible." It was daylight out there. "They've been gone for a few hours."

The three, none too steady on their feet, headed for the front door. It was locked. They had to force their way out of a window. As he fell into the garden, Agent Schmitt became aware that he was being watched. The woman who was watching from across the street had the kind of look on her face that made wise men kowtow. Schmitt staggered toward her. "I need to use your telephone, right now."

"Keep your distance," she said warningly. "I've called the base MPs."

"Ma'am. I'm Agent Schmitt. PSA . . ." With horror, he realized that the ID he was trying to flash wasn't there. And he'd stepped closer as he said it. She kicked him hard enough to make him sing tenor for a month, and retreated from his doubled-up body into her house and locked the door, loudly.

Agent Reno was trying to break into the black SUV. Agent Erskine made the mistake of following the woman and was pounding on the door, when a Humvee with six MPs skidded to a halt, narrowly missing Schmitt, lying in the middle of the roadway.

Aggression, under the circumstances, was probably stupid, but perhaps it was the drug's effect. Schmitt had to admit later—with him bloody, Reno coffee-stained, and Erskine's face looking like he had a terminal disease that vaguely resembled dried Coco Pops, and not a shred of ID among them—it wasn't that surprising that things went badly wrong. One of them did appear to be burgling a car, and another attempting to force entry into Sergeant Jenkins' house. A third person being sick in the roadway didn't help the reaction of the MPs one bit.

Still, they were luckier than Cangi. He was forgotten in the melee and mess that followed, and woke up the next day, when the others were already in Washington, doing some explaining. On an actual carpet that might as well have been The Carpet.

"We could ignore them," said Arachne doubtfully, looking at the soldiers in front of them. They'd come down Midway Plaisance fairly low. The soldiers were unmistakably making gestures to halt and to come down.

Medea had much more experience at judging soldiers by their posture. Those were four nervous men, but not men who would run. You could see it in the way they stood, as clearly as daylight. She shook her head. "They're from the 101st. We'll have to talk to them. Down, Smitar."

The one with marks of rank plainly recognized them. He was suitably respectful, but firm. "I'm sorry, ladies, but we're not allowed to let anyone in past the outer perimeter unless they've been authorized."

"Is that like roasted?" asked Smitar.

"No, silly! Don't you know anything? It means written on," said Bitar, tasting an M16 with his tongue.

"Well, tell him to write on us then," said Smitar impatiently. "We want to see Cruz. We need a good scratch and some birds and bees to eat."

The officer blinked at the dragons. "Sergeant Cruz isn't here."

"Yes he is. Can smell him," Bitar informed the man.

"They can smell a man a thousand cubits off," said Medea. "Those people from the PSA took him and Mac. They're coming here, if they're not here already. We need you to authorize us to find them. They're not going into the pyramid."

She folded her arms. Neoptolemeus and Priones took one look at that and took a step back, wide-eyed and silent.

That move obviously did not pass this young officer by. He would go far, decided Medea. He had survival potential.

"I can't do that, ma'am," he said.

She downgraded his survival potential. As he was about to discover what dragon dinner felt like, first hand, from the inside. He continued, "But I can have you taken to see Professor Tremelo."

"Who is he?" asked Medea, pausing.

"Remember, Medea. We met him. It is a rank like Doc Jerry's," said Arachne.

"Dr. Lukacs? He's here too," said the young officer. "He came in to see Professor Tremelo this morning, and Lamont Jackson just arrived too. Look, ladies, let me escort you there. They'll sort something out."

Medea looked at him, long and hard. "Very well," she said. She turned to the dragons. "Wait. If we do not come back with this authorization very soon, eat these others and come and fetch us."

The two dragons nodded obediently and rose to settle on a nearby building like two enormous, shiny gargoyles. Gargoyles that watched the checkpoint very carefully, as Medea, Arachne and the children climbed into the lieutenant's Humvee.

"Dragons!" exclaimed Miggy Tremelo.

Arachne, Medea, Priones and Neoptolemeus burst into the room. "Doc," said Medea, with no real attention for the rest of them, "They have taken Cruz and Mac, and they are making them go back! Back to fetch someone called Harkness. You must help us. The dragons say they can smell Cruz. He is near. They will take him back into the pyramid and I will never see him again. And he is such a wonderful husband. Such a good father."

She sniffed and dissolved into tears. Liz patted her arm and fished out a Kleenex for her from the new portmanteau-handbag, as Arachne continued in her musical voice. "We need authorization to get past the soldier guards. Help us, please. Mac will be killed without me to look after him properly."

Miggy Tremelo cleared his throat. "You say the dragons smell Sergeant Cruz inside the outer perimeter? That they're going to 'fetch' Harkness? Tom Harkness?"

Arachne and Medea nodded. "They have been taken by the PSA. They have held us as hostages for days, until we escaped from them this morning."

"Hell's teeth! There is a presidential directive putting the entire inner perimeter area off limits to anyone without prior consultation with PSA *and* the National Science Advisory Council. And that means me. They're not authorized to do any such cowboy crap on their own. Rachel! Get me that woman—ah, Ms. Garnett—on the phone. Meanwhile—"

He looked at the paratrooper lieutenant's name badge. "Lieutenant . . . Evans, is it?"

"Yes, sir. Rich Evans."

Miggy gave the young officer a quick inspection and decided he liked what he saw. Not so much Evans' size—although he was a big fellow, well over six feet tall—as a certain indefinable something he thought he read in his blue eyes. Still . . .

As a scientist, "indefinable" made Miggy edgy. He had to be careful here.

"Tell me something about yourself, Lieutenant. Personal, I mean."

Evans' eyes widened slightly. "Sir?"

"You heard me," said Miggy. "I'm entering a political gray zone here, Lieutenant, and you may—or may not—be one of my chosen instruments. I haven't got time to subject you to a battery of psychological tests. So tell me something about yourself that might give me a handle. On you, so to speak, not your uniform."

Tremelo knew it was a rather outlandish demand, but . . . if his assessment of that "indefinable something" was accurate, the lieutenant would give him an answer.

And, indeed, after a moment's hesitation Evans shrugged, unbuttoned his right sleeve, and rolled it up to expose a very striking tattoo. A large Celtic Cross with . . .

"I got this after I married Tricia. She's a Jewish girl from Wisconsin. Then"—he pointed to some lettering under the cross—"I had our two daughters' names added. This one's Kennedy Lynn and that one's Madeleine Grace."

Miggy recognized the script, if not the names themselves. "In

Hebrew!" he said, half-laughing. "Why do I think I'd never find such an idiosyncratic tattoo on the arm of a PSA agent?"

Smiling thinly, Evans rolled the sleeve back and began rebuttoning it. "I believe, sir—so I've been told, at any rate—that PSA agents are strictly forbidden from getting tattoos of any kind."

"Wouldn't surprise me. Fine, Lieutenant Evans. Will you accept my authority, under the circumstances?"

"Yes, sir." That came with no hesitation at all.

"Good. Get onto outer perimeter security. Check if any PSA vehicles have gone into the exclusion zone."

"I'll do *that*," said Marie decisively, heading for the outer office. "Put the lieutenant outside where he can do what I can't."

"And get me the director of the Fish and Wildlife Service!" Miggy hollered after her.

Evans frowned for a moment, and then smiled. "Fish and Wildlife, huh? Correct me if I'm wrong, Professor Tremelo, but I don't believe their authority is limited by the Alien Pyramid Security Act."

Miggy was grinning outright—and starting to rub his hands together. "No, as a matter of fact, they aren't, Lieutenant. I really, really detest *that woman*. And I do believe she just stepped over a line she couldn't afford to cross."

But Evans didn't hear the last sentence, since he was already out the door.

The two black SUVs drove up to the checkpoint, at speed. The driver held up a PSA ID and drove into the outer perimeter area, towing his horsebox. The vehicle behind towed an even larger trailer. Uncertainly, without their commanding officer present, the paratroopers let them through.

"That's Throttler!"

"And Cruz!" said the other dragon.

They looked at each other.

Then at the paratroopers manning the checkpoint. Then at the departing SUVs. Then at each other again. Then they launched into flight.

"We're going after Cruz and Throttler!" said the dragon, leaning his head down to shout at the paratroopers.

"We won't be long. Don't worry, we'll come back and eat you," said the other, flapping.

Lieutenant Evans drove up just in time to see the SUVs heading further into the exclusion zone. Then, he looked up at the
seventy feet of sinuous reptilians, undulating after them.

Private Marc Henderson raised his rifle.

"Hold," commanded Evans. "Don't fire. I doubt if a 5.56 mm
bullet would have any effect on a dragon anyway."

"But, Lieutenant, they're entering the fire-zone."

Evans put his hand on the muzzle of the rifle and brought it
down. "They're animals, Henderson, don't you know that? Wildlife.
Endangered wildlife. We don't even shoot pigeons flying in here,
let alone something that is rarer than an American bald eagle."

"But they talk, Lieutenant," protested Henderson.

The lieutenant shook his head sadly. "So do parrots. Like boots,
they're hardly human, are they? We stop *human* ingress. Those
are our orders."

One of the other soldiers spoke up. "Lieutenant, on the news
last night they said that they believed those critters had been
taken by the Pissants, uh, the PSA. The conservation guys were
appealing for any information."

"Yes, I know," said Lieutenant Evans, smiling more widely still.
"You're right. I'd say we'd better report to Fish and Wildlife that
they're here—except I happen to know that's already being done. I
guess the Pissants are going to have to do quite a lot of explaining, especially after Ms. Garnett's denials last night."

Private Henderson nodded earnestly. "I found that out when
I got arrested for the pizza."

At any other time Evans would have loved to know how even
Henderson could have managed to get arrested for pizza, but
right now he had to get a report in to Tremelo.

"She's not available," said Marie. "I threatened to rip an extra
asshole in her secretary, but I reckon she's genuinely not there."

"The President . . . What is it, Rachel?"

"Checkpoint CZ alpha on Midway Plaisance. Lieutenant Evans
reports two PSA vehicles have just passed the outer perimeter,
towing two large trailers. Horse trailers, they think. The dragons
have chased after them. The lieutenant says the dragons insist
Sergeant Cruz was in one of the vehicles."

"With their sense of smell, I don't doubt it." Miggy grabbed his
jacket and was heading for the door himself. "God only knows

why the bastards have horse trailers—but it won't be good. The call to the President will just have to wait. Marie, tell Lieutenant Evans those PSA agents have to be stopped from whatever they're doing. With deadly force if need be, dammit! I'm getting down there. And get on the phone to Senator Abrams of the Pyramid Oversight Committee. Senator Larsen from Montana, too. Tell them we've got the dragons, the sphinx and the PSA running some kind of cowboy rogue operation. Tell them I've gone to try and put a stop to it."

Lamont pushed past Miggy. "The car's out front, Miggy. I'll drive you."

"Rachel, you make the calls," said Marie, grabbing her children's hands. "I ain't letting that man of mine out of my sight ever again, not as long as I live."

A minute and a half later the stretch limo was racing toward the inner exclusion zone around the University of Chicago's Regenstein Library. Or what was left of it, anyway.

Sitting in the second black SUV, the one towing the larger trailer with a sleeping Greek sphinx within, not the one towing the double horsebox, Cruz could only wish that he'd had a proper chance to say goodbye to Medea, and that they'd put him and Mac into the same vehicle. Well, he had a pack full of the sort of things he'd wished like hell he'd had last time. And in BDUs he was a lot warmer than these jerks in leather skirts. They looked a lot more like a cheap remake of *Ben Hur* than the real thing. The inner exclusion line was just ahead. There, according to Agent Supervisor Megane, they'd stop, hitch the horses from the horsebox to Throttler's trailer, and, linked hands touching the still somnolent sphinx, make their way into the snatch zone.

By now, Cruz was pretty sure the PSA agents must have drugged the sphinx. How they'd managed that—or how they'd persuaded her to enter the cargo plane that brought them here from Las Vegas—he still couldn't figure out. They had to be absolutely crazy to do something like that. Leaving aside the legalities, Throttler was *dangerous*.

But . . . he'd also been around Agent Supervisor Megane long enough to have gotten a sense for the man. And just that one brief contact with Helen Garnett had been enough to give him a sense of what *she* was like. So, although he didn't know any of the details, Cruz was sure he knew how the whole thing had unfolded. Garnett would have talked tough in front of Megane, not understanding that Megane was to a real "tough op" what a semi-delusional drugstore cowboy was to John Wesley Hardin. If she said "inch," Megane would interpret "mile"—not knowing himself the difference between a mile and a kilometer.

The rest would follow, like an avalanche—or a train wreck. It would actually be rather funny, in a gruesome sort of way, if Cruz and Mac hadn't gotten stuck in the middle of it. Cruz was pretty sure that he could break free of the two assigned to be his contacts, but whether Mac could was another matter. And whether they'd get themselves shot on the spot, was yet another matter. It might be best to go, and let Throttler bring them home . . . if this worked.

He wished he could talk it over with Mac first, though. This bunch of PSA security flakes didn't have a snowball's chance in hell of surviving the other side. They just didn't get it. He just couldn't penetrate that armor of *know-it-all*. The only trouble was that the Krim might drop them into a place where even Throttler might get killed or separated from them.

Just then decisions were taken out of his hands by an impact that knocked him sprawling onto Agent Bott. With the raw sound of screeching metal the SUV fishtailed and came to a stop. Struggling to sit up, Cruz saw why. The trailer carrying the sphinx had been knocked over sideways. The roof had been torn clean off and Throttler had been rolled right out onto the street. Now, looking somewhat groggy, she was lurching to her feet.

Looking up, Cruz gave a lopsided grin. He saw now what had knocked the trailer over. A blow from a dragon's tail. It was a good thing that they'd been slowing to stop just outside the inner exclusion zone.

"Looks like the Seventh Cavalry arrived just in time," he murmured to himself. It might make things more complicated later on but it took decisions out of his hands, for now.

Agent Supervisor Megane hauled his helmet straight. "Out. We need to recapture that animal!"

"Are you utterly crazy?" said Cruz.

"That means you too, soldier!" snapped the PSA agent. The doors to the vehicle opened and pseudo-Greek hoplites spilled onto the roadway.

Willy-nilly, so did Cruz.

⊙⊘   ⊙⊘   ⊙⊘

It wasn't hard for Liz to work out where they were. The two dragons were wheeling overhead, just above the black SUVs and the now-smashed trailer. The stretch limo slewed around, and people—led by Arachne, by a short head—exploded out of the doors. She and Medea ran full tilt toward the redhead and the stocky dark man, both in camo battledress, surrounded by Greek hoplite warriors who seemed to be frantically trying to pull their swords apart.

Liz ran toward Throttler instead, with Jerry and Lamont—and Marie and a trail of kids in hot pursuit—across the broad yellow line painted across the roadway. They ran past the *Exclusion Zone—Danger!* signs. "Are you all right?" yelled Liz.

The Greek sphinx was still groggy, but at least she recognized them. "When does the great contest start?" she demanded. "I hope we're not too late. I'm bound to win the gold medal."

Liz looked up at her. "Huh? What contest?"

Throttler frowned. "The World Riddling Olympics, of course." She nodded her huge head toward Megane. "The one that Mr. Bara over there is . . . what's the word? Emcee, I think."

Liz, Lamont and Marie stared at Megane, who was lying on the ground now. Apparently, he'd tripped while trying to duck one of the dragon's swoops.

Marie suddenly laughed. "God, you know—he *does* look a little bit like Dave Bara."

The name vaguely registered on Liz. Dave Bara was the master of ceremonies for one of those idiotic television quiz shows that Americans seemed addicted to, for no reason she'd ever been able to fathom.

Lamont laughed, too. "So *that's* how they did it." He shook his head. "Throttler, there ain't no such thing as—"

"Lamont!" Liz half-shrieked. She now understood how the PSA agents had managed to finagle the sphinx onto that cargo plane, too—but she hadn't forgotten, as Lamont had, just how deadly Throttler was. As much as Liz detested the PSA, she still didn't want to see half a dozen of them eaten alive right in front of her and several children.

Sure enough, the frown on the huge sphinx's face was starting to look positively thunderous. But before Liz could figure out a way to deflect Throttler's murderous fury, one of those same idiot

PSA agents—disguised as a "Greek warrior," to make everything as absurd as possible—rushed up and tried to push her away from the sphinx.

Liz lost her temper and gave the bastard a mighty swat with her handbag. Unfortunately, he flinched at the last moment. Instead of the solid corner of the bag smacking into his head, it simply knocked his helmet askew and she stumbled off-balance into him. The next thing she knew she was wrestling the jackass.

Jerry and Lamont tried to pull them apart, only to have more "Greek hoplites" run up and join in. Marie and her kids did too. There was a massive free-for-all just in front of Throttler—whose teeth were now bared.

Cruz was the first to realize what was happening, as he emerged from an enthusiastic hugging by reptilian and human agencies. "Smitar!" he yelled at the dragon. "Herd them back across the line!" He struggled to free himself from the embrace of his loved ones.

Then there was a brief purple flare of light. Jerry, Liz, Lamont, Marie, four children and five "Greek hoplites" had vanished.

Miggy Tremelo was making the air turn blue with his swearing.

Lieutenant Evans and his soldiers arrived a few seconds later, spilling out of their Humvee with their weapons ready.

"Arrest that son of a bitch," Tremelo snarled, pointing at Megane.

The agent supervisor had managed to get back onto his feet. "You can't—"

But by then Lieutenant Evans had his rifle muzzle right under Megane's chin.

"Can't what?" he asked. "And what kind of odds do you want? I'll give you ten-to-one, but I wouldn't take them if I were you. I really, really wouldn't."

"Should I shoot him, sir?" asked Henderson. Quite a bit more eagerly than was really proper for a trained soldier.

Megane cocked his eyes at the private. Henderson's gun was pointing right at his upper chest, from a range of maybe eight feet. He couldn't possibly miss—and whatever else Megane was ignorant of, ballistics was clearly not one of them. He'd be dead before his body hit the ground.

"It grieves me to report that Private Henderson here once got arrested for pizza," Evans said solemnly.

Megane's eyes swiveled back to Evans. By now, they were the only part of his body that was moving at all, besides his mouth.

"Huh? That doesn't make any sense."

"I know it doesn't—and he's the same soldier who just asked my permission to shoot you. I recommend you contemplate that juxtaposition." Evans held up a hand. "Not just yet, Private Henderson. I think negotiations are still possible. So, Agent Whateveryournameis, I repeat: What odds do you want to give me that—what was the expression—'you can't do that,' I believe? Like I said, ten-to-one's the going rate."

Megane's jaws tightened. "I'm not talking."

"How wise of you. Private Henderson, you may lower your weapon. I do not believe it will prove necessary to shoot the imbecile after all."

Henderson did as commanded. "Well, damn," he said. "It was lousy pizza, too."

"I tried to point out that the sphinx could have taken them there, without all the dangerous stuff with the pyramid," said Mac. "When we were in the SUV on the way here. But they weren't listening."

Miggy shook his head. "The Greek sphinx would probably not have helped them get where they've gone anyway. According to what we've established from Dr. Lukacs, the Krim have been excluded from ancient Greek myth, and ancient Egyptian myth. I'm not sure where they've gone, but it isn't there."

"So . . . where *have* they gone?" asked Cruz.

Miggy pulled a face. "Name a mythology. There are hundreds to choose from. Probably thousands."

At last! The Krim device sensed a rich crop, full of credulity and anger, just in range. It activated the prukrin transfer mechanism. This Ur-Mythworld had been a huge problem, with too few new meme-carriers and huge problems with the local gods. It had thought the Greeks venal and unreasonable, to say nothing of lazy. The Egyptians had been far too independent and intransigent. This place, underpowered as the Krim device was now, was worse still.

It was only when the translation was too far advanced that the Krim device realized that it had been gulled. The meme-flavor of some of those coming through was the same as the group of denialists it had had such a hard time with in Greece and Egypt. The one who had eventually driven the Krim-masters out of their new playground in Greece.

The group would have to be killed. But it would have to avoid direct contact!

As if it had not been having a bad enough time with the Krim-primary in this world. He was very strong. It was questionable just who was in control any longer.

PART II

MY KINGDOM
FOR A NORSE

CHAPTER 7

@@@@@@

Again there was no moment of transition, no time between places. Jerry just found himself in an alien world, falling flat on his butt, with a large "Greek" on top of him. That almost certainly saved his life, though. A hissing white-hot ball of metal hurtled overhead and smashed clean through a huge rusty iron pillar.

Frightened, yowling, misshapen creatures yammered and ran around them, and over them. They were in some kind of enormous hall, lit only by fires running down the length of it, and filled, right now, with panic. Some of the panic came from the man on top of him. "What in hell is going on?" he yelled. And then he repeated himself in bad contemporary Greek.

"We're in a Mythworld. Now get off him, you idiot," said a woman with a slight Germanic-Dutch hint to her English.

Never had Liz's accent sounded so charming. She pushed the PSA agent off Jerry and hauled him to his feet. "Come on, Jerry. The others are back there. We've got to get out of this place. There is a passageway."

It was the kind of Liz-practicality that Jerry found he really could use. Unfortunately it didn't seem to be working too well this time. The passage led into a warren of others, an absolute maze of rock-hewed passageways, poorly lit by pitch-soaked brands that burned in iron hoops along the way. It was also

61

full of panic-stricken men, and creatures that definitely weren't human. Humans were in the minority, and they had that half-starved, beaten look that said "slave" even without the dirt and the ragged clothes. The ragged clothes always included some form of breeches, and, despite numerous attempts by the PSA agents still badly disguised as "hoplites," they did not speak Greek.

What was worse was that the passageways all eventually seemed to loop back to the great hall. And someone was throwing white-hot iron around in there, with considerable force. Force enough to make holes in walls, and start several fires, which didn't make things any easier.

"That's enough," panted Marie. "Let's stop running and try and get organized."

They stopped in a little alcove off the main passage, and Marie sat down on a stone bench. She looked a little gray-faced even in the ruddy torchlight. Her kids clustered around her, the youngest boy climbing down from Lamont's back to hug her. And then Marie's eyes went wide. "Where's Tina?"

The little girl swallowed. "She didn't come with us, Mama."

"Are you sure?"

The one twin who was present nodded. "She let go my hand just before it happened." A tear leaked down her face. "Will she be all right?"

"Just fine, honey. I promise," she said, hugging her. "Better off than us, here."

Marie looked at someone standing next to Jerry. Standing so quietly that Jerry hadn't even noticed him. "And you, boy?"

In jeans, sneakers and a Chicago Bears sweatshirt, Neoptolemeus looked like any American kid, not the son of Medea and a Greek hero. A scared, miserable kid, right now. "This is Medea's son," said Jerry, putting a hand on the boy's shoulder. "Neoptolemeus."

Lamont nodded. "We'll take care of you, boy."

The child bit his lip and leaned into the shelter of Jerry. It was an odd feeling, that. Jerry squeezed the shoulder. "You'll be fine. We're all friends of your mama's."

In the background, five "Greeks" were attempting to assemble firearms from their spears and swords, with a notable lack of success. One of them cleared his throat. "Um. Dr. Lukacs, I presume?"

Jerry looked at the man and noted his hoplite outfit was from around the rise of the Persian conflicts—which was rather a lot later than the Achaeans that they'd fallen in with on their first venture into the Ur-Mythworlds. "Yes. And who are you?"

"Besides the jerks that got us into this mess, that is," said Liz, swinging her shoulder bag dangerously.

The PSA agent straightened up. "You interfered with our mission—"

A huge squalling howl from the hall interrupted him, and perhaps recalled him to where he was. "I'm Agent Stephens. Can you tell us where we are? We've lost our guides and we still have an assignment to complete, if possible. Sergeant Cruz said you were the leading expert in this field, you and someone he called 'Sir.' So could you tell us where about in Greece we are?"

"We're not in Greece," said Jerry as calmly as he could.

This appeared to tax Stephens' intelligence. "But Agent Supervisor Megane told us—"

"Haven't you figured out *yet* that your goddamned boss is a nincompoop?" demanded Lamont angrily. "What does it take? A two-by-four across the head?"

"We're in another Ur-Mythworld, Agent Stephens," said Jerry, less heatedly. "Another mythology entirely. We had succeeded in banishing the Krim from the Greek Ur-Myth. Looking at the dress of the people we've seen so far, and what I would guess are giants and trolls, I would suspect Norse. It's not an arena I am overly knowledgeable about, other than in general terms."

"What are you group of morons attempting to do with those spears?" asked Liz.

The agent looked warily at her. "We have covert-ops weapons, Miss. We'll just get our weapons together and establish radio contact with HQ and move out."

"That's Dr. De Beer to you, not Miss. Unless you also want to call me 'Sir,'" said Liz with a nasty smile. "You really don't understand what you've gotten into, do you? Thanks to your idiocy, what we're all into, I should say."

He bridled a bit. "Look, Miss, um, Doctor . . . I'm sorry you got caught up in this op, but you shouldn't have interfered."

"I probably saved your life, you fool. Throttler would have killed you, and probably eaten you, in another few seconds. You had to be utterly insane to meddle with a sphinx like that!" She took a deep breath. "However, that's over and done with, for good or bad. Now, we've got children to get out of here. You'd better put those spears together again, and give them to me, Jerry and Lamont. We at least have a little experience in using them."

He drew himself up rather scornfully. "We've got enough fire-power to deal with unarmed savages. We just need to get the rifles screwed back together. I don't see any need for subterfuge at the moment."

"First, they're not unarmed," said Liz. "They have very effective spears, swords, bows and arrows and knives, which they know how to use a lot better than you do. Second, *you* are unarmed, because firearms won't work here. And by the looks of it you can't even get them assembled, let alone try them out."

"Having some trouble with the screw mechanism," admitted one of the men.

"The Norse probably didn't have threaded screws, and certainly not precisely machined ones," said Liz. "And third, I don't have the time and patience to shepherd you around. I broke in one set of paratroopers, who had the great advantage over you of functioning brains. I'm not prepared to do it again. You either take orders from me or we part company. Now."

"I'd do it if you want to stay alive," said a grim-faced Marie. "Or I might be tempted to deal with you myself for what you done to my kids, bringing them into a place like this."

The answer of the agent was to dig into his leather shoulder bag and produce a large pistol. "Ma'am, we've got a job to do in the interests of the National Security of the United States." Somehow, like Megane, he managed to pronounce "national security" with capital letters. "You people shouldn't have got yourselves involved. But this is more important than the lives of a few citizens or children. You'll just have to look after yourselves."

Liz looked at him and laughed. "You still don't get it, do you? I gather you were supposed to 'fetch' some high panjandrum called Harkness. Well, there are no guarantees that he's in this Mythworld. And short of dying, there is no way you can get yourselves out of here, let alone him."

The agent nodded. "We're considered expendable. We knew that. But it is vital to make sure Mr. Harkness does not remain in enemy hands."

Liz snorted. "Good luck. I suggest that you keep a diary, so that when your dead body arrives back in Chicago they'll know where you went. You still don't have a clue where you are, or where to go."

Neoptolemeus began to cry. "It's all right, son. We'll get you out of here," said Jerry awkwardly, wishing he knew just how that could be done. He'd worked it out once before. He'd work it out again. Last time he'd just had the responsibility for adult lives on his hands. Now . . . with Medea's son and Marie and Lamont's own brood . . . it just got harder.

"But *she* said that there is no way back," said the boy. He was plainly used to taking a female word as final. With a mother like Medea, that was understandable.

"I worked out a way back before," Jerry said, with a confidence he didn't really feel. "It's different this time, but I'll work it out. And if I can't, Liz and Lamont and Marie will." He pointed at Tyrone. "I remember your mother telling me that she wanted you to make friends with other American boys. Here's your chance."

"Good thinking," said Lamont. "Will you take care of him, Ty? And Neoptolemeus, Ty doesn't know anything about swords and dragons and magic. Things you grew up with, and we're likely to have to deal with here. I'd appreciate your help with showing him how to deal with that stuff, huh?"

Neoptolemeus looked at Tyrone a little doubtfully. "Are you high-born, Ethiope?"

"Chicago South Side," said Lamont with a wink to Marie. "You don't get much higher than that." She seemed to be choking a little.

"Do you know anything about trucks?" asked Neoptolemeus, accepting this assurance cheerfully.

"I guess," said Tyrone. "And Emmitt," he jerked a thumb at the live-in cousin. "He knows everything. What's your name again, kid?"

Neoptolemeus left the shelter of Jerry's arm and walked across to Tyrone. "Neoptolemeus. And you, Ethiope?"

"Tyrone . . . Neo what? What kinda name is that?"

Neoptolemeus shrugged. "I suppose you can call me Tolly. My little brother does."

Jerry felt oddly bereft, although he'd have said that he was the least paternal guy in the universe. Still. What did he know about kids?

The "hoplite" agents all had handguns out now. It looked to Jerry as if they might just abandon pretense and their swords and spears. If they did, then Jerry was all for looting them immediately. They had to be better weapons than the pistols would prove to be.

Each of the agents pulled a hinged piece of cheek-piece across their mouths. "Control, come in for strike-team alpha," Stephens said, then waited.

It didn't look like he was getting a reply.

"Control, are you receiving me?" There was a hint of desperation in that voice.

"It's not going to work," said Liz. "Now run along, while we try and work out how to get out of here. Any ideas, Jerry?"

He shrugged. "My field is the Middle East. I know something about Norse myth, I suppose." A bit hastily he added, "But I'm not a specialist, you understand?"

Liz laughed. "God, Jerry, you are *such* an academic. 'Not my field' translates into, 'I know ten times more than all but twenty people in the world, who *really* know the stuff.'"

Jerry gave her a nervous smile. "Well...okay, I remember all the basic stories. The apples of Idun, the death of Baldr. The binding of the Fenrir wolf...Enough to guess we're in some fight between Æsir and giants right now. Although these look more like trolls. Mind you, size and shape do seem to be things that the Norse pantheon changed at will."

"I suppose the education system in the old South Africa was sadly lacking. All we ever learned about was the Great Trek, six times," said Liz resignedly. "So who were the good guys?"

"Anyone but the giants and Loki. Some of the giants were friendly with the Æsir. Lamont, do you know any of it?"

"A bit," admitted that fount of useless knowledge. "I read a book about the ring of...I think it was Andvari. The source for that opera."

"Wagner?" said Liz with faint traces of alarm. "Don't tell me I have ended up in Wagner. That's too cruel."

"In the gravy...the sauce for it, anyway," said Jerry, grinning.

"It's an Odd...un," Lamont immediately came back.

"Oh, I 'Woden' say that," said Jerry, rubbing his hands.

Liz cocked her head "Look, it sounds like that fight is getting closer. I think we need to go elsewhere, before my beating you for making any more terrible puns becomes academic."

"Why don't we go up there?" asked Neoptolemeus, pointing

to a rickety ladder, made of crooked rived wood with roughly lashed crossbars, standing in the shadowy corner. It led up to a dark hole twenty feet higher up. "We could pull up the ladder when we're up."

"And pelt them with rocks or bricks or something if they try to follow us," said Ty, gleefully.

"What about this lot?" said Lamont, nodding toward the nearby gaggle of agents. They now had their helmets off, peering unbelievingly in the poor light at what their radios had become.

As he said that, a bar of near-molten metal smashed through the wall and removed one of the agents from the equation permanently. The bar went right through his chest and into the wall beyond. And then, as with all of those snatchees killed in the Mythworlds, he suddenly wasn't here anymore.

That had the rest of them pushing the kids up the rickety ladder in a real hurry. Getting back home was on everyone's minds. But not dead.

By the time Jerry got up the ladder, Lamont was yelling for Tyrone and Tolly. "Where the hell have those damn kids got to?"

The damn kids in question stuck their heads out of a doorway, and scampered out. "We thought we might find something we could throw down on the bad guys. But there is some fat guy with a red beard asleep in there," said Tyrone in a stage whisper.

"We thought he was dead," said Tolly.

"But he's snoring fit to bring the roof down," said Tyrone with a giggle. "Worse than my dad."

"You should hear *my* new dad!" said Tolly, proudly. "He's the champion! There is a window on the other side of the guy."

"It's open," said Tyrone.

"And it's snowing out there."

"How far is it from the ground?" asked Liz, standing next to the ladder that the four surviving PSA agents had decided to climb up too. "Hurry up, you lot."

"Dunno. We didn't want to go too near the sleeping man in case we woke him," admitted Tyrone.

Anyone who was still asleep in this racket was probably not going to be awakened by two small boys, Jerry decided. Even ones like these two, with broken volume controls.

"There are bound to be other rooms. And you two kids will

stay close to us. We are not getting separated, you hear me?" said Marie, in her best *don't-argue-with-me* tone. "Emmitt. Ella. Keep an eye on them, for heaven's sake."

"Haul that ladder up," Liz said to the agents. "Put your backs in it, for goodness sakes. Are you scared you're going to get a breeze up your skirts?"

If looks could have killed, Liz would have been stone dead right there. But the ladder came up with speed, hitting the stone roof. A plate-sized flake of rock nearly brained Liz. "Hells teeth! Turn it, shit-for-brains!" Then she looked guiltily at the kids.

But there was no room to maneuver the ladder. They had to leave it propped half up, half down.

They moved down the passage past the open doorway, from which stentorian snores of truly epic proportions were issuing. Jerry had moved himself to the front—"point," he thought soldiers called it—while Liz brought up the rear, tailed by the four worried looking PSA agents. As they came to where this passage intersected another, Jerry nearly walked into a man who was hurrying around the corner the other way.

There was a torch just there and so Jerry got a really good look at the man, before he turned in a swirl of blue cloak and sprinted off down the passage. It was not the kind of face you forgot, strong, lined, with an eagle-beak nose, a sour turn to the mouth . . . and an empty eye-socket.

And a pyramid-pendant around his neck.

With a cold shock Jerry knew that he'd just met the Krim's local flunky. To make things worse, his name happened to be Odin. He'd not been pleased to see Jerry, and there had definitely been a look of recognition in that solitary cold blue eye.

"We're in trouble," said Jerry. "This is Norse myth, all right, and the Krim is definitely in control. That was Odin."

Lamont's eyes widened. "Let's see if we can find a window. Before we run into Loki, next."

"Loki? You mean like Thor's evil half-brother from the Marvel comics," said Emmitt, eyes wide, slight sulky look forgotten. "So . . . is Thor around too? Throwing thunderbolts . . ."

Jerry nodded. "I think they took some liberties with the mythology, but yes, probably. They won't be the sort of characters they are in the comics, necessarily."

"Way cool!" said Ty happily.

Jerry didn't have a chance to explain that it probably wouldn't be. Liz bustled up. "Jerry, I think you should let me take the front. You're leading us in circles."

It was said with a smile, and a militant swing to the new shoulder bag. She probably wanted the chance to give any other Norse gods a kick where it hurt most and a swat across the head with that bag. It didn't have the weight—yet—of her old one, but it had metal corners and a good solid strap. Liz believed in finding weapons where you could. She was also, from a youth spent in the African bush, someone with senses honed to a degree that Jerry knew he couldn't match.

He cheerfully moved to tail-end Charlie . . . well, not including the PSA men. Poor fellows. They looked a little out of their depth here.

It rapidly became apparent that, inside a building at any rate, Liz's sense of direction was no better than Jerry's.

She'd brought them back to the ladder. Only it wasn't half up anymore, and a group of men in Norse-style helmets and mailshirts were climbing it. By the shout that went up when they saw her, the chase was on.

Liz sat down and kicked the ladder outwards, with all the strength in her powerful legs. The sounds of cascading men, cracking timber, and screams of pain and fury came from below.

"I think we'd better find a way out before they find another way up," said Lamont.

"I think we'd better take our chances with that sleeper," said Jerry. They hurried on. But at the door, Liz paused, shook her head and put her finger to her lips. She pointed onwards. Jerry realized that there were no snores.

"He looked at me," said Liz, quietly motioning them to the other side of the passage. "He looked at me and said something like 'Sif,' and lay down again."

"There's one of him. We could overpower him," said one of the agents.

Liz shook her head. "He's enormous. I don't think you could shift him, let alone overpower him. We'll try the passage your Odin came from."

They did, and soon realized just what Odin had been doing there. It led to a bridge—a sort of sideless hanging gallery—across the hall below with its long lines of fires. The hall was virtually deserted now, except for dead bodies and two standing figures.

One of them was one-eyed Odin, wearing a swirling blue cloak. The other figure wore a girdle of iron and metal gauntlets, and held a metal rod in one hand, clumsily. His red beard appeared to have a problem—it wasn't attached on one side.

Odin pointed at them and said something that included the word "Thjalfi."

Whatever he said stirred the other person to hasty action. He ran to get underneath the bridge and raised the metal staff.

"Run!" yelled Jerry. He couldn't shove, because the PSA agent would have tumbled off.

The man blinked and said, "Why?" just as the staff began to somehow grow and push the whole stone structure up toward the rafters, sending the arch-bridge's keystone tumbling. Trapped with the PSA agent on a piece of rock that was somehow balanced on the metal rod, Jerry saw one agent fall toward the fires, and Lamont and another agent haul Ella up onto the crumbling stones on the far side. Then he was hard against the great stone beams of the ceiling.

There was a narrow gap between the stone beams and the crooked wooden purlins. Jerry forced his way up there, but then realized that wasn't going to help. He was going to be crushed into the rotten thatch.

Luckily, the thatch turned out to be really, really old and rotten, cracking and splintering—and trickling icy water down his collar. Jerry managed to squirm his head up and through the rotted reed. Then, he got an arm out and pulled himself up, away from the crushing rock. Beneath him the stone beam groaned.

It was bleakly gray out here, and *cold*. The bitter wind brought flurries of snow to join that which already lay in drifts wherever it could find purchase on the steepness. Heaving—cautiously, because this thatch was centuries old by the feel of it—Jerry hauled himself out onto the roof. It was apparently merely thatch over a hole, because he could see rock, gray and snow-corniced, and wind-bent little alpine bushes off to the side.

Just below him was the head and shoulders of the PSA agent. The man's face was contorted with pain, and he was struggling to get up. Jerry could no more leave him there than he could have deserted a book. Cautiously he edged down and helped.

"My leg is trapped," said the man, weakly. "Ahhh. I can't move it. Pull me!"

Jerry did his best, but the thatch was truly rotten. He put his foot right though—onto a stone beam. That gave him something solid to stand on so he could pull properly. Which he did, with the result that when the slab of stone of the 'bridge' was dropped inside—or at least, by deduction and the crashing noise, Jerry imagined that must have happened—the PSA agent came free abruptly. Together they rolled, slid and cascaded down the thatch. It was probably the only safe way to have gotten off that rotted surface without falling through it, down into the hall—a fifty-foot fall, very possibly into the fires.

They landed together in a tumble of snow, filthy rotten straw and the debris of centuries, at a point where the runoff was plainly intended to go off down the hillside.

By this time the PSA agent was groaning and white-faced with pain.

Jerry knew he faced some very awkward choices. The others were in there, somewhere. But what did he do with an injured man?

He settled for examining the injury. He was no anatomist, and the man was no help. The sandal-clad foot had plainly been trapped between the stone beam and the rising bridge-piece. Only the fact that they were both very roughly hewed could have saved the man's foot from becoming jelly, but plainly it hadn't saved several bones. The injury itself shouldn't kill him. But given the temperature out here, exposure would. Bare legs, except for brass greaves, bare arms and a skirt of peltoi and a brass cuirass, were fine for Mediterranean summer warfare. Here the man was going to die from the shock and the cold.

"Can you lean on me and we can try to get to some shelter?" asked Jerry.

The PSA agent nodded. "Lost my gun."

"That's the least of your worries right now," Jerry grunted, helping him up. They followed the watercourse down. It ended in a short cliff—the sort of thing Jerry might have been able to climb alone, but the injured man wasn't going to manage.

"Sit here." said Jerry. "Let me look around."

Unencumbered, he was able to move easier and faster. Just over a small ridge he spotted a structure made of huge slabs of stone, chinked with mosses. There was a hole-window and Jerry managed to get up to the sill and look in.

Inside, the large, fat, red-bearded man snored and bubbled from the floor. Beside him was the room's only piece of furniture, an enormous stone chair. The room wasn't the ideal place to find shelter, but the air coming out was quite warm. And it would give him a chance to try to find the others. So Jerry went back and helped the PSA agent up and over to the hole-window.

They had to approach the sill along a path that wasn't wide enough for two men. The sill was shoulder high. It all made for a somewhat epic and monumental effort, but Jerry got the man into the room.

He was just helping him off the sill when someone spoke. "Well, well, look what the cat dragged in. *Einherjar!*"

Jerry turned to find himself being grabbed by the man with the loose beard and the iron gauntlets and girdle who had been talking to Odin. The hands in those gauntlets were enormously, crushingly strong. But their attacker only had two arms—and two people to hold. Back at grade school Jerry had only once ever hit someone. The class bully had poured milk—Jerry's milk—onto the book Jerry had been reading. Jerry had been quite accustomed to being the butt of various jokes and pranks. He usually just read on and ignored them. He was not that attached to milk anyway. But one didn't mistreat books like that. He'd punched the bully in the eye, a reaction so out of character and unexpected that the kid had backed off, despite being twice his size, and despite it being a totally ineffectual, feeble blow.

Jerry tried it again. Like the last time he hit the offender in the eye. Like last time he also hurt his hand, but the physical exercise he'd been forced into by the Greek myth adventure paid dividends. The man who had grabbed them with those incredibly strong hands did not quite let go, but he staggered back, to fall into the stone chair. The chair began to rise slowly from the floor on the backs of two enormous women who had apparently been hiding under its legs, in a hollow there. They'd been covered with a blanket, sprinkled with floor-filth, to make it invisible.

"Damn it!" cursed the man with iron gauntlets. "Not me!"

He let go of Jerry, just as Jerry took another swing at him, and pulled the iron rod from his belt. It grew as he held it and pushed the chair back down, with the two gigantic women yowling. Jerry took this opportunity to get away. He fell over the still-snoring Red-beard, who, for his part, muttered and rolled over—sending

Jerry staggering to the door and into the arms of some burly Norsemen, backed up by the one-eyed one.

Whatever One-eye said in his foreign tongue, it did stop them from killing him.

It didn't stop them being tied up like Christmas turkeys, though, both him and the PSA agent with the injured foot. The corpulent red-bearded man slept through all of it, even fake-beard kicking him and shouting at him, and Odin rebuking him for it. Jerry would have liked to ask him why he spoke English but the gag was fairly effective, and very dirty.

A few minutes later, with one less shoe than he'd had earlier and half the sleeve torn off his windbreaker, Jerry found himself being carried outside and bundled onto a cart, and left there, under guard, next to a moaning but barely conscious PSA agent. The guy had at least tried to fight. Kicking someone with that foot probably came under the heading of less than clever though.

Distantly, Jerry could hear the sounds of mayhem and search continuing.

CHAPTER 8

❀❀❀❀❀

"Jerry! Jerry!" screamed Liz, watching in horror from the crumbling edge as the rod in the gauntleted man's hands had grown, widening and raising the stone slab out of the bridge, and crushing it into the vast dim beams.

Lamont pulled her back. "We've got to run, Liz. There are more of those goons coming." He pointed. Sure enough, running along a sort of balustrade-ledge was another group of the Norse warriors she'd tipped off the ladder.

Liz found it hard to care. They'd been through such a lot . . . and . . . and . . . she was just getting know him and love him for all his crazy habits. She was vaguely aware that she was being hustled along, and that Lamont was crying too. Jerry and Lamont had been close friends a lot longer than she'd known him. A now ex-maintenance man was not the most likely of friends for a visiting professor of mythology, but that was Jerry.

She swallowed. That *had* been Jerry. So blind to ordinary things that he saw right through to the person on the inside. Okay, capable of wearing his pants back to front, but what was that to someone of his quality?

She sniffed angrily. Damn fool! She should have been at the back, not him.

"There are more of them that way," said someone.

"Quick, in through here. There's a staircase."

There was. But it was not designed for humans. The steps were one and a half times too high, forcing Liz to try to concentrate on actual circumstance or tumble headlong down the stairs onto everyone else.

When she got to the bottom, she was in a gloomy cavernous room. Her first thought was that they had strayed into some kind of Norse giant's torture chamber. Then she realized it just smelled that way, and that the implements could just as easily belong in a giant's kitchen. One without much house-pride . . . or any idea of hygiene. The floor was ankle deep in slushy stuff that she didn't want to think about too much.

There was bellowing from up the stairs. And more, answering bellows coming from outside.

Someone said "*psst!*" from calf height. Looking down, Liz saw a very black face in the ruddy firelight from the ox-roasting-size open range. It wasn't the sort of black face to inspire any confidence; it had a big warty nose, snaggled teeth, and a lot of black, wild hair. But the owner of the face was beckoning.

"*Svart*," he said looking at the Jackson family. And then some more Norse that was above Liz's ability to guess.

"What's he saying?"

"I only get one word, but I think he wants you to go in there because you're black," said Liz. "Like him."

"In," said Marie, pushing children forward. "I can't run any more. And he does look as black as the ace of spades. If that gets us help, I'm not too proud to accept it."

The gap was narrow and the space inside, dark. It seemed to be dusty and full of hard lumps of stuff.

"It smells like coal," said someone.

"Hush," said someone else.

Outside, they could hear the clatter of searchers. They waited silently in the utter darkness of a giant coal-cellar.

The wait gave Liz time to reflect and to regret. To cry too, in the darkness. She didn't have very long though, because a little hand found hers. "Come," it whispered. "Mom says."

The tunnel was dark and narrow, and hot. It came out at a river, near a dock beneath the cliff. The broad, cold green-water river was rimmed with ice. The water bobbed with the heads of swimmers, many of whom were as black and furry as their guide. He pointed and dived in.

"Do we swim it, Lamont?" said Emmitt, looking doubtful.

Lamont felt the water. "No way," he said. "It's like Lake Michigan in midwinter. Those guys might be able to swim in this and live, but I don't think we could."

Liz leaned down and felt. Sure enough, it was finger-numbing cold. The bitter wind made it worse when she took her fingers out. "I agree. That's hypothermia material, and you'd be too cold to swim in it. I'm not sure if you'd die of cold or drown first. We'll have to find some other way."

"But . . . where?" asked Marie. "I don't think we could find our way back down that tunnel without that little hairy guy to guide us. He might have been as ugly as my old boss, but he sure knew those tunnels and got us out of a jam. I saw someone even opened that coal-hatch, just when we were leaving."

"I guess we'll just have to try," said Lamont. "We can't stay here for very long; it's too cold. At least it was warm in there. Come on, everybody, take hands."

Liz found herself walking back into the dark little tunnel holding Neoptolemeus' hand and that of one of these moronic PSA agents. She desperately wanted Jerry's hand, but his body would be back in Chicago now. That thought was enough to start her crying again. You never knew how much you needed someone, until they weren't around to be told how much you needed them.

It soon became apparent that they needed a guide down there, too. They ran into several dead ends and had to reverse back down one passage and try another. It was as black as pitch, and hot and seemingly airless. Liz was beginning to wonder if they'd ever get anywhere, except lost forever, when she saw a gleam of firelight ahead.

This time they really had come out into the torture chamber. What was worse was that there was nothing much they could do for the two wretches they saw in barred cells. Lamont looked grim, and looked around at the torture tools. He found a file and a crowbar, and passed them through the bars to the astounded looking creatures trapped there.

"We don't know if they've searched down here, and I'm getting the kids away from this place. But you can get away down there," he said, pointing to the trapdoor they'd come through.

He got a gabble of amazed Norse in return. The language was Germanic enough to sound familiar to Liz without being intelligible. But pointing at the knives set next to the rack was clear enough. She passed them each one, feeling sullied just by the touch of the metal. Going up the winding stair out of here might be more risky but at least it felt cleaner. And it wasn't just filth underfoot that she was thinking about.

After more wandering in dark tunnels, they found themselves in a familiar looking passage. Sure enough, it was the one leading to the alcove with the ladder. And there were voices again, coming toward them. It felt almost as if they were trapped in some kind of horrible repeating cycle. "Up the ladder again," she said.

They hauled it up and jammed it halfway again, and crept down the passage past the snorer. He was still at it. Liz didn't even look. But Ella tugged hard at her sleeve. "You've got to come look," said the child in a whisper.

She did, not out of any real desire to, but just to oblige the kid. Ella normally talked nineteen to the dozen, with her twin filling in the other nineteen, on the occasions that Liz had met them before the incident. Liz wondered briefly, sadly, if Jerry and she had ever had kids . . . what would they have been like? Morose Emmitt? Sparky little Ty?

And then she saw.

The huge sleeper was still there, but the stone chair had fallen over and a hole—a shallow foxhole—was revealed where it had been standing. And on the floor lay a hoplite helmet and something that made her heart leap like a klipspringer on amphetamines. The torn sleeve of that ratty old jacket of Jerry's.

No blood. Just a piece of torn fabric, and, now that she looked . . . one shoe. Jerry's.

It had to have gotten here *after* the incident on the bridge. Had to!

Ignoring the sleeper, she went into the room. Looking around, she saw a lot of old straw on the floor, and the mark of a human hand in the snowdrift next to the window.

It all came together now in a wild surge of hope. Impossible! But it *had* to be. He must have come here . . . through the roof! She found words were just too difficult. But she hugged Ella so hard the poor child probably had difficulty breathing.

Lamont and the others bundled into the room too. "Can we get out of the window? They're coming from both sides."

Liz looked. "Yes. The ledge is a bit narrow, but we can."

She vaulted out to prove it, nearly choked on her hooked shoulder-bag strap, then almost fell over the cliff yanking it free, and still couldn't stop smiling, especially at seeing the footprints in the drifted snow outside the window. Whatever had happened to Jerry, he had been alive, well after she thought him dead. Hope was like a wild fountain inside her, as she helped Ella down and was pushed aside by young Ty. He didn't need help! How old did she think he was?

More out of a desire to see where Jerry had come from than any other reason, Liz led them off, following the occasional footmarks. They seemed to go in threes for some reason. Not very straight threes. But that was a left and there a right sole pattern. Despite herself Liz started to sing "Oh, my soul is on the line . . ."

Lamont caught up and shook her, his face worried. "What's up, Liz?"

She pointed at the footmarks in the snow. "Jerry. He didn't get killed, Lamont. He got away, somehow."

A huge smile split Lamont's face. "Well, I'll be dipped . . . uh," he looked at his kids. "Are you sure those are his prints?"

Liz nodded. "His jacket sleeve and shoe were in the room with the sleeper, and a Greek helmet. No blood. He might have been killed since then, but he didn't die when I thought he had. He may be a captive . . . he may be dead. But he wasn't. He wasn't!"

Lamont gave her a squeeze. "He's quite a man, that. Makes good puns. Even sings better than you do."

Liz laughed a little unevenly. "Everybody sings better than I do. And there is no such thing as a good pun." She smiled, feeling rather weak with the aftermath of the emotion-storm. "So what do we do now? I really can't think straight."

"That's a first," said Lamont.

"Well, it is the first time I've admitted it, anyway," said Liz.

Lamont stuck his chest out, plainly also infected by the relief. "You just leave it to a sensible man to sort things out, li'l woman," he said, with suitable condescension. "We men know how to do these things. Let me show you how it's done."

He turned to his wife. "Hey, Marie. Where do we go now?"

She shrugged, looking a little puzzled. "I guess a bit farther away, Lamont. Even if it is cold out here, those locals weren't jumping into that damn river for a wash."

"We all look like we could use one of those. But at least it isn't snowing right now."

"At least you have an advantage, being black," said Liz.

Lamont laughed. "Liz, right now, you are too."

Liz couldn't see her own face but to judge by her hands that was probably accurate. "So do we just go on, Marie?"

"Yeah."

So they did. They wound up skirting a low cliff-top until they came out at some scree, and then into a shallow valley. Looking back they could see that the hall they'd come from looked exactly like a hill—except with a huge chimney, spewing black smoke across the landscape.

"If we go over the next crest we can watch it, without being seen. We might have to go back if it gets any colder, later," said Lamont.

Looking at Marie, Liz wondered just how easy that was going to be. But Marie caught that look, and shook her head, just as Liz was about to open her mouth. Well, they could always use those two PSA jerks who were following them like lost sheep. There was no real cover out here, and if there were places to look out from the Norse giant's hill-fort they simply had to be seen. Being coal-dust blackened from head to toe made them stand out against the snowy patches, and the burnished carapaces of the PSA men didn't help either.

The far hill-crest was farther than it looked. By the time they got there, they were all panting and tired. Just over the ridge-line, out of direct sight of the smoke-spewing hill, they flopped down.

Liz found a rock to rest her back against. Now that she'd come this far, she wanted to go back and look for Jerry. It was dangerous there, true, but, looking down the valley they were now above . . .

She grabbed Lamont's shoulder. Marie was lying with her head on his lap. Liz pointed.

There was a black cave-maw near the bottom of the valley. . . . A steaming maw. Something was emerging from it. Something scaly and gleaming in the weak sunlight. Something enormous.

She'd seen dragons before, but Smitar and Bitar didn't look like this thing. It was three times their size, for a start.

"I think we just stay very very still," said Marie, putting a restraining hand on her youngest son.

On the whole, that seemed like a very good idea, especially as a party of Norsemen in their chain mail had just come into view below, in the valley beneath the hill with the smokestack.

CHAPTER 9

〰〰〰〰〰

"He's mine!" said Throttler, swaying over toward Agent Supervisor Megane. "Answer, mortal!

> "When my first is a task to a young girl of spirit,
> And my second confines her to finish the piece,
> How hard is her fate! but how great is her merit
> If by taking my whole she effects her release!

"Name her!" the sphinx finished. By now her jaws were less than two feet away from Megane's own, which were gaping as widely as hers, in proportion—but it was a very different proportion. She'd snap his head off as easily as a man bites the top off a carrot.

"Huh?" said Megane.

"Wrong answer!" Throttler's jaws gaped still wider, as she started the bite.

"Stop! Stop!" shouted Cruz. "Throttler, you can't eat him!"

She paused, frowning toward the sergeant. "Why not?" she demanded irritably. "I followed the rules."

"Uh . . ." Cruz tried to think up an answer.

Fortunately, Mac's wits were working faster than his. "He's poisonous, Throttler. You'd probably survive, big as you are, even though a bite out of him would kill one of us in a few seconds. But it'll make you really sick."

She drew her head back a little, looking down at Megane with eyes that were a bit crossed. "Really? Humans usually aren't."

Cruz picked it up from there. "He's not actually human," he said, shaking his head. "It's what they call evolutionary camouflage."

"Like some toads in—in—the Amazon, I think," added Mac.

Miggy Tremelo weighed in, using his very best academic demeanor. "I'm afraid they've got the right of it, Throttler. There's quite a literature on the subject, in fact. This one"—here he gave Megane a disdainful look—"is a member of a species called *Securitus cretinii*. They grow like weeds in the swamp areas of Washington, D.C.—inside that dreaded zone known as 'the Beltway.' Because of their appearance, they're able to infiltrate jobs where they can mimic human beings. Especially jobs in the Pyramid Security Agency, where it isn't hard to imitate cretins. But, as a last defensive resort in case they get caught, their flesh is highly toxic."

Throttler pulled back a foot or two farther. "Really?"

"Oh, yes. It's quite a public health problem, because they're so obnoxious that people naturally want to gobble them right down when they catch one. We have to give school children special classes on the subject."

Riddles aside, the sphinx wasn't actually the sharpest pencil in the box. So Cruz thought there was a good chance this might work. And since Throttler's next course of action was obvious, he had the answer ready.

"Well, then," said the sphinx, drawing back an enormous—and very deadly looking—lion's paw, "I'll just swat the life out of him, then."

As stupid as he might be, Megane at least had enough sense to finally realize the sphinx was perfectly serious and he was on the very edge of mortal existence. Naturally, though, all he could manage himself was an inchoate squawk of protest and an upraised hand that would have sheltered him about as well as a toothpick.

"No, don't!" said Cruz. "You'll scatter his contents all over the place. Those are even more toxic than the outside."

Blessedly, the lieutenant joined in. "He's right, Sphinx. We get trained in paratrooper school on how to dispose of them. They have to be carefully quarantined first—every part of them intact." Evans grinned. "Then we bury them alive in a special place. It's called Thule Air Base. An Air Force buddy of mine was stationed there for a few months once, on *Securitus cretinii* disposal duty. The temperature in the winter gets down to forty below zero and they once recorded surface winds of two hundred miles an hour."

He was now giving Megane a look that could only be described as evil. "Yup, that's where this fellow is headed, sure enough." He jerked a thumb at the two other PSA agents who'd also managed to avoid the snatch. They were standing a little ways off, being closely watched by the paratroopers. "These two also."

Throttler was starting to look mollified. "That's pretty good. A bit grisly, actually. It'd be a lot more merciful if you just let me—"

Firmly, Evans raised his hand. "Can't, Throttler. Yes, I know it's a terrible fate. But those are The Rules, when a *Securitus cretinii* gets caught."

The sphinx had a great respect for The Rules. "Oh, well. In that case, you have to do your duty."

Evans nodded, then gave the Humvee a quick scrutiny. "Don't really have room for all three of them in the Humvee, Professor Tremelo. Not with a proper guard on them. Might I . . ."

"Oh, certainly, Lieutenant. By all means use the limo." He sighed heavily. "Lamont won't mind, wherever he is."

"And where do you want me . . ."

Tremelo tried to figure out the best place to keep Megane and his two fellow agents under detention. That was a tricky question, actually. Whatever black eyes Helen Garnett was going to come out of this with, the woman still had enormous power and influence. Not to mention an instant readiness to use bullying tactics.

Fortunately, the problem solved itself that very moment. Two more vehicles came racing up and screeched to a stop. They both had U.S. Fish and Wildlife Service insignia.

Best of all, Miggy recognized the man who immediately climbed out of the passenger seat of the first vehicle. The director of the service himself, no less, Mark O'Hare. Miggy had never met him personally, but he'd seen photographs of the man. Fortunately, unlike all too many of this administration's appointments, O'Hare actually had real credentials for the job.

He also had a temper, clearly enough. When he came up, he gave Megane a look that was every bit as evil as the one Rich Evans had given—but had not a trace of the lieutenant's humor.

He didn't have much of the lieutenant's protocol, either.

"Is this the rotten motherfucker?"

Megane looked very offended and started to say something, but a growl from Throttler put a stop to that. The sphinx was still not more than ten feet away.

O'Hare gave her a very friendly look. "Hi, Throttler. Sorry about all this."

"Oh, it's okay, Mark. I'm feeling a little sorry for them, actually. Ever since the soldier here told me they were condemned to being buried alive at Thule Air Base. Sounds horrible."

O'Hare now glanced at Evans. "Is that what you told them?"

"Yes, sir. The, uh, Throttler was about to . . . well. Eat him."

The director nodded. "I can believe that." He was back to giving Megane that very evil look. "And you know what, Pissant? Under the law—if you'd bothered to check—she'd not suffer any penalties, either. There's a completely different set of rules that apply to the sphinx"—he glanced at the dragons—"as well as Bitar and Smitar."

Throttler looked very smug, at that point. So did the two dragons. Megane was obviously furious, but he still had enough sense to keep quiet. At least, as long as Throttler was within jaw range.

"I've got a problem concerning custody, Director O'Hare," said Miggy. "Under the circumstances . . ."

"Professor Tremelo, I believe?" O'Hare stuck out his hand and Miggy shook it. "Yeah, I know, it's a little tricky. However, under *these* circumstances—you should know that I've been in touch with both Senators Abrams and Larsen, and they've been in touch with the media—I've got quite a bit of latitude. The Fish and Wildlife Service does have police powers, and we're not restricted to federal property when endangered wildlife is involved."

Again, he gave Megane that very hard look. "Which it certainly is, in this case—and with the nation's best known endangered species, at that. Most popular, too."

He lowered his voice enough that the sphinx couldn't hear him and growled at the PSA agent, "You stupid, arrogant asshole. You'll be *lucky* if you wind up reading a thermometer and recording wind speeds at a military base seven hundred miles north of the Arctic Circle. Did you—or that shithead boss of yours—really think you could get away with something like this?"

Abruptly, he waved his hand. "Never mind, don't answer that. Who cares what you think?"

He gave Evans an appraising look. "I've got police powers, but we're not really set up to keep prisoners. Normally, we'd just take an offender to the nearest police authority and turn them over. However..."

Evans smiled. "I'll have to check with the commander of Fort Campbell, of course. But I'm pretty sure the 101st Airborne will be willing—delighted, rather—to provide our fellow federal toilers with the wherewithal to keep these Pissants under guard for the moment."

He transferred the smile to Megane. "You wouldn't believe how popular these fellows made themselves at Fort Campbell. And seeing as how it's *officially* Fish and Wildlife making the arrest—we're just lending a helping hand, so to speak—I can't see where Ms. Garnett can squawk."

"Oh, she'll *squawk*," said O'Hare, who was now smiling himself. "But the thing is, right about now I think she's mostly squawking in fear, not fury. Okay, Lieutenant. Talk to your commander and ask him on my behalf if he's willing to put these bums up, so to speak, at the 101st's base. If he wants to talk to me personally"— O'Hare pulled out his wallet and extracted a business card—"this has my cell phone number on it."

Things were moving much more quickly than Miggy expected. So quickly, in fact, that he realized those first calls he'd had Rachel make to the senators had stirred up a firestorm. What else could explain how quickly O'Hare had gotten here? He couldn't possibly have made the flight from Washington, D.C., on that short a notice—not even if he'd been flown in on a fighter plane. He had to have arrived in Chicago already.

Like a shark, smelling blood in the water.

It was easy to forget, sometimes, how an overly powerful agency like the PSA—especially one prone to bullying—could pile up a huge number of enemies. And how fast those enemies could move, once they saw a chance to take them down a notch.

Or ten.

"I've got to get back to my office, people," he said quietly. "I think everything's blowing wide open. And this area's not safe any longer, anyway. With those new absorptions, the pyramid's certain to have expanded again. We'll need to move the perimeter out another hundred yards, probably. Maybe two hundred, with that many idiot PSA agents going in."

"But . . . Neoptolemeus . . ." protested Medea.

"Is in a Mythworld with Dr. Lukacs and the Jackson family," said Miggy gently. "You know Jerry Lukacs and Lamont Jackson well enough, ma'am, and I know Marie Jackson. Your boy couldn't be in better, more careful hands. Now will you all get in the vehicle and get back, please? There is no guarantee that if you got snatched you'd end up in the same place or would be able to help."

A corpse fell from the sky. It was wearing a brass cuirass, and a Greek-style horsehair-crested helmet. A ten inch by five inch piece was missing from its chest. Smoke still rose from the hole.

One of the dragons leaned in and sniffed. "Chargrilled."

Agent Supervisor Megane gaped in horror.

Miggy turned to Evans. "Load that corpse up and let's get out of here, now. Some of your men may be snatchables."

Lieutenant Evans realized that might well be true—especially with a private who'd somehow managed to get himself arrested over pizza. However, he knew the essential trick of military success. Sergeant Cruz might not be part of his squad, but he was the best NCO around. "Sergeant," he said with a nod, which was all that was necessary to say.

"Sir," said Cruz.

A minute and a half later they were all heading out, the Humvee first, one SUV abandoned and the other driven by a paratrooper, the remaining agents under guard in the limo. Megane probably wished desperately that he could call in to his own authorities—but his helmet and those of his remaining "hoplites" had been left behind to talk to themselves.

CHAPTER 10

⟨◉⟩⟨◉⟩⟨◉⟩⟨◉⟩⟨◉⟩⟨◉⟩

Lying in the back of the chariot in the cold, Jerry could only be glad of the body—presumably still alive because it was warm—stacked against him. He wouldn't have minded if the man had not had a cuirass on. Brass seemed to transmit cold better than it did body-heat.

Time passed. In the way of time when you were worried and helpless to do anything, Jerry was sure that it was passing very slowly. It was getting to be a question of whether he froze to death or worried himself to death first. He worried about the others, let alone about his own fate, at the hands of a guy with metal gauntlets and fake beard, and Odin.

He tried to distract himself into remembering as much as he could about Odin. Not all of it was comforting. Yes, Odin was the leader of the Æsir who had hanged himself on the tree for nine days and given his one eye for a drink from the well of Mirmir. He was also—a stray scrap of information in the sea of stuff Jerry had waded through in a bibliophile's life—known by many names, or "kennings" as the Norse put it. They often gave clues to origins and nature of the god in question. This one was known variously as the Allfather, which was a delusion of grandeur from what Jerry remembered, the Wanderer from his habit of wandering about incognito, and Baelwerker—evil worker.

There were lots more, but those were the ones that came to mind. Odin was known to be fickle with his favors and had fathered a fair number of children on women other than his wife, Frigg. About normal for a boss god, in other words. There seemed to be more of an element of sneaky cunning to him than was typical of someone like Zeus, though.

Jerry knew less about the other Norse gods. A stray memory brought up Geirrodur the troll king and bars of white-hot metal being flung around, but Jerry was almost sure that myth had been about Thor.

Finally, a group of Norse warriors came past, and then Odin on horseback. An eight-legged horse. The man with iron gauntlets came and got into the cart.

"Well, I'm not carrying him down from there myself. He can sober up and get himself home," muttered the man sulkily. "Damned Einherjar won't do anything I tell them. But if he says it, then they jump."

He kicked the two prisoners aside, took up his stance. "Tanng-njóst, Tanngrisnir, away!"

Nothing happened.

Iron gauntlets swore. "Move, damn you, goats!"

Jerry had put two and two together now. This was Thor's goat-pulled chariot—only it lacked the ornamentation you might expect of a thunder-god's chariot. This English-speaking person was also a pretty poor stand-in for Thor.

Odin returned with a double-clatter. "Tanngnjóst, Tanngrisnir, Bilskríner!" he snapped, walloping the goats with his spear-butt.

The goats and the chariot took off like a rocket ship heading for orbit. Fake-Thor landed hard on Jerry as the chariot leapt and bounced down the rough track at terrific speed. The goats seemed to want it airborne, and the chariot didn't have springs of any sort.

It was a hellish journey and the charioteer's efforts to slow it down were met with no success. Neither did his efforts to stand up. To add to the joy of the journey, icy sleet showered down on them. Jerry could only be grateful, when, after an eternity, the bone-shaking slowed and then stopped, pulling into a barn made of rough rocks.

Iron-gauntlets got out staggering, stepping on Jerry and his companion. They were at least out of the freezing rain. Iron-gauntlets didn't bother with unhitching the goats, just left everything.

They lay there for a long time, as dusk gathered outside. Presently someone with a burning brand came along and unhitched the goats with a lot of grumbling. Norse was a fine grumble-language by the sound of it, with plenty of gutturals to help you sound really cross and miserable. It reminded Jerry a bit of Liz, when she started swearing at the Immigration and Naturalization Service in Afrikaans.

Eventually, the muttering grumbler noticed them. He hauled them out bodily, and dumped them on the straw, then pulled the chariot away and left, ignoring Jerry's yells.

The straw seemed a better place than the back of the chariot, anyway, although that made no difference to his co-sufferer. The PSA agent had lapsed into unconsciousness. Jerry was suffering from extreme bruising and cold, and some light-headedness, but that appeared to be the worst, apart from being tied up and left in a Norse stable.

He strained at the cords futilely. Well, maybe he could at least burrow his feet into the straw. The shoeless foot felt as if it might be about to lose toes from frostbite, and the other one didn't feel much better.

He was just about half into the straw, and thinking that this had to be an improvement on the chariot, when it became obvious that still being in the chariot had one thing going for it. Goats—huge goats, the size of ponies—could not come and sample your clothing.

Just when he thought nothing could get worse, Jerry got Wagnerian laughter and a kick in the ribs. Two Norse warriors had entered the barn. They pushed the goats away, examined the PSA agent, and then hauled Jerry to his feet.

One said something to Jerry, accompanied by a prod from fingers the size and hardness of a rifle barrel, that obviously meant "walk," seemingly oblivious of the fact that his feet were tied together. So Jerry did his best. He hopped. And fell over. The new outburst of Wagnerian laughter was worth enduring just to have his feet cut loose.

They walked him out, and onto a rough trail. They mounted horses and rode, chatting merrily, pausing their cheerful dialogue only to occasionally lean down and belt him with the flat of a sword, if they thought him to be walking too slowly. A numb foot and his giddiness didn't help.

Coming over the ridge in the sunset Jerry could be excused for halting and staring. The hall below was huge, even by mega-mall standards. Being thatched with spears and with literally hundreds of doors also would have made it stand out.

"Valhöll," said one of the warriors, apparently finding justification in Jerry's halting abruptly. Not, of course, for too long. A swat with a sword-flat urged him on, toward what, from here, was already quite a racket—a very drunken party, by the sounds of it.

Jerry blinked. He was hardly a warrior who had died in battle. And a drinking party with nubile Valkyries was not actually his idea of a good time, especially not for eternity. Once in a while, maybe.

It soon appeared that the joy of drinking himself senseless was not for him anyway. He was led through a corner of the huge hall of roistering men. The hall was decked with shields and axes, and reeked of boiled pork, mead, and the aftereffects of too much of both. The two escorts pushed in through a doorway and off toward some private chambers beyond. They came to a door at which they knocked, very respectfully.

Jerry found himself in the presence of Odin, in Odin's own chamber. The one-eyed god sat slumped in his chair, a drinking-horn in one hand and a pair of ravens perched on the back of the chair. There were two other people in the room, a golden-haired and bored-looking woman and a man with a short stubbly beard and a rather weak chin.

Jerry realized that the latter was Mr. Iron-Gauntlets, without the fake beard, gauntlets, or the broad iron girdle. He looked about twenty-five years old and with incipient jowls already developing. He also looked as surly as bull-beef right now. The blonde looked ready to take him out of the Mythworld and send him back home with a blow from her tambour-frame.

Odin stared at Jerry, his one eye cold and penetrating. The stare was plainly intended to intimidate. It might have worked too, if the raven behind Odin had not chosen that moment to lift its tail over the blue cloak. Lightheaded and shivering, Jerry couldn't help a bit of puerile laughter.

Plainly Odin had not expected that response. He said something in Norse.

"Pardon?" said Jerry. His legs felt as if someone had taken the bones out of them, and the room seemed oddly wobbly.

Odin's solitary eye narrowed. He raised his hand and said . . . something. Which became an understandable, "Answer, Thrall."

Jerry blinked. It must be some kind of translation spell. "What was the question again?" he asked, swaying.

"None of your insolence!" snapped the man who had been using the iron gauntlets. "Answer Allfather Odin!"

Well, that established his pedigree. "Shut up, Thjalfi," said Odin offhandedly. "I have not yet forgotten that you left Thor behind. Now, foreign thrall, answer me. Or I'll make the blood-eagle out of you."

Jerry's reply was to pitch forward on his face.

He was vaguely aware of voices talking after a while. ". . . Sif, find me two that are not too drunk and have this one hauled to the dungeon. Put him in with the son of Laufey. He'll be keen enough to talk after he sees what happens to those who oppose us."

The woman said something indistinct, but clearly petulant.

"Hel take it, woman. If he hasn't staggered home by tomorrow I'll go back and look for him myself. We still need him. You know that by this time of night the Einherjar are not capable of riding to the gates of Asgard, let alone all the way to Geirrodur's castle. Now get me someone to heave this carrion away."

"If I go out there they'll think I'm another Valkyrie for them to deflower. And I have enough trouble with one drunken sot," she said.

"By my eye . . . Thjalfi."

"They don't listen to me, Allfather," said Thjalfi sullenly. "They say I am just a bondsman."

"Humph. I'll do it myself then," said Odin.

A door slammed. "Do you think he suspects?" said Thjalfi.

The woman laughed. "Him? He's far too vain."

"Best to wait until he's well asleep before . . . Stop that."

"Oh. Don't you like it anymore?" she teased.

The man coughed. "He'll be back soon. And you never know when those birds of his will show up."

"I'm still going to poison those ravens."

"I tried," he said glumly.

A little later two large grumpy warriors picked Jerry up, and transported him down many flights of stairs, and tossed him down into a pit. It seemed to be a place of strange shadows, monstrous, fearful shadows, as Jerry faded into unconsciousness. Those had been quite some blows he'd taken to the head, and it had been a long day.

တၜ   တၜ   တၜ

When he awoke, Jerry realized that there were very few bits of
him that didn't hurt, but that at least he was no longer cold. He
began to slowly take stock of his surroundings. The surface he was
lying on felt like stone. Opening his eyes a crack, he saw that the
wall looked like stone too, stone with odd shadows leaping on it.

Firelight! No wonder it wasn't so cold. But . . . wasn't he in a
dungeon?

He opened his eyes properly and saw that, fire or no fire, he
was in a dungeon, and a place of torment. There was a very
large snake high up one of the walls, and although it could not
quite reach the man below who was bound to three huge slabs
with what looked like thick red-brown rope, the snake could spit
venom at him. There was a harassed-looking woman crouched
next to the bound man, holding a bowl.

The bowl was now almost slopping full of the poison. She
darted with it to the fireplace. The snake spat and the bound
man writhed and screamed. He must be enormously powerful
because the very floor shook. The woman hastened back to hold
the bowl in the way again, wiping his ravaged face with a rag.
There were tears on her own face.

After a while he said, "It's all right, Sigi. It's just pain. It'll
pass." The voice was thick with agony, but there was no mistak-
ing the affection.

Jerry sat up, with difficulty, as they'd not seen fit to untie his
hands.

"Ah! Our visitor has stirred. So nice of you to drop in," said
the bound victim sardonically.

Jerry was beaten up, mildly concussed, and half frozen. But he
knew enough mythology to realize that the speaker could only
be the bound god, Loki.

Loki, the father of lies, the architect of Baldr's death, general
maker of trouble . . . and occasional savior of the gods of Asgard.
A great cell-mate.

"There is some water there, in that rock-bowl," said the woman,
gesturing with her elbow.

"Poor hospitality," said Loki, with a wry smile. "But there is
something of a shortage of mead in these palatial quarters of
mine, I'm afraid."

Jerry staggered to where trickling water dribbled into a small depression in the floor, drank some of the cold water, and then washed his face. It was awkward with bound hands, but at least he could kneel and dip. The icy water hurt, but it did wake him up. He wasn't that sure that he wanted to be awake, but it seemed that he didn't have a lot of choice in the matter.

"So, stranger," said Loki, when Jerry had finished his ablution and stepped uneasily nearer to them. "What brings you to this delightful spot?"

Jerry looked at the snake above them, very warily, but the serpent seemed to be ignoring him completely. "A certain one-eyed . . . traveler had me sent here."

Naming gods was a poor idea in the Mythworlds. It was never wise to call their attention to oneself. "And you, Son of Laufey?"

It was a wry smile, but it was a smile. "I see my reputation, and my fate, have gone before me, mortal. I have been many places, maybe not as far as the wanderer, but far enough. There is that about you that speaks of further places. Places beyond even One-eye's ken. That must have rubbed him raw." Loki definitely took some savage pleasure in that last statement.

"He asked me a question, perhaps about that," admitted Jerry. "He asked in Norse, not in my tongue, so I was not able to reply. So he sent me here. To learn a lesson, I think."

Now those eyes were bright and mocking. "Heh. Not to answer him is to survive, mortal. He can't bear not knowing. I'd find ways to avoid telling him, if you can. He's nearly as tricky as me, though."

It made sense. The Krim didn't seem to place any value on the lives of the human victims it wasted during its reenactments of myths. It would only keep him alive if there was something to be gained from doing so.

"I was almost free, and my repayment and Ragnarok the terrible had almost begun, when I would have destroyed all that lives," said Loki conversationally, "when Odin's power was renewed. Is this anything to do with you, man from a far place?" That was said calmly, but there was a terrible hatred, barely masked, underneath the words.

Jerry shook his head. "No." He was glad to be able to say that. "It's the Krim."

"These are a people of whom I have not heard. When *Naglfar* sails, they too will not be forgotten."

"No," said Sigyn, "they will not," and she was just as grim as he was about that.

"The Krim is a thing, not a people," explained Jerry. "It's that pyramid that One-eye wears around his neck. Or at least that is its symbol. It is a machine. A device. I believe it seeks the destruction of my people. My world."

"And it has enlisted One-eye to do it," said Loki admiringly. "It couldn't have made a better choice, really."

"Except you," said Jerry with equal urbanity.

That actually got Loki to laugh. "Except me, indeed. But what do I have against your people, your world?"

Jerry was surprised to see Sigyn wink at him. "Oh, what does that matter," she said. "Loki will destroy everything. He's bad."

The bound god shook his head. "You do know how to ruin my lines, Sigi. I've got a reputation to keep up."

"Ah, husband," she said quietly, a hand soothing his brow. "What does it all matter now? They have killed one of our children, and changed the other into a wolf. What do we care what they think? It has been many centuries since I saw you laugh. I had forgotten. You used to make me laugh all the time."

"There is not much to laugh about, Sigi," said Loki, the grimness returning.

"That didn't used to stop you," she said, caressing him with one hand while she kept the bowl positioned to catch the snake's dripping venom with the other. "Even when they were all united against you, you mocked them and laughed at them. Only Thor dared to stand up against you."

"I never understood that. Why did he let them do this to me? The Thunderer has no brains, but he's not unfair," said Loki.

"I don't know," answered Sigyn. "He played no part in your binding. But what I said was that back when you laughed at them, they could not stand against you. This mortal made you laugh instead of wallowing in our bitterness. Maybe if you can laugh again, we can break free."

"It has to be worth a try," said Loki. "Talk, mortal."

Jerry took a deep breath. It hurt his ribs. He wished he had Liz's brashness and courage. But she wasn't here, so he'd just have to do his best. "My name is Jerry, Loki. Not 'mortal.' I've defeated one set of gods already, and if I have to beat another I will. I'm only interested in helping you break free on certain conditions."

"You make me smile already, mortal that dictates to gods, and claims to defeat them. And Sigyn is right, with that comes hope. Not a lot of it, but a tiny spark. Why should I negotiate, Jerry? Ragnarok is sure. The Wanderer himself knows he cannot win when the Time comes."

Jerry shrugged, as nonchalantly as he could. "Nothing is sure, this time around."

"It *is* all happening again!" said Sigyn. "I was sure of that."

"And," continued Jerry, "if I am right, this is the pattern. It will happen again, and again, until the Krim's masters get tired of it, unless we stop them."

"That's a powerful argument," conceded Loki, with a crooked grin. "Once is bad enough. So, name your terms, Jerry."

Jerry could understand why Loki had got away with blue murder so often in Norse myth. His smile went all the way to his eyes. There was mischief in those eyes, but there was also a trustability to it. In some ways it reminded him of Lamont's youngest child's smile. It had the same childlike quality to it. Not heedful of consequences perhaps, but with no true intent of evil. And yet . . .

Loki led the forces of giantkind against the Æsir in the final battle. The gods had bound him, but not killed him. Odin had by this time known that Loki and Loki's offspring would kill him, and the other Ás. Why had he allowed him to live? There had to be reasons. Odin was not known for fairness.

Jerry swallowed. "First, my girlfriend, my best friend and his wife and children are out there. I won't have them hurt."

Loki nodded. "We place our values in those we know and love most. Many are the men who would kill a stranger."

"But when the world falls, those close to us must fall too," said Sigyn.

Jerry started realizing that she was more than just loyal. Well, to cope with a man like Loki you'd have be clever and subtle at manipulation.

"I will have vengeance for my sons, Loki," she continued. "You promised me that." There was an implacability there, that Jerry could feel was as unstoppable as the tide. "You promised me Asgard would fall."

Loki sighed. "Never make promises to women, Jerry. Not even in your cups. They have a way of remembering everything you have said, in exactly the way that suits them." Despite the sarcasm in the words, Loki's smile at her contained both affection and acknowledgment of the agreement. "I said that I would destroy those who did what they did to Narfi and Váli."

"And to do that we must bring down the walls of Asgard," she said.

Loki shrugged. "Which I arranged to have built, and which will withstand the mountain giants and the frost giants, among which I have my kin."

"But not the sons of Muspellheim," said Sigyn quietly.

Jerry had it now, that elusive trace of memory. Surtur the fire demon, who had spread his fire and darkness all over the nine worlds at the end of Ragnarok. Surtur, the lord of the fiery South, that balanced Nifelheim of the frozen North. There was a certain symmetry to Norse myth. Sigyn might not want to have Loki destroy the world, but she would let him, if that was the cost of her vengeance. And if Jerry had it right, Ragnarok was something that virtually nothing had survived.

CHAPTER 11

Watching from among the heather and rocks on the ridge, Lamont saw how the dragon wound its way down to the burn and drank from the dark water, and then turned and made its way back. It huffed as it went, emitting clouds of yellowish noxious-looking vapor from its nose.

"Where are those kids?" asked Emmitt.

Ty and Tolly had disappeared again. Lamont was beginning to regret pairing them up. It had seemed like a good idea at the time, but Ty was enough of a handful on his own. He just had to be one of the most inventive and creative eight-year-old fabricationists in the United States. Marie called it lying, but Lamont suspected that to Ty the line between truth and fiction was somewhere in the Cartoon Network.

"Darn those kids. Where did you last see them?"

"They were just down slope from me. Playing some game. I told them to lie still."

Lamont studied the slope. No Chicago Bears sweatshirt visible. There was a slight indent, an incipient stream-bed, with more cover in it than on the rest of the hillside, just below where the kids had been. "They must have gone down the gully. I'll go and look."

"We'll stick together," said Marie firmly. "There's nowhere else they could have gone."

So they made their way down. They found them in a small cave—along with two other people.

One was a man who could have passed for Arnold Schwarzenegger's body double, except that he was blond and had a naked sword in his hand. The other—a short and stocky bearded dwarf—had not drawn his weapon, but looked decidedly nasty.

"—ling you the truth," Ty was saying. "The power-rangers are coming. We're just scouting for them because Dracona the green transformer has their scent. I wouldn't touch us if I were you."

"Tyrone, you come here this minute!" said Marie, startling the two strangers out of any action they might have been contemplating.

Lamont kept a firm hold on the rock that he'd picked up. It wasn't much against that sword, but it was all there was to hand, here. Admittedly, by the look on the face of the tall guy with the sword, he wouldn't need it that much. The big blond looked positively relieved to see them. He lowered his sword, pointed at a stack of implements against the wall, and said something in a lordly gabble.

What was that saying architects were so fond of? *Form defines function*, if Lamont remembered right. It was true, Lamont reflected. Those things might be Norse era tools, but they were still spades, and the blond sword-swinger plainly was expecting people who didn't have swords to do the digging, especially coal-dust covered ones.

Well, a spade—even a wooden one with metal edge—was still a better weapon than a rock. "Take a spade, people," said Lamont in a very even voice. His son and Medea's were still too close to a man with a naked sword. "And try to look like that's what you came here to do."

A spade is a good disguise. See a man with a spade and you assume that he's a workman, thought Lamont, looking at the blond swordsman's casual stance as he attempted to talk to the now blue-kneed PSA agents. It had been a fairly brisk early autumn day back in Chicago. Lamont, Marie, Liz and kids all were dressed for that. But it was much too cold for the gear the PSA agents were wearing. Sandals, brass greaves, the skirty thing—a *peltoi*, he thought it was called—and a cuirass didn't do too well in this temperature.

Lamont almost grinned. A pity Jerry wasn't here. He'd like to have pointed out that they looked mighty cuirass . . .

Blondie looked a bit scornful about their outfits, but seeing as they'd brought him some serfs to do his digging he wasn't making a fuss. He and the dubious-looking dwarf led them down into the valley, across the burn, and to the dragon's path. He pointed. Lamont added the Norse word for *dig* into his vocabulary.

"A hole big enough to trap a dragon?" said Liz quietly. "You've got to be kidding me. Let's get out of here, Lamont. I'll distract him, you hit him. We can deal with the dwarf."

"Okay."

She paused, seeing someone new appear on the scene. From nowhere, it seemed like. "Um. On second thought, better keep digging. That's the guy we saw in the castle. Odin himself, if Jerry was right."

It was Odin indeed, in his blue cloak and broad hat, and with just one eye. Fortunately he was not really interested in labor unrest. He was pointing at the ground. Maybe he was saying that Blondie didn't have a building permit. Lamont noticed, however, that Odin's arrival had led to the dwarf's abrupt departure.

And Odin's departure led to the pit digging being moved too. They were now to dig a trench up the slope. Fortunately, it was fairly soft loam. Unfortunately, their chances for rushing the blond muscular warrior were considerably slimmer. He was sitting on a high rock, sharpening his sword. He tossed a fragment of wool into the air and held the blade out as it fell. The sword appeared to split the drifting wool.

Surely nothing could be that sharp? On the other hand, did they really want to find out?

"There'll be a chance to sneak off later," said Liz quietly.

It certainly seemed a safer option, and fortunately Blondie wasn't after much in the way of entrenchments. He was not watching his diggers but keeping a wary eye on the dragon's cave. He obviously saw something that made him decide that now was the time to leave and suddenly they were herded back up to the shallow cave. The dwarf had made a fire. The PSA agents looked like they were going to kiss him. Blondie didn't seem to be planning to stay and enjoy it though. He took up a folded piece of brown coarse fabric and turned toward the mouth of the cave.

"When he's gone," whispered Liz.

But then Blondie turned back, beckoned to Lamont, and tossed the fabric at him. It was a lot heavier than it looked. Lamont's knees almost buckled.

Now, Blondie gestured for Lamont to follow him. So they all

started trooping out, but he waved the rest of them back with that bright sword of his.

Lamont followed him back down the hill to the shallow pits. Blondie got into one, pointed at the rough cloth, and said something in Norse. Lamont got the message, even without the Norse. He covered up the hole, with its warrior inside, and pinned down the edges of the cloth with rocks. Now was the perfect time to hit Blondie so hard with the shovel that he couldn't use his sword, and depart hurriedly.

But Lamont couldn't bring himself to do it. The idiot was plainly planning to stab the dragon from underneath, and that dragon made Bitar and Smitar look kittenish.

From under the cloth the blond warrior said something that Lamont guessed to be "vamoose." Looking at the belch of yellow smoke coming from the dragon-cave, Lamont didn't need any further invitation. He legged it across the peat-stained stream and ran for the cave. Now, maybe, they could get out of here. . . .

Looking back, he saw that the huge green dragon was slowly making his way out of his lair. Lamont ducked behind a handy rock and wished there had been a very much bigger handy rock. Peeping out through some fronds of dead fern that still clung to the stone, he watched the dragon ponderously advance down the path toward the pit where the blond Norseman lay hidden.

Lamont could see three possible outcomes. First, the man might just succeed. Second, the dragon might just find him and kill him. Third, he might wound the dragon. It was the third possibility that worried Lamont the most—and, unfortunately, it seemed the most likely. This was not a very large valley, it was not a very deep cave that his family was hiding in, and this was a very small rock he was hiding behind. And a wooden spade wasn't going to make much of an impression, if a sword that sharp couldn't.

He watched. And waited.

In the cave Liz cursed under her breath. The dwarf whose name was apparently Reginn, judging from what she thought the blond guy with body-builder build had called him, had drawn his sword and was intent on the scene down below. If it hadn't been for Lamont being stuck behind a tiny rock a good two hundred yards closer to the dragon than any sane person wanted to be, this would have been the perfect time to make a sharp exit. She had a boyfriend to go looking for, and she had a feeling that the blond guy and this Reginn were up to no good, even if dragon-killing was a traditional knightly practice.

Besides, she was a biologist. There were probably *far* more knightly types than dragons anyway. She watched Reginn's intent face. It held an expression that seemed a combination of fear and nasty delight. Liz could probably swat him with one of these heavy wooden shovels, but there was no way that Marie would leave and let Lamont catch up. Actually, there was no way Liz could just leave him down there, for that matter, no matter how sensible it would be.

The dragon appeared to be crawling slowly toward the holes they'd dug. It stopped and puffed some of that sulphurous yellow smoke, then turned its great head, as if tasting the air. For a brief, wild moment Liz considered yelling a warning. But that would most likely be terminal for all of them.

The dragon continued its slow pace forward.

Suddenly, a great gout of the yellow smoke roared and gushed out of that fangy mouth and surged across the valley. The dragon reared up and Liz could see a spurting fountain of black blood. Its blood hit the grass, and the grass withered and smoked. The dragon twitched and clawed the ground, its great tail thrashing as if it was about to do a lizard trick and come right off.

The dragon jerked spasmodically. And then again, and reared up trying to reach the place from where its black life-blood leached out onto the ground.

Even from here she could hear that it was saying something. To Liz that made the dying worse, somehow.

They watched and waited. And then the blond man emerged from the side of the dragon, his great sword held aloft, and it seemed to catch the sun like some shaft of silver. Liz wasn't surprised that the others clapped. The dwarf was capering in glee. He waved his sword at them and bellowed something that was probably "out." Before Liz decided to take *him* out, he chopped a solitary spruce—perhaps four inches thick—with a single cheerful swipe.

He shooed them ahead of him like he was herding geese. He was soon happily engaged in kicking the dragon, and loudly congratulating his knight, who was cleaning his sword, and beaming toothily himself.

"Now do you think we can just slip away?" said Marie. "Where the hell are those children? Come here, you two. Don't you dare go near that cave!"

Unfortunately that yell, while it had turned the two boys back, had also reminded the dwarf and the blond dragon slayer of their presence.

They found themselves lifting a very heavy foreleg while Reginn and the dragon slayer took part in some gory butchery. At length the two of them hauled out a heart the size of a steamer-trunk. It was speared onto a spruce sapling, and they were sent walking up the hill with it back to the cave and to the fire. Reginn waved cheerfully with a snaggle-toothed smile and left them to make a dragon-heart barbeque.

By the way Ella had stopped to be sick, the dish might not catch on in the U.S. Liz suspected it might be a better hit back in South Africa, where the men doing the barbequing—"braai-ing"— believed in alcohol marinade, principally applied internally to themselves, because the meat was too hot. This blond dragon slayer was their kin in spirit, anyway. He had dug out a flask of something and was applying it liberally internally, and not offering to share, either.

Liz had spent much of her adult life working with commercial fishermen. She was used to out-toughing and out-drinking men. And right now she wouldn't have minded showing this fellow how it was done. Still, after dragon-killing, a drink was probably a fairly reasonable thing to want.

Liz tried to turn the meat, more on principal than out of any real interest in cooking dragon heart properly, burned herself, and sucked her fingers.

"Ow! Give me a hand with this, will you," she said, putting her fingers back in her mouth. It was some indication of how long ago breakfast had been that dragon heart tasted quite appetizing.

Emmitt responded, after a prod from Lamont. He had the bright idea of using another stick. It didn't work too well either on the lopsided weight of heart. He ended up burning his fingers too, and instinctively sucking them, before they got the meat propped the other way.

The blond dragon slayer now tried his hand at singing. You'd have thought that a noise like that would have frightened off birds and any other wildlife, but Liz noticed that two ravens fluttered in and perched on a ledge near the entrance. They eyed the grilling heart with greedy, beady eyes.

"Where are the others?" one raven asked the other.

"Probably still flapping along."

"Probably flapping in the other direction, Hugin," cawed the first. "You were supposed to watch them."

"I was tired," said the raven grumpily. "Do you know what it was like trying to find a single nuthatch, let alone five? Here on Gnita-moor of all places."

"I know," said the first raven. "That's why you should have kept a better watch on them."

"I forgot, Munin. I was too busy looking out for trolls. This is too close to Geirrodur's castle to be comfortable for a bird. There's nothing trolls like more than raven-roast."

"You'd forget your own head next, Hugin," said the other raven, with a disapproving clack of its beak.

Hugin scratched his poll with a black claw. "Memory is your job. Anyway we'll just have to do it without them. When is the idiot going to burn his hand and lick the hot blood, if he has thralls doing the cooking?"

Emmitt looked incredulously at Liz. "They're talking," he said in a frightened whisper.

Liz had been trying to come to terms with them saying anything but "Nevermore," herself. She'd already worked out that they weren't speaking English, but that she was understanding them. "I know," she said quietly. "Now, for a tasty piece of dragon heart, they might like to explain."

Hugin bobbed his head forward. But Munin—the one on the left—clacked his beak angrily. "You're not supposed to taste the hot blood."

"Why not? The human is blond, *and* it is offering us some," said Hugin eagerly, hopping from one foot to the other.

"Because it is not Sigurd the Dragon-slayer, the killer of Fafnir the Great. He's the one with the sword and the ice-brew. Go and peck that stuff out of his hand. I'll chase off these thralls."

"No chance," said Hugin. "If that's Sigurd, then that sword is Gram. I might not be you, but I remember that much. I don't want to be half a raven. You do it. I'll chase the thralls. Peck their eyes out."

"Emmitt, pick up a rock," said Liz, doing it herself. "If one of these dumb birds even takes to the wing, I'll have to show you how to pluck ravens for roasting."

She reached into her bag and pulled out a pair of shades, and passed them to the boy, who now had a rock in his hand. She perched her reading glasses on her nose.

"How straight and how hard do you throw, Emmitt? I killed a crow or two, from a lot farther off than this." She noticed that Lamont had put down the spade and picked up a rock too. Emmitt might look a bit sulky, but like Lamont the boy was quick on the uptake.

"I practice my pitching on sparrows, Liz. I never miss." He hefted the rock, as if gauging it for a throw. "You get the one on the right. I'll kill the left-hand one."

This boy was good. He sounded convincing too. The attitude came through.

Munin squawked indignantly. "You're not supposed to do that! We'll tell Odin."

Sigurd started singing again. Liz reflected that obscene songs hadn't changed much, and then realized that she could understand the words.

"If you live that long," said Emmitt disdainfully.

"And, even if we let you live, Odin is going to really like the fact that you've botched it," said Liz, keeping her voice calm and even. "So you might as well talk to us and tell us what's going on here. Maybe we can reach a deal. In the meanwhile, Lamont, you all need to have a taste of this heart. It does translation magic."

"You can't do that!" squawked Munin. He was definitely both the more intelligent and the more conservative of the two.

"Why not?" said Liz.

"Because Sigurd is supposed to," said the raven.

"We'll leave him some," said Emmitt.

"But . . . he's supposed to eat all of it," protested the raven. Lamont came forward with one of the PSA agents' rather useless short swords and sliced a piece off. Sigurd concentrated on squeezing the last few drops out of the skin he'd just drained and swayed out past them to relieve himself of some of his one-man party.

"And then drink Reginn's blood," the raven concluded.

Liz shuddered. "He's welcome to that. All of it. You Norse are so sweet. We just need a bit of translation skill and we'll happily get out of here, okay?"

"I suppose it'll still work," said Hugin, as Lamont gingerly tasted a bit of the heart.

Marie was far more pragmatic when she was told what to do. She closed her eyes and ate it.

"I don't see why not," said Munin. "A drop of dragon's blood does the trick."

Marie blinked at the raven. "Lamont," she said. "You hear what I hear?"

He nodded. "Yeah."

"Cut another piece for the kids. Quickly now, before that blond lunk comes back."

"I don't want to eat that, Mama," protested Ella, in girlish horror.

"Just close your eyes and pretend it's medicine, which is what it is," said Marie. She pointed a finger at the PSA men. "You, fat ass, you and your friend better get a piece too."

Ty and Tolly tried to outdo each other with he-man noises of enjoyment, and Ella gagged on her fragment.

"I'm a vegetarian," protested one of the PSA agents.

That was nearly too much for Liz, and, she noticed, for the ravens. They nearly fell off their ledge.

"*Caw!* Vegetables . . . *Caw. Caw. Caw.*"

Back on Earth in the United States, there was no reason why you couldn't be a PSA operative and a vegetarian—or a homicidal maniac, for that matter. But to the Norse, Liz was willing to bet, it was as funny as it must have been to the Zulu the first time they encountered the idea. She wondered what the word "vegetarian" translated into. By the way the ravens were behaving, it was really bizarre. Liz knew from the farm the idea was still a joke to the rural people whose life centered on cattle herding. Meat was as much of a part of their life as Kleenex wasn't.

"Shut up," growled Lamont. "It's part of your cover. Put some in your mouth and pretend."

The agent looked pale, but took the piece of hot meat. Put it to his face. Seemed to be chewing.

"*Het jy dit geëet?*" asked Liz.

He looked at her blankly.

"You've got to really put it in your mouth," she snarled. "Ass. The spell doesn't work otherwise. Your buddy understood me, didn't you?" she said to the other PSA man.

He nodded, startled. "Yeah. Look, Stephens, you've got to do it."

"I can't . . ."

Liz took a fingerful of the hot bubbling juice and pushed it into his mouth, which was still open. He spat and retched. But when she said *"Moeshle nyama!"* at least he understood her, even if he did not agree.

"Right," said Marie. "Birdies. Are you going to talk us out of here? We'll get this Sigurd guy to taste this stuff when he comes back in."

The two ravens had almost gotten over the vegetarian business. "It's a deal, black-elf. So long as we get a piece of heart too," said Hugin, plainly the greedier of the two. "What do you say, Munin?"

"I suppose. I want a rare piece," said Munin. Lamont obliged.

"Will it work?" said Liz. "Look, we could just sneak out now."

"He'd chase you, and cut off your head with Gram," said Hugin. "It's what you do to runaway thralls. And that *is* Sigurd. He's a one-man army."

Munin tore a fragment of meat off the piece between his claws. "No problem. Look, we need you out of here to do our job. And he's a pushover for us corvids. Trust me, it'll be easy. A guy who will take advice from nuthatches hasn't got much in his brain-box."

"Good meat," said Hugin. "Sure you won't have some more, grass-eater?" He cawed at his own humor, as Sigurd walked back in.

Liz pointed at the meat, which was charring on the one side. "Try, master."

He shook his head. "Reginn's supposed to eat it, thrall-wench. Otherwise I end up with the blood-guilt for killing Fafnir his brother."

"See if it is done then, master," persisted Liz, wondering how long she could keep up the "master" bit.

"I suppose so," he said, prodding it with a big forefinger. Hot juice obligingly burned him, and he licked his finger.

"Here stands Sigurd," said the raven Hugin. "Cooking a dragon's heart for someone else. If he ate it he would understand the speech of all, even the birds and the beasts."

"He really should chase these thralls out of here," said the other. "They're here to help the evil Reginn who murdered his father with Fafnir and got the great Sigurd to kill the dragon Fafnir, the brother of Otr, for whom the gods paid weregild of Andvari's hoard."

"Yes," said Hugin. "Send these thralls away. Half of them are black-elves anyway."

"Reginn probably needs them to do his dwarfish magic," said Munin. "Send them away."

Sigurd looked at them. "Shall I kill them all? I fancied keeping the one wench for a tumble."

Liz lifted the rock still in her hand just enough for the ravens to get the message. "*Caw.* Wouldn't do that. No, never. The black-elves would be angry. Send them away now. And give us a piece of meat."

Sigurd blinked. "Did you speak my language before?"

"No, you now understand ours," said Munin.

"I meant this thrall-wench."

"Only after, master," said Liz with a false smile. "Can we go?"

Sigurd cut himself a slice of hot heart. "I suppose so. I thought I'd get you lot to carry the dragon's treasure, but you and those men without any pants on can get gone. I worry about men without pants."

They left, hastily, with Hugin saying in a wheedling voice, "You could spare us a bit. Come on!"

Outside the cave it was apparent that both evening and the weather were drawing in. "So where do we go now?" said Lamont. "You're the outdoor expert, Liz."

"And can I take these off now?" asked Emmitt, tugging at the wraparound dark glasses. "I can't see much out here in them. I couldn't see anything at all in the cave except that fire."

"Sure. It was just to stop those ravens pecking out your eyes." She grinned at him, giving a thumbs up. "You did pretty well in there. And Lamont, I think we have to find shelter and warmth, before the agents' knees fall off and we all freeze to death tonight. This is about as different from my part of Africa as is possible, but that's just common sense."

As usual it was Marie and the department of common sense that took over. "Practically that leaves us with the dragon's cave—and that bozo Sigurd is going to go back there, or return to that place the birds said was a troll castle." She pointed back the way they'd come from. "I'm for the castle. It was fairly warm with those fires, and I think all of the trolls ran away."

"Besides, your average troll is an improvement on Sigurd," said Liz.

Marie nodded. "And it looks like it's about to start snowing."

As they walked back over the hill it began to do that, in unpleasant wet sticky flakes. By the time they got to the troll castle, Liz was fairly sure they were safe from any sort of pursuit. They were lucky to find the place themselves.

The room where Red-beard was still sleeping had delicious warmth seeping out of the stone window, although the two PSA agents in their sandals were almost too cold to climb in there. They had to be hauled over the sill.

"First things first—we ought to block that hole," said one of them.

"With what? Fatso's cloak?" said Liz, sarcastically. She leaned over and gave the ratty garment in question a tug.

The snoring stopped abruptly. The huge red-bearded man sat up and looked at them, with bleary road-map veined eyes.

"Who are you?" he asked. "Where is Thjalfi? And has anyone got something for me to drink?"

CHAPTER 12

@@@@@

Marie could smell the wave of old booze sweating out of the man. She'd got a whiff of it on their way out, but at the time there had been other things to think about. Now the smell and the sight of the tremor in his hand brought it all back, sharply. It didn't take a glance at Emmitt to realize that it would do the same to the boy. Her sister—Emmitt's mother—had been in that state often enough.

The big red-bearded man looked at the broken stone chair. "I did that?" he asked warily.

"I reckon so," said Marie. There was frost in her voice, despite the situation they were in.

He actually looked as if he was about to start crying. "I didn't mean to. I don't remember . . ." He trailed off.

"I never can remember." He sniffed. "Look, I'm sorry. I'll try and get you another one, but I'm . . . er, a bit broke right now."

Marie looked at him silently.

"There's more, isn't there," he said, looking uneasy.

"There always is, isn't there?"

He hung his head. "Sometimes," he admitted.

She still stared at him.

"Look. I'm sorry about the chair." He started wringing his huge hands.

"It ain't my chair."

He stood up shakily and groaned. "Oh, my head. Then what's the problem?"

"You are," said Marie. "Or rather, your damn drinking is. It's not just chairs you're wrecking. It's yourself."

He held his head. "That's not something I can fix. I wish I could."

"It can be done. If you want to enough. If you're determined enough. If you're strong enough."

He staggered over to the rock window, took a handful of snow and wiped his brow with it. Then took another handful, stuck it into his mouth and sucked on it.

He looked down at his clothes. It was fairly plain he'd been sick on them. He swallowed. "I, Thor, am the strongest of the Æsir. I will do this thing, or die in the effort." He looked at his clothes again. "I don't like waking up like this."

"It's a first step," said Lamont dryly. "But do you think you can keep it up?"

"Thor?" said Emmitt incredulously. "You mean, like, the hammer-thrower?"

Thor nodded. And then plainly wished he hadn't. "Yes. I am the master of Mjöllnir." He went and sat down again, leaning against the wall. "Never again," he groaned.

"So if you are Thor . . . let's see the hammer!" demanded the boy.

Thor shook his head carefully. "I . . . er, sold it."

"What for?" asked his audience.

Thor looked sadly at them. "Drink."

"Look, I can accept this part about powerless over alcohol. Every one of the Æsir is unable to stand against something. Frey is weak against the frost Giants, Heimdall against Surt's minions. And it's true my life has become unmanageable. It's a mess."

Thor now gave Marie a stern look. "But this second step nonsense! This 'we came to believe that a power greater than ourselves could restore us to sanity' nonsense. I *am* a power greater than myself. I am one of the Æsir. I'm a god, you idiotic woman. And I've tried, and I couldn't restore me to sanity. Sif tried. Heimdall tried. Idun tried with curative apples. Nothing works! When the drink gets in me nothing will calm me down but another drink."

"Strongest? You don't look that strong," said Ella doubtfully.

Thor attempted to haul his belly in. "I am Thor of the Æsir.

Mighty Thor!" He patted his midriff. "I admit I have let myself get a
bit out of condition, lately. But with my girdle of strength . . ."

Liz laughed. "Girdle. It'd have to be super-strong to keep that
gut in."

"I think he means a sort of belt, like a boxing champion's belt,"
said Lamont, with a grin. It was hard to take this wasted bleary
slob too seriously, even if in this world he was a god.

"Heavyweight champion," said Liz. "And there I was going to
ask where he bought it."

"Well," said Thor, completely missing the sarcasm, "it was given
to me by the giantess Grid, when she heard we were coming to
Geirrodur's castle." He lifted his tunic and looked in puzzlement
at the acreage of white belly. "It's not there," he said, worriedly. "I
promised I would return it. I, uh . . . seem to have lost mine."

"You seem to have lost this one too."

Thor looked around, more worried than ever. "You haven't seen
Thjalfi anywhere around?"

"Is it a person or a thing?" asked Ella.

"My bond-servant, along with his sister Roskva," said Thor.
"I don't see the gauntlets of iron or Grid's rod anywhere either."
There was the edge of panic in his voice.

Pieces began to fit together in Liz's mind. "This Thjalfi. Has he
got a fake beard? About the same height as Lamont, but fatter.
Wearing a bilious green tunic thing?"

Thor looked puzzled. "Nay, Thjalfi has but a little wispy beard.
Barely fit for a weasel, let alone a man. He is of a height with the
svartalfar here"—he pointed at Lamont—"and I think his cloth is
green. Yes. It is. It made me feel very unwell the other morning.
Something always makes me feel unwell in the mornings."

"And what is this 'Grid's Rod'?" asked Marie.

"A staff of iron which can neither be bent nor moved. It will
grow, too, to press against the foe, be they ever so far. We used
it to cross the Vimur river. Geirrodur's daughter Gjalp was making it flood."

"Ah," said Liz grimly. "I think we can tell you, then. It's your
servant Thjalfi who has your iron gloves, and your rod. I'd guess
that he probably has your belt too. He tried to kill us. Damn
near succeeded, too."

Thor looked at them in puzzlement. "Thjalfi? With my gauntlets of iron?"

"Unless they're common fashion items around here, I'd give you long odds that your servant has helped himself to them." Liz's voice began rising a little. "*And* tried to kill us, *and* we've lost Jerry because of it, to say nothing of one of those idiots." Liz pointed at one of the PSA agents.

Thor looked doubtfully at the man. "Even in a Valkyrie such skirts are hardly decent."

"He's a man," said Lamont, enjoying the discomfort of the agent. He was still quietly furious with the PSA and its agents for having gotten his family into this mess.

Thor blinked. "Is it customary among you svartalfar—the pale ones, anyway—for warriors to dress like that? Does it make them more courageous, because of the mocking? Loki and I got ribbed for months when we dressed as Freyja and her bridesmaid."

"They thought we were going to a place where the men dress like that."

Thor made a face. "Lucky you came here, eh? But I still want to know more about what game Thjalfi thought he was up to. He's getting above himself, acting on his own like this. We don't want him picking needless fights with svartalfar, too."

"Oh, he wasn't alone," said Liz.

"So he had a bunch of his low-life friends around and he was showing off," said Thor with enormous tolerance. "I've done the same myself. You get a bit carried away."

"This was a tall man with just one eye," said Liz. "Sound like someone you know?"

"*What!*" bellowed Thor furiously.

"And a bunch of warriors he called 'einherjar.' They were hunting for us."

"How dare he!" Thor's face, florid before, was now beetroot-red. A huge meaty fist slammed into his palm, like a thunder-crack. Suddenly making fun of him being the most physically powerful of the gods seemed a stupid idea. Energy seemed to almost crackle from him.

"Thjalfi is my bonder! What's Odin up to messing with my man, and bringing his men here. Where the Nifelheim is he? This time I'll—"

"I don't think he's around anymore," said Marie. "We saw him giving advice to Sigurd, and then he rode off in the other direction."

Thor sighed. "Don't tell me. I was drunk and he's been . . . and gone, hasn't he? It always seems to happen that way these days. And now I'm the one who has to try to explain to Grid. At least I know I have to start on Thjalfi. I don't remember him being like this, before. I wonder where he's got to?"

"We didn't see anyone," said Tolly.

"And you can see the whole hall from the place where that bridge thing broke off," said Ty. "The fires look like they're going out."

Marie sighed gustily. "What have you two been up to this time! Why must you always wander off the minute that no adults are looking at you?"

"Maybe we should nail one foot to the floor," said Liz, giving the two boys her best basilisk stare. Ty seemed to find the idea funny. His friend Tolly looked a bit more wary. With Medea as a mother, you never knew if things like that were a real threat or not.

"Look, you two just stay in sight from now on or I'll be tempted to let her do what she threatened," said Marie crossly. "I've got enough to worry about without chasing around after you."

"I thought we saw Babe Ruth being abducted by aliens. We had to check that it was for real," said Ty.

"In an eighteen-wheeler," corroborated Tolly.

"Babe Ruth? Aliens? Are you crazy?" demanded Emmitt. "Can't you even come up with a believable lie, Ty?"

Ty did his best look hurt. "Any myth can be true here, Dad said . . ."

"Myth, yes," said Lamont, rolling his eyes.

"We were looking for something to eat," admitted Tolly.

Lamont nodded. "We're going to need to feed everyone. Especially these kids," he said. He turned to the two surviving PSA agents. "The paratroopers had rations last time that we could share. What have you got?"

Thor thought that they were addressing him. "Goats," he said. "Tanngnjóst and Tanngrisnir. They pull my chariot . . . Well, they used to pull my chariot back when I had a chariot. Thjalfi had to borrow one last time I needed one and we had to walk this time, because of the little accident I had with it. So we can eat my goats."

"Goats. Oh, we can't . . ."

Thor interrupted, waved a generous hand, completely misunderstanding her reaction to goat. "So long as the bones are intact I can bring them back to life the next day. And the way those two goats eat it's just as well to kill them at night. One of them ate my bed-clothes one night. . . . I'd, um, perhaps had a little more mead than I should. I nearly froze to death before I woke up. I'll call them."

He turned to the window and bellowed. How one pair of lungs could produce such a volume of sound was beyond belief. Even the walls seemed to vibrate.

Thor turned back to them. "They'll be here presently. Why don't we go and find those fires the boys talked about. We'll need a spit of some kind."

"It has to be warmer there," said one of the agents. "And then we really need to look at strategies for us to get back. We have an . . . assignment to complete."

Liz snorted. "Trust me, someone else will have to 'complete your assignment.' The only easy way back is death. And thanks to you we're all stuck in this mess and thanks to one of your idiots we've lost Jerry, who was our best chance of getting home. I want to find him. And if you want to survive you're going to have to give up playing tag-along and be useful. And get with the local clothing. You look like you've escaped from a circus to the locals."

"Don't take that tone with us, ma'am," said one of them testily. "You're not an American citizen, you know."

"And this isn't America, you jackass, in case you hadn't noticed," snapped Liz. "Now shape up or ship out, whatever your name is. We're going to look for heat, and a spit. You're sort of pretend-ing to be a warrior. Act like one. Now, lead out. We'll keep you on point, and maybe you'll get back to the U.S. sooner than you thought possible. Move!"

Lamont chuckled. "You better listen to 'Sir', mister. And you'd better introduce yourselves. If we need to yell a warning, a name helps."

"Agent Bott."

"And Agent Stephens," said the other, as if providing ID to people of no importance was physically painful. "Look, it is unfortunate that you people got involved but our assignment is vital to national security. We need your cooperation."

"Let's put it this way," said Liz, shooing them ahead of her like hens. "You certainly need *our* cooperation. Now you've just got to convince us that we need yours. And so far, you've been more of a liability than an asset."

They went out, arranged the ladder and descended. "Don't stand under the ladder when Thor comes down," said Marie quietly.

Only the last two rungs broke.

The fires in the huge main hall were definitely dying. Patches of dead coals shared space with the sullen glow.

The place was eerily quiet in the half-light. Here and there the fire flared, sending shadows chasing. The few remaining torches guttered in their sconces, and the huge, dim hall seemed even dimmer. It was an eerie place and the dead trolls did not make it any more appealing.

The clatter of goaty hooves nearly frightened Stephens into an early grave and a quick transfer back to Chicago. Goats, in Liz's experience, were evil-minded cantankerous creatures. These ones looked the part. And they were huge. More the size of a pony than a goat.

One of them took a long goaty look at the strangers surrounding Thor and lowered its head. It raced toward them at full acceleration. "*Tanngnjóst!*" yelled Thor, loudly enough to stir the embers to flames.

"Get out of its way!" yelled Liz. They scattered, Lamont assisted by a sideward toss by the goat that shunted him some ten yards across the floor. Thor stopped the goat with a solid thwack against the head that made it sit down on its goaty tail.

Liz felt something tugging at her skirt. It was the other goat. Liz took it by the horns and leaned into its face. "I see by your beard that you are a billy goat. You're billy goat gruff right now, but you'll be billy goat treble after I've finished with you."

It was apparent that the dragon's heart gave her the power of speech with birds and animals, as well as lower life-forms, like a local Norse god turned into a drunk. Tanngrisnir let go hastily, before Thor even got there.

Marie helped Lamont back to his feet.

"Well," said Thor. "We have dinner, although I must admit my stomach doesn't really feel much like red meat."

Lamont felt his derriere. "More like a revenge killing than dinner."

The goats looked decidedly wary, and started looking around for the best way out. There were some disadvantages to this translation spell, Liz realized. It didn't make the animals any cleverer or more human—things like the ravens were clever to begin with—but it did allow them to understand what their destiny was about to be.

"I feel like fish," said Thor. "But Thjalfi never brought any. He likes eating goat. It's a pity we don't have a cart or we could just head home to Bilskríner. Thrúd always sees that there is a bit of fish for me. She's a good girl, really. Not like my sons Modi and Magni. I hardly ever see them these days."

"What about having a good look around first?" said Liz. She had no love for goats, either alive or as dinner, and she wasn't squeamish, but having your dinner eye you warily was a bit off-putting. Besides, they might just get some idea of what had happened to Jerry. He could still be here, or there could be a clue as to where he'd got to. "We might find a chariot or a cart or something you could hitch up to them. How far is this Bilsk . . . this home of yours?"

"Were I to have my chariot, we could ride there fast enough. My goats do not entirely tread on the earth," said Thor, with a twinkle.

"All right. It's chariot hunt time, then," said Liz.

They didn't find one.

"Trolls don't really approve of the wheel," said Thor gloomily. "They're very conservative. They think the horse is too much progress and a bad thing, except as dinner."

"They make metal things," said Lamont, gesturing with the smoky torch he was carrying. Fortunately they'd found a supply of pitch-soaked torches early on. "This is a smithy, obviously enough. Those are chains. Those are tools . . ."

"They're capable enough craftsmen," said Thor. "Not a patch on the dwarves, of course. But they have tools."

"For making weapons and things to imprison people," said Liz.

Thor blinked. "That and brewing kettles, naturally, woman. What did you expect? Plows?" He seemed to find the idea funny.

Lamont shook his head. "Some people would find plows more useful. Me, for one. I could make you a cart here, but I think it would take too much time."

"What about a sled?" asked Liz, looking thoughtful.

"Not enough snow," said Marie. She was sounding tired and in pain again.

Liz wagged her hand back and forth. "That's not really a problem. In South Africa all the rural people use sleds. And most of South

Africa doesn't see much snow. They use oxen to drag sleds made out of a fork of a big tree."

"There is much snow between here and Asgard," said Thor thoughtfully. "If we go west."

"And it was snowing when we came in, Ma," pointed out Ella. "Quite hard, remember."

"I guess. But we still need to eat and stay warm. If it is snowing, it's no weather for going out."

"But soon enough Geirrodur's troll castle must freeze. The fires die without the trolls to feed and stoke them," said Thor. "While, ahem, my Bilskríner is not as well maintained as it used to be, Asgard is warmer, or it least it will be until the Time."

"We could pick a room, close it off, and at least wait until morning."

"This one would be good, but we still need food."

Lamont turned on Stephens. "What's in the pack?"

Of the two surviving agents he was the only one who still had his "authentic Greek leather bag."

The vegetarian agent looked wary.

"It's that or goat. Nice meaty goat," said Liz cheerfully. "And if we have to eat it, you will."

Agent Stephens blanched. "I do have some K-rations. And some ramen noodles."

Liz slapped her head and burrowed into her own bag. "I forgot. I have some candy bars I picked up for the kids when I heard you were coming." She blushed slightly. "And a box of multiflavored jelly beans. Let's see what the transition to this place has done to *those*."

"Transition . . ." said the agent, frowning.

"Yep," said Lamont. "In case you hadn't noticed, it affected the assembly mechanism on your weapons. I reckon you'll find that they're still threaded. The threads would just match the engineering skills of the Norse. In other words, as good as a blacksmith working them by hand could make. You'll find the same has happened to your other toys. The paratroopers found that their stainless steel had suddenly started rusting."

Liz nodded. "And my lighter, which used a flint—which the Greeks knew—and lighter fluid, which they didn't. It changed too. The flint part stayed the same, but the lighter fluid became moth-ball smelling stuff. Jerry said naphtha was the basis of some flamethrower fuel that they used to call Greek fire."

The agent dug into his pack hurriedly. His K-rations had become hard biscuit. The ramen . . . a sort of coarse-ground meal.

Thor sniffed it curiously. "Barley. We can make gruel out of it. Some goat soup maybe? That'd be easy on my digestion."

Liz's candy bars were some sort of honey and nut confection. She could almost see the lightening of mood and the improvement in attitude among the snatchees as the sugars hit their bloodstreams. Liz still wanted to get on and search this place thoroughly to see if Jerry might be hiding somewhere. Now, after one of the candy bars and one of the agent's hard biscuits—which had a definite tang of pork-fat, to Stephens' distress—getting the search organized and remotivated was easier. Braving the rat-infested kitchen was not so daunting, even if it was just as smelly.

All they found there, however, was a cleanable small cauldron— and, in an antechamber, three brace of rock ptarmigan, still with the feathers on. And some salt that didn't seem too dirty.

"Do you think it'll be all right?" asked Emmitt, looking at the grayish stuff doubtfully.

Liz grinned. "Possibly. Salt kills most bacteria. Mind you, any self-respecting bacteria would have left a while back."

But the best find was a storeroom full of furs, carefully packed and baled.

"Trading stuffs," said Thor knowledgably, inspecting it. "Trolls are good hunters. Good loot."

"Warm loot," said Marie. "And we'll need it."

Thor pointed at the two agents. "You could make them trousers. Good fur trousers."

But of Jerry there was no sign. And it was now completely dark and snowing hard outside the troll castle. Reluctantly, Liz had to admit that now was not the time to be venturing out, not to look for Jerry or even to avoid goat-dinner. So they retreated on the forge, and set about preparing a supper and keeping the place warm. Having bales of ermine helped, as did a plentiful supply of coals that they found in the smithy.

"Right," said Liz. "I suppose I am the only person who has ever plucked and drawn a game bird. You two"—she singled out Tolly and Ty who were investigating a rack of sharp implements—"come. You're about to learn how to do something quite revolting which will delight you."

That was enough to get their cooperation. And prepping the

birds would get her out of sewing. Or, hopefully, cooking. She'd rebelled early against learning anything about either art.

For the next hour it was quite a happy little domestic scene. Three people sewing together with leather thongs enough furs to bankrupt a royal house, and give the entire "beauty without cruelty" movement collective apoplexy. Well, if they'd been here, the ladies would just have had to come to terms with reality. In that period of history, fur equated with warmth and everyone wore them. And, cruelty or not, the garments that were being roughly stitched weren't beautiful anyway. But they would be warm.

Lamont was dividing his attention between supervising Agent Stephens' attempts at sewing and Agent Bott's attempts at cooking. Neither was going to win any prizes. Thor was bemusedly stirring barley gruel and also keeping a weather eye on Agent Bott trying to grill birds.

Liz and her team were trying their hand at nailing a platform of riven oak together, using crude iron nails they'd found. And Liz was trying hard not to throw up at the lingering taste of one of the jelly beans she'd tried, too incautiously. What it had turned into, in Norse terms, didn't bear thinking about. At a guess it had been the same dirty trick some Swedish fisheries scientists had tried on her in repayment for the *mampoer* trick she'd played on them. The memory of a *rakfisk* flavor bean would remain with her for always. Why couldn't she have gotten arctic cloudberry, like Lamont? Still, even *rakfisk* was better than whatever flavor Agent Stephens had got. He *had* thrown up.

The plan—if they could get through the night without Thor going into the DTs—was to proceed to this Bilskríner of his in the morning on the sled they were constructing. Despite Lamont's obsession with puns and useless information, he was a really good maintenance man when he wanted to be, genuinely good with his hands.

CHAPTER 13

⊛⊛⊛⊛⊛

The afternoon was sultry. Yet the new body that had fallen out of the pyramid onto the street outside was cold enough to have come out of a morgue. Condensation began to form on the brass breastplate and the solitary grieve. The helmet radio chattered and the GPS tracker came on.

In the PSA operations control room in Washington, there was a loud cheer.

PSA Director Helen Garnett leaned over the shoulder of one of her assistants, who was studying the information coming onto the screen. "I take it we've made contact finally, Jim. Which agent is it?"

Assistant Director of Operations James Horton was leaning over the woman's other shoulder, studying the same screen. "I think . . ."

The woman sitting in front of the console provided the answer. "It's Agent Sternal, ma'am. No question about that. But he's not responding to our signals."

"Why not?" demanded Garnett testily. "I thought the man had been properly trained. There's no excuse for—"

"Uh, he's dead, ma'am," said the operative. She pointed at some data in one corner of the screen. "Those are his vitals. Flat as a pancake. Agent Sternal is dead, ma'am."

Garnett straightened up and stared at Horton. "Dead?" she said, as if it were a word she'd just encountered.

Inside the inner perimeter the medics who still did patrols might have gotten to the man faster if the PSA had thought to set up a liaison with them. As it was, by the time Agent Sternal was found the corpse was well on its way back to ambient temperature. The man was so well dead that all they could do was load him into a field ambulance and drive out.

The ambulance was met at the outer perimeter by a team of PSA operatives, but not until the paratroopers stopped it first. The PSA vehicle and its four occupants had been forced to remain thirty yards away. Cruz and Mac's story had got around, and the paratroopers were in no mood to put up with the PSA trying its usual bullying tactics. The lieutenant insisted that the perimeter was under the control of the 101st—and the PSA could damn well wait in line.

For their part, the PSA operatives were insistent that no one except them was to handle the matter of Sternal's reappearance. No one there, on either side of the controversy, had any doubt that telephone calls and e-mails were being exchanged like gunfire between offices in Washington, the Pentagon—and the various offices maintained in Chicago by all parties involved.

The two agents still in the PSA van got out, and one of them tapped the agent-in-charge on the shoulder. "GPS says he's in that vehicle, Senior Agent Moran."

"Let's get him, then," said the agent. "I've had enough of this crap."

The four of them went across to the field-ambulance, where the lieutenant from the 101st was consulting with the EMTs. Senior Agent Moran flashed his ID at the driver. "We're here for the man you have in the vehicle."

The driver blinked, and looked at the lieutenant.

For his part, the lieutenant didn't blink. "The hell you will," he said pleasantly. "Professor Tremelo will handle this."

Moran gave the lieutenant's name plate a quick glance. "Evans, is it? Well then, Lieutenant Evans, let me explain to you the facts of life."

"Fuck you," said the lieutenant, every bit as pleasantly. "The only 'fact of life' that matters here today is that we are paratroopers and you are punks. If you give me any shit at all, you're dogfood."

Moran gaped at him. "You—you—" He took a shaky breath. "You can't!"

"Don't be silly. I told you. We're paratroopers. That's what we do. And I guarantee you we're a lot better at it than you are."

Evans turned his head slightly. "Sergeant Andersen, if any of these PSA agents makes a threatening move, kill him."

"Yes, sir," said the nearby sergeant stolidly. "Private Henderson, lower your weapon. The lieutenant said *if* they make a threatening move." He gave the PSA agents a glance. "Which they won't."

A bit reluctantly, the rifle barrel of one of his soldiers came down. Maybe two inches.

Moran was still gaping at Evans. Then, realizing how foolish he looked, snapped his mouth shut.

"I'll have you cashiered for this," he hissed. "At the very least."

Evans shrugged. "Maybe. But I doubt it, and you want to know why?" The lieutenant jerked a thumb at the ambulance. "Because this operation of yours is already coming apart at the seams, that's why. You Pissants might have gotten away with breaking half the laws on the books if you hadn't gotten caught in the act and if your operation had succeeded. But you did and it isn't. In Washingtonese, do you know what word that translates into?"

Moran stared at him. "What?" he finally asked.

"Wa-ter-gate," said Evans, drawling out the syllables. "There's blood in the water, Pissant—and it's yours, not mine. So guess who the sharks are coming after? They ate a president, once, after snacking on a bunch of flunkies and plumbers. You think they'll choke on a quarter-ante agency director—much less a penny-ante field agent?"

Moments later, the PSA vehicle departed. The lieutenant turned back to the ambulance driver.

"So what did he die of?"

The medic shrugged. "Hypothermia, maybe," he said, wiping the sweat off his brow. "The only other thing obviously wrong with him was a broken ankle. But he had frostbite."

"Examination of the material on the corpse's sandals revealed fragments of plant material, mostly fairly far gone into decay." The young forensic scientist spoke calmly, as if he weren't addressing an audience that included an eagle-winged, lion-bodied individual with the upper body of a naked woman. "However, we have identified the remains of bracken, *Pteridium aquilinum*, and also cloudberry."

"Not exactly what you would expect to find in Greece, even mythological Greece," said Miggy, steepling his fingers.

"No, Professor, it isn't. The pollen analysis from the mud paints a picture far more congruent with a paleoarctic origin for the material. I have a crew doing composition comparisons with various locales in Northern Europe and Asia, at various historical dates." He scratched his chin, obviously debating whether to extend comment past what was certain.

"Spit it out," said Miggy, who, as a career scientist, was an expert at dealing with scientific caution.

"It looks like Scandinavia, Professor. Tenth or eleventh century."

Miggy Tremelo grunted. "Norse myth. Rachel, get me someone with some expertise. Actually, get three or four. I'll talk to them on the phone, and see if I can pick out someone I can actually communicate with."

"Norse. You mean like the Vikings and Thor and Odin and all that stuff?" said McKenna.

"Yes. And I'm afraid I know a lot less about that subject than I do about high energy physics," admitted Tremelo.

"I know a little about it," said the paratrooper. "Ma was an Olsen before she married. Danish roots and proud of them. It's pretty wild stuff. Fenrir wolf and Ragnarok. And Loki. And lots of giants and trolls and snow and ice."

"Perfect spot for a bunch of Greek hoplites," snorted Cruz. "Well, at least they've got the Doc with them—if they'll have enough sense to listen to him."

"And my child," said Medea.

"And my mother," said Tina, "and Ella, and Daddy and Emmitt and Ty. We need to get them back. I want them!"

"We're doing our best, child. And, well, they *are* the best. They're the only people who have ever come back alive before." What Miggy didn't have the courage to say, was that the means they used last time—the sphinx—wouldn't work. Without a lot more data about Norse mythology he wasn't sure what would work, if anything could.

The phone rang. Miggy was relieved.

And then, as he realized what the call meant, a lot less relieved.

He stood up. "I have to go to Washington to testify to a Senate select committee. That woman—Ms. Garnett—has apparently been very busy. I guess it's going to be a political slugging match, after all. I thought she'd have enough sense to cut her losses and run. I'm going to need some witnesses. Rachel, get me Colonel McNamara on the line. Patch him through to my cell phone, since I've a plane to catch. You all stay right here, until I contact you."

"What about the dragons?" asked Medea, pointing to the parking lot, where the dragons reclined.

"Yeah," said Cruz. "Fish and Wildlife are getting pretty shrill about taking them back to their reserve. Still, Bitar and Smitar are a major deterrent for those PSA goons. Whether or not they'd be dumb enough to start a physical conflict with us paratroopers, the dragons just plain scare them. I'd like them near at hand."

Miggy smiled evilly. "I have taken steps. A special guard for them and Throttler is flying up from Vegas. I believe they're accompanied by several news crews. The dragons will stay exactly where you want them. You are not alone in the belief that Ms. Garnett would like them, you, and certainly me, to disappear. In the interests of national security, of course."

"Of course," said Cruz. "Actually, I'd better go out and talk to the dragons. They're not very bright, but they tend to listen to me."

"For about as long as it sticks in their heads," said Medea, squeezing his shoulder. "Which is, generally speaking, not very long."

"You need to pat them gently with something," said Cruz. "An oar is good."

The dragons greeted him with their usual enthusiasm, as if they hadn't seen him for three months and he was their only possible source of food. Literally, of course. They tried to wrap their coils around him and taste him with their tongues.

"Lay off, let me breathe! The food arrived yet?"

The dragons looked at him with kicked puppy eyes. He was obliged to wallop their heads a few times to reassure them.

"No food, Cruz," said Smitar mournfully.

"Poor little us," said Bitar, accidentally squashing a SUV. "Nobody loves us. Not even the chicks."

"And I've nothing against chicken," said Smitar. "It's nicer than goose. Not so many feathers to get stuck in your teeth."

"If you eat them before barbequeing them, that is," said Bitar, licking his chops. "They're nice with fries, I believe."

"What are fries?" asked Smitar, tasting a piece of SUV bumper.

Bitar thought about it. "It's tricky. Anything that can't get out of the way, that you cook in grease."

"Never was that fond of Greek food. I preferred the flavor of Egyptians. More tender and spicier," said Smitar. "Anyway, we're starving."

Cruz swatted them affectionately. "You can't believe everything a dragon says. They speak with forked tongue. I know from Arachne that you ate at the truck stop. And I've got to have a word with you about that. You have to stop snacking on people's cars."

"Can't help it," said Bitar. "I'm craving metal. And the stupid officials here don't wear armor like they should."

"It's a breach of tradition," agreed Smitar. "It shouldn't be allowed. Officials need armor. And I must admit I really feel the need for a bit of bronze. This chrome lacks flavor."

Cruz wished like hell he had Liz to ask about the biology of the creatures. Maybe they really did need to eat some metal.

"There is something missing in our lives, Cruz," said Smitar.

Bitar nodded. "Besides grilled chicken. Or goose."

Smitar coughed awkwardly. "It's about . . . you know . . . Lady dragons."

Bitar nodded. "You haven't got a sister, have you, Cruz? You did say your mother could be a bit of an old dragon."

CHAPTER 14

Loki was, in many ways, the architect of Ragnarok. Jerry faced an interesting conundrum here. Did he try to help the god who had brought about the end of everything? Or was that playing into the Krim's hands? The answer seemed to lie in gaining an ally . . . and changing the course of the myth. "So, why does Uncle Fox not find another way?"

"Uncle Fox. I had almost forgotten that," said Loki appreciatively.

"It is a good name for the cleverest of tricksters," said Jerry. Flattery was supposed to be something you laid onto royalty with a trowel, and he suspected that for gods a steam shovel would be good. Anyway, in this case, it was accurate. Loki was supposed to be the arch-trickster. But, besides his mischief, he was supposed to be the source of most evil and the eventual destroyer of the entire world. Despite the charm of the man, Jerry knew that he had to treat him with caution. A good trickster would have to have abundant charisma, after all.

"The cleverest of tricksters lies bound until the end of this cycle of time," said Loki with a wry smile. "Anyway, I did not know I had competition."

Jerry shrugged. "I am an expert of sorts on the competition. The trickster is a common motif in mythology. Nearly every culture has one, from Hanuman to Glooskap. They are usually neither good nor evil, but do help men when the fancy takes them. Loki is held as the greatest of them all. They are all thought to be at least in part created as good bad examples."

"Maybe," said Loki dreamily. "Maybe once they were chieftains of small tribes on leafy islands, who helped their people to survive by guile and cunning, when strength would not prevail. Yes, I was the friend of humans once. But did they come to my aid when the Ás killed my son and used his entrails to bind me?"

"Did they know?" asked Jerry. "And could they? Your enemies made sure that they would not wish to."

"That is true enough," admitted Loki. "One-eye found me a useful thing to blame for most things."

"Almost half of which you had nothing to do with," said Sigyn.

"Well yes. But the other half I did, often as not," said Loki, with disarming honesty. "It usually seemed worth it, at the time."

"And now?" asked Jerry.

"Well, some of the tricks were worth it," said Loki. "I probably shouldn't have done Sif's hair. It served her right for being a tease, though. But Freyja deserved what she got. Even she admitted it later. And Skadi deserved it too, I don't care what she says."

Jerry nodded. "And, if I recall right, a fair number of those pranks of yours involved changing your size and shape?"

"That and my powers over fire are my aspects, mortal. Uh, Jerry. That is how we have a fire in this damp pit, though we have little else. Fire is my name and fire is my nature, they say. Friend and destroyer both."

There was indeed something very flamelike about the mercurial Loki. "Well, how about we try the friend part on these thongs tying my hands together?"

"An easy gift to give," said Loki, fixing his sparkling eyes on the thongs. They began to smolder, and then, as Jerry strained against them, they broke and burned fiercely.

Jerry flung them away hastily, and the fire promptly died. It was good to have his hands free. "Thank you." He gave Loki a bow. "Now all you have to do is transform yourself and we can be out of here."

"If it were that easy, O man from a far-off place," said Loki, "I would have been gone for many ages and Ragnarok would have been. Odin has bound me here with a tie that cannot be broken. A blood tie. A tie that goes deeper than the iron that

Odin changed Narfi's entrails to, once they had bound me. I am bound by my son. I cannot break or escape that bond."

Jerry pondered the matter. "I think I understand. It is symbolic magic, isn't it? The chain that bound Fenrir is much the same thing. Tangible things can be broken. Intangibles . . . are much harder."

"Indeed," said Loki. "I should have guessed from what they did to my Fenrir. It was that that turned me against them, finally. As you say, any fool can break a leg or a sword. To break the spirit or destroy hope is indeed much harder. The bond between father and son is not easily broken. Odin used that to shackle me, as nothing else could. Sigyn cannot free me of the entrails of our son, either."

Jerry chewed his lip and put more effort into thought. If only he knew Norse myth better! "Then how did you get free before . . . you would be free at the end of this cycle of time, if I have it right."

"By slow determination," said Loki. "I cannot break the iron which was Narfi. But I can wear through the rock. And if that is what must be done to avenge my fine sons, I will."

By his face Jerry could tell that was no exaggeration. The rock would eventually crumble. "There is one other possibility," Jerry said cautiously.

"And what would that be?" asked Loki with gentle irony. "That I burn myself free as I burned your bonds? That too I cannot do against my own child's body."

Jerry shook his head. "No. That *I* could free you. To you . . . those are your son Narfi's guts. To me it is just iron . . . or am I misunderstanding this?"

"No. You have it right. There is just one detail. It *is* iron, and you are not the biggest or strongest of mortals, unless your looks deceive me—in which case I do apologize."

The iron bonds were only about an inch thick. Nothing to Thor, perhaps. "I'm feeling a little poorly at the moment," Jerry admitted. "Normally, it'd be like a few strands of wool."

Loki smiled. "You are quick, for a mortal, Jerry. I suppose if you weren't, you'd be dead."

Jerry realized he'd just met up with the god of Norse punsters, which, all things considered, was both alarming and hardly surprising. The various sagas, as he remembered a colleague complain,

were just about impenetrable to outsiders because of the various
word-plays or "kennings." He supposed that long Scandinavian
and Icelandic winters lent themselves to that. "It's one of those
things about being mortal, Loki, although it cuts me to the quick
to admit it. And the pain of that makes me lithp. Then I'll be
Thor, and Thor being thtrong, I could break your bondth."

Loki laughed helplessly. Eventually he got control of himself.
"Don't tell the Thunderer. He's a bit slow and always suspects
people are making fun of him. It is a good thing I understand
the tongues of all mortals or some of it would have been wasted
on me."

"Yeah. Well, its a good thing my friend Lamont didn't get
nabbed and put in here too. Or we might just end up making
bad puns while your Ragnarok comes and goes. I wish like hell
he was here. Him or Liz, although she'd have killed me for that
pun. They're both better at practical solutions than I am. And
there has to be one. Here I am—free, able to avoid Odin's spell
and help you, and I haven't got the strength or the tools to do
anything about it."

Jerry felt through his pockets, hoping against any kind of logic to
find a file or a crowbar, or a pair of bolt-cutters . . . instead of . . .

A couple of pens that felt like goose-quills, a used handkerchief, a small pocket diary that Liz had given him in the vain
hope that it would help him remember appointments, a plastic
bag that Liz's candy supply (officially for Lamont's kids) had come
in, his wallet, and a remarkable shortage of bolt-cutters or even
something as useful as a penknife. Of course, transition would
have changed the items. The plastic bag felt leathery.

Loki sighed. "If wishes were enough to bring them here, or any
others that might befriend me, I would have this place so full
of my kin among the mountain and frost giants, and my living
children, that we'd have to stand on each other's shoulders. This
place is proofed against the magics and summonsing of both the
giant-kind and of the Ás. Even if we were free, only that vindic-
tive bitch Skadi can get in and out of the pit."

"And she does not come down here when the bowl is nearly
full, or I would dash it in her eyes," said Sigyn. "She knows I
have to protect my husband from her snake's venom."

"Speaking of bowls, how much time do we have left?" asked
Loki.

"It nears full, beloved," she said despondently.

He sighed. "Friend Jerry. You had better find somewhere well clear. Sigi. Try to note where he is. He's a mortal, and that poison would burn him far worse than it does me. It might kill him and we need him. Even if it takes a little longer, have a care throwing the stuff out. I can endure a little longer. Jerry. It will take me a while to recover, before I can be rational again. And my writhing shakes the place. I am sorry."

Jerry felt the contents of his pocket again. "I think . . . I think I have something we can try." He pulled out the once-plastic bag, the couple of quills, and the handkerchief. Liz might prefer Kleenex but there were things you could do with handkerchiefs that defied Kleenex. He could tear strips off them and use them to hastily lash two goose quills into a cross, and then use that to hold open the oiled leather bag. He felt around and found some of the burned thong . . . Now all he needed was something to tie it onto, and he'd have a sort of bag-on-stick to hold over Loki's face. There was nothing remotely sticklike in the prison. Then it occurred to him that he was being needlessly inventive. He pulled the bag of out his pocket, and flattened it out. "If I can just put this over your face, Loki."

The bound god grinned. "It'll improve it. Try it."

"And quickly," said Sigyn. "The bowl grows heavy."

Jerry eyed the snake warily, but the huge serpent resting on the ledge above seemed semitorpid. The creature seemed content with just dripping its venom onto the face of the bound god below. So he put the bag over Loki's face and backed off hastily.

Sigyn took her sheltering bowl away, and poured it out. And Loki lay . . . still. And then spoke from under the bag. "Sigi. Rest your arms for a while. I don't like the view under here, but there is no pain. There is no pain," he said again, almost incredulously.

"We will make something of a tent of it first," said Sigyn, holding her now empty bowl back in place, and flicking the moisture off the bag. "It would have run down onto your face soon."

She smiled at Jerry, and he could suddenly see that under the exhaustion, under the sorrow and the bitterness, she was a very beautiful woman. "Thank you. You have been the first good thing to happen since Loki was trapped."

"The second," said Loki. "You coming here to sit with me was the first, and the greatest."

"He always did have a silver tongue," she said, smiling again. "Now. With those quills, can you make some kind of prop to make the bag into a sort of tent?

Jerry had taken out his billfold. The credit and bank-cards were ivory by the feel of them. "If I made a V of this above his eyes. And I have some coins . . . we could weigh the edges down with that."

"A personal face tent," said Loki.

"You will have to lie still, husband."

"I'll do my best, if it will give you a rest. Keeping still when I know I have outsmarted Helblindi and his tart Skadi will be a pleasure."

"Who is Helblindi?" asked Jerry, ever curious.

"Our One-eye. My accursed half-brother. Just one of his myriad aliases. It means Hell-blind, which is appropriate."

That explanation left Jerry puzzling at the genealogy of the Norse gods, as he organized Loki's personal face-tent. He wasn't that familiar with the relationships of the Norse pantheon, but he hadn't known that Odin and Loki were related. Loki was one of the giants—and Odin was one of the Æsir . . . wasn't he?

A little later Sigyn triumphantly lowered the bowl. "My arms. It has been centuries. Thank you, Jerry."

"Hey," said Loki. "She's mine." You could hear him laughing under that tent.

"Keep still," said Sigyn sternly. "Why I put up with you, I do not know." And when he started to speak again, she said, "Hush." And he did.

Jerry was impressed. One had to be careful around women who could shut someone like Loki up. "I want to explain something," he said calmly, knowing that it was her that he had to convince, not Loki.

"For the favor of a rest from holding the bowl, I will happily listen. Loki will too, but he is not going to say anything."

"Right. Well, it would seem that your Mythworld—your Asgard, your gods—have somehow been taken over by this device called the Krim. It takes humans from our world—the world you once called Midgard—and reenacts the old stories with them to see and believe. This revitalizes the old beliefs. We know from our last encounter that it can do the same scene many times. It does this, not for the old gods, but for some reason of its own. It takes over for purposes we do not fully understand."

"So?"

"I suspect the myths, the stories and sagas have to be reenacted over and over again," said Jerry. "You want vengeance. I can understand that."

"But you cannot understand the depth of that desire," said Sigyn grimly. "I do not mind if we destroy Odin many, many times."

Jerry nodded. "I accept that. But do you want your son Narfi to die many times? Do you want Loki to suffer many times?"

She was silent for a long, long time. The only sound was the splash of venom on the oilskin bag. Then she said, "No. But I want my vengeance, Jerry."

"And I want mine," said Loki quietly, forgetting his injunction against talking. "Thph. The bowl, Sigi. Quick."

She had it ready, and Jerry carefully rearranged the face-tent. It gave him a chance to think.

"I'm not saying that you can't have your vengeance," he said eventually. "It seems that the right way to stop the pattern . . . is to stop the myth being reenacted according to the pattern."

"So?" said Sigyn.

"So I need to break Loki out of here . . . and let you succeed, without Ragnarok. You would accept vengeance without destroying the world, would you not? It would stop all this repeating, again."

She was silent for a long time. "Yes. But a number of the Æsir were involved. I want them all."

"We can agree on principle, though. And sort out the terms between us." Jerry said that last with a confidence he didn't really feel.

"Spoken like true trickster," said Loki. "Now please hold the bowl for a bit, because I need to talk."

Sigyn held the bowl over his face. "Poor love. To have to hold your tongue for so long!"

"And I almost succeeded too," said Loki, with mocking self-admiration. "Oh, I am great! So what do you plan, Jerry?"

"My first project has to be to deal with that snake."

Sigyn shook her head. "Skadi would know if you interfered with her pet. It's not intelligent enough to tell her what goes on, but she'd know if it were killed. And the huntress is probably stronger than I am," she admitted reluctantly.

Jerry tugged his ear thoughtfully. "We'll need her to get out of here then, won't we?"

"It'd be one possible way," said Loki. "Odin has given her the *galdr* that allow her in and out. But if need be I can burn my way out. It might take a while though."

"Longer than a mortal can do without food or drink," said Sigyn. "Besides, as I have explained to you, lava has to go somewhere."

"And if I burn upwards it will be here that it comes to, if I recall right," he said with a grin.

"What about steps or pockets in the rock?" asked Jerry.

"That could work. Less lava. Still, it takes rock a while to cool."

"You can melt any kind of rock?"

Loki nodded. "Burn rather than melt. Some things are harder than others, but everything burns . . . after a fashion."

"Even iron?"

Loki snorted. "Yes. But if I don't pay attention to it, it just rusts."

Jerry strained to remember shreds of the chemistry that he'd never paid that much attention to anyway. Rust. It had to be that Loki could somehow cause oxidization reactions. He only remembered redox reactions because his first take had been to wonder if school lessons had finally wandered into the fascinating realm of mythology, and whether he could explain it had actually been a red bull . . .

He recalled, vaguely, being told that rusting was exothermic. So what caused rust? Salty water, obviously. Heat? He'd attended an archaeological seminar on some Greenland dig once, by accidentally wandering into the wrong room and then being too embarrassed to leave. They'd said something about the rates of corrosion. But that could also have been because of the cold causing dryness.

It didn't matter too much, though. Loki's "binding" could rust because it would be the sort of iron that the Norse had had—not precisely stainless. But it would take time. And time was not on his side, unless he could somehow think of a way of making it pass a lot faster for the iron than it did for him. That'd be some magic trick!

And that had to be the answer, he suddenly realized. He'd learned to command Pan's sprites. He learned to deal with the magic of the Egyptians—where belief had bound magic to words and names. Even their gods could be compelled. The Norse, like the Greeks, had had a troll or a dwarf or a giant anthropomorphism for everything from the sea to thunderstorms. Their magic was definitely at least partly symbolic—hence the guts of Narfi binding Loki. And there were chants, and appealing to the gods, if he remembered right.

So all he had to do was learn some Norse magic. Free Loki. Find Liz. Stop Ragnarok. Help Sigyn get her revenge on the lords of Æsir. Defeat the Krim, and get home.

Easy, really.

chapter 15

〰〰〰〰〰

"Dashing through the snow,
On a two-goat open sleigh,
Over rocks and bumps we go,
Shivering all the way.
Oh what fun it is to ride
On a two-goat open sl—"

A particularly large bump knocked the breath out of Liz. Lamont didn't know if he should be relieved or not. Liz was to singing what Pavarotti was to the construction industry.

But at least she'd made Ella laugh. His little girl was troubled. She'd had a bad night. Dreams about, not surprisingly, her twin. Well, Lamont would have had a bad night himself if he hadn't been too exhausted. There was enough to worry about.

Looking at Liz, he realized that exhaustion or not, the blond Amazon had had a bad night too. She was more upset and worried about Jerry than she was ready to let on, and there was not a thing she could do about it. It was anyone's guess as to where he was. Privately, Lamont knew, there was a damn good chance his corpse was lying on a slab back in Chicago. Privately too, he was glad to be here, doing something, rather than hanging around Chicago, waiting for Marie's condition to worsen. The downside was Tina not being here . . . or maybe the other kids being here. The Mythworlds were dangerous places. And he'd have to look after them, now that his vaunted luck had run dry.

Just how dangerous it was, was suddenly apparent as the sled slewed sideways and spilled them all into the snow. One of the PSA agents almost vanished into a snow drift. It took his partner two minutes to help him get out.

The figure rising from the snow and towering over them looked seriously unimpressed at having had two goats run onto his face. "Can't a body sleep in peace?" he said, in a gravel-crusher grumble. He peered shortsightedly at them as he hauled his fist back.

Thor stood up and shook the snow out of his beard. "Why do you sleep in the middle of the road, Hrímner?" he bellowed.

The giant paused. Squinted. Blinked and lowered his fist. "Because it is flatter than sleeping on the rocks?" he answered.

"I should knock your head off for that," said Thor crossly.

"There's no need to be so hasty!" said the giant. "It's not often that I get guests riding over my face. Let's have a bite and something to drink, eh?"

Something about the way he said it started danger signals in Lamont's mind. The giant obviously didn't want to fight with Thor, who had a certain reputation. But Thor lacked some of his tools of the trade—that strength belt and his famous hammer. And he'd gone to seed a bit. Lamont was sure by the way the giant said "drink" that he knew all about that. If he'd had any doubts, they were erased by the way the giant opened the huge flask and shook it so that the smell of alcohol and honey washed over them like a tide.

Thor made a weak noise and reached out for it. But the giant and the Æsir had failed to factor Lamont's wife into the equation. Lamont had to grin. A few people had made that mistake before. A couple of them even lived.

"You stop that right now!" Marie hollered at Thor, stepping between them. "And you, put that away, before I put it away for you."

The giant blinked myopically at her. "Are you refusing my hospitality?"

"Yeah—and you know why, too." Marie planted her hands on her hips and stared up at him.

The giant looked at her, and then at Thor, and then more

carefully at her, and then at Thor, whose reaching hand was still weakly wavering. "Hey, Öku-Thor, where is Mjöllnir? And who is this woman who looks like a svartalfar, but smells like one of those Midgard worms?"

"You mind your language, motherfucker," snapped Marie. "And take that booze away. Or do I have to make you?"

"Do you wish to refuse my hospitality and fight?" Hrímner peered at Marie more closely still. He was at least thirty feet tall. The size of a double story house.

"If that's what it takes," said Marie, seeming unaware of her husband and daughter trying to haul her off in opposite directions.

"It'll have to be a duel of wits," said Thor, rubbing his temple. "It wouldn't be fair and I would have to deal with you myself otherwise, Hrímner."

The giant looked thoughtful and a little wary. "Three questions then. I'm not Alvis."

By the looks of it Thor was managing to keep a straight face with difficulty. "I wondered if you'd heard about that. Maybe you should just let us pass," he said, appearing to go off into a paroxysm of coughing.

"If you're absolutely sure you don't want a little drink for that cough," said Hrímner, "I suppose I could just do that."

Thor hauled the sleigh back onto its runners and nodded, keeping his head down.

"I think that sounds quite wise," said Lamont, bodily lifting Marie and putting her onto the sleigh before she did any more insane things.

"Right," agreed Hrímner. "You black-elves are tricksy ones. Is that how you got it right, Thor?"

Thor, coughing so much his shoulders shook, nodded, and got back on the sleigh. "Tanngnjóst. Tanngrisnir. Away, Bilskríner," he managed to croak. The goats hauled them away from the giant, at a speed that Lamont felt was not fast enough.

When they were a good hundred yards off, Lamont turned on the red-faced Thor, who was doing a good imitation of a fat walrus having an epileptic fit. "What was that all about?"

Thor's laughter nearly started several avalanches on the surrounding hills. When he eventually managed to speak it was pretty asthmatic. "I'm not the sharpest file in the box, but those frost giants . . ." He started laughing again.

"Will someone please tell me what is going on," said Liz crossly.

"I think Thor just put one over that frost giant," said Lamont, still holding Marie.

Thor nodded happily. "They have ice for brains. He never figured out that I wasn't the one that tricked that smart-ass Alvis. My poor daughter Thrúd. She should never have agreed to it."

Lamont could believe that Thor would never have managed to outwit any smart-ass. "So . . . um, who did trick this . . . Alvis?"

"And what did your daughter agree to?" asked Marie.

Thor smiled. "Gold-teeth was getting a little particular in his attentions to my little girl. He's a real philanderer, that one! So she said she'd only entertain the advances of someone who could defeat her old man in a duel. That's my girl! I hear it put off a fair number of Ás, including old One-eye. Then up comes this smart-ass black dwarf, ugly as sin—and he says he has come to take up the challenge for my daughter's favor. Only since he is not the challenger, honor says that he gets to choose the weapons. And he chooses a battle of wits. A test of knowledge."

Thor coughed. "It's not exactly my strongest point, I reckon Odin put him up to it, because who else would have thought of it?"

"So what did you do?" asked Lamont.

Thor grinned. "The trickster stood in for me."

"Loki, you mean," said Emmitt. "I thought he was the bad guy."

"Nah. Well, yes. But not on purpose, a lot of the time. He's just . . . kind of heedless. And he loves making mischief, just to see what happens." There was a troubled note in Thor's voice.

"So what did he do?" asked Ty.

"Loki asked the dwarf a question as long as the Midgard serpent's tail . . . and kept the smart-ass showing off until sun-up. Smart-ass turned to stone, then," said Thor, cheerfully. "I have the little bastard's head as an ornament. Thrúd likes to go and sit on his head from time to time. You'll see it when we get to Bilskríner."

Liz had to admit that the goats made good going across the snow, despite her impatience. At least they did not encounter any more giants. Instead they came to a vast causeway of light that led to the gates of Asgard, and the end of the snow. The goats just kept right on going, cloven hooves clattering across the solid rainbow, to the giant-built walls of Asgard.

"Did you sell the wheels?" demanded the tall, slightly sneering man at the gate-arch. He cradled an enormous horn with a silver mouthpiece and silver chasing around the rim in his arms. "And why are you bringing a bunch of your Midgarders to the home of the gods?"

Thor shook his fist at him. "Shut up, Heimdall. I'll take whoever I want to Bilskríner." They bumped past, under the disapproving gaze of the watchman of the gods.

"He needs a T-shirt that says 'honk if you're horny,'" said Marie disapprovingly. "He looks a bit like fat-ass, my old boss."

"He doesn't like me much, but he's still too scared to make something of it," said Thor. "So he contents himself with sneering at me and kissing up to Odin. Smarmy bastard."

The sled continued to bump and slither its way down an earth track. Liz's American companions seemed a bit startled by that, but she wasn't. All over Africa people still used sleds towed by oxen, in a total absence of snow. And those two goats were nearly as big as oxen, and amazingly strong.

They came over a slight rise and saw a huge thatched hall. "Bilskríner," said Thor proudly. "It has five hundred and forty rooms."

"Any of them bathrooms?" asked Liz, noting that the thatch was in less good repair than it might be.

"Water washes away your strength," said Thor, earning himself instant popularity with Ty and Tolly. "But we have a steam room."

"That'll have to do, although it wasn't quite what I had in mind." Liz was almost at the point of twisting her legs around each other, and wishing fervently that the sleigh didn't bounce quite so much. There was no smoke rising from Bilskríner. Liz was willing to bet that most of those five hundred and forty rooms, including the sauna, were unoccupied.

She was quite right about that. There was a stable thrall, who by the looks of him had been asleep in the hayloft a few moments back. But then all he had to care for was two goats. The huge place was conspicuously empty.

"Where is everyone?" asked Ty eventually, as Thor led them in from the stables.

"Probably over in Valhöll," said Thor, gloomily. "But Sif, Roskva and Thjalfi should be here. As often as not, they're not, though. Thrúd always pops in. Modi and Magni spend all their time over at Valhöll. So: as I said, welcome to my humble home. What can I offer you?"

By the looks of it, thought Liz, nobody had better ask for much. But what she said was: "What I really want is information. I want to know if they brought . . ." she thought how best to put it, and settled for "my man, here. You said those warrior types . . ."

"Einherjar," said Thor, his expression bleak. "Odin's chosen warriors. Once many of them cleaved to me. But he and his Valkyries have lured them hence to Valhöll with boar meat, mead from the goat Heidrún, fighting and their ever-renewed virginity."

The ever-renewed virginity sounded a pain, but Liz could see the attraction of the rest compared to this cold hall. Obviously Thor's thoughts ran down the same direction. "I suppose I did let things slip a bit," he admitted, kicking aside a pile of debris. "The drinking got out of hand. Well, let's start by asking Thjalfi." He bellowed into the dusty emptiness of the hall. "*Thjalfi!!*"

There was no reply. No sound of running feet. Thor scratched his beard. "Hmm. *Sif!*" He tried Roskva next. Still no reply. He shrugged and bellowed back toward the stable. "*Lodin!*"

The man who had taken the goats came dogtrotting in and bowed. "Yes, Master?"

"Where is everybody? Where is that man of mine? I've got some awkward questions to ask him." Thor slammed a huge meaty fist into his palm.

Lodin looked a little surprised. "He came in last night with the two prisoners."

Liz pounced on him like a cat. "Prisoners. Where are they?"

Lodin shook his head. "Two of the Einherjar came and fetched the one."

"And the other?" demanded Liz.

"He's still back in the stable, I suppose," said Lodin, jerking a thumb in that direction. "I thought the master must have taken them prisoner. I don't mess with his deeds."

"Show me," said Liz, taking a firm grip on his collar. "Now."

So Lodin led them back into the stable—to a pile of straw. "He *was* here, somewhere. Maybe the goats et him."

That was said with perfect seriousness. Considering the two goats, it might very well not be a joke at all.

Looking around, one of the children found a brass grieve, with the leather strap gnawed.

"Them goats have a taste for leather," said Lodin. "The one the Einherjar left here was wearing those. I guess he must have got loose. Nasty looking coves, both of them." He scratched his head. "Wonder where he could have got to?"

Liz suddenly had a very good idea where the "Greek Hoplite" agent had got to. Probably a mortuary-shelf back in the USA. But that meant that these Einherjar must have taken Jerry. And at least at that time . . . he must have still been alive or he too would have disappeared.

"These Einherjar. Where did they take him?"

Lodin looked at her as if she was a little simple. "To Valhöll, naturally."

Liz took a deep breath. "I suppose I'd better get along to this Valhöll place too. Go and sort these guys out."

Even Thor looked a little taken aback. "I suppose you could pass for a Valkyrie," he said. "But this is not the best of times for going looking for anything at Valhöll."

"And a bit of caution might just be called for, Liz," said Lamont. "There's no point in you getting killed trying to find Jerry."

"I've got to try. He'd do the same for me. He has before, crazy fool," she said fiercely, trying not to cry.

"For sure, we have to try. But if I have it right this Valhöll place is Odin's hangout. And it's supposed to be chock-full of his warriors."

Thor nodded. "The Einherjar. The lone warriors, who spend each night in feasting, fighting and drinking and sport with the Valkyries. And each morning the slain are as good as new and the Valkyries are virgins again."

"Sounds like a great place for those dragons of Medea's," said Liz. "So what do you suggest, Lamont? Besides me running off half-cocked into a bunch of these hungover warriors. I suppose it is a big place too, and there are a fair number of them?"

"Each gate is big enough for eight hundred to march abreast," said Thor.

"Hmm. It must be fun to clean," said Liz, who had long since figured that the best reason for a small apartment was that you didn't have quite so much to vacuum. "So what do you suggest? I dress up as one of these Valkyries? Can do, I suppose."

"I could go over there and ask," said Thor. "He's not going to pick a fight with me. But, well, Odin always talks rings around me. I can never get a straight answer out of him, and somehow I always end up doing things his way."

He scrutinized Liz for a moment. "You'd need a breastplate and a sword and a shield."

"Master," said Lodin tentatively. "I could go over and ask."

"You?" said Thor gaping. "Ask Odin?"

Lodin nearly fell over backwards into the dung-heap. "No, master! Ask the other stable hands. They always know what's going on. And they always give me a horn or two of ale. They like you, master."

"Odin gets the noblemen who fall in slaughter, but Thor gets the kin of slaves," said Thor, sighing. "Ah, well. I think that could work. Find out if Thjalfi is there too, Lodin. If you see him give him a clip around the ear from me and send him home."

Lodin grinned revealing good, solid pre-orthodontistry skew teeth. "Now that'll be a pleasure. He's changed, master. Not the same man at all that used to come down for a drink with me. And he was sick all over the chariot."

"Chariot?" said Thor.

Lodin looked wary. "Uh. Lady Sif said I wasn't to say anything about the chariot—after last time."

Thor scowled. "I'm Öku-Thor. The charioteer. If I crash it, it's my look-out. Now get along to Valhöll with you! Try to come back sober enough to muck out here. And don't come and tell me what good beer they've got. I'm craving a drink really badly myself."

Liz noticed that his hands were shaking quite a lot. She wondered just how you dealt with a god who was seeing snakes and pink elephants. Thor might be flabby, and have let himself go, but there was still a superhuman quality to him, besides the smell.

"How about if we tried this sauna," she said determinedly, turning him. "And Lodin."

He bowed. "Yes, Lady?"

"Don't stay too long over those horns of ale. Please."

He nodded, looking as if this were the first please ever to come his way, and turned toward the stable door, briskly.

"Don't run. Slouch along like normal," said Thor. "You never know when those damned ravens of Odin's will see you."

Dead on cue, two black birds fluttered in. "One of them said 'Odin,' Hugin. I heard it," said one of the two.

Thor glowered at the birds. Liz was much more practical. She picked up a piece of broken yoke and hefted it for weight.

"*Caw*! You wouldn't dare," said one of the ravens. "We are Odin's ravens."

"I did earlier," said Liz. "Or have you forgotten the dragon's heart?"

"Good eating," said the first raven. "You haven't got any more, have you?"

"We've got a job to do, Hugin," protested the other raven. He sounded exasperated, as if his partner's greediness was a long-standing issue between them.

"Yeah. *Caw*. Anything that says we can't eat on the job?" Hugin perched on a rafter. "You speak good raven for a human."

"Ah," said Liz. "And there I thought you spoke good human for a raven."

"If you can speak to them," rumbled Thor, "tell them if they're not out of my stable by the time I say Vanaheim, I'll try a lighting bolt on them."

"*Caw*. He must be more hungover than usual. Come on, Munin. I'm not that interested in who Thor is drinking with."

The ravens fluttered out with what looked to Liz like a careful show of not being too hasty but really moving rather fast.

"They all spy on me," said Thor blackly.

Liz could see why, even without suspicion about what the Krim was up to in this Ur-Mythworld. In a way it was a good thing Thor had a drinking problem. It was probably why he hadn't been recruited by the Krim. And the ravens turning up to see who Thor's "drinking buddies" were smacked of the gatekeeper telling tales. They walked back through to the great hall. Thor had a visible tremor in his hands and shoulders as he opened the door.

Liz was surprised to see Marie putting a hand on his arm. "You can do it."

He was panting a little. "It's bigger than me."

And suddenly Liz realized that he wasn't exaggerating. And he was seeing snakes.

So was she. Well. One snake. More like a dragon, but without wings. And quite big enough to make up for there only being one.

It'd be a pink elephant next.

It wasn't. It was a wolf. A wolf pretty close to the size of the elephant, though.

CHAPTER 16

⊚⊚⊚⊚⊚⊚

"Magic has bound him. Magic has to be the way to free him," said Jerry. "And as you two can't do it, it does depend on me. Magic isn't exactly my field of expertise. I was looking for some advice."

"And there I thought you were a gifted practitioner of Seid," said Loki mockingly.

"Shut up, Loki," said Sigyn, with the amiability of a wife who has said this very often. "The mortal comes from another place and time. He is ignorant of many things. He probably doesn't even know what Seid is."

"Um. No. Actually, I don't."

"Don't you dare say 'I told you so,' Sigi," said Loki ruefully. "Seid, Jerry, is a magical art practiced by Odin, and by women, because it would be a dishonorable thing for men."

Jerry raised an eyebrow. "But okay for Odin?"

"Well," said Loki. "He is the oathbreaker. Maybe he feels no need of such honor."

If Jerry had it right that was an insult of rare order for one of the Norse.

"Maybe he's just a bearded lady," said Jerry lightly.

He sat down rapidly. He had to. Loki was making the floor shake with his laughter. Sigyn was laughing too, so much so that she was actually crying.

147

Jerry tried to work this one out. Someone had once said to him that the Norse had been a homophobic culture, and argued that was what accounted for the disdain in which Loki was held for his various cross-sexual shape changes. He'd been the mare that had lured the giant builder's stallion away, causing the giant to lose his deal on the building of Asgard's giant-proof walls. The result was Odin's eight-legged horse.

That was a less than clinching argument, Jerry thought, given that Odin still seemed pretty keen on the horse. But one thing was certain: Women were second-class citizens in the honor stakes—hence allowed to use this "Seid"—and honor was everything in this social milieu. The image of the master of Asgard as a bearded lady obviously had appeal.

"If only I had thought of that when I gave the Æsir their flyting," said Loki. "I mocked them well, but that's a rich insult. For that and that alone I would give you what help I can. But not with Seid. There are other arts."

Jerry looked at the tear on the cheek of Sigyn—and began to put it all together.

"I think . . ."

"No! Thor did that once and his head caught fire," said Loki mischievously.

"I thought you were going to help me?" said Jerry, head askance. He got the feeling that once Loki got into this frame of mind he would only stop . . . too late. Best stop him before he started.

"Ah. A point," admitted Loki, readily . . . too easily, contrite. "What help can I be?"

Jerry turned to Sigyn. "Lady Sigyn. Would you give me some of your tears?"

She blinked, and touched her cheek. "You are less ignorant of magical things than you would have us think, Jerry."

The secondary symbolism of tears, especially tears of laughter, liberating things, had not occurred to Jerry until that moment. He'd actually been thinking of salty water. And rust. But Norse mythology and poetry was full of multiple symbolism, so their magic was bound to be also.

Jerry collected some of Sigyn's tears onto a quarter he found in his pocket. It wasn't a lot of liquid, but it would have to do—since the only other possible container was being used to catch snake-venom.

He wanted all the elements of rapid oxidation: salty water, heat, and rust itself. He felt around for the thongs that had tied him. Symbolic again, if he could get them to burn again by sticking them in the fire.

Rust . . . well, rust would just have to be rust. Ideally it should have come from a broken shackle, but rust would affect everything. He'd just paint it in that shape. And the Futhark . . .

The runes had each had meanings, evolving much as hieroglyphics had into hieratic script. "I need the runes for water and time—or days. And chants. You can tell me who to appeal to."

"A good sorcerer in the making," said Loki. "Vidólf was the mother of all witches, Svarthöfdi the father of sorcerers. And Sigyn will show you Dagaz and Laguz, the runes for water and days."

She scratched them out.

"This one is 'day.' And this one is 'water.'"

"Years?" asked Jerry.

She showed him another, and then added a fourth. "And this one is 'Ansuz,' which could be useful too."

She said the last with an absolutely straight face. Even Jerry, normally oblivious to hints, could catch an elephant like that. He began to draw the runes, scratched into the rust on the iron bonds. A great many years. And fair amount of water, drawn with tear-wetness, and, using the burned ends of the thong, the symbol Ansuz. He hoped that it would give him some, and that he wasn't just being stupid. But Loki's silence was telling. The mischief-god was the original motormouth. He was so quiet it was hard to tell if he was even breathing. And both he and Sigyn were staring with a fierce intensity at Jerry.

Jerry just hoped that his hair wouldn't catch fire before it was all done. To judge by the sagas, the spells would be in verse. Probably sung . . .

Well, he'd better pass on that part. His singing was good—if compared to Liz's. She sang in the bath. Fortunately, he'd never really liked the tiles in that room anyway.

> "Svarhöfdi, spell master,
> Dagaz passing ever faster,
> Make us Vidólf wise,
> reduce and oxidize
>
> *Rust!*

Laguz, tears sweet and salt
mix with iron, mend the fault
Blood tie broken be by water
liberation from the child's slaughter.

Rust!

Rust consume, heat, eat and devour
Iron bonds as if the second was an hour
turn pure metal to our side
Make of it an iron oxide

Rust!"

It was lousy poetry, but not too bad for the spur of the moment, he thought.

He took the little pocket diary, which was now thicker than it used to be since vellum was thicker than paper, and was inscribed with runes. He used his thumb to flick the pages over—a symbolic passage of days. The smoldering thong burst into flames, and somehow water dripped from the runes he'd painted.

The iron that bound Loki flaked red. And flaked again. And burst with erupting splinters of rust.

Loki sat up suddenly with a small crow of delight, his bonds falling into red dust. "Free! Free at last. Let Asgard quake!"

Now his eyes blazed with a truly inhuman glee, which, as he definitely wasn't human, was as it should be. It was also rather alarming, when you were stuck in a hole with him that wasn't more than twenty by twenty feet wide.

Sure enough, his first act showed that even by accident Loki's thoughtlessness was a danger to himself and everyone else. He hugged Sigyn—and nearly upset the bowl of venom over the two of them.

"Careful!" Sigyn shrieked, trying to hold the slopping bowl away from the two of them and nearly dousing Jerry instead.

Loki backed off, and then ducked because the snake spat at his face. The serpent, heretofore almost dormant except for the dripping venom, was coming to life. Loki tripped over the slabs he'd been bound to, and fell flat on his back.

"He hasn't changed much," said Sigyn, smiling broadly.

To prove that he could still change, the god blurred—and a mouse skittered across the floor.

That was too much for the snake. When had it last had a tasty mouse? Even a mouse with Loki-eyes?

It flung itself off the rock shelf and down onto the pit-floor; then, across the floor at the mouse-prey. Jerry desperately looked for something to deal with the huge snake. Why did Loki have to be some damned precipitate? Jerry was sure that, if he could work out spells to deal with iron bonds, he could have come up with something for snakes.

The snake struck. It struck so hard that it hit the wall, and bounced back slightly stunned.

It had missed its prey, which was surprising in a way, because the prey was now a lot larger. The hawk still had Loki's eyes. It also had its talons dug firmly into the snake's neck, just behind the head. Sigyn calmly stepped onto the snake's tail as the snake attempted to lash that up and around the hawk.

Loki changed again, back into himself. He was still holding the snake behind the head. Now, with the other hand he grasped it behind Sigyn's foot, and held it aloft. He grinned at them. "Roast snake, anyone?"

"You might tell me next time," said Jerry, keeping a good safe distance.

Loki shrugged, still smiling. "It is that way with me, I'm afraid, my sorcerer friend. I tend to act first and think later. It has gotten me into a fair amount of trouble over the years."

That was in character, Jerry supposed. Trouble and Loki would never be that far apart. The secret was to avoid having trouble with Loki when he turned nasty.

Sigyn shook head ruefully. "That is true enough. Now what are you going to do with that snake?"

"Spit in its eyes?" suggested Loki.

"Dash its brains out," said the more practical Sigyn.

"I thought I might save it and put it down Skadi's front," said Loki evilly.

"Huh. She'd probably enjoy that. They're her pets, Loki. Kill it and be done with it."

He did, with a whip-crack. He used the snake itself as the whip, which was singularly effective if not something Jerry ever wanted to try himself. Uncle Fox was a lot stronger than he looked. He could have broken the bonds had they just been made of iron, and not magic.

"Now why don't you transform yourself and fly out and drop us a rope?" suggested Jerry, as if such shape-changing was something he saw every day. That was one thing about the Mythworlds—you became quite numb to the impossible.

"A good thought," said Loki, blurring again. The hawk flew upwards . . . and stopped.

Loki dropped down. "Not quite so easy. And not knowing the nature of the spell Odin has set there will make it harder. Oh, well. Roast snake while we wait for Skadi? She won't be long, now that her pet is dead."

"Better that you go and lie on the slabs again and pretend to still be bound," said Sigyn.

Loki nodded. "I'll put the snake back on the rock-shelf, and lie in wait for our huntress." He looked at Jerry. "You'd better contrive some kind of binding for the bitch, friend sorcerer."

"And take cover," said Sigyn. "She's nearly as strong as Thrúd."

Jerry sincerely wished that he could follow either instruction. There really wasn't any cover, and as for a binding . . .

Loki plainly wanted him to come up with some kind of magic, and right now his mind was a perfect blank. All he could think of was how nice some handcuffs and a secure cell would be. He could have hidden in the cell.

True to Sigyn's prediction, Skadi was not long in coming. And the giantess daughter of Thjazi was not a small woman. Actually, she wouldn't have been a small man, either. She took one look at her snake and reached into her girdle—for another.

Sigyn gave her a bowl full of venom right in the eyes.

And then things got really ugly.

Skadi plainly couldn't see. She was screaming, both in pain and rage. Neither stopped her from attacking them. There wasn't a lot of room to dodge. Loki attempted to grab her, and got himself knocked back against the wall. Sigyn threw the empty bowl at her head and it shattered. That didn't seem to give Skadi any pause at all. Loki grabbed the dead snake and flung it around her neck and started trying to throttle her with it. Skadi grabbed the snake also and was doing her best to pull it off her neck. The snake from her girdle had escaped and was now cornering Sigyn. The two fighters had staggered close to the fire, and were now standing next to it. Which one would win—or whether the body of the snake would give first—was a moot question. The snake certainly was no normal creature or it would already have been torn in half.

Jerry searched desperately for a way to intervene. All he saw were some pottery shards. And the fact that Skadi the huntress was wearing top-boots—quite wide at their top—and she was right next to the fire.

Using two scraps of the broken bowl, Jerry scraped up some of the coals and poured them into one of her boots. Then, hastily, he did the second boot. Skadi was too busy straining at the snake to notice. Smoke started coming out of her boots, and Jerry shoveled a second load in, for want of any better idea.

The dead snake broke. Loki tumbled backwards and Skadi suddenly realized that her feet were on fire. First she danced frantically, in the process stepping on her live snake—which latched its fangs into her leg. She sat down hard, grabbed the snake and flung it at the wall—narrowly missing Sigyn. Then she tore at her boots, hauling them off, scattering coals.

But Loki had seen enough. Grinning like a fiend he took a whole handful of live coals and poured them down the back of her neck. His hands seemed completely impervious to their heat.

Skadi jerked backwards and Loki assisted her with a mighty shove. Her head hit the floor with an audible crack. She lay still for a moment, before she rolled over screeching, pulling her smoldering dress away from her body and standing up to scatter more coals. She stood on a coal, yowled, leapt backwards, and tripped over Loki's prison-slab. She landed with an even louder crack. This time, before she could move, Sigyn was onto her, pressing a sharp fragment of pottery to her throat. "Lie still, bitch, or you will die right here."

Blinded, stunned, snake-bitten, and obviously in a lot of pain, Skadi moaned weakly—but did not move. How could she know it was just a piece of pot? Jerry actually felt a little sorry for her. She had tortured Loki for centuries, so Loki and Sigyn plainly had a grudge. On the other hand, Loki did tend to bring things on himself.

Skadi was a fairly minor and obscure member of the Norse pantheon, and Jerry didn't know much about her. But the way Skadi was reacting to the pottery shard that she couldn't see, and his memory of the most famous binding in Norse myth had given Jerry an idea. What was it that the chain that bound the Fenrir wolf was supposed to be made of? Ingredients such as the sound

of a cat's footfall and a fish's breath. If he could fool this giantess
that she was under duress of similar intangible bonds . . .

"Hold the knife steady, Lady Sigyn," said Jerry, as calmly as
he could. "It wants but a few more chants and scratching of the
runes until we have her bound with the invisible net."

"Will it hurt her?" asked Sigyn, in a voice which said that she
wanted it to.

"Not unless she moves," said Jerry. "If she stays still, it will
feel as light as the finest cloth. But the more she struggles, the
tighter it will bind. It is woven from the teeth of birds, moonlight
gathered at noon and the . . ."

Inventiveness failed him, The best he could come up with was
"tomb dust from an ancient king," and hope that Skadi hadn't
read much Gothic horror.

"Who is that?" Skadi's said through gritted teeth. "Curse you—"

Loki held a coal close to her cheek. Not quite touching but
close enough for her to feel the heat. "Now, now," he said in a
mockingly cheerful voice. "You wouldn't want to make a sorcerer
powerful enough to undo Odin's works angry, would you? He
already conjured up hot coals to help you dance. It is a shame
that you are so clumsy that you fell over. I would lie very still and
silent in case he decided to do worse." He took her knife from
her girdle—a precaution they should have thought of earlier—and
toyed with it.

"Sorcerer?" said Skadi, digesting that. She didn't seem the
quickest thinker around, but then she'd been through some harsh
treatment in the last few minutes.

"Of course, Skadi. A very powerful one. How else do you
think I am free? Yes, Loki is free, and Fimbulwinter begins," he
said savagely. "Now, while my sorcerer spins his magics, I will
ask you to give me the *galdr*. I need the chant to see me free
of this place."

"You will not get it from me," she said with savage satisfaction.
"Odin is more powerful now. He won't need Thor and Heimdall
to catch you any more, Father of lies."

"That is an interesting description coming from you. Njörd
would be impressed to hear of your honesty, adulteress."

Skadi snarled. "Hel take you, Loki."

"I hope so. She is my daughter, after all," he said, quite urbanely.
"Now, tell me the *galdr*."

"I'd rather die."

"That can be arranged, Skadi," said Loki grimly. "Not quickly of course, but it can be arranged."

Skadi sniffed. "Then you will never get out."

"I still have my sorcerer. He has defeated Odin's Seid runes. He may get us out. Why not reach a bargain? When Ragnarok comes, you are one of the giants. One of my kin. If I win . . . I will set you free. Or Odin may come looking for you. Otherwise, you are dead."

She was silent for a while. "I suppose so," she said at last. "Vegtamr Gungnir Fjallar. Nine times."

Loki shook his head, his eyes narrowed. "You won't mind my holding the knife to your throat while I say it then, will you?" he said, his voice full of a gentle irony.

Skadi ground her teeth.

"I know the names of One-eye better than you do," said Loki. "Try again. Or I'll have such a spell put on you that Lumpy himself would not fancy you. Your face and eyes may heal, but there'll be no going back from this curse."

She ground her teeth again, and clutched at the pouch from whence she'd pulled the replacement snake. Loki raised an eyebrow and cut the strap with her knife. She moved as he plucked it away. "Uh-uh! Hold still now." The shard of pottery pressed harder . . . and a spot of blood appeared.

Loki drew out a small bottle made of hammered metal. "A potion. And what do we do with this? Drink it? Of course if something goes wrong it would be very sad for Skadi."

"A drop on the eyelid," she said sullenly. Loki nodded, unstoppered it, and wet the tip of his finger and put it to his eye. "Ah," he said. "So the *galdr* was a feint. Still, we shall have to put a stop to that summoning spell. Sorcerer, can you weave that into your net-spell."

"I have done so already," said Jerry, taking his handkerchief and putting it over her face.

"Now can I kill her?" asked Sigyn.

"I'm afraid not," said Loki. "I am not an oathbreaker like Helblindi. Let her enjoy my prison. There is a hidden ladder here we can climb. Let me put a drop of this on your eyelids."

When he'd done so, Jerry found himself looking at a rope ladder. Sigyn examined it carefully. "You first, husband. If you get away you can always come back for us. And this one had no part in the killing of my sons, so I will forgo my vengeance . . . on her. For now. But not so with the others."

Loki grabbed the ladder. "Not so with the others," he said, as he began to climb.

"After you, Lady Sigyn," said Jerry, although the last thing he wanted was to be stuck alone with a giantess trapped under a handkerchief.

She shook her head. "It would not be seemly. And I think you should take her boots." Jerry looked at his one stockinged foot and did—taking very good care to shake out the boots first.

They were at least three sizes too large for him. And rope ladders turned out to be a lot harder to climb than he'd been led to believe by Indiana Jones.

Sigyn followed, and they hauled the ladder up and began making their way cautiously along the rock-hewed corridor.

"It's to be hoped that that is a powerful spell-net you've cast on Skadi," said Loki, quietly.

"Um," said Jerry. "It's . . . uh, well, it's just a piece of cloth. Not a spell-net. Not a spell at all. She just thinks it is."

Loki stopped dead in his tracks, and grinned wickedly. "It might make getting away more dangerous—but, oh, what a tale! The skalds will love that one. It's a trick worthy of the greatest of tricksters! If only I'd thought of it first."

"Don't worry," said Jerry, "they'll probably blame it on you anyway."

The Krim device's computational circuitry was proof that even Moore's law must have an end somewhere, whether it is by postscription or in the ability of computing power to double. Right now it was going through several iterations of probability planning . . . and meeting the unexpected. The gods of the Ur-Mythworlds that the Krim had parasitized before were less recalcitrant than these ones. It offered a renewal of power—an irresistible bait, or one, that if resisted, simply meant the Mythworld was heading into a slow spiral of fading down to extinction. But the labor in this world was hard to control.

And very frighteningly self-willed.

PART III

TO SLEEP, PERCHANCE TO DREAM . . .

CHAPTER 17

⊚⊚⊚⊚⊚⊚

"Got anything to drink in this place, Thor?" said the huge wolf.

The presence of the creature and the serpent-dragon seemed to trouble Thor a lot less than they bothered Liz.

"If Sif sees you here she'll have a fit," said Thor grumpily. "And no. You should know by now that we finished every drop in this place in that last drinking session."

"She hasn't been here for days. I keep hoping someone might restock," said the serpent-dragon. There was something female about that sibilant voice, somehow, and she spoke in the sort of tone that said she thought it ought to be him doing the restocking.

"Anyway. I've given it up," announced Thor.

The wolf sat down hard on its haunches and let its cavernous mouth drop open. Liz could see that it was terribly scarred. It shook its vast head. "That's going to go down really well in those fatuous sagas."

Liz might be alarmed by the wolf and the serpent-dragon—but at least one person wasn't. Neoptolemeus danced forward. "You're beautiful. Do you know Bitar and Smitar?" he demanded.

The serpent-dragon looked at him, and shook her gargantuan head. "No. Don't know you either. Got anything for a girl to drink?"

The disappointment written in the boy's face was enough to make Liz want to hug him.

"So," said the wolf, eyeing them curiously, and possibly a little hungrily, "who are you? Do you have something to do with Thor suddenly deciding he doesn't drink?"

"They're friends of mine, Fenrir," said Thor. He sat down on a bench next to the wall. "I feel awful. There might be some food in the kitchen, Wolf. Thrúd usually restocks that."

The wolf grinned toothily. "There won't be, when I'm finished."

Marie put her hands on her hips. "Well, then, let the children get some first. You're ugly enough and big enough to catch your own anyway."

The wolf blinked. Then cocked his head sideways. "I thought they were appetizers?"

"Trust me," said Marie. "Those little boys would disagree with you." The way she stood made it clear that the disagreement might just be Marie Jackson.

"And we really aren't little boys," said Ty. "We're from the planet Krypton. We just look small." He flexed a minuscule bicep. "But try and eat us and POW! WHAM!" He windmilled the air.

"And you wear your underpants outside your trousers," said Emmitt derisively.

"They're cute," pronounced the serpent-dragon. "You're not to eat them, Brother."

"Hmph," said the wolf. "Jörmungand, one of them just has to say you look pretty, and you put me on diet. I'm always hungry."

"Except when you're asleep or thirsty," said the serpent-dragon. "What's wrong with Thor?"

The thunder-god's arms and legs were starting to thrash around and he was muttering something about spiders on the walls.

"Delirium tremens," said Liz.

"Oh. He looks like a berserker after they've been eating mushrooms," said Jörmungand. She looped a coil around Thor, basically enclosing his whole body. "That'll keep him from hurting himself."

It wasn't exactly a padded cell, but it was a kind of restraint, Liz supposed. The wolf had walked closer and was sniffing them. "You smell unlike any other prey I have hunted across the nine worlds."

Liz had spent her life with big dogs. She knew as well as anyone that what she shouldn't do was show fear, or even think fear. She grabbed the sniffing muzzle with both hands. They were barely big enough to go around it. She stared into the yellow eyes. "That is because we're not prey. Got me?"

Fenrir wrenched himself backwards and free, growling at her. Then, probably because—by the smells of his breath—he'd had the better part of someone's ale-barrel already, tripped over his own feet and fell over. Liz was above him in a flash, grabbing his jaws again, this time in an armlock. Having an older brother who had been keen on wrestling was useful from time to time.

"You wouldn't be growling at *me*, would you?"

He looked at her with wary eyes, and she stared straight back at him. After a brief pause, she released his jaws and he growled, "You're quite some boss-bitch."

There was a little grudging admiration in that tone. He wagged his tail. His tongue lolled out and he turned his head turned at a slight angle. "Sexy, too."

That wasn't *quite* what she'd had in mind as a response. But this was a big dangerous animal, and she could use an ally like that. "Yeah. Well, you need a good brushing before I can call you anything but scruffy. Lie down and I'll do that."

She delved into her bag, and dug out her hairbrush. She could possibly get another hairbrush, but this beast could bite your leg off.

The startled wolf lay down, and Liz started to brush his manky fur. He stretched and rumbled, but there was no malice in it. Belatedly, Liz remembered there was a social aspect to grooming among wolves too. Oh, well. She'd worry about that when the time came. In the meanwhile, wolfie needed half a ton of winter fur brushed out. And there was something very therapeutic to grooming a big dog, even if his snake-dragon sister was looking rather puzzled at the entire performance.

Fenrir was skinny, she discovered. Still young and growing, by the looks of his teeth. He had a gap just behind his vast canines where the carnassials were beginning to cut through. Liz had specialized in fish, but she would bet that this enormous wolf was still less than full-grown.

Someone coughed. Liz turned her head and saw that it was Thor's stable thrall. He had a silly grin on his face which suggested that he'd had a few horns of ale in a hurry.

"My lady . . ."

"Just Liz."

"Justliz, I have found out what happened to the prisoner. He was taken before Odin, and then was flung down into the pit with Loki." Lodin seemed to think being eaten alive might be preferable.

"He'll be all right, then," said Fenrir. "The old man isn't a bad sort even though he has prehistoric tastes in Skaldic verse."

Jörmungand nodded. "Positively ninth century. He's a real old fuddy-duddy. Thinks Starkadian meter is all the rage."

Whatever or whoever this Loki was, besides someone with a moribund taste in poetry, being flung into a pit didn't sound too good. "Well, we need to get him out," said Liz determinedly.

"Can't be done," said Jörmungand. "Not that we haven't tried."

"Yeah," growled Fenrir. "Sigyn isn't your typical literary-fiction step-mom. She was kinder to us than Angbroda."

"And mostly better at keeping Papa Loki from doing anything too crazy." There was some resignation in Jörmungand's voice.

Liz blinked. This was the world of myth, where science, and, indeed, genetics did get a little twisted. But this Loki would have to be a really weird creature to father such a diverse pair. "Tell me about this pit."

"It lies in the caves deep under Asgard. Odin has magically imprisoned Loki there."

"There is another entrance through Skadi's place," said Fenrir. "But it goes through a gap too narrow for me to fit through."

"And if Loki can't escape," added Jörmungand, "it must be the greatest prison ever built. He has always got away before, sometimes just by talking his way out. He has a silver tongue, even if he has a dated taste in music."

Fenrir nodded. "Still likes the lughorn!"

"Awful noise. Sounds like me with a bellyache," agreed Jörmungand.

"Would I fit through this gap that you can't, Wolf?" asked Liz.

Fenrir studied her briefly. "Maybe. Be a bit tight around the top, I reckon. But it wouldn't help you much. There is a maze of caves down there and you humans don't have anything that passes for a nose."

"So that leaves going in through Odin's lair."

The wolf and the serpent blinked at her in unison. "Lair is too flattering," said Fenrir.

"And while it is true that Fenrir and I would stick out and get noticed . . ."

"Maybe not in the early morning," said the wolf snidely.

"In Valhöll," continued Jörmungand, "I gather a woman in that place needs to be a Valkyrie."

Fenrir nodded. "One-eye was always too cheapskate to hire enough, and I gather the job is . . . uh," he looked warily at her, "pretty wearing. Odin gets half the slain and the rest go to Freyja, and she's got the monopoly on trollops. Odin relies on the Einherjar getting drunk and fighting for entertainment, and it doesn't work that well. I'd go with you, except that then they would work out that I was free again, and that Thor had taken his sword out of my mouth."

"Oh." Not knowing anything about mythology was awkward at times. She must make some time to talk to Lamont about it. He wasn't Jerry's ore-grade as a mine of useless information, but he was a long way from being as ignorant as she was. Everyone was. She could swear like a bosun, identify fish by their otoliths, do the math for Von Bertalanffy growth curves, and even cope with public transport in foreign cities. But it was only when she had found herself plunged into the Mythworlds that she'd realized that she'd neglected her education.

"In the meanwhile we will need some food," said Marie, practically. "And we got invited to help ourselves. I'm betting that there won't be any coffee."

"And there I thought this place was the Norse idea of heaven," said Lamont. "Which way is it, Lodin?"

"I'll show you, master," said the stable thrall. "But you'd better get them out of here." He pointed to Jörmungand and Fenrir. "I saw Thjalfi and gave him Thor's message. He said he would be back with Lady Sif soon. And she'll give Lord Thor such a hard time if she sees them, that he's likely to drown himself in a barrel of mead, just to shut out her voice."

Jörmungand looked at him. "And what am I supposed to do with this shaker?"

"Let me out," Thor said. "I'm all right now."

He didn't look it, and Liz had her doubts. Usually the DTs lasted for days . . . but then Thor wasn't really human either. Maybe it affected Norse gods differently.

"And I'm not going until I've eaten," announced Fenrir. "I got invited, remember."

Thor sighed. "At least go across to the old side of the house, where we always used to meet. I'll bring you something. Or send Lodin with something, if I can't get away. She never goes there."

"I'm not surprised," said Jörmungand. "It's feet thick in dust. Come on Brother, we know when we're not wanted."

"It's knowing when we are wanted that's a bit more difficult. Like getting enough drink," said Fenrir with a wolfish grin. "We only tried you because we've been thrown out of Gjálp's place."

"Did you break the place up?" asked Thor curiously.

"No, she just keeps insisting that we pay up or get out. So if you've got any money . . ."

Thor scowled. "I seem to be a bit short. I haven't got anything left worth selling. Get along with you. I don't think I could stand another scene with Sif, truly. She has hair of gold and a voice of brass."

"Did I hear my name mentioned?" A golden-haired woman stood in the doorway, posing artistically so that the sun could catch her hair and dazzle them. A man and a woman stood behind her, obviously servants.

"Er. Hello, my love," said Thor, sounding as if he had a frog in his throat.

"Visitors, dear?" She gave them all a saccharine smile that was as genuine as a Dior dress with a *made in China* label.

"Just . . . just some people who were about to be leaving," said Thor.

"Oh, nonsense. We must ask them to stay for a drink and bite. Some of them look fascinating." She cast a steely gaze over the group. "Jörmungand and Fenrir . . ."

"No," said Fenrir. "I'm Freki. Odin's been overfeeding me. And I don't know who this is." He looked at his sister. "What did you say your name was again, dragon?"

"Orm," said Jörmungand.

"Ah," said Sif. Her tone registered absolute unbelief. "You looked so much smaller when I saw you minutes back at the Allfather's side, Freki."

Fenrir grinned wolfishly. "Everything looks smaller than it is next to Valfödr."

"What were you doing there?" Thor asked his wife suspiciously. "I've asked you not to go there."

Sif tossed her hair. It really was like spun gold. "I know. But I needed provisions for this house. It's strangely empty," she said pointedly. "And tributes from Thrúdvangar are also . . . late. So *somebody* had to do something."

She smiled toothily at him. "And so? Are you going to introduce me to your guests? Svartalfar and a Valkyrie? And these are perhaps Einherjar?" She pointed at the two surviving PSA agents. "Such charming little boys. I have missed the patter of tiny feet since Magni and Modi grew up."

"Magni couldn't patter . . . ever," said Thor. "Made more noise than any giant from the day he was born. And where are he and Modi?"

Sif waved an airy hand. "Out and about."

"At Valhöll. Partying," said Thor crossly.

"Well, you can't blame them for wanting to spend time with their grandfather," said Sif. "Now, Roskva. Where is that food and drink?"

The dark-haired maiden standing two paces back from Sif bowed. "Waiting, my lady. They'll need to come in through this door."

"And I am blocking it. Tch," she clicked her tongue. "Now I must go and clean up after my journey. Have them bring it in. Have a feast prepared."

"It's at least a mile, that journey," muttered Thor.

Sif chose to ignore that and swept regally past them. Behind her came a stream of thralls rolling barrels and carrying meat.

"Just three barrels of that and I'm anybody's," sighed Jörmungand mournfully, looking at the hogsheads of mead going past. She sniffled. "If anyone would have me."

At a mere fifty gallons of mead a barrel, Liz guessed that she wasn't most dragons' idea of a cheap date. "Not a lot of talent out there?" she asked, sympathetically.

Jörmungand snorted. "They're all old enough to be my grandfather! You read all those sagas . . . and you know what? I am the only dragon who was ever born in them. The others were all around already. So what am I to do? Except eat . . . and now I'm bigger than all of them too. Like that really helps." She sighed gustily. "You don't know any dragons, do you?"

Liz looked speculatively at her. She was—to a biologist anyway—a superlatively beautiful animal. "I might just be able to fix you up with someone. You wouldn't mind if they were maybe a little younger and smaller than you, would you?"

Jörmungand stared at her wide-eyed. "Younger . . . listen, as long as they're under a millennium, I'm interested." She paused. "Or do you think I need to play a bit hard to get? You know, suave, sophisticated . . . a dragon-girl who has been around, that sort of thing."

"Honey, I don't think Bitar and Smitar would know 'sophisticated' if it bit them on the leg." Candor might do best, thought Liz. "They're a little thick, actually. Handsome beasts but . . . not your deepest thinkers."

"Male dragons are always a bit slow," said Jörmungand. "Or that's what Papa Loki said. He always said that he was glad I was a girl. Anyway. Beggars can't be choosers. So . . . um, can you set something up?"

Jörmungand looked around uneasily to see if her brother was listening and then whispered sibilantly . . . "and maybe give me a little girl advice?"

Liz hoped that it would be on reptile biology and not on dating behavior. She'd never been too good at how you were supposed to behave. Reptile biology had to be simpler. "The only problem is that they're back where we come from. We just need to take you back with us."

America could cope with another dragon, she figured. Maybe this one would eat a few INS officials for her.

Thor wandered over, shaking his head. "I think Sif's up to something."

Another one of your great thinkers, thought Liz, but kept her opinions to herself.

"But she did make one good point," said the red-bearded god. "We never really got properly introduced." He bowed. "Thor, god of warriors and thunder, at your service. I know the black-elf lady Marie, but I have not been introduced formally to you. And here in Thrúdvangar we like to at least meet formally. After that things tend to get more muddled. This here is the Midgard serpent, Jörmungand, and the famous Fenrir the wolf. We're . . . ah, drinking companions. But I have given up."

"Well, I ain't no black elf," said Marie forcefully. She cupped her ears in her hands. "See? No pointy ears. We're Americans. I'm Marie Jackson, that's my husband Lamont and these are our kids. Tyrone, Ella, and Emmitt. He's sort of adopted. My sister's son. She had the same sort of problem you got. And that there is Neoptolemeus. He's with me until we can get him back to his Ma."

"And I am Dr. Elisabeth De Beer," Liz said, wondering what that title would translate to. "Call me Liz."

"Or 'Sir,'" said Lamont, with a shadow of his usual smile.

Thor nodded with deep respect. "A skald must always be welcome."

Skald? Liz hoped it didn't mean scold. She tried not to be... too much.

"And you two?" Thor asked looking at the two agents in their breastplates and roughly cobbled furs.

"Special Agent Bott. PSA."

"And Special Agent Stephens. PSA."

Thor looked at them with a jaundiced eye. Liz wondered what *special agent* translated to.

She was answered by Thor's next comment. "Tax collectors, eh? Well, I suppose there is need for your ilk. Listen, I'm having some problems with the revenues from my own kingdom, Thrúdvangar. If you're in need of a job... or do you already work for the Americans? And how came you Americans into the land of the trolls? I had not previously heard of Americans. Is Americanaheim beyond Vanaheim?"

"We were transported magically from our own place. It's a lot farther than Vanaheim," said Lamont. "We'd like to get back home."

Thor blinked. "But do you not like Asgard?"

"It's a great place," said Lamont. "But one of my daughters got left behind. And Tolly here got separated from his Ma."

Ella burst into tears. Neoptolemeus swallowed and nestled into Marie.

Then Thor started to cry too. He came and knelt before Ella, looking like some kind of cross between a fat cabbage-patch kid and red-haired troll. "It's all right, child. Thor will see it gets fixed," he said earnestly, a tear running down his red nose.

"He always was hopelessly soft with kids," said Fenrir, loftily disapproving.

"It's why he didn't tear your head off when you were little and the others wanted him to," said his sister. "It's his better aspect, if you ask me."

Now Sif's manservant coughed and said: "Platters have been laid in the small feasting hall, lord."

"Thjalfi! Where have you been, you rogue?" demanded Thor, focusing on him. "And where is my belt of strength and Grid's rod?"

Thjalfi looked at his master with amazement, impressively so for someone Liz had last seen with a fake red beard and the aforementioned rod. "But they were with you my lord, at the evil troll Geirrodur's castle. Didn't you bring them back with you?"

Thor looked uncertain. "No."

"He had them on. I saw him," said Marie, pointing at Thjalfi.

Good, thought Liz. *At least I wasn't imagining things.*

"Me?" said the faithful retainer in hurt tones. "My lord. That's ridiculous. I am your body-servant and loyal bonder. I've served you for years..."

"S'true," muttered Thor. "But I thought you got killed. It's all vague now..."

Thjalfi bowed. "I am a very solid ghost."

Thor frowned. "Disir are female."

Thjalfi waved his hands airily. "Anyway, my lord, Lady Sif awaits with dinner."

Thor blinked and gestured at Jörmungand and Fenrir. "Yes, but my friends..."

"Orm and Freki," said Fenrir.

"Uh, Orm and Freki won't fit there. You will have to have the food moved to the greater chamber," said Thor.

It was Thjalfi's turn to look taken aback. "I, er, thought something could be brought to them."

"No," said Thor largely. "Friends of mine. They eat with me. Have the platters moved. It's only a few sword lengths."

Thjalfi looked—very briefly—mutinous, but then he bowed and dogtrotted off to go and do as he was bid. So a little while later they all trooped through to a huge hall that would have been big enough for fifteen simultaneous *platteland* weddings—the kind where every relative living gets dredged up to fill every inch of space with people you'd rather not meet.

Sif was doing that job single-handedly, and doing it very well, Liz thought. Thor's wife was the sort of lady bountiful that would make the average recipient of condescending kindness ready to starve to death rather than take a mouthful of the bounty.

But then, Liz admitted, maybe her antagonism to the woman was just a case of not liking someone with real golden-blond hair. The damned stuff really looked as if was made of gold, and it made Liz feel very unwashed and unbrushed. Maybe she should have done her hair before Wolfie's.

Sif's gown, too, was an embroidered thing of beauty, studded with seed pearls. It was surprising Thor hadn't sold that. But then, she probably hadn't let him get his hands on it.

Servants ghosted around with jugs of mead, filling the drinking horns. Marie, seated at Thor's left hand, reached out and covered Thor's horn. "We're resisting one drink one day at a time, remember."

Thor nodded. "Uh. Well. I suppose so."

"We have no control over alcohol," she said firmly, quoting.

"Right." The thunder-god's lips quirked. "And you are a power higher than I am." But he turned the horn over, and adopted a firm-chinned look of red-bearded determination.

"But, my dear, you must have a drink to the health of our guests!" insisted Sif. "It would be rude not to."

"Right," said Thor weakly, turning his horn the right way up again.

"Wrong," said Marie, glaring at Sif. "Get this into your head. From now on he can't even have one drink because one drink leads to another."

"But he is Thor! Thor the mighty drinker who even lowered the ocean when Utgardaloki put the end of his ale-horn into the sea." Sif gestured to the waiting Thjalfi and his jug.

"He can drink as much seawater as he wants to," said Marie.

"Uh. It made me throw up," said Thor. "What am I to drink if I can't have mead or beer . . . or small beer? There is nothing else."

"Water," said Lamont.

"That stuff kills you," said Thor. "Really. And fish . . . well, they live in it."

Liz could believe that the local water might easily kill you. Like the Greeks drinking wine, almost everyone here probably drank something with alcohol in it to keep the waterborne diseases limited, if not completely at bay. Boiled or spring water it would have to be.

Thjalfi tried to pour some more of the mead into Thor's horn. Marie plucked the jug out of his hand and emptied it over his head.

Sif smiled sweetly at her. "You say she is a power greater than you, husband?"

Thor looked at Thjalfi, dripping and gaping, and nodded. Marie grinned. And then her face spasmed with pain, briefly.

"So don' push me," she gasped. "Gimme one of those pills, Lamont honey." The pills had altered, but still seemed to work.

Thjalfi had backed off to the now open mead-barrel, which stood beside the other three unbroached ones. He was about to refill the jug, despite his dripping, when Marie caught sight of him.

She whistled at the dragon, to get Jörmungand's attention. "You. Go and finish up that lot."

Jörmungand didn't wait for a second invitation. She surged up and plunged her gargantuan black-lipped mouth around the first barrel, and up-ended it down her throat. The next one she just swallowed whole . . . as she did with the last two. And then she gave a little ladylike burp, and said "'scuse me."

Sif watched with little red spots of furious color blossoming on her cheeks. Liz was sure, now, that Thor's wife not only understood Thor's drinking problem, but had come here with just one purpose in mind—to get him drunk. She was also certain that Thjalfi was up to his plump neck in whatever Sif was up to.

The real question was *why*? Liz could only think of one plausible answer. The Krim had lost two prior encounters with some of this set of humans, so it was treading more cautiously now. One of its aims was presumably to get any allies they might have made out of the way.

"All right," growled Fenrir. "She got to drink all the drink. Can I eat all the food?"

"No," said Liz firmly. "You need a properly managed diet, or you'll end up with all sorts of growth problems. And we don't want that."

Fenrir stared at her, his bucket-sized toothy mouth wide open. "Diet . . ." he said, as if he might be pronouncing a foreign word. "Did you say 'diet'?"

"Not starvation. I just need to adjust your protein and calcium input. You're growing too fast. You'll end up with weak bones. Wolfing down everything is just not on. I want you a strong and beautiful wolf, not one crippled with joint pains."

"Just one roast ox?" said Fenrir pleadingly.

Jörmungand began to hiccup.

"So what we do now?" said Special Agent Bott to his companion.

"They're treating us like amateurs and pariahs," said Stephens.

"Yeah, I know." Bott examined what his laser sighting device had become. He tossed the piece of pitch-pine and flint aside. "Trouble is, they do know more than we do. And they don't seem very interested in cooperation."

That was at the root of their problems here. Cooperation. These guys seemed to have no loyalty and worse, no respect. The scary thing was that the others were in control. Well, more in control than Stephens or he were.

"That Thjalfi . . ." Bott mused. "The local factotum fellow. He seemed more friendly."

"At least he brought me a loaf of bread, and took away the meat," said the vegetarian. "I don't see why they all find it so funny."

"I suppose it is very odd in this culture. Anyway. I think we should cultivate this Thjalfi."

His companion shrugged. "Why not? We can't complete our primary objective. If I understand it right we don't have much of a chance of getting back to the U.S. either. Except these guys did manage it before."

Bott nodded. "That's why I think its worth sticking with them. Even if means putting up with their nonsense."

"Until we get home."

"Yeah," said Bott, rubbing his hands together. "It'll be quite different then."

"Shouldn't have drunk that stuff so fast," admitted Jörmungand, a bit later. Liz was no expert on the proper color of dragons, but that particular greenish tinge didn't look right at all.

"A mistake," she agreed, nodding. Liz felt genuinely disoriented. Women going off in pairs to the bathroom was something she hadn't actually thought of across the species-divide. And Jörmungand being sick was something she could have passed on entirely.

"Just . . . drink helps me to forget my sorrows. Helps me to forget that I'm a freak."

"You're not a freak! You're a very fine dragon!" *Who has just puked up four hogsheads of mead, the barrel staves, a roasted ox, and some large sharks,* but she didn't say it aloud.

"I'm too fat," sniffed Jörmungand. "These dragon friends of yours will never like me. I need to diet!"

At this rate, thought Liz, *I'll have an anorexic dragon in my life.* "Nonsense," she said robustly. "Who told you that rubbish?"

Jörmungand sniffed again. "It says so in all the skaldic sagas I've read. They say I am so big I have to live in the ocean. And I've read all of them. They . . . help me get away from myself."

"I wouldn't believe everything you read. I mean, who wrote them?" asked Liz.

"Some of the greatest skalds in history, and some of the worst," said Jörmungand. "You must know more about them than I do, being a skald yourself."

"Um," said Liz. "I just think that what I really am is lost in translation. And I promise you that I've written a lot of things I didn't believe myself, and they're supposed to be true. I was writing about fish—and I'm not a fish. Naturally, I get some things wrong. If these skalds were writing about dragons, unless they were dragons, they probably got things wrong too. Trust me. My skills are not skaldic poetry . . . well, not any kind of poetry, but I know a lot about zoology." Liz saw the puzzled look. "Take it as the study of animals."

"Like hunting?"

"No. More like understanding how they work . . . look, just trust me, I'm an expert. You are *not* fat. Just . . . very big. The skalds have it wrong. I'm sure, if you think about it, you'll find they get other things wrong."

"Oh, all the time. And most of them can't write for old rakfisk. I mean take that stupid death scene in the Völsung Saga. Could it be any more contrived? Here is Atli dying, having been murdered by Gúdrun, and they stop to have a long pointless bicker about her temperament not always having been what it should have been. Artistry," said Jörmungand sarcastically. "I could do it better myself."

"Spoken like a true critic," said Liz.

"I think it goes with a serpentine body," said Jörmungand, flicking out her forked tongue.

Marie turned, too late, to try and pull the sharp thing out of her. It must have killed her, she realized. Consciousness was fading like the light seemed to be. All she was aware of was that golden-haired woman smiling toothily in triumph as she fell.

Regret. She hadn't even been able to say a proper goodbye to Lamont and the children. . . .

She'd come into the room looking for Thor. At this stage, the guy was going to need near constant support, but he was doing well. She'd found him—and Sif and Thjalfi. Thor had been in a chair, lolling, drool running down his chin and the air smelling like 'shine.

CHAPTER 18

⚬⚬⚬⚬⚬

"Marie's missing," said Lamont worriedly, as soon as Liz and Jörmungand returned. "So are Sif and that bum Thjalfi. I think they kidnapped her. And Thor's useless. He got into the booze again. Got drunk faster than you can believe."

Liz took a deep breath. "If they did kidnap her, there's only one place she can have been taken, Lamont. Valhöll."

Lamont's eyes narrowed. "That's what I figure, too. I'm going to have to ask you to look after the kids, Liz."

"Don't be stupid, Lamont."

"She's my wife, Liz. She's my . . . she's . . ."

"I know. It is kind of obvious. And she's great. But she wouldn't thank you—or me—if I let you get killed. She's living on borrowed time, Lamont."

"That's why I've got to get to her."

Liz shook her head. "I know that makes it even more precious. But it also means you've got to stay alive. For your children." She made a face. "It's not that I'm unwilling, but, well, I've all the parenting skills of a shopping mall."

Lamont clenched his fists. "I can't just leave her. I can't just do nothing. I *can't*. Marie . . ."

"I know," said Liz. "So I'll go, instead."

Lamont blinked. "You?"

173

She shrugged. "For a recce anyway. Look, you stick out in this place . . . like a bar of Ivory soap in a coal scuttle."

Lamont managed a crooked smile. "More like the other way around, but I take your point."

Liz patted her chest. "For once being built like a milkmaid and having . . . uh, blond hair does make me look like a local. My ancestors were mostly Dutch, which is just a bit closer to Norse than yours. And I gather there are these Valkyries wandering around. So I'll just go and wander. By the sounds of it they're all half-smashed on this local brew anyway. Let me go and see what I can find out. I was planning to go anyway, and I might find that they've put her in with Jerry. We'll send Lodin to the stables again. A two-pronged attack. In the meanwhile you can get Thor sobered up and get ready for whatever action we have to take."

"If we can take action." Something about the way he said it suggested that he was preparing himself for it to be too late, and was already thinking of payback. And that you didn't want to be the guy on the receiving end.

Liz put a hand on Lamont's arm. "If they just wanted to kill her, they could have done it here. And you looked for signs of a struggle, didn't you?"

Lamont nodded. "Nothing obvious, anyway. I'm not exactly a forensics team, Liz. But, well, this Valhöll doesn't sound like a healthy place for a woman to go 'wandering,' as you put it."

"I can take care of myself. I used to work on fishing trawlers, Lamont, not in a seminary for refined young ladies from genteel homes. There are several guys walking around at home who have three Adam's apples and lovely soprano voices."

"What?" He looked puzzled.

"Guys who used to have baritone voices, one Adam's apple and two balls," said Liz cheerfully. "Now, I think I need a suitable outfit. And helping myself to that woman's best clothing has appeal, especially if I can wreck it before I get back. You go and locate Lodin while I dress. And keep an eye out for the children. If they want hostages, those are the best."

"I suppose I'd better take the kids with me everywhere I go," said Lamont in sudden fear. "I can't ask those waste-of-breath agent types to do it."

"Bring the children to me," said Jörmungand. "And I'll get Fenrir. There aren't any Ás around except Thor who would take me and my brother on. I'll keep an eye on them." As an afterthought she said, "And I won't let Fenrir eat any of them either."

Marie felt as weak as a cat. Had the cancer suddenly taken some kind of giant leap forward? The last she remembered was the potent smell of distilled liquor, and yelling at Thor. Too late. He was already far gone, damn the bitch. And then that thing being stuck into her . . .

Opening her eyes, Marie saw the bitch in person looking down on her. Her arm was linked with the old guy with a missing eye.

"I knew she was no good," muttered Marie, a muzzy determination in her mind to take at least one swing at Thor's wife, somehow. She'd backed down from pretty damn little before she knew she had the cancer. There were times when it wasn't worth your job or the other sort of trouble. She had a good man and family to look after. Since the diagnosis, she'd decided that she would back down for nothing. Not ever again.

The one-eyed man viewed her wild swing dispassionately. She'd come nowhere near the golden-haired blonde, but it hadn't stopped Sif from backing away.

"A warrior-woman," said the one-eyed one.

"Thor says that she is more powerful than he is, Odin," said Sif warily.

"Perhaps in determination," mused Odin, as Marie tried to get up from where she'd fallen.

"She stopped Thor from *drinking*, Odin. That's why I had to get her out of there. I have managed to get him full of the drink again with Thjalfi's help. But she'd gotten him to stop earlier, and she'd do it again. That has to be some kind of magic."

"Nonetheless, she's a human, even if she's colored wrong. Not one of the ones that thwarted . . . the other before. I can detect no signs of godlike power. She is no danger. Her death and pain can merely strengthen this Ur-world. I will use her in one of the myth recreations."

"I thought we might want her as a hostage," said Sif doubtfully.

Odin tugged his beard. "We can do both." He picked up a long thorn, that Marie now remembered Sif stabbing her with. "The thorn of sleep. Let her lie, without breath, but without death, inside the ring of flames. I seem to have lost Brynhild."

He pushed the thorn into her, and the place whirled into oblivion again. The last thing Marie heard was him saying as if from some incredible distance:

"Valkyries. Bear her to within the hall I have prepared on the mountaintop, inside the wall of flames. And see she gets a mailshirt."

Thrúd walked out to go and fetch a mailshirt. It seemed impossible that her own mother had not recognized her, even in these thrall-rags and a hood. But then she'd hardly recognized herself in them, in the sword-blade mirror.

She was incredibly pleased to have an excuse to get out of the room. How disgusting could Sif get? Odin! He was sort of her grandfather! It was sick enough when the old lecher had tried to feel her up. But Sif was all over him, just as Modi had said! And by the sounds of it, the black-elf woman had managed to stop Papa-Thor drinking. So Sif went and kidnapped her!

Thrúd ground her teeth. She'd find out exactly which flame-mount the Valkyries were going to transport this black-elf to and then get back to Bilskríner to see how Papa-Thor was doing. She swallowed. He was such a big idiot. He'd never believe Sif was doing anything wrong.

Who could she turn to for help? This black-elf? Getting her free would be quite some task. She was paler skinned than the black-elves that Thrúd had met in her travels through Nifelheim. And they had had straight, greasy black hair, rather like that know-it-all, Alvis, nothing at all like hers.

Thank all the gods for Loki! Uncle Fox would have been her first choice, if Odin hadn't chained him away somewhere. Sif hadn't liked Loki, which, after he'd shaved her hair off, was hardly surprising.

Thrúd ground her teeth again. It might just have made him the ideal ally.

CHAPTER 19

⊚⊚⊚⊚⊚

"Yes, you do have to wear a mailshirt," said Jörmungand firmly. "All the Valkyries do."

Liz held the offending garment at arm's length. "You realize that if it was going to do any good, there is no way I could hold this out like this? It's too light."

"I could bite through it like fine vellum," said Fenrir, licking his lips. "But I think it is for the look of the thing. No one expects Valkyries to actually fight."

"Even for the look of things," insisted Liz, "this is designed for someone with smaller shoulders. And a smaller bra-size. It's metal and it doesn't stretch."

"I'll see what I can do to the side straps," said Lamont in a subdued voice. "Not much I can do about the chest part, though. Is there no way you can fit into it?"

Liz looked at his face and nodded. "I was just complaining for the sake of it, Lamont. It'll be a bit of a squeeze but I'll manage. But you might need tin snips and pliers to get me out of it again."

Lamont managed a slight smile. "Maybe a can opener."

"There is one in my bag. I don't like leaving that behind."

"Hit them with the sword instead," said Emmitt.

Liz felt the Norse sword at her side. "It doesn't weigh as much. Besides I don't know too much about fencing. I thought it was something you had around the game-paddocks until I was about twenty-five."

"Hit them with the sharp bit," advised Fenrir, his tongue lolling as he stretched in front of the fire. "Does anyone else feel that it is much colder tonight?"

"Not compared to Geirrodur's castle."

"Maybe so, but it is cold for Asaheim. Maybe Fimbulwinter comes at last." There was a look of bloody joy in his eyes.

Liz had felt no guilt about helping herself to Sif's wardrobe. She did feel uncomfortable about taking a horse from Thor's stable without his permission. There was only one. It was a gentle look-ing chestnut, about fifteen hands high, with a long mane and tail. It turned an enquiring head toward them as they entered.

"Thrúd's," said Lodin. "She's used to a woman's touch." The stable thrall looked warily at Liz. "Not . . . that Thrúd was too good at being ladylike. You can ride, lady?"

Liz nodded. "So long as it isn't sidesaddle. Even that I did once or twice."

So, a few minutes later, Liz was trotting across Asaheim in the dusk over the low ridge to Valhöll. She had strict instructions from Lodin about Thrúd's mare. The stable thralls at Odin's hall would care for her, especially if she dropped a word or two in the right ear. She wondered how you got to be thrall in the afterlife. It didn't seem like much to look forward to, really. An eternity of forking dung. If that was your reward in paradise . . . life on earth must have been pretty grim. Mind you, you had only to look at the special offers from most religions—a cloud, a set of wings and a harp, or seventy white raisins with transparent flesh—to understand why preaching hellfire as an alternative was so attractive.

When she reached Valhöll, the noise coming from within told her the party had already got to the hitting-each-other-is-fun stage. Wonderful.

She stabled the mare, said appropriate things to a certain bald stable hand, as per her instructions, took a deep breath and headed for the nearest door and the mayhem.

The rock-hewed tunnels under Valhöll were steep. At least you knew when you were going uphill toward daylight. That was the only direction they could be sure of. The tunnels were dark and, worse, branched. Jerry was beginning to wonder if they'd ever find a way out.

"We need a light," said Sigyn. "We could wander forever in the dark."

She said that without much thought, but it provided a spark of inspiration. Or just a spark . . . on the end of a piece of rock, which became a flame. "We've been fading away in that pit for far too long. I should have thought of this ages ago," said Loki, his teeth gleaming in the darkness.

It made it easier going, but it took a while before it occurred to Jerry to ask Loki if he could smell like a bloodhound if he turned into one?

Loki nodded. And laughed. "Now, would you be implying that the bouquet of even a dog would be better than mine?"

Jerry shrugged, grinning back. "There is a certain in-scent-ive to that aspect too. But I must admit it was getting out of here, that was my first thought."

"You shouldn't have even hinted at the idea of getting clean," said Sigyn, longingly. "The first century was the worst, though."

"After that our noses went numb," said Loki. "You get used to pretty nearly anything. It will mean darkness again, but Jerry's idea is a good one. Stand beside me. And then, when I change, keep a hand on my back, both of you."

So they did. Loki was a fairly tall dog, fortunately. He led them back and down—the direction they'd been avoiding—and then up again. At last Jerry could hear the distant sounds of a huge, very raucous party. And there was a torch burning in a wall-sconce.

Loki transformed into himself again. "Good thinking, Jerry. Except I kept wanting to lift a leg. Now, I will go and scout ahead. The trouble is that even transformed, the Ás would rec-ognize me."

"It's the eyes. Something about them does not change. They remain the true Loki," said Sigyn. "Go then. But go carefully."

A large buzzing gadfly went.

He came back a little later. "It's early yet. If we can wait until they reach the fall-down drunk stage we can pass through the hall with a bit more ease. Follow me. We need to slip through the sculleries, and up a little stair. I have found us a perfect spot to watch and wait."

He had indeed. It was a little gallery, plainly intended for musicians. They could watch the whole debauch within the vast hall with ease.

"Odin's not there," said Loki. "But there is Heimdall-goldteeth. And there is Magni. Thor's son. They're likely to recognize me."

"Heimdall is not likely to ever forget you," said Sigyn dryly. "And let's hope that he doesn't try that hundred mile vision of his."

"I thought he was out keeping a watch for giants," said Jerry.

"Well, yes, but not at night," said Loki. "So it must be after nightfall. Good. I thought so by the drinking, but it is hard to tell. Now all we need is a little more drinking and a good distraction. A big fight. There is always one. Then we'll be out of here before they drink the minni-toast. I'd like to be gone before Skadi finds out she was tricked, and before Odin starts looking for us."

That made every kind of sense to Jerry, although he wasn't sure what a "minni-toast" was. He was willing to bet it wasn't a small piece of lightly carbonized bread, or a drink to the health of Mickey's bride. But he had something of the measure of Loki now. "And then?" he asked.

Loki chuckled. "You think far too far ahead. Next thing you'll be asking me if I have thought of the consequences."

Sigyn shook her head. "We're not that ignorant about you! But what *are* we going to do? We need to get out of the gates of Asgard. Once we have reached Jötunheim or even Midgard, they will not take us with ease. So how are we going to get out of Asgard?"

"I haven't thought that far ahead yet," said Loki cheerfully.

"That's what we'd like you to try," said Jerry dryly. "If it is not beyond you."

"Of course I can, but it is so dull . . ." said Loki. He caught the look they were both giving him. "Oh very well. We need to get to either Thor's or Frey's homes. Thor has those vile goats and a chariot. Frey has his boar Gullinborsti and his chariot. I could fly over the walls to Midgard, but we'll need fast transport to get you two away. There'll be hue and cry of course, but I thought I could do my act as a gadfly and bite Heimdall. Or if we hit the gates early, he might not be there yet. The child of nine mothers is dipping very deep."

Loki pointed to where Heimdall was half slumped over a table with a Valkyrie on his lap trying to get his head up to pour more mead down his throat. With shock Jerry realized that he recognized that face. His first reaction was of intense relief. Liz was still alive! His next reaction was of fairly violent jealousy. As a rational and serious academic Jerry hadn't even known he could feel like that.

Liz realized the error of her ways about ten seconds after entering Valhöll's smoky and noisy halls.

For starters, the place was enormous. It looked bigger than ten O'Hare's put together, and full too. The only answer as to how Dark-Ages architecture stood up to these demands was by magic, because there was no other possibility. It had looked big from outside. From inside it looked, if not like a sea of people, like a reasonable sized lake.

There were rows and rows and more rows of tables and bench-seats full of the butts of Norse heroes. In between them staggered thralls carrying platters of steaming hog-meat, and of course, foaming jugs of booze. The raucous bellowing and laughter was like a solid wave of sound.

It appeared that Oktoberfest had had its origins here, complete with low-cut mailshirts as an early version of the dirndl. Valkyries, accompanied by a train of thralls, poured foamy stuff into the drinking horns. Impatient yells for service added to the Munich feel of it all. The Valkyries were understaffed. By the looks of it, it would get a lot worse before midnight. Well. Jerry wasn't going to be in this room. It was kind of a pity. She'd enjoyed Oktoberfest.

Then an arm snagged her around the waist and deposited her derriere on a lap, and she realized that it was less fun for the waitresses here. For starters you might get a lot more than a tip. And, looking at the face of the man who had hauled her onto his lap, you could forget some gallant gentleman stopping him from harassing the hired help. From what Thor had said, Heimdall-with-the-gold-teeth was one of the boss's cronies. Maybe he enjoyed partying with the hoi polloi. Or maybe this end of the hall was for the major league heroes. Most of them were big enough to have done well in any rugby team.

Heimdall blinked owlishly at her. "Shwat you looked f'milar, wench. I'm better c'mpany than that slob, Thor. Drink with me."

He held the horn to her face, clumsily slopping a quarter pint of the stuff down her mailshirt. Mead was a lot nicer than she'd thought it would be, but she still didn't want to shower in the stuff. His arm was still around her waist, and he held her so firmly that there was no escape without a major struggle. Mailshirts did have one advantage on your average dirndl, in that squeezing private property was less intrusive. His fingers were strong enough to dent the metal, though.

Liz took the only option available. She drank. A lot less of the stuff than Heimdall had had in mind for her, as he attempted to pour the whole horn down her throat. It was a big horn. Silver-chased. It was the same thing he'd had for a tootle-pipe at the gates! There was a stopper in the bottom. Well, you could probably drink out of a trumpet if you didn't mind wrecking the thing. And there were no valves on this.

Liz managed to pull the stopper loose. A stream of mead urinated unnoticed into Heimdall's cloak. Liz, with the stopper firmly clasped in two fingers, used both hands to stop herself being drowned in mead. All she had to do was to keep Heimdall from tipping it too much, and pretend to drink. She still got a fair bit more down her cleavage, but doubtless this oaf thought that added to her charms.

She was able to upend it and drain the last dregs so that it wasn't too obvious. Heimdall and several of his Viking-type buddies cheered her. Heimdall showed no signs of letting go, although she tried to pull free. So she snagged a jug from a passing thrall. This was what was expected of her, so she was allowed to pour it into the enormous twisted horn—and quietly push the stopper home. It took another half of a two-quart jug to fill the darn thing. But now it was her turn to pour it in his face. As he leaned back she saw the pyramid-pendant under his blond beard.

He drank all of his hornful. And bellowed for a refill. For Liz.

Liz could see no way out of it . . . yet. But when the horn was full again, she leaned forward and kissed him, as she pulled the plug. She wasn't quite as lucky this time, as some of it was dribbling down her leg. She'd take this big sot on at down-downs, and drink him under the table, but not while Jerry and Marie needed finding. She gave him some tongue as mead spilled onto the rush-strewn floor. By the looks of old Gold-teeth's face that hadn't happened too often lately.

Then she used two hands to chug the empty horn full of mead, ignoring his clumsy efforts to give her a feel up and wishing they'd issued her with chain-mail pants, with a small bear-trap strategically placed. She pushed the bung back in and "accidentally" whacked his fingers with the end of the horn.

While he was still sucking his fingers she called for more mead. "Two to one," she said, lining up jugs. "You're bigger than me, big boy."

"By the Allfather, Valkyrie, you can drink!" said a man with a plaited walrus moustache next to her.

"Not as much as me," said Heimdall, putting it away. Liz hastily refilled while he was still belching and wiping his beard. And while he was drinking she snagged two more jugs off a passing tray. Heimdall's counting was getting a little weak. "Wasn't that my two?" he asked, taking the horn anyway.

"No, this is the second," said Liz, pouring it down his throat. She raised her eyes to heaven. Wouldn't this oaf pass out?

Then she nearly passed out instead. There, standing on the little gallery, as bold as Beauchamp, was Jerry, looking ready to commit murder.

She tried to stand up. And that was a mistake. Heimdall sat up and made a grab at her. "Time for loving!" he bellowed, pushing her back onto the table and sending the bench flying along with a full load of Norse warriors as he tried to lift her dress. Liz kicked him. As hard as she could. Unfortunately, only in the belly. He did crash into the next table, via a platter of steaming boiled pork.

"S'playing hard to get?" he said, sitting up and tilting his head at her, ignoring the fight that had broken out next to them. He surged forward again, grabbing her dress. He was so drunk he missed. Liz flung a leg of fatty pork at his head. And then swung that horn of his at him, as she tried to get up, and slipped on the pork-fat and spilled mead. He grabbed her with one hand, and Liz knew that, drunk or not, he was stronger than she was. And no one around here was about to lift a finger to help, despite her scream for it.

Except for Jerry Lukacs. He'd wrenched the upper rail off the little gallery and jumped the twenty feet down to the tables. The table went over, but not Jerry. He'd already gained the next one, swinging an eight-foot long piece of two-by-two rail, whacking blond heads. He brought it down, edge on, on Heimdall's head, just as Gold-teeth managed to hitch her dress up.

Liz rolled frantically away.

Jerry slipped on the horrendous mixture of grease and mead, lost his grip on the two-by-two, and fell onto plaited walrus moustache's head. The heavy oak table went over.

Liz rolled across the floor, seeing Jerry wrestle with walrus-moustache, who must have been three times his size. And then Heimdall sat up.

He was a god. *But didn't he have the decency to fall over and stay down?* thought Liz furiously, struggling to get up with her wet skirts tangled in someone's feet. They fell, just as she saw Heimdall grab Jerry . . . and the torches winked out.

There was nothing but darkness and pandemonium. Liz tried her best to add to that by hitting anything in reach with what she had in hand—the horn.

Then something hit her. If it hadn't been for that stupid mailshirt it would have been a lot worse. As it was the breath was knocked out of her, and she was sent sprawling, gasping, into a space that was fairly free of legs.

There was light again. The torches were being hastily rekindled. Liz, peering out from under the table, could see the profile of the man with one eye talking to Gold-teeth. They were holding Jerry. Holding him in such a way as to make escape highly unlikely, even if his head were not lolling. He was moving, though, so he probably was still alive.

Liz tried to get up, to follow her first instinct to see if he was all right. But her legs were trapped under a bench that appeared to have a few elephants sitting on it. She bashed her head hard on the oak of the table above her as she tried to sit up again. Seeing stars, she heard Odin say, "I gave orders for this one to be put into Loki's pit. What in Hel's name is he doing here?"

Heimdall blinked owlishly. "Maybe he 'shcaped."

"Or maybe he never got there. I'll question him, either way."

"Can't I finish killing him?"

"No. This is not one of the Einherjar, Heimdall. I need him alive to get some answers out of him. Where is your horn?"

Heimdall scratched his head. "I had it with me. I was having a drinking competition with some new Valkyrie . . ."

"There are no new Valkyries," said Odin, his eye narrow with anger. "Fool. Don't say you've lost it. You'll need it at the Time. No other horn will be heard across all of the nine worlds to call our allies!"

"It mus' be here somewhere," said Heimdall.

Liz looked at the item in her right hand.

Odin turned, pushing Jerry in one of his escort's arms. "Look for it. In the meanwhile I'd better send someone to check on Loki. Actually, I'd better go and check myself. And I'll see this one bestowed. With guards. Sober ones."

Liz crawled deeper into the shadows under the table. There was a platter under here. A huge one, that had obviously got lost in the melee. Well, so Gold-teeth and Odin wanted the horn back. It was not her heartfelt desire to oblige the bastard. And it was still smoky, half-dark and chaotic out there. She wanted to follow Jerry, to find out where they were going to put him. There was something to be said for a weedy academic who would take on a whole hall full of these warrior types with a two-by-two for her. That something was probably "crazy idiot," but still.

She bit her lip. Explaining what she was doing kissing Gold-teeth might just be interesting.

She crawled out from under the table, held the horn under the platter and set off toward the doors where Odin was heading, hoping Heimdall didn't spot her. Risking a quick glance back she saw most of the people in that area of the hall were on hands and knees. Horn hunting, no doubt.

The trouble was that there were a lot of doors in the wall at the hall end, just below Jerry's gallery. At least three of them were possible, but if she hesitated she was probably lost anyway. So she walked through the nearest one. And nearly collided with a load of more boiled pork. This plainly led to the kitchens. One of the thralls looked at her and the empty platter and pointed with an elbow to a stair leading down off to her left. "Scullery."

She had very little choice but to go into it, or crash into half a boiled pig. The passage wasn't wide enough for both of them. And there were more food-carriers coming.

The scullery stair was obviously not the main access to that area, as there was no traffic. She might find somewhere to stash this horn. She couldn't come out of the kitchen doors with an empty platter. She walked down and round. And collided with a ragged thrall. The platter and Heimdall's horn were knocked flying.

"What are you doing with that?" demanded the thrall, in a very un-thrall female voice. "That's that jerk Heimdall's Gjallarhorn. How did you get that?"

Liz was grabbed by a pair of strong hands. Very strong hands. She tried to pull free and failed. "Let go, damn you!"

The thrall snorted. "Not until I work out where you're running off to with Gjallarhorn. Asgard needs it, even if I don't need Gold-teeth."

"I don't need him either," said Liz, shuddering. "I have to agree with what Thor said about the creep this morning. And you can have the horn. I just took it to spite him."

The ferociously strong grip on Liz's wrists eased slightly. "You saw Papa-Thor this morning?"

"Yeah. We brought him back from ... watchamacallit ... Geirrodur's castle." The part about "Papa" registered. "Thor is your father?" asked Liz incredulously.

"I think," said the woman holding her, "that we need to talk. There is a storeroom back there. Do you have anything to do with the black-elf that Sif had kidnapped? That made Papa-Thor stop drinking?"

Liz nodded. "Yes. That's why I'm here. To try and find her. Now let's get into this storeroom before they find us."

The "thrall" let go of her and scooped up the horn. "This way."

It was only few yards to the unobtrusive door. "In here."

The door closed. It was pitch dark in there. "Who are you? I did not know my father had any friends among Odin's Valkyries." The voice was thick with suspicion.

"I'm not a Valkyrie. I just disguised myself as one to come and look for Marie. And my boyfriend."

There was a long silence. Then Thor's daughter said, "Are you quite crazy?"

"I think I am," said Liz ruefully. "I didn't realize that it was a bulls party, and that I was dressing up as hooker. But what are you doing here? And what do you know about Marie? And who are you actually?"

There was another long silence. Finally the other person replied. "I'm Thrúd. I thought that was obvious. And what I'm doing here is my business." Her voice was stiff with a "don't ask" tone. "But I can tell you what has happened to the black-elf woman. One-eye has sent her to lie inside the wall of flame, like the Valkyrie Brynhild."

"He's killed her?"

"No. She lies as if dead, but she is not. She is somewhere between death and life. She will lie like that forever, unbreathing, but undying, untouched by the passing of days, forever, until the Time itself."

"Where . . . Lamont will go spare. Is there any way of getting to her? Of waking her?"

"Oh yes," said Thrúd. "If you can get to her. She lies in a great hall on a mountaintop in Midgard, guarded by a wall of flame. If the thorn of sleep is drawn out of her neck she will wake to be the bride of the hero that has dared this mighty deed."

"Her husband is going to be mighty unimpressed, if it's anyone but him," said Liz dryly. "But at least she's not dead. I'm less sure about Jerry."

"Jerry?"

"My boyfriend," said Liz. "Your one-eyed friend took him off to question. He was just going to check on someone called Loki first."

"Then we'd all better get out of here," said another voice, nearly startling Liz out of ten years' growth.

"Uncle Fox!" said Thrúd incredulously.

A flame flared in the darkness. Liz found herself looking at an impish grin that dominated an otherwise handsome but scarred face. "Liz, I presume?" he said coolly. "And my little Thrúd." There was considerably more warmth in that.

Thrúd hugged him.

"Easy on my ribs, girl. You don't know your own strength."

"Where is Sigyn?" demanded Thrúd. "If you've left her behind . . ."

"Behind these boxes," said a female voice.

Loki looked at Heimdall's horn. "Payment for services rendered? We were watching your little carouse from the gallery."

Liz swallowed. "It wasn't what it looked like," she said. "And now if you'll excuse me I must go and see if I can get Jerry free."

Loki shook his head, and put himself between her and the door. "Explain what it was then," he said, standing there with his arms crossed. "Before you go out and call One-eye and his henchmen down on us."

Liz shrugged, feeling herself coloring. "I got dressed up in this Valkyrie outfit and came across from Thor's home to look for Marie and Jerry. I didn't . . . quite realize what I might be in for. Heimdall pulled me onto his lap when I tried to walk past. So . . . I played the part. And tried to get him fall-down drunk. We were having down-downs competitions out of this stupid horn. Only I kept pulling the plug out, while, uh, distracting him," she coughed, "and letting the drink run out, before I pretended to drink it. See. The side of my dress is soaked."

"And then?" said Sigyn, coming out from behind the boxes.

"Then I saw Jerry, and that ass decided to rape me. Jerry came to rescue me, I got knocked under the table. And the lights went out."

"My work," said Loki. "When Helblindi thinks about it, he'll realize that. And then?"

"Then the guy with one eye was there. I was under a table with the horn, and I saw them take Jerry away. More to stop Gold-teeth from finding this horn of his than anything else—One-eye told him to—I hid it under a meat platter and tried to follow them. But I took the wrong door and collided with Thrúd. She brought me in here."

Loki looked at Sigyn. "Well, I don't know. I suppose it is possible. Look, we'll take you with us. And the horn. That's a prize and a half."

"Leave me behind," said Liz.

Loki shook his head. "When Odin finds I am gone there will be a manhunt such as Asgard has never seen. Jerry, to whom we have sworn an oath, will be guarded by enough of the Einherjar to stop Thor, let alone you. But that horn might do for the ransom."

Thrúd looked a little doubtfully at it. "Maybe," she said, "but Ragnarok comes. And the Ás will need the horn, Uncle Fox. "

Loki's eyes danced in the flame-light. "Ah. But I reached a compromise with Jerry, Thrúd. A compromise that will hopefully avoid the need for Ragnarok entirely. It does rather depend on getting this Jerry free to fulfill his side of the bargain. If I swap the horn for Jerry, I won't mind, because Gold-teeth won't need to use it. It'll do him no good."

Thrúd still looked doubtful. "I suppose we can take it along," she said, reluctantly. "But I don't trust you, Uncle Fox. I like you, yes, but I don't trust you. Not that you always cause ill on purpose," she condescended, "but it does follow you around."

"But you can trust me, Thrúd," said Sigyn practically. "And this Midgarder did convince me. I agreed. I will settle for vengeance on those who killed Narfi, and who bespelled Váli. If I can have that without Ragnarok, so be it."

Thrúd raised her eyebrows. "That makes this 'Jerry' the most valuable hostage in the nine worlds."

"That's the way it should be," said Liz.

"The way it should be is that we get out of here," said Loki. "With Gjallarhorn, or he's doomed and not worth anything."

Thrúd nodded. "Through the kitchens. I wish we had horses, but we'll just have to steal some from the Einherjar."

"Lodin gave me your little mare to ride over here," said Liz guiltily. "She's lovely."

Thrúd blinked. "Old Stumpy let you ride Snowy?"

"Yes. I'm sorry. He did make special arrangements for her to be looked after."

Thrúd shook her head. "It's all right. I'm just surprised."

"Well, can you be surprised later," said Loki impatiently. "I hear shouting."

Liz did too.

"Put the horn in that little kettle," Thrúd said decisively.

The "kettle" was what Liz would have called a pot. And yes, it was black, and so were the contents. Loki picked it up, frowned, and said, "You'd better take it. I might need to organize a distraction."

"No wholesale destruction," said Thrúd.

"I had thought of setting the kitchen ablaze."

Sigyn and Thrúd raised their eyes to heaven.

"No," said Liz firmly, pushing him ahead of her. "Jerry is somewhere in the building. And if part catches fire, it will all burn."

"The fires under the pork," said Sigyn. "And make everything else go out."

Loki smiled nastily. "It'll be a pleasure to ruin their dinners anyway. Let's go."

Liz found herself hustled down the passage. There was definitely something going on in the main hall. It sounded like an enormous disturbed beehive.

At the door to the acre of kitchen—a well-orchestrated bedlam of fires and enormous pots, spits and other mysterious implements of torture—Loki paused. He fixed his gaze on a huge black pot in the corner. It reminded Liz more than anything else of one of those cartoon pots that had four missionaries boiling in it.

The pot erupted into a fountain of flames. Loki shrugged

apologetically to the others. "Spontaneous pork combustion. Walk. Don't run."

With the kitchen staff trying to put out the fire in the pot, and smoke as thick as tar pouring from it, and the torches and fires in the place somehow burning less well than they had been, they edged their way to a small door at the back, and out into a passage that led to the stables. They paused in the doorway.

By the sounds of it, the stable hands had already adjourned for the night to the hayloft with some beer. The Einherjar obviously did not go night-riding.

Loki transformed into an owl, fluttered up to a trapdoor and obviously took a look around. He transformed again on the ladder as Liz tried to persuade her brain not to disbelieve her eyes. The Mythworlds were hell on a hardened empirical scientist. Still, it was useful to have someone quietly close the trapdoor, and take the ladder down.

They walked the horses out as quietly as possible, and two minutes later were on the grassy slope leading back to Bilskríner.

CHAPTER 20

The one-eyed god shook Jerry so hard that he was afraid his head would come off. "Where has he gone?" he demanded, bubbly spittle spraying Jerry.

There was no point in trying to pretend that he didn't know who Odin was talking about, and anyway Jerry was less than sure that he cared. He didn't really care about anything right now. He thought it very odd that this hall decked with shields seemed to look like a weedy parking lot with the very recognizable Museum of Science and Industry in the background. If only the pain would end.

The one-eyed god stared at him furiously. "Who stabbed him?"

"It must have happened in the melee, Allfather," said a distant voice.

"Hel. I need answers out of him. I can't let him die yet. Get me Idun. And put him down on that bench. I will need my gambanteinn. . . ."

And it all faded into darkness. Noisy darkness, with occasional visions of a sunny parking lot, with dandelion heads nodding, spreading their seed like drifting stars across the great darkness. Then there was a taste of spring, scents and flavors he'd never known that he'd encountered, but stirring things from the recesses

191

of his mind. Smells of wet dogs, and mushrooms and blossoms, and somehow the icy freshness of a water drunk from a mountain stream. It was from somewhere in his youth. Somewhere very early in life with his grandfather, and his grandfather's dog, neither of which he had a conscious memory of. Something had triggered all these things with a feeling of wellness . . . and apple.

Apple? He wasn't even that fond of apples. Well, not store-bought ones. He could remember, now, picking one and eating it straight from the tree, together with an old man with white hair and a wet dog that seemed to grin at him. This apple in his mouth tasted more like that. He chewed, weakly, and the juice flowed into his mouth.

Somehow with it came strength. Not a lot, but enough to chew again.

He'd been stabbed. Surely he shouldn't be eating? He swallowed the juice anyway. It was both sweet and tart, and something about it had brought an old man and his spaniel out of a photograph he'd barely remembered back to mind. Jerry's grandfather had died before Jerry turned four. So why was he giving his grandson an apple again? This one was even better tasting than that one had been. Jerry swallowed the mouthful. He could remember, now, that he'd implicitly trusted the old man. So he swallowed. It was all an illusion anyway. He was dying. Funny. He hadn't realized that you'd feel better when you died. He opened his eyes to see if there really was a clear white light at the end.

The woman was beautiful enough to be an angel, which was awkward for a self-avowed atheist. But Odin, standing behind, her bore no similarity to either Jerry's grandfather, or Saint Peter.

"You have some questions to answer," said Odin grimly.

"Not until he has finished eating the apple," said the woman, her voice calm and sweet. She handed him an apple, with one slice off it. "Eat," she said.

So Jerry took a bite. He just hoped that Idun's apple wouldn't take him all the way back to teen acne again. But he was sure that it had brought him back from the very brink of death. He chewed very slowly and very deliberately. He might not have a lot of time to think after this. Besides, it was a very good apple.

"Thank you," he said, once he'd swallowed. "It is the best apple I've ever eaten."

She dimpled. "Asgard forgets. Enjoy," and she walked away.

Jerry took another bite. Odin wasn't going to wait for him to finish it though. He grabbed Jerry again, and lifted him with two hands by the remains of Jerry's jacket. "Where. Is. Loki?" he hissed into Jerry's face.

Jerry still had half of the apple in his hand and a fair amount in his mouth. And this apple was just too precious to waste. He managed to push it into his pocket, and store the bite in his cheek. Jerry was sure Loki would not still be on the gallery. "Minstrel's gallery," he managed to gasp out.

Odin put him down. "Bind him and guard him. We've searched every inch of this building, and I think that Loki has escaped, from what happened in the kitchen. But I'll check."

So Jerry was tied up and left to finish chewing the piece of apple. He had a feeling he'd better enjoy it, and that the next while was going to be rough.

He was dead right.

Odin came back, fuming. And then began a long, exhausting, unrelenting interrogation. The only thing Jerry had to hold on to was what Loki had told him: to tell Odin what he wanted to know was also to die. And there were no two ways about it, that bit of apple had done him the world of good. He wasn't ready to die.

Gradually the questioning shifted. Now Odin wanted to know how Jerry had helped Loki to free himself. And just what Jerry had done with Kvasir's mead and Heimdall's horn.

At least it was easy not to betray anything about the last two. But what he did say was enough to convince Odin that he was a very powerful sorcerer. Or maybe it was whatever Skadi—still apparently stuck in Loki's pit under an enchanted and only slightly used handkerchief—had said to Odin.

Eventually, after what seemed like several eternities, Odin stopped questioning him, and Jerry was put into a fairly ordinary cell under constant guard. It would appear that whatever Odin had said to his Einherjar it had included some pretty harsh words on the value of staying sober and not ending up in the pit with Skadi.

The Krim registered protests with the device. The Krim-possessed god needed some self-will. It was no pleasure, no vicarious experience otherwise, to enjoy the pain and death energies, to revel in the flesh. But this one had far too much and it was as stupid as it was devious. Yes. There was a need for the belief-constructs necessary to animate this Ur-world, but this prukrin-energy source had threatened the Krim before. It must die, and die soon. As soon as possible!

The device was not designed to agree or disagree with the masters. But if it could have nodded its head it would have. The energy requirements of keeping a prukrin transfer portal active were too high when there was no fresh material to input.

Fortunately, from what it had gleaned of the physiology of the victim species, what the local god planned would perhaps not be fatal for a god, but was going to be rapidly so for a man.

CHAPTER 21

⊘⊘⊘⊘⊘⊘

"I've been thinking," said Cruz, herding them all ahead of him like a flock of geese, "that we'd better stay indoors and away from the windows for a while. Professor Tremelo says we can camp out here in his Chicago headquarters for a while. And, uh, I told the dragons they could hold, and probably eat—with permission and ketchup—anyone they caught sneaking around this place. We're awkward witnesses. And I got the feeling from the PSA crowd that this business they dragged us into isn't really legit. And the other thing I got was that they don't care about staying within the limits of what is. That Megane clown, for sure. Whether he's acting on orders from higher up or not, who knows?"

Mac hugged Arachne again. "If the Pissants don't go over the colonel's head and suddenly get us posted to Colombia or Afghanistan or something."

There was a tremendous uproar outside.

"Keep back. Keep low." Cruz moved up to the window along the wall and took a careful look outside. Then, grinned. "It's okay. The next wave of the Seventh Cavalry just arrived. Maybe Prof Tremelo should have told the guys on entry control that Bes was on his way. I'd better go down and get him to put them down."

"Bes!" said Throttler delightedly. "Let's go."

The dwarf-god from Punt, the Egyptian god of protection, was standing just outside the building with two MPs and they were making the racket for him. People tend to do that when you hold them upside down by one leg and swing them around.

Bes still wore a loin-cloth and a cloak made from a very short, wide leopard. He still had a top-knot with bobbing ostrich feathers. He'd acquired a broad wrestling championship belt, and an awful lot of gold bling since they'd last seen him. His laugh and his beard were as broad as ever. "Cruz!" he said delightedly. "And my favorite lady friend!"

Throttler blushed. "Hello handsome," she said coyly, as Bes dropped the two dazed men and leaped to hug them. It was almost as dangerous as an affectionate squeeze from a dragon.

"The Prof sent for him," said Cruz to one of the victims, who was reaching for a side arm.

Bes looked sternly at the man. "Never ever call a man 'shorty' unless you are very sure that he is."

Cruz shook his head at the MP. "Man, are you crazy! Look, confirm it if you like, but this is Bes. As the guys from the WWF will explain, you don't get in his way or mess with him."

"He assaulted us!"

"So you've got a story to tell your grandkids one day," said Cruz with a grin.

"And you're alive to tell it," said Bes with a growl. "It appears that I'm acquiring believers here. So . . . how does that American saying go, friend Cruz? Yeah. Go ahead," he said cheerfully to the MP fumbling with his side arm. "Take that weapon out. Make my deus."

"Don't let's get hasty, Bes. He was just trying to do his job," said Throttler. "I wonder how many riddles he knows?"

"He's not kidding," said Cruz, quietly, to the other MP. "Nobody got too badly hurt, yet. Let's just call it a day. He's a sort of special bodyguard the Prof called in."

The guy blinked and shook his head. "I saw him on *The Best Damned Sports Show Ever.* I thought it was faked. Hey, Dodson, cool off, willya? It's just a misunderstanding, I guess, and like you said, nobody got hurt too badly." He turned to Bes. "You wouldn't autograph something for me?"

"Sure," said Bes, showing how fast Las Vegas had accustomed him to certain American customs.

After Bes signed the man's gunbelt, they moved into the building to fill Bes in on developments, using the service garage entrance at the back. The garage had the only door big enough for Throttler to pass through. Cruz couldn't help noticing that Throttler had a wing protectively over Bes. As if anyone needed it less!

When Bes had heard the whole story, in various choruses, and had somehow gotten Tina to sit on his knee—when she wouldn't go too close to anyone else—he said, "Well? When do we leave? The sphinx-image in Vegas will do for a point of departure. It's about time I popped back in to Egypt anyway. I need to tell Harmakhis to sit on anyone he sees going near his nose. Best way to teach them the meaning of 'fundamentalism.'"

Cruz had to think who Harmakhis was—oh, yeah. The Egyptian sphinx. With a nose, Jerry had explained, that had been hacked off by some Muslim fanatic in the fifteenth century. Being sat on by a sphinx might put his ideas about defacing other people's monuments into a new perspective.

Mac shook his head. "It's not that simple, Bes. They haven't gone to Greece or Egypt. Prof Tremelo thinks it's Scandinavian myth."

"Got any giants for me to beat up?" asked Bes curiously.

"Lots. And lots of other dwarves there too. But it's kind of a tricky question just how we'd get there."

"Can't you fly there, my dear?" asked Bes of Throttler.

"I don't think so," said Throttler. "They're heathens. They don't believe in the sphinx."

"We'll have to get there and do some missionary work then," said Bes, rubbing his hands.

She nodded. "And some riddling."

The secretary came in. "I have a call from Professor Tremelo for Sergeant Cruz," she said, trying not to look at the Sphinx's exposed frontage. Cruz had to admit that he'd almost forgotten that she wasn't wearing anything.

Miggy Tremelo sounded exasperated. And like he wanted their company with whatever was making him feel that way. Which was why he was ordering them—in the politest fashion—to get everyone, including the dragons, to Washington.

"I've spoken with the Air Force. They're arranging air transport. Someone will be in touch shortly."

Cruz had encountered dragon feelings about air-traffic before. The skies belonged to them, not these upstarts. "Uh . . . Professor. Wouldn't it be more sensible to fly everyone here?"

"Much," said the professor. "But it would also be easier to take a tortoise out of its shell."

Or get a dragon into a plane, thought Cruz, but he didn't say anything. There was a dangerously explosive quality to Professor Tremelo's voice, that said "don't argue."

They did, after a while, settle down to sleep that night in their jury-rigged bedrooms in Tremelo's offices.

Well, most of them. Bes, the protector, sat like a gargoyle, silent and unmoving on the roof of the building. Cruz felt genuinely sorry for any Pissant who might try anything during those dark hours. Bes would just take them by the scruff of the neck and give them a shake. It was a quick and efficient way of dealing with rats.

But the night passed with no untoward events. So, the next morning, the dragons on flat-beds ("don't want them flying in city limits") and the rest in appropriate vehicles were whisked off to meet their airplane. The Air Force cargo plane would be landing at Midway airport instead of O'Hare, since that was closer. Nobody—certainly not the drivers—particularly wanted to be hauling two dragons all the way across the metropolitan Chicago area.

Cruz was dead right. Once they got there, the dragons were not impressed. Not impressed to the point of open rebellion.

"If the gods had intended us to fly in one of those devices they would have given us hand luggage, not wings," said Smitar, so convincingly you might almost think that he knew what hand luggage was.

"Besides, I want to accumulate those frequent flier miles. I can't do that if I'm not flying," said Bitar, showing that he too could eavesdrop without understanding a word.

"It flies. You don't have to," said the misguided fellow they'd sent to organize this flight. "Now please get your animals in the plane, Sergeant."

"With respect, sir," said Cruz. "They're not my animals. And even if they were how do you expect me do that? I can't carry them on my back."

"Soldier, if I needed your cheek..." He stopped because Bes

had stepped between them, reached up, and pulled him down to Bes height.

Bes had an airplane wheel chock in his other hand. He let go of the air force officer, took it in both hands and squeezed it flat. "I don't think I can carry a dragon that doesn't want to go either," Bes said, "and I'm fairly strong. So why don't you show us how it is done, eh? You get Bitar in and we'll follow with Smitar."

He twisted the steel wheel chock into a pretzel. "Now. We'll watch."

The officer stepped back.

"Piece of advice, sir," said Mac. "The dragons are a rare and protected species. And don't argue with Bes. He's got no respect for rank. No real understanding of it, in fact."

That, thought Cruz, was the understatement of a lifetime. Bes was a gen-u-ine god—so what did he care about the difference between a captain, a major and a colonel?

But all he said was, "Bitar, don't eat him."

"Phtt. Too small and smelly," said Bitar, tasting the fellow with his tongue.

Now looking nervous instead of belligerent, the officer took a walkie-talkie from his waist-band. "Look. I'm just doing my job. But if you want to make it difficult, I'll need some heavy equipment."

Cruz kept his face impassive and said nothing. When the low-loader device came trundling along, along with a team of burly loaders, the officer said, "Now get on, beast."

"Why?" asked Bitar curiously.

"We need to move you. Or we can hoist you on with a crane."

Bitar brightened. "Cranes are biggish birds. Do you mind having it plucked first? The feathers get stuck in my teeth."

He leaned over and took a small nibble at the lowbed-forklift thing. "Terrible flavor. Anyway, you're supposed to carry me. Not put me on that thing. And I am not going into that flying machine. Not into its mouth." He swung his tail, putting a twenty-foot-long, six-inch-deep dent into the hangar's steel door. Then he tipped the lowbed-forklift onto its side with negligent ease. The operator had to hurriedly clamber out of his little cubicle, onto the ground.

Cruz took pity on the man. "Sir, can I suggest something?"

The officer took a deep breath. "Besides telling me that I have just made a fool of myself? But it can be done, Sergeant. I'm not beaten yet."

"Yes, sir. It probably can be done. But Smitar will probably also knock the airplane apart if he doesn't want to be in there. And they haven't got a tranquilizer that can deal with the dragons either."

"Oh." The officer studied the dent in the hangar's steel door and the tonnage of his loader.

Cruz cleared his throat. "Generally the dragons are pretty fond of food, sir. And you can reason with them. You could try bribery."

"You said 'food,'" said Bitar. "Don't tell me you didn't, Cruz. I heard you!"

"Yes, I did," said Cruz. "You were just going to tell me about in-flight catering, weren't you, sir?"

Smitar licked his lips. "Do you serve maidens?"

The officer took a deep breath. "We serve nearly anyone, as long as they're over twenty-one, and on the airplane. And I hear you're going first class. Food and drinks on the house."

"Now can you put the drinks trolley back on its wheels?" said Cruz.

Bitar did, nearly effortlessly. "Is it normal to eat on a house?"

"Of course," said Smitar. "Bigger than a plate, isn't it? How do they get the house inside the plane?"

It took a lot more cajoling and a substantial menu, with ketchup and hot sauce in industrial quantities, before the two dragons were persuaded aboard. And there was no way they were staying there without the others for company.

The dragons filled up a lot of floor space, and persuading them that they could not leave their tails out, and then strapping them down took even more diplomacy. It would have taken the dragons a few days to fly to Washington under their own steam. But it might have been easier.

The rest of them were at least cooperative about getting on and strapping in, but finally they and a small mountain of dragonish delicacies parted with a sweating officer, and taxied onto the runway.

"I need to go to the bathroom," said Priones.

"Tie a knot in it and pray the dragons didn't hear you," said Medea nervously. "Otherwise they'll want to go too."

That wasn't a pretty thought. But it was only when they were coming in to land at the end of their journey that Cruz realized that there was another ugly thought he hadn't had. Dragons need to eat to fly. They produced huge volumes of lighter-than-air biogas that made them bulge like oversize balloons. Liz De Beer said that was the only possible way they could get airborne. It was a smelly if effective solution to getting something really big to fly under its own muscle power.

Only now they were stuck in an airplane with them. And not only was it not going to be nice to be here—that gas was flammable. It was also toxic.

And by the looks of it, their in-flight greed had seen to it that the dragons were not likely to fit out of the cargo bay. Cruz, his mouth suddenly dry, ignored the seatbelt warning and went up to talk to the pilots.

The copilot came and had a look. And then there was some very hasty consultation with the flight-controllers.

It was not a textbook landing. But it was a wise one. So was opening the nose cone and the tail bay . . . and retreating a long way to a fire truck while the C-5A rocked . . .

Miggy Tremelo appeared to be in a far better temper when he met up with them upon their arrival in Washington. "Easy flight, I trust?" he asked cheerfully. "Let me introduce you all to our Norse mythology consultant, Dr. Lars Gunnarsson."

Mac had expected all mythology experts to look like Jerry Lukacs. It was a bit of a shock to find that this one looked as if he'd be more at home in a Norse myth himself. Okay, so he was a little old for it, with some white hair in his beard, but you sort of expected him to be wearing a mailshirt and a bear cloak.

"Very Norse-looking dragons," he said professionally. "More serpentlike than the modern pictorial image is usually."

"They're Colchian," said Medea.

"We've got indigestion," said Bitar.

"From the Caucasus, are they?" said the scholar. "You know, we all tend to think of the Scandinavians as a bunch of bloodthirsty Norse Vikings raiding England, but it was their trading voyages that spread their influence across Europe and even in my opinion, America. Huge numbers of traders plied the rivers in what is now Russia. Ibn Fadlan, the Arab traveler and diplomat, records meeting them on the Volga. And although his description was hopelessly sensationalized, the Scandinavians were there, to the northwest of the Caucasus, as well as on the Dnieper. They would have brought memories home to influence their culture. I wonder if these were not the source for the prows on all those longships?

Medea shrugged. "The females live in the water. They only come out to breed."

"Even more plausible," he beamed.

"It would seem," said Tremelo, "that our friends probably have ended up in a place called Geirrodur's castle. Anyway, we're scheduled to appear before the Senate committee charged with overseeing Krim pyramid affairs. I have organized hotel accommodation, and for the dragons, this hangar—"

"I think we'd all better stick together, Prof," said Cruz. "Here is good for all of us, if we can get some camping gear."

Tremelo looked at them, taking in the children, and the concrete floor. "You don't think that's a bit extreme? I had ordered some hay for the dragons."

Mac shook his head. "You don't know, first hand, what these PSA guys are like, Prof."

Tremelo hesitated, then shrugged. "Okay. I think the PSA may have cut its own throat, but they've got enough loose screws rattling around inside that organization that it's hard to predict what they'll do. I'm also getting the feeling that support for this clandestine operation went deeper than we'd like to think it did. Very well, you stay right here. I'll get the camping gear delivered. Is there anything else you might need?"

"Maybe some sleeping tablets for Tina," Cruz pointed at the Jackson child. "She's taken this pretty hard, Professor. She's fallen asleep a couple of times and seems to go straight into nightmares about her twin."

The mythology expert smiled. "As it happens I am a psychologist. Or I used to be until I retired to focus on my first love, Scandinavian mythology. Let me have a talk with her. She is naturally very traumatized."

A few minutes later a very troubled looking Scandinavian mythology expert came back from the corner where he had been talking to Tina. "I am afraid I must strongly recommend against using any sleeping tablets," he said shortly. "She isn't having night-mares. I have read Dr. Lukacs' reports about the Mythworlds they found their way into last time. This girl is dreaming about things she could not possibly know, but that her sister in the Mythworld may be experiencing."

"Telepathy?" asked Tremelo skeptically.

Dr. Gunnarsson shrugged. "We don't exactly know where they've gone. It may be contact with a spirit medium for all we know. But she knew details about Geirrodur the troll-king's castle, Thor, Grid's rod and the belt of strength and gauntlets of iron, as well as about Fafnir and Sigurd—none of which a girl her age would have known, and all of which goes well beyond coincidence. And I am as skeptical with regard to telepathy as you are, Professor Tremelo."

"I guess the Mythworlds—and the denizens of them," Tremelo said, nodding at the Sphinx in animated conversation with Bes, "should teach me not to be so skeptical." He grimaced. "Somehow I don't think I'm going to introduce that into testimony at the hearings, even if I do believe it."

CHAPTER 22

It was a cold clear night. You could actually hear the frost-crisp grass crunching under the horses' hooves. Loki noticed it and laughed. "Fimbulwinter. Loki is free. The clouds are massing in the west."

Thrúd's face, white in the moonlight, looked as if it had somehow gone a paler shade. "No!" she said.

Loki shrugged. "It will mean the return of Baldr."

Thrúd scowled at him. "Is there any bit of mischief and gossip you don't know, Uncle Fox? It was just a little-girl crush. I had one on you, too."

"What appalling taste you had, girl," said Loki. "Anyway, I am willing to avoid Ragnarok if I can."

"The question," said Sigyn, "is whether Ragnarok is willing to avoid you. Great magics are tied to the Time."

Loki raised an eyebrow. "I don't play with great magics, ladywife. That's One-eye's province."

"Exactly," said Sigyn. "A reason to be suspicious, especially after what Jerry told us."

"About what?" asked Liz as she tried not to shiver. This was no weather for damp skirts, whatever Fimbulwinter and this Ragnarok were.

"About being trapped in a cycle, which repeated and repeated to give power to some foreign god. The 'Krim,' he called it."

Thrúd peered intently at her. "It does have a strange feeling that I have been here before. But I remember great Bilskríner becoming a place of ruins."

"It's true enough," said Liz. "Jerry and I and our friends fought the Krim before. We defeated it . . . but it fled. This is obviously where it came to. It reactivates old myths. Old beliefs. Jerry's the expert. All I can say is that I'm very cold."

"Bilskríner lies just ahead," said Thrúd comfortingly.

Lamont Jackson was almost beside himself with worry. Should he leave the children in the care of a pair of monsters and go and look for Marie . . . and Liz too? The waiting was going to kill him, for sure.

The sound of hooves was a welcome one. Even bad news had to be better than no news. It took him a few seconds to realize that there was more than one horse out there. He wondered if he should find a weapon . . . and then Liz came in.

With several others.

Not Marie.

He forced himself to be as calm as possible. "What news?"

Liz took a deep breath. "Well, she's not dead, Lamont. Thrúd here saw her. But I couldn't rescue her. Odin has put her into a kind of suspended animation. She's in, well, like a coma, inside a wall of flames on a mountaintop."

It was Lamont's turn to take a deep breath. "At least she's not dead. Come in to the fire, Liz. You're blue with cold."

She nodded weakly. "I think I'm about to fall off this horse."

Lamont caught her, set her on her feet, and gave her his arm to lean on. "Let's go into the main hall and the warmth and we can get introduced. Thor is still out of it. That stuff was distilled, and potent as hell," he said grimly.

Lodin arrived, and beamed at the stocky individual in the tied-up rags that the local peasants seemed to wear. "Lady Thrúd," he said, bowing respectfully. "Whose horses are these?"

"Einherjar's, Stumpy. See that they're well rubbed down and that they have some oats. We'll turn them out at first light. It is too cold outside now."

Thrúd was a little worried by these strangers who had taken over her father's hall. They seemed a little short of respect for

Papa-Thor. But she could always reestablish that! He didn't seem to be too good at doing it himself these days, she admitted ruefully. She remembered how it once had been. At the same time she began to remember what it had become. It was strange how that memory had faded, of the immortal Ás trapped in the downward spiral of Asgard. That was when Papa-Thor's drinking had really got out of hand. That hadn't changed. Well. If these strangers—she really was not at all sure they were black-elves—could help, then a little disrespect was a small price to pay.

They walked through into the main hall, where a number of small trees were blazing merrily in the hearth. Three children were fast asleep against dread Fenrir's side. The wolf was trying to look as if he was quite unaware that the girl-child—who looked remarkably like the woman sent to be a stand-in for Brynhild the Valkyrie—didn't have an arm around his neck. The fourth was sleepily looking at them from next to the great Jörmungand. Two other men in roughly cobbled furs were fiddling about with some strange helmet on a table off to one side.

"Any news?" asked the black-elf boy who was still awake.

"Well, Marie is still alive," said the black-elf man whom Liz had addressed as Lamont. "But she's trapped behind a wall of flame in a coma."

The boy began to cry. Big tears starting suddenly from eyes that had had the Loki-flame of rebellion and trouble moments before. "I never even had a chance to say . . ." His chin quivered and he dissolved into a flood of tears.

Lamont went over and put an arm around him. "Easy, Emmitt. It's not that kind of coma." Plainly, by his voice, he was hurting too.

Close family ties, plainly. That was good. Thrúd approved. "It is a magical sleep, child. If the thorn of sleep is drawn out, she will wake. Even if a thousand years have passed."

"And we'll get her free," said Liz. "And get it out of her. Promise."

"You have Loki to help. And what is a wall of flame to me?" said a man who had entered behind them.

Both the Midgard Serpent and Fenrir surged to meet him. The wolf, suddenly realizing he had children using him as a hassock, stopped dead, and waited until Lamont set them down. Then

Fenrir danced around Loki and Sigyn like a terrible puppy dog, jumping over the sinuous coils of Jörmungand.

"I thought that it was extra cold tonight," said Fenrir, panting. "Fimbulwinter comes!" There was red joy in his eyes.

Then in walked Thor, bleary-eyed and puzzled looking.

"Papa-Thor," said Thrúd, going to hug him.

"Hello, littlest one," he said, squeezing her back. "Where is your mama? And where is Marie?"

Emmitt was not yet entirely recovered from his emotional shock. He walked up to Thor. "You," he said, waggling a forefinger. "I thought you were Thor. But you were so weak you couldn't even stop them kidnapping Marie. You can't not drink, can you? I thought you were someone I could rely on." His tone was bitter, plainly hurt to the core.

"Sif told me it was medicine. It would stop me craving drink," Thor said humbly. "Look . . . I won't do it again."

The black-elf boy looked him in the eye. "Promise?" He sighed. "My mama promised." It was plainly something too painful to think about, by the way he bit his lip.

Thor nodded. "It's not easy. But if you'll help me, boy . . . I'll do it."

The boy looked at huge Papa-Thor. The lad had good shoulders on him when he put them back like that. He looked for a long time. Then he said, "Deal."

"You can train him up as warrior," said Thrúd. "It'll keep you busy. Get you to lose some of that"—she poked him in the belly—"because Fimbulwinter is here. So is Loki."

Thrúd was not too sure what she expected from her father at this point. Actually, she had to admit that her feelings were a mess. Trust Loki to stir everything up, especially the bit about Baldr. But he had been, to all intents and purposes, a sort of uncle all her life. He'd helped her out, and saved Freyja, and for that matter Odin, and half a dozen others out, and helped Thor recover Mjöllnir.

Yes, he'd caused a fair number of problems too. But she knew Thor considered the defense of Asgard a sacred trust—even if he seemed to be giving house room to two of the Asinjur's greatest enemies, Jörmungand and Fenrir. It was he who had put a sword in Fenrir's jaws, and very nearly caught Jörmungand while fishing, after all. And now he seemed unsurprised to see them here.

She was surprised to see her father looking embarrassed and uneasy. "I didn't know what he planned to do," said Thor. "Odin told me what you'd said about Sif. And Baldr."

"Well, I did say it," said Loki, obviously not going to give Thor any room for comfort.

"I had to do something after that," said Thor. "But I thought it would be a good beating..."

Loki shrugged. "He would never have caught me without your strength, Red-beard."

"I know. But I should have stayed after you were caught in the net. Heimdall was getting up my nose, and I thought I should get out of there before I hit him. He's the Allfather's favorite... And someone offered me mead." Thor sighed. "It was true about Baldr, though? You caused his death."

"It was all true, and that was true too. But I had reason. And I had help. Help that betrayed me. Help that I will destroy." Loki smiled thinly, viciously. "And while I might have sent Baldr to Helheim, I wasn't the one who kept him there. I swear to it."

Everyone had assumed that the giantess Thökk—who had refused to weep for Baldr, and thereby condemned him to remain in Helheim—had been Loki in disguise. So who had it been then?

Thor looked troubled. "Sigyn. What is this all about?"

Thrúd had a terrible feeling that she knew, now, why Loki had done it. But Papa-Thor was in no condition to go and fight Odin, and all the other Asinjur who would rally to him. She just hoped Sigyn wasn't going to give it all away.

Yet.

She'd have to explain it to him sometime, and it wasn't going to be easy. Everything that Loki had said at the flyting was true. Even the parts about her mother, which were painfully obvious now that she'd seen Sif with Odin.

Sigyn held out her hands. "I am not being drawn into this, Thor. But you know Loki. *He* is not an oathbreaker. A trickster, yes. But he does not lie to you. He had reasons."

Thor sighed. "What you said about me was true, Loki. Hurtful but true. But I can't let you loose to bring Ragnarok."

"What I said about everyone was true. I left some of the best bits out though," said Loki with a wicked grin. "I'm saving those. But I've had a little talk with a sorcerer. A little Midgard fellow who called himself Jerry."

Thor shook his head. "I knew a Jelling once. At a place in Jutland."

"Not quite the same, Red-beard. This Jerry talked me into forgoing Ragnarok and settling for revenge."

Thor shook his head. "Can't be done. You know Odin as well as I do. He'd rather bring Ragnarok than lose. Loki, I must hold you. This time I'll see to it that it's at least comfortable. Otherwise . . . give it up. Give me your word and go into exile in Midgard. It's not so bad. I spent a few years cadging drinks there. I'll be going too. This mortal's wife"—he pointed at Lamont—"was captured and taken from my house. I owe him a double debt: for the evil done to his wife and for help that she has given me. I honor my debts."

Loki shook his head ruefully. "You never change, old friend. You remain honorable . . . and a bit dim. Has it occurred to you that you're standing with my son and my daughter, and without Mjöllnir, or the Megingjörd, or the gauntlets of iron, or Grid's rod?"

"He has me," said Thrúd.

"And me," said the boy black-elf.

Liz walked into the fray. "Excuse me," she said crossly. "Stop this, right now."

She turned on Loki. "You owe Jerry. He got you out of your prison. You owe it to him to get him out. You won't do that by starting a fight with *my* friends. Now just put a plug in it. You've been looking for a fight ever since you got here. And Thor, I know Jerry Lukacs. Trust me, just because *you* can't think of how to do something, doesn't mean he can't. Jerry has out-thought two sets of gods already. So you just concentrate on hard stuff like staying sober, and then if Jerry can't produce, then you worry about it. Got me?"

Whatever else Papa-Thor had got, he hadn't quite gotten used to women like this. He gaped.

But Loki started to laugh. "You know, Öku-Thor, she's right. I was looking for a fight, I suppose. And yes, this Jerry was clever enough to get me free. That means that he is technically cleverer than me, because I couldn't."

"And Papa-Thor," said Thrúd, taking the bit between her teeth, "Uncle Fox was telling the truth about mama."

"I know, little one," said Thor gently. "I'm not all that clever, but I knew something was going on. He didn't have to shame her in public though. Things . . . things haven't been too good between your mama and me for some time now. But she's still my wife."

Thrúd took a deep breath. "And . . . maybe . . . I think I understand about Baldr. It . . . well, it was my fault, Papa."

"Oh, I had my own axe to grind too, Thrúd," said Loki. "And don't pester Thrúd about it, Thor. We all do things we regret later. I'm an expert at it."

Thrúd found herself getting a squeeze from her father. "If I understand this right, and I'm not quick about these things, it's a good thing Loki got to him first. And you can tell me about it if you want to, when you want to. It's over now."

"Even Mjöllnir wouldn't have hurt Baldr, Thor," said Loki.

"Umph," grunted Thor irritably, knitting his brow. "True. You could have told me, though."

"I don't want to rub you up the wrong way, old friend, but I do things my way, and you do them in yours—which is charging in like a bull at a gate. That wouldn't have worked."

"This is very interesting," said Liz, "and you can all talk about your misunderstandings, and kiss and make up . . . later. Jerry is still a captive over there. We've got that horn. We need to arrange a trade. And we need to rescue Marie."

"Horn?"

"That gold-toothed creep's tootle-pipe," said Liz.

Loki nodded cheerfully. "Heimdall must be swearing most beautifully by now. Take my advice, Thor. If that wench kisses you, don't hold her, hold onto your pouch with one hand and your hammer with the other or she'll steal both."

Thor rubbed his head. "This is all too fast for me. Let's take it slowly. The Allfather has this Jerry prisoner. You have Heimdall's horn. You want to exchange the two."

"Yep," said Liz. "For starters anyway."

"Well, I'm not that clever," said Thor, "but I think most of the Asinjur will just come here and take it from you, and imprison you or kill you."

"Even here? Take someone from Bilskríner?" Thrúd said incredulously.

Thor nodded gloomily. "Loki's right about the state of things. My halls are empty of warriors. I don't know what's happened to the belt of strength. I can't find my iron gauntlets. I'm afraid

I, uh, sold Mjöllnir for drink. And Odin can call to muster all the Ás, all the Vanir. I don't have a lot of friends left. I know. It's my own fault."

"Well, it's gonna change," said Emmitt belligerently.

Loki nodded. "Well said, boy. But for now, we need to flee this place. There are places in Midgard and yes, in Jötunheim, where we can find shelter. Where even the Ás will not follow. And there is always Helheim."

Thor shuddered.

"There is just one awkward detail. We have to get there," said Jörmungand. "And getting out of the gates of Asgard could be tricky. I can go by water, but you can't."

Thor shrugged. "We hitch my goats to the chariot, and charge."

"And end up full of Ull's arrows," said Loki, "spitted on One-eye's spear, and getting chopped into dog-gobbets by Heimdall and the rest of the Einherjar. Remember we have mortals here. And they can be killed very easily."

Thor sighed. "All right, Loki. You always come up with some sort of plan. But I am just not dressing up in women's clothes and pretending to be Freyja again."

Loki chuckled. "And you looked so good in a dress. You've got such pretty ankles."

Thor took a swing at him.

"He's just teasing you, Papa."

"I know. But it's like that damned punning. The only way to get him to stop is to hit him."

"Punnish him," said Lamont.

Liz groaned.

Loki smiled. "And you must be Lamont. Jerry said you were a man after my own heart, but hopefully not on a platter. He also said that you were a practical man. How would you get us out?"

Lamont shrugged. "Camouflage. The ladies' dresses might even work, but I also swore that they'd never get me to do it again. A distraction would help. A few smoke grenades. I gather archery is a problem. Something to keep the heads down for a bit. Are these gates closed?"

Thor nodded. "Between dawn and dusk, yes."

"And when do you think they'll get here?" asked Liz.

"Possibly before dawn. Not much, though. They will assume that Loki has taken one of his forms and flown. After first light someone may track the missing horses."

"But it is pretty dark out there. We can go out and get ready to rock and roll on those gates at dawn," said Lamont. "Now, we're going need to get some things ready. Have you got a smithy and some tools?"

"And how do we stop them chasing straight after us?" asked Liz.

Loki shrugged. "Let them try."

"I plan to discourage it," said Lamont.

Thrúd had more faith in the black-elf. Loki tended to leave the ends of his plans to chance.

CHAPTER 23

〇〇〇〇〇〇

Liz might have guessed that Lamont's plans would involve a serious shortage of rest. He had her and Thrúd making caltrops. At least in Myth-Greece they'd kept him away from a workshop.

After a while Liz's curiosity got the better of her. She asked Thrúd what all this stuff about Baldr was about.

"I was . . . involved with Baldr." She sighed. "I was still quite young. We Æsir do not age as you mortals do. And Baldr was even more handsome than Loki was before Skadi's snakes. But Baldr was married to Nanna. And Papa-Thor and Uncle Fox were like two old mother hens about me. From what I can work out, Loki went to Odin to get Baldr to back off, before Papa-Thor found out. I was still quite young. The mistletoe . . . well, it grows on the oaks. Odin's grove-trees. Baldr was protected against harm from anything else. Papa-Thor would have fought Baldr. Thor could not win, so Loki dealt with him. I don't know if he meant to kill him. He doesn't always think of consequences."

Liz thought that was the understatement of the generation. "But what did all of this have to do with Odin?"

"He is Baldr's father. And Baldr is foretold to rule the Æsir after him. What Loki is saying is . . . horrible. He is saying Odin plotted for Baldr's death so that there would be no challenge to his rule."

Liz gaped. "His son?"

"One of them," said Thrúd. "And no, I'm not still in love with him, whatever Loki thinks. Baldr broke it off just before he was killed. I . . . I was *glad* he got killed. He used me. I was just another bit of fun, and a way of getting at Papa-Thor. He taunted me with that," she said, colors flying in her cheeks.

Mocking Thor's daughter was probably a seriously bad idea.

They worked on while Loki and Lamont competed in ingenuity and puns. Liz had to be glad of it. It might keep him from thinking too much about Marie.

"The big problem," said Loki, "is Jörmungand. She's not very fast on land, and her wings are too small for her to fly with. I can transform myself, and her. It's not easy, but I can do it. I transformed Idun into a nut once." He grinned. "Mind you. I am not sure that she got better. Of course if we get Jörmungand into the water there is no catching her. Fenrir can outrun even the arrows of Ull."

"We need to attach some armor on this cart," said Lamont, "that's not going to weigh it down too much."

"Don't let Thor hear you call it a cart, for Hel's sake. He's terribly proud of his title Öku-Thor—charioteer-Thor."

Lamont shrugged. "Call it whatever you like; it could use some improvement. Leaf springs for starters, and a better way of attaching the goats."

Loki laughed. "He's a traditionalist, is our Thor. And spring is the time of leaves, yes, and they would hide us, but this is Fimbulwinter. It will be snowing before morning. Asgard is unused to snow."

"Snow . . ." mused Lamont. "Chariots don't do too well in deep soft snow, do they?"

"Depends on how deep," said Loki. "It was clear out when we rode over, but the snow is coming. There are long watches to the night."

"That's going to make tracking horses tricky. And Marie . . . will she be all right?"

"She lies behind an eternal wall of flames. She will be warmer than we are."

"She's not well," said Lamont, biting his lip. "I need to get back to her."

"All the more reason to get out into Midgard, snow or no snow," said Loki.

Lamont's eyes narrowed. "I'm going to have a look."

It might have been clear when Liz had come back from Valhöll, but now it was as black as the inside of a cat out there, and snow was falling as if it had a deadline to meet. It was a regular blizzard now. If it kept up like this it was going to be axle deep on the cart in no time. Lamont refused to call that thing a chariot. It was more like a two-wheeled farm wagon. And the snow was soft and powdery. The goats would almost have to swim through it. What they needed was a skidoo . . . He might as well wish for a ski-plane.

And into his fertile mind an idea was thrust. The Midgard serpent's tail was definitely a lot higher than it was wide. "Just how well will Jörmungand cope with that soft snow?" he asked Loki. "It won't be quite swimming, but no one is going to walk on top of it for a while."

Loki shrugged. "Let's ask her."

Jörmungand went out and showed them. A patch of the floors of Bilskríner were never going to be quite the same again, but Lamont had the design for a giant mythological skidoo. All they needed was a broad sled, with one wide skid with a high but gently sloping prow. Jörmungand could put her head and a little of her upper torso on that, along with them. A hundred and fifty feet of tail could push the skid along.

Now all he needed was to construct it before morning. Fortunately, there was a half-built boat in Thor's workroom. It had plainly been abandoned long ago, when the bow had been completed and the rest still needed to be clinker clad.

Thor was easy about the idea of them using it. "A snow dragon-ship! I like that idea. I'm never going to finish the ship anyway. And the timbers are old already."

Jörmungand liked it too. "I tend to dig in to drifts," she said. "This should stop that."

At length they were ready, and Lamont went to have another look outside. It was still snowing, but less heavily. The snow was lying nearly four feet deep. There was also a hint of sullen daylight. They'd been at the preparations for longer than they'd realized. He sighed. Well, he'd better wake the children. Emmitt had passed out quietly in a corner a few hours back. Thor had carried him to sleep with the others. Red-beard liked that boy.

When he went through to the room where the straw pallets and goose-down covers had been laid, Lamont realized two things.

First, he was very tired. Second, he had real problems because Tolly and Ty were not in their beds. Just as he was setting out full of panic, the two came in.

"There is snow! I had never seen snow until I came to this place. And there is so much of it!" said Tolly excitedly.

"We found this belt thing, Pa," said Ty, hefting a broad gold and leather belt. "It's pretty cool, hey." He held it against his waist and grabbed his father's arm . . . and pulled Lamont off his feet.

"I think Thor is looking for that," said Lamont in a controlled voice. "And now do you think you could put me down? That's his belt of strength."

Thor was delighted. "Where did you find it?"

"I'll show you," said Ty.

They followed the boy to a room on the back of the huge hall.

"Thjalfi's lair," said Thor. Already, with the great belt—it looked like a championship prizefighter's belt—he looked less like a has been and more like Thor, god of thunder.

The room yielded quite a trove. There were the iron gauntlets, and an iron rod. "He told me I'd lost them!" said Thor, incensed.

There was also something that meant nothing to Thor and a great deal to Lamont.

A still. A homemade copper still.

Which went a long way to explain Thor's "medicine," and where it had come from. There were still several skins of the stuff, which Lamont looted. It might come in useful, even if he had to keep it a long way from Thor.

They went back to the room where Ella was still fast asleep. And smiling in her sleep. Lamont hated to wake her, poor child. She wasn't used to coping with a world that didn't have her twin in it. He didn't want that smile to go. Maybe cuddling that wolf had done it. It had been damn funny how the wolf had taken to her. He'd be embarrassed if he thought they'd noticed it, but as long as no one was looking . . .

Well, Liz said wolves were a highly social species. And there were those Mowgli stories. Giving Ty to the wolf to raise was not an unattractive thought! Although the wolf probably wouldn't think so. But it definitely allowed Ella more liberties than anyone else.

She opened her eyes. "Daddy, Tina's been flying in a big jet-plane. Huge. Big enough for the dragons to lie stretched out!"

She started giggling. "And the dragons ate too much while they were flying and then they wouldn't fit out. They got stuck in the door because they both tried to get out together. And Cruz said some rude things . . ."

"What?"

"They've gone to Washington, D.C. Will you take me sometime, Daddy? It's not fair that Tina gets to go on her own."

"Uh." Lamont really didn't know how to deal with this. But at least she was smiling. Part of the way back to the talkative girl-child she'd been. He picked her up and hugged her. "Liz and Thrúd are organizing some food. And as I know Liz's cooking skills, I think we'd better go and see that we get something edible," he said. She was her mother's daughter. And at least he had her.

"Is there any news about Mom?" Ella's worries and fear came back with a sudden rush and she clung to him.

"The news is not too bad," he said. "She's a prisoner, but she's okay. We'll free her soon. Come. Got some new people for you to meet, that are going to help us."

Thrúd plainly did not have the culinary deficiencies that Liz did, because the oatmeal was edible. So was the smoked salmon and the rye bread, and the gammon. Looking at the size of that side of salmon, Lamont felt like going fishing for the first time since they'd found out about Marie's illness. But since his luck had deserted him on other things, it probably wouldn't allow him to catch fish any more either. That was too bad. He'd really *enjoyed* catching fish. He'd never caught a thing before Tyche, the Greek goddess of luck, had blessed him, despite a fair amount of trying. The novelty had been nearly as nice as catching the fish. Besides, it stopped you thinking about other problems. If they ever got out of this mess . . . well, even trying might provide him with some solace.

"I've left Thjalfi as much detail as I can," said Agent Bott.

"Well, we hope he's as good as his word. He's certainly got the ear of the powers that be in this place," said Agent Stephens.

"Yeah. Do you think we should try and lose these guys? Stay here?"

"How?" asked Bott. "They'd find us here. That wolf-thing could smell us out. And it's snowing outside—hard enough for us to get lost and not fast enough to fill in the tracks. We should have gone last night."

"We weren't even sure of which direction," said Stephens, picking up a helmet with an utterly useless sealed GPS unit in it. All that there was now was a piece of parchment. He'd love to know how the hell the switch had been pulled. It must have been back in the van, on the way into the pyramid zone. He'd been next to that big paratrooper. The son of a bitch must have done it somehow. "And when did we really get a chance to get out from under the eyes of those monsters?"

"If there is one thing I really like about them, it's that you and I are not monsters in their eyes," said Jörmungand. "You've got to admit it, Brother. It makes a change. Loki and Sigyn were always good to us. Thor . . . well, he was so far down the slide to being a stumblebum he didn't care any more. He wanted company to drink with. He only took the sword out of your mouth because he was blind drunk and wanted to sell it for more booze."

"He admitted that, yes," said Fenrir. "And I used to get on with Tyr. But these people are still mortals, Sis. Whether Loki admits it or not, Ragnarok is coming. I don't even know if he can stop it if he chooses. And in Ragnarok all mortals will die, and we'll stand beside our father in battle against the Æsir."

"Hmph. You're not even full grown yet, Fenrir. Ragnarok isn't due for centuries. If things can change that much, we can change them some more. Besides, I like having a girl for a friend. There's all sort of woman talk that I never had a chance to do before."

It was Fenrir's chance to snort. "Soppy stuff. But, fair enough, I like Liz too. And the kids have brought out a big brother side I never knew I had. But there's no sense in getting sentimental about it. Ragnarok will end all things."

"So this is where you two are," said Liz, coming through the door. "Time for us to get going."

She looked faintly guilty. "We're going to need a hand to get the half-boat out. I didn't think of that."

"Hands are something I'm a little short of," said Fenrir.

Liz found getting the half-boat out was an easier task to accomplish than she'd thought. Actually, it displayed the kind of thinking she wished she'd employed in her various house-moves. Do not fight the queen-sized bed-base around corners and up the stairs. Just have the world's biggest snake swing its tail once at the wall, and push the thing straight through the new hole. Easy really, if not the sort of action that pleased landlords—or Thrúd.

"You should treat Bilskríner with some respect!" she said, as Jörmungand pushed the half-boat through the hole.

"Why?" asked Jörmungand.

"Because it is home of the god Thor," said Thrúd.

"It's a house. Big and badly built. It can be fixed. It's not exactly an architectural treasure, Thrúd. And in the last little while he hasn't actually spent much time here. I know because I spent most of the time drinking with him."

"You should respect it because he has lived here," said Thrúd stiffly.

"Oh?" said Jörmungand skeptically. "I'm inclined to respect people, not things. But I live in the ocean, mostly. Call that my home. I'll thank the Ás and the Midgarders for not making water into it."

Thrúd found something else that needed doing, and Liz had to grin to herself. She was not a bad kid, but was obviously used to being the strongest female around—which you could believe if you'd seen her carrying a few "essentials," like a metal mirror that must have weighed a hundred and fifty pounds. She had her father's strength, but packed into a smaller female body. Mixing with Jörmungand would do her the world of good.

Jörmungand slid herself into the rope and strut harness that Liz and Lamont had constructed. She had a good look at herself in Thrúd's mirror and arched her neck up proudly. "All aboard."

The Mythworld-skidoo moved fairly slowly at first, very sinuously and with enough lateral sway for Liz to wonder if Jerry would have been seasick on this craft too.

"Chariot goes faster," grumbled Thor. It was still snowing, but not with the force it had had the night before. The snow lay about four feet thick and was still loose and powdery. Perhaps Thor's goats could have coped with it. But the Mythworld-skidoo was accelerating as they hit a slight downhill, with their back-track straightening out and the half-boat rising onto its keel instead of digging its way through the snow. Now they went fast . . . and then still faster.

Straight toward a party of warriors struggling their way through the thick snow. "Wheeee!" shrieked Jörmungand. "This is fun!"

By the way Odin's Einherjar were diving into drifts, they didn't think so. Just because you're a Valkyrie-chosen brave warrior does not mean that you want to be flattened by a half-boat moving at least forty miles an hour, by Liz's estimate. It went on accelerating, spraying powder snow and racing ever faster on the downhill toward the gates of Asgard.

"Thor had better be right," Liz yelled, "because if those bloody gates are closed we'll be jam at this speed!"

An arrow winged over her head, and skittered off Jörmungand's scales. The gates were open—but Heimdall and a dozen others were trying to close them.

"Faster!" yelled Liz in Jörmungand's ear. "And the rest of you get down!"

But Loki and Thrúd had already taken up bows, and were shooting back at the frantic gate team. Another black-fletched arrow sprouted in the boat-timbers as Jörmungand churned the snow behind them. Through the snow-arch Liz could see that the gate-closers had run away. But the gap was a narrow one. Liz just hoped that Jörmungand was keen sighted. It wasn't a major reptile trait.

Sure enough, they hit the gate edge with a shriek of splintering wood because Jörmungand's aim was not that good. But at least they were through.

And then Jörmungand was turning. Was she taking them back? Was she crazy? Best not to ask.

The entire half-boat lifted—all twenty feet of solid oak—and Jörmungand turned across the gateway she'd been racing straight toward. The half-boat slid sideways, a good seventy feet. A sheet of snow, several tons of it, sprayed straight at the Einherjar. One moment there were thirty warriors with swords, battleaxes and spears, bracing themselves, archers ready to fire.

And the next there were only snow-men, and Jörmungand was turning again, racing across the flat and away.

"I've done that at sea, but it's even more fun on the snow!" said Jörmungand happily. "Swamped a few longboats like that, I have."

Liz could well believe it. She was just very glad that she hadn't been on the longboats, or standing in the snow.

They were away from Asgard.

But they had left a trail that even a blind man could follow, if he didn't mind getting his knees wet.

CHAPTER 24

Liz was not the only one who could see that the trail would be easy to follow. Loki was up on the prow talking to Jörmungand. They immediately began to throw a series of s-bends that Liz just knew would have made poor Jerry lose his breakfast.

"That won't stop them following us," she said to Loki, as she clung to the gunwale.

"It might just put them off doing so on horseback," said Loki, with a wicked grin. "Look."

Liz could see what he meant. The trail was no less clear, but now there were huge ridges of snow—real powder drifts—seven or eight feet high to wade through. As a South African from an area of that country where it never snowed she had no idea how much it would affect the horses. But it didn't look like it was going to be pleasant. And galloping down their back-trail, which would have been easy a little earlier, was going to be impossible now.

"We'll reach the sea before they reach us," said Loki. "I have arranged a vessel."

Liz was impressed. Either Lamont or Thrúd or Sigyn must have leaned on him, hard. Loki wasn't much of a hand at preparation.

The sea, when they got there, was cloaked in a clinging sea-mist—the ocean plainly warmer than the frigid air. Liz wondered what sort of little unseaworthy tub she was going to encounter. The poor thing she and Lamont had vandalized in Thor's workroom had been well built, she had to grant. And weren't these Norsemen Vikings? It had to be better than that Greek boat, or that blasted Egyptian floating banana, stuck together with linen strips. And at least she was used to going to sea in small boats.

The vessel loomed blackly out of the mist, at least the size of a supertanker.

"*Naglfar*," said Loki. "She cannot come too close to shore."

Thor and Thrúd both shuddered.

"At the moment she carries no cargo," said Loki, urbanely. "And what other ship did you two think I could get?"

"I suppose a cruise liner was too much to hope for," said Liz. "Or even a battleship."

Loki chuckled. "On *Naglfar* we need fear no warship. She is the biggest ship in all of the nine worlds. I have to have the biggest and best of something."

"So they let you have the corpse-ship," said Thor, a little tersely. "Well, let's go to her then, if we must."

It looked like a long cold wade and then a longer cold swim to a ship that even Thor seemed reluctant to board. But the Midgard serpent had shaken herself free of the Mythworld skidoo. "I'll take you out to her," she said. "Get up on my back."

It wasn't quite as wet as swimming might have been, although stowing all of Thrúd's bundles was less than easy. In some ways Thrúd was a woman after Liz's own heart. She also didn't believe in that silly "traveling light" idea.

When they got closer to the great vessel, Liz realized that it might just be bigger than she'd thought . . . and a lot weirder than the Egyptian banana boat. In the sea-mist it almost seemed to be constructed from tiny scales.

"Okay, what is it made of?" asked Liz, as Jörmungand got closer to the vessel that loomed like some vast cliff over them.

"Nails," said Loki, ghoulishly, plainly relishing telling her. "The nails of the dead."

He was rewarded by suitable shudders from some of Jörmungand's passengers. Liz wasn't going to oblige him. "Lousy building material. What do you do for struts?"

Loki looked darkly at her. "You and Sigyn are two of a kind."

Jörmungand reared up out of the water and deposited them on the deck.

The ship really was at least the size of supertanker. "A lot of nails," said Liz.

"The godar are encouraged to make their people be sure that no man dies with untrimmed nails, as Æsir would have Loki's ship take a long time to finish," said Thrúd.

Liz sniffed. "Smells like old toenails. Maybe washing their feet before they died would have been nice too."

Sigyn gave a snort of laughter at the hastily turned back of Loki. "Now he's gone off to sulk. He's very proud of *Naglfar*."

"She's certainly big enough," admitted Liz.

Sigyn shrugged. "She will ferry the enemies of the Æsir to Ragnarok. So Thor will tell you that she is too big, and I would have her twice the size."

"Well, let's see if we can skip Ragnarok. It does sound as if I could pass on it."

"All that lives will pass, or so it is foretold, either in flood or by fire," said Sigyn, with a hint of sadness.

"A lovely grim prediction," said Liz. "Packs them into the churches, does it?"

Sigyn looked a bit nonplussed.

Liz took pity on her. "Look, back where I come from there are dozens of religions, and preaching that the end of the world is at hand is good business. So far their gods have been a bit of a let-down, because the end keeps being delayed. It's probably because the dead are now working to rule or something."

Sigyn looked at her and shook her head. "Here the end comes. Fimbulwinter has begun. There will be no spring for three years."

"And no hay fever. Look. Things have to change. And if you believe in them, they won't." *Just don't stop believing in this ship of nails until we get to disembark*, she thought to herself.

Sigyn shrugged. "Nothing really changes in the nine worlds. We live in the great cycle of time. And here the dead do not work to rule, they fight to rule."

Jötunheim lies to the north and east of Asgard. Liz thought it was probably a good place for hunting snarks. It was a place—if she remembered her Lewis Carroll correctly—entirely composed of chasms and crags. And even finding that the snark was a boojum was easier than taking another voyage on *Naglfar.* The nails formed a flexible armor, very like fish scales. But unlike fish scales they did not have anything inside them (like a fish, for example) to stop them flexing with each and every wave. Liz was an old sailor. She didn't mind the ship pitching or rolling. But the deck moving in parallel with the waves under her feet was too much! She understood now why Thor and Thrúd had been so unenthusiastic about the corpse-ship. It wasn't squeamishness. It was just a liking for being able to remain standing up.

At least the children had enjoyed it as much as Loki did.

"So where now?" asked Liz, as they sailed into a deep bay that would have made the average Nordic postcard photographer orgasmic and the average sailor very wary. Snowy pines clung to the cliff edges above the midnight blue water. *Naglfar* touched and scraped her way slowly in toward the shore. Liz had yet to work out what moved the great ship. She was a little afraid to ask.

"I must consult my kin," said Loki. "And then we will need to find a messenger to send to the Æsir."

"And we need to set about getting to Marie," said Lamont. "As I explained to you last night, Loki, she's . . . sick."

Loki nodded. "I have thought about what you told me, and I have thought about where you are and her health. I must explain fully what the thorn of sleep does. It may be that Odin has unwittingly blessed you. He may have given you hope."

"Don't play the fool about this, Loki," said Lamont harshly. "We had the best doctors in the U.S. examine her. It's too late. It's gone too far. There is no cure known to man."

"I do not jest." There was none of the usual mockery in Loki's voice. "Odin has not given you healing. He has given one thing that you did not have before, though. And that is time to seek that healing."

"What?" Lamont's head bobbed forward. He stared intently at Loki.

"The thorn of sleep. It is a magical thing. The victim will lie without breath, but without change or death either, until that thorn is pulled out. I do not know this illness that you speak of. But there is much wisdom to be found in the nine worlds. This will give you time to seek it. Were you from the nine worlds your Marie might go to rest with my daughter Hel, if she died.

But from what I can understand, if she dies she will go beyond the reach of men and possibly gods. This way, that won't happen while you search."

Lamont sat down on *Naglfar's* deck with a thump. Looking at him, Liz wanted to start crying herself. Tears were streaming down his face.

Liz bit her lip. It had always seemed that the Mythworlds were places to escape from. Where time rushed past, and death and danger were the best reward. Suddenly she could think of several million people who would settle for as much of a chance as Lamont Jackson had just been handed.

"So who is our hostess?"

"Ran."

"It's an odd name," said Liz.

"I wouldn't let her hear that," said Thrúd, with a wry smile. "She's quicker tempered than Papa-Thor, even if Loki does have her wrapped around his thumb. The mother of the waves is she who normally deals with drownings."

They were inside the cliff dwelling of the giantess Ran, which was where Loki had been heading with *Naglfar.* Liz was engaged in her least favorite pastime. Waiting.

Fair enough, Loki and Sigyn had a lot of organizing to do. And Lamont, having been handed something of a possible lifeline, was trying to work out where he could track down any wisdom that might just help Marie.

Thor was training Emmitt. Jörmungand had gone off on some errand for Loki, and Fenrir had been sent off on a similar mission into the hinterland. The two younger boys were happily engaged in boy-mischief, and Ella was asleep. That left Liz and Thrúd to entertain themselves, as their hostess was off about her watery business.

Thrúd embroidered. It was what a noble Scandinavian lady did. Liz's mother would have approved too, so Liz had carefully avoided learning any of that type of art. Which left talking and being irritated. Liz and Thrúd were swapping stories of very different worlds—with strong similarities in places. Hunting, for one, wasn't that different.

The window—no glass, just a sturdy shutter—was open to provide Thrúd with light and Liz with the fresh air she craved.

But she'd been advised not to go out, alone. This was Jötunheim. Mortals walked here with trepidation.

A raven came to perch on the sill. "So this is where you are." It hopped from one leg to the other looking at them with intelligent dark eyes.

"Close the shutters," said Thrúd urgently.

"Too late," said the bird with a clack of its big beak. "Hugin saw you already. Clever Hugin, even if Munin doesn't think so."

Liz smiled at it innocently. "Want some more meat, bird? I gave you that delicious heart before."

The bird nodded greedily. "More dragon heart?"

"On the table." Liz pointed to the far corner, sitting calmly on her chair.

The raven looked suspiciously from one of them to the other, cocking its black head from side to side. Then it launched into the room—and quick as a flash, Liz swung the shutter closed.

"How do you feel about grilled raven, Thrúd?"

"I prefer them boiled."

"I'll peck your eyes out," said the raven crossly.

"And what good will that do you?" asked Liz. "You'll still be stuck in here. Now where is your other half? What's his name? Moron?"

"Munin," said the raven. "He's around somewhere. Odin gives him all the best tasks to do."

Ah, thought Liz. This was the greedy one who didn't remember too well. "I really do have some food. Not dragon heart, unfortunately. If you were hungry I might give you some."

"I'm always hungry," said the plump raven in a self-pitying tone. "But I don't trust you."

"Oh, come now," said Liz. "What have we actually ever done to you?"

"Threatened to throw sticks and stones at me. Shut me in a dark room. Promised me food you didn't give me."

"Well, you've threatened to peck our eyes out. And we'll let you out now. We just didn't want you to have to share with moron, uh, Munin."

The raven clicked his beak. "Would you believe that he found a stag that got killed by a runaway log-wagon, nice and mature, and he didn't tell me about it. So what food have you got?"

Liz turned to Thrúd. "You packed half a larder. All I have is multiflavored jelly beans. And that could make enemies." She thought of the rakfisk jelly bean experience and felt decidedly unwell.

"What about some smoked salmon?" said Thrúd.

"How do you feel about that, bird?" asked Liz.

"Too salty and not ripe enough," said the raven.

Well, if it wanted ripe ...

The jelly bean had been pink. She dug out the box from her shoulder bag, and found a pink sweet in the new wooden box. She cautiously sniffed it, and then held it out to the raven. "Try that."

Hugin's greed exceeded his common sense by several orders of magnitude. He snapped it in half with his beak—and by the bouquet Liz knew she'd got it right. The other half of the jelly bean fell to the table.

The raven stood stock still, ruffling all its feathers up and closing its eyes. For a moment Liz thought she'd killed him. Then the bird opened his eyes wide and stabbed the remaining half of the jelly bean with such ferocity that he left a quarter inch dent in the table.

Hugin stood there with his raggedy black feathers all fluffed out, with a raven expression of absolute beatification on his ugly beak. He stayed like that for at least three minutes. Then he shook himself back to normal, and eyed Liz and the box with his black eyes full of unalloyed greed. "Would there be any more, O kind and generous and lovely and wonderful lady?"

Liz looked. There were six more pink essence of rakfisk raven's delights. "Some," she said. "Not too many."

"Could I perhaps have another one?"

"Perhaps," said Liz. "Definitely, if you can tell me where someone is and what is being done to him."

"I'm your raven. I can find out anything."

So Liz described Dr. Jerry Lukacs as best as possible.

Hugin nodded. "Odin's got him. He's got plans for him."

"I need to know what they are. Then I definitely have another one of those ... delicacies for you."

"Open the shutter," said Hugin impatiently. "And look after those things until I return. Guard them very carefully."

He flew off, making as much haste as a plump raven could.

"I think we have our spy," said Liz.

Thrúd nodded. "That's powerful magic that. What are those things?"

"Believe it or not, it is a sort of sweetmeat for children. I don't think we know what we're giving them sometimes. I wish I had a few more."

Thrúd looked thoughtful. "Well, let us see if the raven returns. And then we can talk to Ran."

"I'd just like to know what the other raven is up to," said Liz. "I think we'd better go and tell the others about this, eh? Especially Loki and your father."

Loki proved elusive, but they found Thor coming back from the sauna, looking glum.

"I need to get back from giantish parts," he said. "The Jötun are laughing at me for not drinking. And water will kill me soon anyway. I want to die in Bilskríner."

Liz absorbed the fact that he was perfectly serious. Well, Jerry had said as much about water in Myth-Greece. "It's time to introduce you to tisanes. And maybe you need to lift a few boulders in public or do something Thor-like to put off laughter."

"It's in his head," said Thrúd. "The giants are all terrified of him. None of them would dare laugh. If anyone can give up drinking and not be laughed at, it's him. So. Show us these 'tisanes.' If Papa-Thor has to drink them, so will I. Will they protect you from the bloody flux?"

She turned to her father. "You may not realize this, but this woman is a powerful witch. She bespelled one of Odin's ravens."

"Oh? Thought or memory? Hugin or Munin?"

"Hugin."

Thor nodded. "A pity it is isn't Munin. Hugin's prone to forget what he's been sent to do if he spots something tasty and dead."

"I can believe that. He has carrion-crow tastes," said Liz. "Now, to make tisanes I need some herbs. Any chance of such things in your stash, Thrúd?"

They found some mint, and after an expedition, some boiling water, a small pot and some honey. The end result was fragrant, anyway.

Thor sniffed it doubtfully, then tasted it. "It's not exactly Kvasir's mead is it?" He took another cautious sip. "But you can drink it."

"It's a very sophisticated drink," insisted Liz, hoping her amusement didn't show.

"Sophisticated?" Thor looked as if it wasn't a word that had been used in his presence too often.

Liz raised her nostrils at him in the way her pretentious mother cultivated so carefully. "Yes, you know, something that someone of refined culture and intellect would drink. Like you. Chugging ale and mead is all very well for the uncultured ones without any finer feelings. But this takes a true connoisseur."

Thor looked warily at the clay bowl. "Oh."

It was a little later in the day, just before sundown, that Loki accosted her. He had a very angry trussed raven under his arm.

"Liz, I just want to know why Thor is wandering around drinking that vile smelling stuff with a sort of constipated expression and his pinky-finger stuck out straight. He looked at me as if I'd crawled out of a piece of cheese when I asked him about it. He said I had no appreciation of the finer things in life. He said I should ask you about it."

"I would have thought you of all people would have a grasp of the intrinsic philosophical zeitgeist and angst that are symbolized by the delicate nuances in bouquet."

Loki grinned crookedly. "Don't let Sigi hear that rubbish or she'll have me drinking it too."

Liz grinned back. It was hard not to like Loki. "It was just a joke. But Thor took it seriously, and to be honest I think that it gives him an excuse to refuse drinks. I told him that alcohol dulls the palate. And it makes him feel good to think he's got such refined tastes. Play along, will you?"

Loki's shoulders shook. "Oh, certainly. But you do realize that Thor is still the greatest warrior of the Æsir? And that many fighters still look to him as a role model?"

Liz smiled. "Culture and an appreciation of the finer things didn't exactly blunt the edge of the samurai. We'll have to introduce him to a tea ceremony next. Now what are you doing with that raven?"

"It's one of Helblindi's accursed spies," said Loki cheerfully. "I was thinking of baking it in a pie and sending it back to him."

"Um. Which of the two is it? Hugin or Munin?" said Liz.

"Hugin, I think. All ravens look alike to me. It thought it was faster than Loki the wild cat."

"Can we find out which one it is? I reached an agreement with

Hugin. He was going to find out where Jerry was and what Odin was doing with him."

"Ah," said Loki. "Let's untie the beak, then."

"This is going to cost you at least two of those magic beans!" said Hugin, crossly.

"I'm sorry. It was a mistake," apologized Liz.

Loki eyed her. "You speak raven. A woman of many hidden talents."

"And some of them even useful," said Liz dryly. Loki brought out the sarcasm in her. "You better untie him, Loki. If he has news, that is?"

Hugin looked affronted. "Of course!"

"Oh?" said Liz.

"Odin's decided that he'll use him in his quest for wisdom. He said he was damned if he would hang on the tree again or part with his remaining eye. Now where is my reward?"

"He's going to *hang* Jerry?"

Loki nodded.

"We need to get moving then," said Liz. "Or at least I do. A dead boyfriend is no earthly use to me. I'm not into necrophilia."

Loki held up a calming hand. "You're not the only one with spies, you know. Although," he said, looking at the ecstatically shivering Hugin. "Mine does it for a love of gossip not for some kind of perverse gastronomic reason. In one way we are too late."

"What!"

"Jerry already hangs from the world tree like rotting fruit." Before Liz could fall over, Loki put an arm around her. "But he will survive. Odin did, and Ratatosk has seen to it that your Jerry will."

"Ratatosk?" said Liz weakly.

"Drill-tooth. The squirrel who lives on the world tree carrying happy little spite-messages between the eagle that lives at the top of the tree and the Nídhögg serpent that gnaws at the bottom of the tree. A friend of mine."

"This is a crazy screwed up universe," said Liz, shaking her head. "Humans die if they get hanged, Loki. We're not built the same as you."

chapter 25

On a limb of the great tree, an ash tree so large that its branches split the sky and its roots went down into the very bones of the earth, Jerry Lukacs was learning how you kept someone in suspense. The spear-wound in his side didn't help either. Hanging by his hands on a rope over nothingness, Jerry wondered if it was going to be his nerve or his arms that gave way first.

And now here was a squirrel climbing down his rope. It had unpleasantly big orange-yellow front teeth. A detached part of his mind said that there was something terribly undignified about having your throat torn out by a rabid squirrel. Another part of his mind said that worrying about dignity when you were about die was just incredibly dumb. But it was so surreal that it cut through the panic. Maybe he was already dead. The events of the last twenty-four hours gave him a sort of detachment about it all.

The squirrel seemed very amused by his predicament.

"Let your feet down," it said.

Very cautiously Jerry did as he was told. If he was already hearing squirrels talk it was probably too late to clutch at the rope around his neck. His hands and forearms couldn't have lasted much longer, anyway. They ached.

Feeling something to stand on under his feet made him feel

really, really stupid. And so incredibly light and relieved that he felt as if he could float cheerfully up into the cold blue sky.

"I suggest you adopt the attitude of the corpses around you."

"Attitude?" Their attitude seemed to be . . . dead. Maybe the squirrel meant laid-back? Dead-pan?

"Position. You are being watched," explained the squirrel.

Jerry hung his head. It was a lot better than having his body hung. Ever since he'd been marched out onto a branch that led out over the cliff-edge, and was wide enough for three to walk abreast, he'd known that he was going to die. There were too many other decaying remains hanging there for him to reach any other conclusion. Why they had dressed him in a wide hat and blue cloak was another matter. They'd put the rope around his neck, and then Odin himself had come forward and sliced the ropes that bound his hands. Jerry's first instinct had been to grab the rope around his neck . . . which had been exactly what Odin had planned. A sharp jab with that spear, and Jerry had fallen into space, clinging frantically to the rope.

A great laugh for the Æsir, no doubt. It had been a slight pay-back to see a large snake drop onto the branch and send them scurrying back to the cliff. It would have been more satisfying if the snake had eaten them.

But what it had actually done was far more satisfying and more terrifying. Jerry finally had the courage to look down. He was standing on the snake's broad back. It was stretched between the branches. He only curbed his normal reaction just in time, or he would have been hanging . . . by the neck.

The squirrel on his chest chuckled nastily. "Góin likes you standing on her back as much as you like standing on it."

"Tell her I am intensely grateful, and I apologize profusely," said Jerry. This was not the time to let ophidiophobia get the better of him.

"Tell Loki. You're going to have hold on again later, when the snakes change shifts."

"Shifts . . . How long do I have to stay here?"

The squirrel switched its tail. "Nine days."

Jerry took a deep breath. "I might as well jump. I don't think I'll manage nine hours."

"Hmm," said the squirrel. "And if I got you a little extra rope and you actually stood on the branch? We could probably get away with that. They can't see that well. They must be oh, twenty-thirty leaps away. And there is a shred or two of fog blowing. Odin cheated a lot. I saw him."

"I . . . I think I could manage to stand for a while on the tree-branch. I'm not sure about nine days. That's a long time without food or water, even if I could stand still long enough. I'm sorry to be so difficult." Jerry felt foolish to be apologizing, and still incredibly glad to be alive.

The squirrel shrugged. "Well, there is some joy in putting one over the Æsir. The problem is thus. There are two branches accessible from the cliff. Both are guarded, night and day. They put the ropes on the upper one, and bring the sacrifices along the lower one. I can run up the trunk, the snakes can wind their way up it, and the great stags can leap between branches. But even if they would carry you, the stags are loyal to Odin. So there is something of a problem in getting you away from here. And before you ask, a fair number of those sacrifice-hanging ropes are rotten. A couple of them broke under my weight."

Jerry hadn't even thought that far. A drift of cloud was blowing cold and damp around them. "Can we try moving onto the branch, and talk about it from there?"

"Surely. I think Góin would appreciate that," said the squirrel.

The huge snake—which made a python look like blindworm—arched its back, lifting him. "Put your legs on either side of her body," said the squirrel. "You humans have absolutely no sense of balance."

So Jerry knelt and then put his legs around the snake, and shimmied his way the few yards to the huge branch. He wouldn't have said no to guardrails, but compared to where he had been, the branch seemed as wide as a six-lane highway. And even if it meant certain death, he wasn't going to endure that thing around his neck one instant longer. He slipped the noose free, and stood with it in his hand.

"Slip it down the front of your shirt and tie it around your waist," said the squirrel. "That's what Odin did. Not with the noose though. Even without a noose I think it will cut you in half after a while."

Jerry was willing to bet that it would do a person damage a lot faster than it would cut them in half, but it had to be more pleasant—and more secure—than a noose around his neck. With painful fingers he set about unknotting the noose that had nearly killed him. There was enough rope to do as the squirrel had suggested. And actually, once he had it snugged around his waist, tight, but not going to tighten any more, it did make him feel a lot more secure. Even if he did fall, the worst that could happen was a three-yard swing—on a rope that he'd proved could hold him.

There was a knot, he noticed now, just above his head. That was how come he'd managed to hold so long. Doubtless it was there for just that reason—to prolong the agony, and let the victim cling to life for a few extra minutes. Jerry stood there absorbing the situation for a while as the cloud broke, letting him look onto a vista of distant branches and still more distant nothingness. He took a deep breath, relishing being able to do so. "Maybe," he said to the squirrel on the branch in front of him, "you'd like to tell me who you are, and just what is going on. I owe you my life. And I gather that Loki is involved."

The squirrel snickered. "Loki is involved in most things, especially mischief, which is why I like him. I am Ratatosk, the drill-tooth, he who carries vicious words of hate between the eagle at the top of Yggdrasil and the serpent Nídhögg in Niflheim. It's a job. And it stops them eating me, which is quite useful as both serpents and eagles like squirrel meat."

He looked at Jerry and narrowed his eyes. "Don't get any ideas. I bite. And I have friends."

"I wouldn't dream of it." Jerry felt the rope-abrasions on his neck. "But what exactly am I doing here?"

"Looking stupid at the moment. By the way you've been dressed, I think you're a stand-in for Odin. I reckon that he intends some quick change of roles, and to drop your body into the void of Ginnungagap. He will emerge as having been a sacrifice to himself, stabbed with his spear, and now with the wisdom of the dead and having lifted the hidden runes."

"Lifted?"

"I think it is a kenning for stolen. Odin's favorite pastime besides seducing maidens. I could like him if he was less self-important. Or if he hadn't tried to catch and eat me."

"I'm making a mental note not to do that," said Jerry. "But is there really no way out of here? I mean if I am still here after nine days, I think our one-eyed friend will just pitch me into the void anyway."

"Beat him at his own game. Odin's a shape-shifter, if he wants to be. He'll come along in disguise just after lunch, I'd guess, and wait for some cloud to come along to toss you over the edge. Then he'll return heroically. But he's expecting a body. You could toss him over the edge instead. That would be fun."

"And very unlikely. If I recall right he has a spear that doesn't miss. I'll have been here for nine days without food or water and my only weapon will be sore feet."

"Gungnir the spear is a problem," admitted Ratatosk. "Oh, well. Beat him to the punch. Come walking down at dawn on the ninth day. You might even get away, pretending to be him."

It was an attractive idea, even if it did mean spending nine days standing on a tree branch, pretending to hang. "It's not going to work," said Jerry regretfully. "I'll be too far gone with thirst, even if I manage the starvation side. I haven't got a supply of food or water." He patted his pockets . . . and felt half an apple. "Except this."

Ratatosk chittered his teeth. "That'll help for the wound in your side anyway. And I can fetch you food and water. And even some extra clothes because it is cold here in branches with Fimbulwinter coming on. Count yourself lucky. The mist will let you sit down most of the time."

Jerry, knowing he had eight and half more days, ate a small sliver of apple. It had a invigorating and rejuvenating effect on him. Not perhaps as much as if he'd eaten the whole thing, but enough to ease the pain of the spear stab and make the prospect of a nine day vigil with nothing but a malicious-tongued squirrel for company seem survivable. "Hey. We have to try," he said. "Maybe you can teach me these runes. I know a few."

"Maybe. And maybe I can be off about my business," said Ratatosk. "Things to do, creatures to insult. The trouble is Nídhögg and the eagle are both lamebrains. I have to strain my intellect to add a bit of spice and malice to the messages, or they'd both have got bored years ago and eaten me. I'll strip some corpses for warm gear for you."

It wasn't quite what Jerry would have chosen as a wardrobe, but the present owners didn't really have much use for them. And even with the hat and cloak and Skadi's slightly too large boots it was going to be very cold on this branch. Cold and a long time in which to do nothing, without any reading matter. No wonder Odin had stolen runes and talked to the hanged corpses.

It would give him some time to do some thinking, he supposed. Thinking of just what the hell Liz had been up to in Odin's feasting-hall for starters. There was nothing formal between them . . . really. Had she perhaps slipped into the spell of this place and its role-play and beliefs? Jerry desperately wanted to believe that she had some reason for passionately kissing a Norse god with gold teeth and a big horn, besides the obvious.

The other thing he could think about was how they could get home. That was possibly even harder to unravel, but it didn't occupy as much of his mind—proving, against all probabilities, that academics can be human too.

"Word for you on that lover of yours from Ratatosk via Nídhögg," said Loki.

Liz turned eagerly. Loki held up a calming hand. "He's in one piece. But reaching him, now, would be nearly impossible. He's going to try to escape at the end of the nine days. Nothing much we can do for him now. However, if your raven informant is right . . . when Odin ventures on Mirmir's well, we'll have him."

Loki made a face. "You do realize that this means that Odin is unlikely to trade your man for any treasure? We'll have to seize him from them. It does leave us with a useful horn."

Liz sighed. "So where is this well?"

"It is at the root of Yggdrasil that spreads itself deep into the lands of the frost giants. We can travel there at will, whereas the place where your Jerry is now is not one that we could reach. Odin will travel with some force, but we will be there before him."

"Just so long as Jerry doesn't find himself as the meat in the sandwich."

"What is a sandwich?" asked Loki.

CHAPTER 26

⊘⊘⊘⊘⊘⊘

The first night on the branch had been the worst night of Jerry's experience. The early hours were just terrifying, with only the sounds of the relentless wind and the moving branches—and things that passed in the night. Something jumped right over him, touching the rope and nearly plucking him into space.

After that it grew quieter and colder. Even with fur over-trousers and a knitted jerkin-type thing that might have been designed for Icelandic fishermen, Jerry was cold. Long before morning he'd untied the rope and huddled into a tight little shivering ball under the blue cloak, in the middle of the branch. The cloak was fortunately a thick weave, oiled and pretty windproof, or he would have died of exposure before dawn. He even resorted to scratching the rune that he was fairly sure was Loki's name on the bark.

Maybe that, or the wind dying down kept him alive. The sky was beginning to pale when he thought of the apple in his pocket. Heaven knew he didn't feel much like eating, but it might just help.

A tiny piece was all he could manage to bite. It might be little furry from his pocket, but it had kept very well. And it did have miraculous properties, warming him like a shot of over-proof whiskey. Warmed him enough to be standing and tied back on to his rope when he spied a couple of cold-looking warriors on the cliff-edge perhaps a hundred and thirty yards away peering at him.

He stood still, except for the shivering—but they probably wouldn't see that from so far off. Eight more days and nights of this?

Ratatosk arrived just after sunup. He spat out a cheekfull of nuts. He also had a tiny skin flask, perhaps a quarter of a pint, slung on a red cord over his shoulder. Maybe for a squirrel it was a feast. But oh for an extra-large jelly donut . . . make that three, and a tall coffee.

"Brisk this morning, isn't it?" said the squirrel rubbing his paws together. "You can eat. The guards have gone back into the little hut at the end of the branch."

"It's very generous of you," said Jerry, looking at the four nuts.

"You're telling me," said Ratatosk. "That's part of my winter store. And in this weather all I want to do is go back to sleep in my hole. It's nice and warm and out of the wind. Cozy."

Jerry realized that the little tree rat was doing it on purpose. "Save it for the eagle and the Nídhögg. I'm half-frozen. I don't know if I can take another night like that."

"Soft," scoffed Ratatosk. "You'll need to toughen up because it looks like we're going to get some sleet." He held out the little flask. "This is water from Urd's well, by the way." He sniggered. "Nídhögg decided Asgard was too busy right now to worry about the Norns. He nearly got one too. They've run off to Mirmir's well. Now. I have to go off and tell the eagle that Nídhögg saw him on high, but he thought he was a runty sparrow. Want anything else?"

A fire, shelter, and the hell out of here, thought Jerry, but what he said was, "More food and drink, I'm afraid. And maybe some more clothes. I was desperately cold last night."

Ratatosk twitched his nose. "There is a knothole a bit further up the branch. The stags go to drink there at night. I'll see what I can do about the rest."

Jerry realized that he'd been there a good twenty hours but had spent most of his time peering toward the cliff, or shivering under the cloak. He'd very carefully not looked down, and he also hadn't looked up or out much.

About fifty yards farther out the great branch divided. A limb went upward and there was a V he could probably shelter in. And out on the outer branches was a great big stag, grazing. So that was what had nearly sent him over the edge last night. Yggdrasil, as he vaguely remembered, had had a good few of them. The tree looked big enough for a whole herd. Well, he'd sworn off squirrel but venison was sounding good, even raw, if not as appealing as a peanut butter and jelly sandwich. Of course, the fact that the stags were not small and he was unarmed, and, unlike Liz, totally inexperienced at any form of hunting, did make the chances of venison nearly as remote as the peanut-butter sandwich.

When a squall of mixed sleet and rain came along, as Ratatosk had predicted, Jerry untied himself and retreated to the V. There was a deeper groove there than he'd realized, and it was virtually out of the wind. Though he hadn't meant to, he fell asleep. He was awakened by the squirrel tweaking his nose and shaking droplets off his damp fur onto his face. "Move. The rain is nearly over."

So Jerry moved, sleepily, and then woke very, very suddenly when he lost his footing on the wet bark and nearly disappeared over the edge. His heart was still doing about four hundred beats to the minute when he reached the rope, tied himself on, and prepared to act dead again. He even had a chance to take a handful of sleet to suck before anyone came along the cliff edge.

There turned out to be one fortunate aspect to the situation. The cliff, which to Jerry's non-outdoorsman eyes looked slightly higher than Everest, obviously caused a lot of updraft. That, in turn, made the tree-branch a place that was intermittently bathed in misty cloud as the air cooled and the water vapor condensed out of it. That meant he could at least sit for a while, hidden.

He had a long day to think about the night ahead, which, in the fashion of events that you are dreading, turned out to be not as bad as he'd expected. When dusk came on he untied and headed first for the huge knothole where he had seen the stag go to drink. He had another half rotten cloak that Ratatosk had brought him, and he was determined to make the lair as comfortable as possible and sleep as much as he could before the cold really set in. He'd just organized his nest when something eclipsed both the dark tree branches and the stars. Jerry had barely time to shriek before the creature landed, and pushed him back into the V.

"Noisy Midgarder. It's going to freeze hard tonight. I was asked to keep you warm."

Under the huge eagle's downy belly, Jerry slept well for the first time in what felt like weeks but was probably merely days. And one of the snakes brought him a bird's egg for breakfast. He would have preferred them cooked, but he just had to switch his mind off and swallow. Pretend it was an eggnog or something.

Only a week to go.

That was a bit much to swallow. Harder than raw egg. Jerry found he coped better by just concentrating on getting through one day at a time.

But he looked forward to Ratatosk's malicious gossip. He'd memorized the runes by now, and he could see the possibilities of using them with sympathetic magic. However, trying it out on flight seemed a little too brave, especially as it would require some powerful symbols like eagle primaries. He wasn't asking his duvet for that! Not after he'd seen its beak. Besides, he had a feeling that flying might be a lot more complex than it looked.

The Krim device had very precise datums on all the sources of life energy inside the Ur-universe. Translating them into physical map-points was more complex as the Ur-universes had their own rules of physics and geography, into which logic did not always enter in the most obvious of fashions. But it was very apparent that one of the life-energy sources, one of the ones the masters had had conflict with in the past, which it had, with mechanical satisfaction seen consigned to sacrifice . . . wasn't dead yet. It seemed to have proved remarkably adept at being hanged without being dead.

The Krim device had reached the stage of being willing to kill the life-source without a shred of the Ur-tradition—a dangerous thing.

Unfortunately, Odin was resisting. Actually, he was giving orders. That was confusing to the machine-mind. It had been built to serve the Krim. Service was its purpose. But was this Odin becoming Krim? Willful and foolish, yes. But so were the Krim.

Wisdom in the world of Scandinavian mythology was not something that was kept conveniently in the Library of Congress, Lamont was discovering, with his new Norse reading assistant, Jörmungand, and Ran's large collection of water-stained manuscripts.

Or from an on-line encyclopedia.

It had to be gleaned in some very bizarre and unpleasant places. Lamont Jackson wasn't going to shy away from that. But it did seem that Odin was the repository of a lot of it, which was more than a bit awkward, as he wasn't likely to be cooperative.

From what Lamont could gather, Jerry was hanging out where Odin was supposed to have acquired a lot of it. Then there was Kvasir's mead of inspiration, fermented from Kvasir's blood mixed with honey, which Odin was supposed to have stolen by drilling a hole in the mountainside and seducing the giantess guard. And the water from Mirmir well, the price of which had been his eye. Wisdom appeared to be something you drank around here. Lamont had known a few folks who'd tried that method, like Emmitt's mother.

Thor . . . The big guy was a few sandwiches short of a lunch-pack, but he was flinging heart and soul into "training" Emmitt. It might just be the making of both of them. Lamont had to smile about Liz's addendum to the way of the warrior. Her actual knowledge of Japanese culture was probably contained in two words—"sushi" and "sayonara"—and her tea ceremony was *two sugars, thanks.* But she was working on Thor and the art of ikabena, as well as tisanes from elderflower, rosehip and raspberry leaf.

Liz found that getting daily reports that Jerry was alive helped. Not enough, but they helped. Her coping mechanism was to get busy. Very busy. And of course to mislead Thor a bit on culture, refinement and good taste. It was for his own good, really, besides being fun. She was fairly sure that she was driving all of them mad, but that was just the way it had to be.

They were gods. They held out for two days, before Loki turned and yelled at Thor. "Go and look for that hammer—and take her with you!"

Thor rubbed his hands together awkwardly. "I don't remember too clearly where I last had it."

Loki looked at him coldly. "I'm preparing the greatest war. You may even be my enemy. But if you ever were my friend, take this woman and make her run across all the hills and valleys of Midgard and Utgard, from the wet gravel plains of Aurvangar to Niflheim. Maybe you will find Mjöllnir. Maybe you won't. And maybe I won't ask Ran to take her into an embrace."

"She's anxious to do some explaining. And worried about him. He's quite frail," said Thrúd defensively. She and Liz had, perforce, done a fair amount of talking.

"Ratatosk says he is as tough as old dragon-leather," said Loki tersely. "Go along with your papa. Just keep away from too many handsome young Jötun along the way. I don't have time to come and get you out of trouble too."

Thor had walked off by this time, his brow knitted, obviously deep in thought about when last he'd had his hammer. Thrúd rounded on Loki. "You make more fuss about me than my father. It's not as if you were a saint, Uncle Fox," she said crossly. "I heard the Lokasenna flyting. Just back off. It's bad enough living with one father."

Loki cleared his throat awkwardly. "If you know the flyting from the Lokasenna, you know that what I said was true."

"Yes," said Thrúd. "Parts of it I know were true."

"True about your mother too," said Loki, his voice quiet.

"I can believe that, now," said Thrúd sourly. "I saw what I saw in Valhöll."

Loki cleared his throat again. "I am sorry I treat you as if you were my child, but you see, I never was too sure—when you were little—if you were my daughter or not. It became pretty obvious that you were Thor's child by the time you were a toddler. No one else's child could possibly break so much. But I'd gotten used to looking out for you by then. And I'd gotten to like . . . and respect your father. Far more than your mother, to be unusually honest. So, looking after you is a habit by now, and very hard to break." He grinned at her. "Besides, you were as lovely a little girl as you are an annoying young woman. But I still love you."

Thrúd blinked. "I love you too, Uncle Fox. But I'm grown up now. I can look after myself."

"It's a matter of opinion," said Loki, raising an eyebrow.

"Coming from you, who never thinks of consequences until it's too late, that's a bit rich."

Loki chuckled. "I'm an experienced expert on bad decisions. Besides, I always was better at looking after others than myself."

Thor still had no idea exactly where or to whom he had sold his hammer. It had been in an alehouse somewhere . . . that had burned down. At least he was sure that it had burned down. Almost sure anyway. He did remember an alehouse burning down, but was less sure if it had happened around the time he'd sold the hammer.

It was probably in Midgard. Possibly. Anyhow ... the taciturn giantess Ran had given him a chest full of sea-jewels to redeem it with. Now all he had to do was to find it.

"You might have lost it in Midgard," said Thrúd practically, "but something of that value would end up in Jötunheim or among the dwarves. What would a Midgarder do with it?"

"Use it in a smithy and break the anvil," said Thor thoughtfully. "Loki would have got wind of it if were in Jötunheim. He might not tell us that, of course."

"Right," said Liz. "Let's go and visit some dwarves, then."

CHAPTER 27

⊚⊚⊚⊚⊚

"I mean, take that Gylfaginning—the beguiling of Gylfi," said Fenrir sagely. "It's never really clear just who is beguiling who. The word-smithing in that question and answer structure is confusing with all of the protagonists in the tale being kennings for Odin."

Jörmungand rolled her eyes. "Oh please, Brother! That's the entire point. The author was just trying to be clever."

Liz found it something of a revelation about Loki, that his wolf-ish son and dragon daughter could and did argue interminably about Norse literature. It had been Loki who had insisted that they should learn to read, Liz discovered. Of course his tastes were antediluvian, and he was wrong about this, that and the next, but it was Loki who shaped them away from being mere creatures of the stomach like Bitar and Smitar.

That would have been easier to deal with than the constant bickering about literary merit sometimes, though. At least Bitar and Smitar agreed about food occasionally.

Still, listening on the sidelines while they traveled across this broad braided flood plain had taught Liz something about the dwarves they were heading for. They were maggots who had feasted on the flesh of the dead Ymir (whoever he was) but had acquired consciousness, and the appearance of men. They were artificers of precious metals and gems. The Norse didn't seem to have any objection to creatures that had, as far as Liz could see, the same origins as politicians and certain members of the legal fraternity. Jerry would have stretched that to bank managers as well. The thought of him made Liz's eyes prick with tears, to the extent that she nearly fell off her horse when it stopped, because the others had stopped.

They'd come to a long, low bluff that ran along the edge of the wash of gravel. It was pockmarked with caves, or, as Liz suspected, delvings. Nothing came out of the first few that Thor bellowed into. But, after trying a fair number, they got a grumpy, "What is it this time?"

A short, stocky man peered out of a cave-mouth. His face was so sooty that it was nearly as black as his hair.

"Are you the sons of Ivaldi?" asked Thor.

Dirty face nodded. "One of them, yes. What do you want?"

Fenrir leapt, knocked the son of Ivaldi down, and put his jaws around the dirty neck. The huge wolf's growl was low-pitched and menacing enough to make Liz's ears buzz.

"Fenrir!" yelled Liz. "What are you doing?"

"The chain that bound him was made by the sons of Ivaldi," said Jörmungand. "Brother is known to carry a grudge. I think that he's about to eat a dwarf smith. I think he should wash its hands first. You should always wash hands before eating."

"It wasn't me!" squeaked the dwarf. "That was Dwalin."

"And who might you be?" asked Jörmungand grimly.

"Sindri."

"Ah. Loki has some words to say to you."

"Look. It was a long time ago. And it was a fair wager."

"It was," rumbled Thor. "One of Loki's more impulsive and stupider ones, and he got out of paying it. And Fenrir, it wasn't this one that made the chain Gleipnir. Let him up. I want to ask if he has seen Mjöllnir, the hammer he made for me."

Reluctantly, Fenrir let go, and stepped off the dwarf's back. "I'll go and sniff in these holes for this Dwalin. I've got the scent of you sons of Ivaldi now."

"Dwalin guards his mine with magic," said the dwarf, rubbing his neck. "Anyway, he was just the craftsman doing the job he was hired to do. We didn't know what would get done with it."

"You find the hole. I'll fill it with venom," said Jörmungand. "Even the maker must realize that there is price to be paid."

"And I still want to know if you've seen Mjöllnir," said Thor.

The dwarf shook his head. "It may have lost much of its virtue anyway in the time of fading, or you would be able to call it to you. But it does not lie among the dwarves. Someone would have told me if my workmanship had showed up."

Thor sighed. "We'll just have to try elsewhere. You dwarves always seemed the most likely people to buy it. Well, we'd better move out."

"What about them?" The dwarf pointed to Jörmungand and Fenrir, now checking out the next cave.

"Their business," said Thor, with a shrug.

"But . . . but . . . we thought they were your mortal enemies?" said the dwarf, betraying that he knew more about what was being done with their products in the wider Mythworld than he'd been prepared to acknowledge.

"We became drinking buddies and sorted out our differences. During the fading. And Fenrir was tricked with Gleipnir. He feels that it was no part of the dwarves' affairs to help to trap him."

"It was a business transaction," protested Sindri.

"Who paid for it? We thought you did it out of respect for the Æsir," said Thrúd.

"Well, yes. We wouldn't have done it without respect. But business is business, you know. Dwalin is not a bad fellow. Besides, he owes me. If he gets killed he can hardly pay me back, can he?"

"So who paid for it, then?" demanded Fenrir, pausing in his sniffing.

"Odin. Like the spear and the boar and the hammer. All the treasures except for Sif's hair. Loki paid for that."

Liz held up a hand. "Wait a minute. What hammer? Do I get this right? You made this hammer Thor's looking for?"

"Yes. One of my best bits of work," said the dwarf, proudly, "even if it was a bit short in the handle."

"How much for another one?" said Liz. "Just like the other one, but with the right length handle."

"Um. Well the price would have to include leaving Dwalin alive. "

"I think we would look for a suitable discount for that. And some blood-price, from this Dwalin. Fenrir could use a suitable collar. A protective one," said Thor.

Jörmungand looked at the dwarf with a thoughtful eye. "Jewelry, or perhaps some fashion accessories," suggested Liz.

෨   ෨   ෨

By the time they got back with a new hammer, a collar of protection against spears and arrows (with warranty) and a sea-jewel necklet that Liz badly envied, but in several sizes smaller, Loki was champing at the bit.

Fenrir was dispatched to Utgardaloki, and Jörmungand to the hag of Jarnvid. And the rest set off for the well of Mirmir.

CHAPTER 28

⊚⊚⊚⊚⊚⊚

It was a good thing that Jerry had made day-counting marks on the bark, because by now he really couldn't have told anyone, let alone himself, what day of the week it was. But on the appointed day, good and early, with the now severed noose around his neck like a necktie, Jerry swayed his way down the branch to the guard-house on the cliff edge. The last scraps of Idun's apple had either lost their charm or had run out of material to work on. The world was a vague place from which Jerry was going to tolerate no back-chat. The guards saluted respectfully. They even helped him up onto a horse.

If only he'd learned to ride one of the damned things. It was a long way down the mountain and to the gates of Asgard. He better stay on the horse until he was out of sight of the guards.

It was very awkward that two of them had respectfully accompanied him.

The next thing Jerry knew was that he was looking up at Odin's face. The one-eyed god looked down sardonically. "You have enhanced my reputation for magic, sorcerer. And I daresay I will live down your equestrian skills. You really are a bit too powerful, just as the Krim device implied. Maybe I need to give Mirmir two eyes and not just one, for his wisdom."

He motioned to a thrall-woman. "Feed him. Then get Thjalfi to load him into the cart. We've a long journey ahead of us."

Jerry was tied up again. But the thrall-woman was very good and patient at spoon-feeding him. And the gruel probably was the right thing for him to eat after his diet of very few nuts, raw egg and a solitary half-apple.

Coming down the slope into the shadow of the great root you could see Mirmir's well clearly. It wasn't, as Liz had expected, a well in the conventional sense at all, complete with a little stone wall and a bucket. It was a natural "eye," a spring etched into the limestone. The green-looking water seethed and stirred and a thin haze of steam rose off the surface. Reeds grew on one edge, and a small lip overhung the other. Three little black figures stood at the edge of the lip.

"What in Hel's name are you Norns doing here?" demanded Loki of the three hooded women.

"We go where the fates dictate," croaked the bent one.

"We go where we must for the deeds of now," said the middle one, in the voice of a mature woman.

"Will dictate the future," finished the third, in a teen voice.

"Oh, Niflheim," said Loki. "You have your own well! This isn't Urd's well at the root of the world-tree in Asgard, where you three dictate the fates of mankind and the gods. Go home."

"We can't," said the three in chorus. "Nídhögg has driven us out."

"I'll have words with him," said Loki crossly. "Now, where is Mirmir?"

"He didn't like what the future held for him," said the youngest Norn.

"So he left," said the oldest.

"And we have been waiting for you, here," added the middle Norn. "You're late."

"As usual," said the youngest.

Loki ground his teeth. "I don't suppose you can be persuaded to leave, and send Mirmir back?"

"It would be of no use," said the oldest Norn. "Munin carried word to Odin. He knows we guard Mirmir's well now."

"But we will leave," said the middle Norn. "We will even leave you with the horn to draw water from the holy well."

"Is that a prophecy or an offer to negotiate?" asked Loki.

"Both," announced the eldest Norn. "We have foreseen it."

"Have you foreseen that if you're not out of here by the time

I count to ten," Liz said, through gritted teeth, "that I am going to use this blunt instrument." She swung her shoulder bag.

Loki gaped at her. "They're the Norns, Liz. The fates. Urd, Verdani, and Skuld. You can't threaten them."

Liz took a firm grip on the strap of her bag. "Watch me. I'm no believer in predestination, but if they are, they know what's coming. One."

"Which is why we have agreed to go," said the youngest Norn. "Provided Loki takes us back."

"Because our powers tell us that Nídhögg will listen to him, and him alone," said the middle one.

Loki sighed. "Do you think you can manage without me? It won't be quite so easy. Mirmir could have persuaded Odin to part with Jerry. Now it'll have to be force."

"Odin comes with a thousand Einherjar as an escort," said the youngest fate, linking arms with Loki. "Besides, Odin would know another power was close." She pointed a long forefinger at Liz. "We could have told you how they would have done it, but now these strangers must contrive on their own."

Liz took a long, hard look at the youngest fate. "Sigyn, I think you'd better go along too. We'll manage. And I can tell that one's future without being a prophetess. She's trouble."

"So what are we going to do?" asked Lamont, after the Norns left.

Liz shrugged. "A thousand of those types I met in that gin-palace-stag-party would be a bit much to handle, head on. So. Odin expects these chicks in hoods and drape-in-the-soup-sleeved outfits. We're going to oblige him. He was expecting them to demand an eye, and was planning to give them one of Jerry's. Let's push the boat out. We'll demand a sacrifice. These guys will drink mead made of someone's blood from what you were telling me. It's obviously lurking in their culture. So: we insist on Jerry being thrown into the well. It's more like a cenote than a well—there is a nice big lip and the water is pretty dark. I'll be waiting in the well, with one of those hollow reeds as a snorkel. We'll claim Jerry, give Odin his water, and let him go."

"It could be a good plan, except for a couple of details," said Lamont.

"Oh? Like what?"

"Like the outfits."

Liz started to swear, bit it off, suddenly realizing the age of her audience. "Sort out the reeds. We'll need at least two. I'll go after them."

She set off at a rapid pace after Loki and Sigyn and the three Norns. She found them a few hundred yards down the trail, with the Norns coming out from behind a large rock, dressed in more typical Norse-Mythworld women's clothing, each with their hooded garments in their hands. Now that you could see them, Urd was revealed to be a tiny wrinkled crone, Verdani a woman with experience-lines around her fine eyes. And Skuld was jailbait. Pouting jailbait. They held out their hooded clothes.

Liz was startled into pausing. "How did you know . . . ?"

"We know," said Skuld loftily. Somehow she managed to look down her nose at Liz, which was quite a feat, because she was tiny.

Liz took a deep breath. "All right. Different rules for different places. I don't suppose you'd like to tell me what is going to happen?"

"No," said Urd. She prodded Loki with her stick. "Let's go, Son of Laufey."

Loki held up his hands and shrugged. "They never tell you anything unless it is to make your life a misery, anyway, Liz."

"Get on with you, Son of Laufey," said Verdani. "The one-eyed wanderer comes into my provence."

"We'd better move then, Liz. Odin is nearly here. You'd better get back."

So Liz hastened back to the rest of the party, inspecting the hooded outfits as she jogged, and realizing that she had a problem.

The Norns were small. There was no way that most adults would fit in those outfits. Thrúd, or her . . . or Lamont wasn't going to get into them with a shoehorn. Thor was not either, not even if they sewed all three outfits together. Besides the Norns had said something about Odin detecting another power—and Thor and Thrúd were powers, too. They'd better back off.

She arrived back at the waiting group next to the well.

"Where is Verdani's provence?" she panted.

"The present," said Thrúd.

"Ah," said Liz, as the situation became clearer to her. "Look,

Odin must nearly be here. And we have a problem. These outfits are way too small for any of the adults. Or even for Emmitt."

"I'll do it," said Ella. She pointed to Ty and Tolly, involved in one of their games that involved a lot of giggling and dodging. "You two! Dress! It's time you did something useful."

"But . . ." said Lamont.

"Somebody has to do it, Daddy," said Ella. Now that she had communication, real or imagined, with her twin, and some shred of hope for her mother, the girl was beginning to come out of the shell that she'd constructed for herself. She'd taken to following Thrúd around. Her announcement had had an effect, not, by the look on Lamont Jackson's face, one he was altogether pleased with. Besides, Liz remembered, Marie had said that both girls flew at anything that vaguely smacked of acting.

"We'll be in the water, Lamont. Right next to them."

"Me too," said Thor.

Liz shook her head. "Kids, scramble into these." She held out the clothes. "Thor, the Norns said that Odin would know if Loki was here. I think the same probably applies to you. And to Thrúd. So I'll need you to back off, with Emmitt. Up there somewhere? If we have trouble . . . well, you could throw a thunderbolt or two. Give us a chance to try to get the kids out."

Thor folded his arms. "I do not flee from a fight."

"Thor, we don't want this to be a fight! That's the whole point. Please?"

"It's the right thing, Papa," said Thrúd. "And I can hear the sound of hooves."

Reluctantly, Thor unbuckled his belt of strength and handed it to Lamont. "Take this. A mortal cannot long survive in a fight with the Ás, but it may give you the strength you need to flee Odin with the children."

Lamont put around his waist. "I'm honored, Thor."

"And I wish it was me," said Emmitt.

"One day," said Thor, putting a hand on the boy's shoulders.

Liz handed Thrúd her bag. "In a pinch, hit someone with it. And we'll need those reeds."

"Fortunately we all cut some," said Thrúd, handing her a bunch of hollow reed stalks in exchange.

"You're stars." Liz smiled, relaxing now that action was finally at hand. She knew you were supposed to get tense, but *not* doing something had been very hard. "We'd better get rid of some of these clothes," she said to Lamont. "And I hope you can swim."

"I hope so too," said Lamont with a smile, patting Thor's belt. "Otherwise I'll be a strong drowner."

Liz stepped out of her green skirt. "It's close enough to the color of the water. I'll take it with us. It'll do to hide behind."

"Good thing that Thor has left," said Lamont. "I hate to think what he'd say about a man hiding behind a woman's skirts, especially when they were wearing his belt of strength."

Jerry approached the end of the journey with a mixture of terror and relief. On the relief side, the journey in the cart had ended. On the terror side, the food had given some clarity to his mind, even if he was woozy at times.

If memory served him correctly, they were heading toward Mirmir's well, where Mirmir had made Odin pluck out one of his own eyes to gain a draft of the well of wisdom. Jerry was no fool. He could only see one reason for Odin taking him along, and it wasn't for his company.

The walk down the steep slope was playing havoc with his eyes. He would have thought that they'd put up a better effort while he still had two! He wasn't even seeing double. He was seeing treble. Three little black-clad hooded figures, standing next to the water. And he'd have sworn that the smaller two were playing scissors-stone-paper.

"Why have you brought warriors to Mirmir's well?" said a high girlish voice. "You know that it is not allowed."

Odin turned to the Einherjar accompanying them. "Go back to the chariot. I thought Loki might be here but he isn't." He jerked Jerry's collar. "I can deal with this one on my own."

As they advanced, Jerry saw that the hoods masked the Norn's faces in deep shadow, except for the tip of one nose. "Stop that," said the tallest Norn to the other two.

"I would have thought Urd had put away such childlike pastimes," said Odin, sounding suspicious.

"It's my second childhood," said the smallest Norn in a quavering treble. "I had a terrible first childhood, and I'm going to enjoy this one. And it keeps Skuld happy."

"That is wisdom," said Odin. "Great Norns, I would give my right eye for a horn of water from Mirmir's well."

"The price has gone up," said the tallest Norn. "The price is now a human sacrifice."

"Push him over the edge into the water," said the second childhood Norn.

"Throw him into the well," said the third.

"To drown and enrich the pool with his blood," clarified the tallest.

"Do you want me to cut his throat first?" Odin pushed Jerry to the lip of the pool.

"No!" said the Norns in hasty chorus.

"He's got to struggle."

"Otherwise it doesn't work."

"Push him in!"

So Odin did.

It couldn't have been more than ten feet down to the water, but it felt like fifty.

Jerry's screaming was the sweetest sound Liz had heard in long time. He hit the water with a terrific splash, and Liz went after him. The water they were hiding in was deliciously warm, and tinglingly effervescent. Unfortunately, the green color was due to the dense mats of water-weed.

Liz battled through the muck, and reached the threshing figure. She tried to grab Jerry and pull him to the edge, under the lip, but got a kick that nearly drowned her instead. It knocked all the air out of her, and she had to thrash for the surface.

Then a strong hand grabbed her.

Jerry had two shocks when Odin casually pushed him over the edge into Mirmir's well. The first was not that unpleasant. He was going to drown in warm water.

The second—that someone was pulling him down—was terrifying. He swallowed a fair amount of water trying to scream, and kicked with all his might. He was rewarded with a meaty impact. Then something grabbed him and flung him in against the lip. Moments later he was joined by a gasping Liz, who was weakly trying to push something into his hand. It was a sort of pipe, and she put a similar thing in her mouth. Then the same strong hand pulled him under. He had the intelligence left to put the pipe in his mouth and try to breathe through it.

He felt a hand find his and squeeze gently. And a layer of something was pulled over him.

"What happened there?" Odin demanded.

Ella couldn't think quite what to say. She'd seen Liz burst out of the water herself. And then a black form—probably, she hoped, her daddy. And a fair amount of splashing.

A sudden horrible thought occurred to her. Maybe there really *was* some kind of monster down in this water. Maybe it had eaten all of them. She leaned over the edge, not caring about anything else except finding out if he was all right. She saw the bamboos in the misty water.

"It's the water demons," said Ty. "It's like . . . this drowned woman that lives in a cave near the bottom of the well, and she pulls them down and sucks their brains out through their noses."

"Oh," said Odin. "But I thought I also saw some dark shape attack."

"That's the water-wolf," Ty explained. "It lives at the very bottom of the well in between all the dead men's bones and treasure and it tries to get them first. It uses the blood to wash the bones and it likes to gnaw the flesh off their toes. And it eats their guts like spaghetti, and . . ."

"Stop giving away our secrets," said Tolly.

"Yes. Go and fetch Odin a horn full of water," said Ella hastily. Once Ty got going he was nearly impossible to stop, especially with anything ghoulish.

Odin drank the horn of water. "I thank you, wise Norns. Now I will escort you back to Urd's well."

"No," said Ella firmly, trying to remember exactly how the Norns had spoken. "Now go. Great danger threatens you if you stay."

"Tell me more," said Odin.

"Only if you give us your other eye," said Tolly.

Odin put his hand over it, protectively.

"Samurai Jack is coming," warned Ty sepulchrally. "And he is a giant giant and he's dead already, so you can't kill him and . . . and he's got snakes for hair. And even if you cut his head off he just grows another two."

Odin backed off.

"Samurai Jack?" said the man with him. Ella placed him. The one that had been there when Thor's wife had come home. He was the creep who'd stolen Thor's gloves and belt of strength and then made the whiskey-smelling stuff that had got Thor so drunk!

"Thjalfi," she hissed, "you are a lowlife asshole." Ma wasn't around to hear it.

Odin was already heading away, so he didn't see a Norn kick his henchman on the shins. Hard.

"Creep. Lowlife. Scumbag. Bottom-feeder," he heard, as Thjalfi scrambled and limped after him.

These Norns were certainly knowledgeable. But Thjalfi was a useful creep, scumbag, and lowlife bottom-feeder.

The Krim device tried furiously to get Odin-Krim's attention. He was right on top of them, positionally!

But Odin was not responding. He was even more strong-willed than Krim. Prukrin transfer selection involved the gullible, the easily manipulated, and those with various emotional energy keys. Odin had none of those features. Instead he was very Krim-like.

Lying under the water, covered in a layer of weed and Liz's skirt, Lamont waited for the inevitable to happen. How could he watch the kids and stay under water? He had to go and look. Had to.

Just then there were two almost simultaneous splashes. Lamont shot his head out of the water like a submarine launched cruise missile. A grinning Ty and Tolly were swimming toward them, splashing and laughing.

"I told them not to," said Ella from above.

"Honey," said Liz. "Why don't you join us too? You were absolutely brilliant." She was hugging a bemused but smiling Jerry Lukacs. "I'm never letting you out of my sight for one instant, ever again. You've got so thin, love."

"It's . . . been a bit of a rough journey." He squinted at her. "And the last time I saw you, you were busy kissing someone else."

Liz blushed. "It wasn't what it looked like. And I think you saved me from getting raped."

"She went there to look for you, Jerry," said Lamont, "without realizing that Valkyries are the Norse equivalent of boom-boom girls. She was acting the part and trying to get her partner blind drunk. So don't make a fuss about it, because she's been tearing herself apart to think how she's going explain it to you."

Jerry blinked. "She doesn't have to explain anything."

"But I want to," said Liz. "First, though, we need to get you out of here, get you dry, fed, and your hands untied."

She looked as if she was about to start crying any moment, with the chin definitely quivering slightly, which was not something you expected from Liz. She also looked as if she was going to devour him with her eyes.

"Sounds good," said Jerry. "Especially the fed part. I've eaten half a magic apple, thirty-six nuts, four bird eggs, and a bowl of gruel in the last nine days. Does anyone know what has become of Loki and Sigyn, by the way?"

"He took the Norns back off to Urd's well. Sigyn went along to keep an eye on Skuld," said Lamont.

"Skuld-uggery! She wanted to make sure he Urd on the side of caution," said Jerry. And then gaped as Liz, instead of groaning, burst into a flood of tears and hugged him fiercely.

"It wasn't *that* bad," he said warily, once he could breathe again.

"It was bloody awful," she said, smiling through the tears. "But it's so very you."

"Are you absorbing wisdom through the skin?" asked Thor from the edge of the water. "What did you do to Odin? He and his troops are still galloping their horses away from this place."

"That," said Ella, with a scowl, "was my little brother. He's a menace."

"I thought it was way cool," said Tolly admiringly. "Especially the part about the drowned woman. How did you find out all this neat stuff?"

Agent Stephens watched the black bird warily. It did have a large beak. It also had a roll of parchment around one leg. "The message is for you," said the bird. "I could peck it off, but it probably would be illegible. I was told to tell you Tom Harkness sent me."

Agent Stephens had had a hard time in the last while, reconciling himself with the fact that his entire purpose in life was now something he had to reassess, in the light of being somewhere where the U.S. was not even a concept, and from where he had no chance of return or even of fulfilling his mission. He and Bott had tagged along with the party of moderns simply because they did not know where else to go. Preparation and briefing for the

Harkness mission had of necessity been scanty. And then not only had they lost their guides, their destination and their way home, they'd also lost their mission . . . or so he'd believed.

Now, unless someone was deceiving them, he had to reassess again. With trembling fingers he undid the little scroll. What he saw there was enough to convince him that Tom Harkness was still alive—and in *this* Mythworld, the Norse one, not still stranded in the Greek Mythworld.

He was filled with righteous indignation. How dare these people mislead him like that? Not only had this Liz, Lamont and these children wrecked the mission, and destroyed his way home, they'd also deceived him about his mission objective.

"I have a message for you from Harkness," the raven continued. "The Americans you are associating with are known collaborators and sympathizers with unfriendly foreign powers. We need you to act as our eyes and ears in their midst."

CHAPTER 29

⊘⊘⊘⊘⊘⊘

"So now we need to know what you plan, Jerry," said Loki, once they returned to Ran's cliff dwelling. "After all, you have now received two of the perceived sources of wisdom in the Norse world. You should be, if not a match for Odin, at least able to see through some of his strategies."

"Yes," rumbled Thor. "I've heard Loki's side of the story. There is some truth in what he says. Actually, to be fair, everything I've looked closely at proved to be true. Not polite, but true. Odin bespelled Loki and Sigyn's son Váli—a blameless boy—and thereby killed their son Narfi. That calls for a blood-price. Loki has put that price as Odin's own life. Many of us, myself among them, played a part in Loki's capture. Odin, Heimdall and Skadi imprisoned Loki for what Odin told us was for the benefit of all. Odin was always too good at talking us into doing things for his benefit."

Loki snorted. "And he was very good at telling us we would not understand his reasons for doing them, because they were high matters which only he could understand."

"It's always a mistake to hand over too much thinking to someone else," said Liz. She nudged Thrúd. "Especially men."

Thor's daughter giggled.

Jerry rubbed his brow. "Wisdom is maybe the wrong word for what I've acquired. Or rather maybe it is the right word, but we understand it wrongly. We all drank from the well. I didn't mean to, but I swallowed enough."

Lamont held out his hands. "And I can't say it gave me any insights into how to treat Marie's cancer or that it made Tolly and Ty any older or wiser."

"If I have my geography right, Mirmir's well is one of the deepest places in this Ur-universe. You've got to understand the symbolism here. The water in Mirmir's well has passed through every place in this world, filtering ever downwards. By the laws of contagion it's therefore still part of all the things it has passed through. You were drinking in the land . . . I suspect you would find it very hard to get lost, or starve now. You wouldn't know precisely how you knew, but you'd know."

"Great. Really useful," said Lamont. "Especially to someone wanting to find his wife, and cure her. Not to mention organizing a great apocalyptic battle."

Jerry raised an eyebrow. "If you think about it, Lamont, it at least would help you find her. And to a general it should be priceless."

"But how does it help us to capture Odin? We should have struck when he was at Mirmir's well," said Thor, cheerfully ignoring the fact that they had been vastly outnumbered.

Counting, Jerry suspected, was not one of Thor's strengths. Or perhaps his strength lay in the fact that he *didn't* count, before he got into a fight.

Jerry tugged his straggly little goatee-beard. "I need to think about it. Asgard's defenses are designed to keep out frost and mountain giants. If I recall rightly, it is the flood caused by Jörmungand and the fire caused by Surt that destroys the world at Ragnarok."

"Surt and the sons of Muspell did figure in my plans," admitted Loki. "An alliance of convenience against a common enemy, as it were."

"A mistake," rumbled Thor. "We've got a sort of common background with the frost and mountain giants. We've married them, had them live amongst us, like Loki, been friends with some like Ægir, and Grid, fought with them, wandered their lands. We share much of the same opinions and attitudes. The South and East are closed lands. Muspell and Surt's dominions have an ancient enmity with the Vanir, but no common blood or traditions."

Jerry was surprised by the perspicacity of Thor's analysis. "Yes, culture," he said knowledgeably. "You know why Americans stir the honey into their tea clockwise, and South Africans like Liz, do so counterclockwise?"

"What is clockwise?" asked Thor.

Jerry demonstrated with a twirling finger. "Like this. Counterclockwise is like that."

Thor thought hard. "To symbolize the movement of the whirlpool . . . but then why the other way?"

"Coriolis force!" said Emmitt. "It goes the other way in the southern hemisphere."

"Nope," said Jerry. "To dissolve the honey and make the tea sweet."

Loki cracked up. Liz scowled. Thor was still standing and tugging at his beard. "So: what you are saying is that we may do things entirely differently for the same reason? That despite our differences we have similar needs?"

"I suppose that's true. But what I was saying was that sometimes the superficiality of culture and tradition stop us thinking about things clearly and differently. They set our patterns of thought and hide the underlying truth. We come from outside your culture without that baggage. Maybe we can find the right answers."

"And there I thought that you had just found an opportunity to make a dumb joke," said Liz. "How I maligned you."

"Well, that too," admitted Jerry, grinning. "But seriously, I need more information, preferably inside information about Asgard, and about what Odin plans."

"I have a spy. A very greedy spy and I am nearly out of his price," admitted Liz. "One of Odin's ravens, Hugin. He's not the brightest, but he did tell us that you were being taken to Mirmir's well."

"What do you bribe him with? Roadkill?" asked Jerry.

"Sort of," said Liz. "You know how all our American stuff changed to being whatever was contemporaneous here?"

Jerry nodded. "It at least has to be within the framework of reference for the Ur-universe."

"Well, I had a large box of those multiflavored jelly beans. I bought them for Lamont and Marie's kids, not just because we don't get them in South Africa," she said defensively. "And one of the flavors they changed to is something quite gross, but Hugin regards it as a sort of gastronomic heroin. But I only have one left."

Loki coughed. "Ran, dear. Would there be any chance of using Grotti's handmill?"

The giantess who had been quietly listening nodded. "If you are careful." She got up and walked out.

"A grotty handmill?" Liz asked.

"As I remember the story," Jerry said, "some king of Denmark bought the mill and two giant slave-girls. The mill would grind out whatever you told it to. So he made it grind gold, but he did not give the slave-girls any rest so they ground out a horde of Vikings."

"Mysing's horde," said Loki. "A terrible menace."

"And Mysing set the slave-girls to grinding salt," said Thor.

"Salt?" Liz looked puzzled.

Jerry grinned. "It was very precious in those days. It was the chief preservative before we had deep freezes, Liz."

"True. We still salt tons of fish on the west coast in South Africa."

"And in those days the sea itself was not salty," explained Thor. "So Mysing made them grind salt."

"But once again he neglected to give them rest," said Loki, in a sing-song voice. "So they ground faster and faster until Mysing's ships sank under the weight of the salt, and they went on churning the wheels in a whirlpool, spilling salt into the sea."

"That's labor activism!" said Liz. "So what happened next?"

Loki shrugged. "The giantesses Fenja and Menja fell into Ran's embrace, which is what happens if you cling onto a millstone in the open ocean. The stones stopped turning before the sea became solid salt, and the stones found their way into Ran's net, as all the treasures lost under the sea do."

Ran came back carrying two enormous millstones linked with a rusty contraption.

"And here I thought I'd said goodbye to rusted bolts forever," said Lamont. "Give it to me. I'll do my best to fix it." He looked critically at the rust. "No guarantees, though."

"Lamont, if anyone can fix it, it'll be you," said Liz.

"Flattery gets you time sanding and oiling." Lamont tried to pick it up, and failed. "And I'll need some help from Thor and his belt of strength to carry it to the workshop."

Lamont restored the handmill to working order with some patience, a lot of swearing, more oil, and a grave shortage of Miles Davis to listen to. It was the latter he complained about most. "Unfortunately, I didn't find any giantess attached to it to restore. And the idea was plainly that with the heavy wheels, inertia would keep them turning. But trust me, starting them is not going to be easy."

"A job for you and me, Papa," said Thrúd.

Thor looked alarmed. "It's hardly a job for a warrior. Or even a male, working a mill-stone."

Liz prodded him in the kidneys. "The times they are a changing."

"And not always for the better," Thor grumbled, taking the handle.

"Consider it an opportunity to get in touch with your feminine side, which every artist needs to do," said Liz. "You need it for your ikabena skills to flourish. And if you need more help with it I'm sure I can find you a mop."

Thor strained to look over his shoulder.

"What are you doing?" asked Thrúd.

"Trying to look at my back," answered Thor.

"Why?"

"Well, I've seen my front," explained Thor, "and that's not the feminine side of me. It must be in the middle of my back where I can't reach."

For someone without a feminine back-side he churned the wheel very effectively. Perhaps he had one after all.

"It seems to have made them in all the flavors," said Liz, inspecting some of the jelly beans. They'd made an enormous pile—about thirty yards wide—and they'd barely set the wheels spinning.

"That's a relief," said Loki, "as you said the ones that the ravens liked were revolting, and you have enough here for bribes for half the ravens in Midgard." He picked up one of the beans. "What are the other flavors like?"

"Some of them are delicious. Lamont, lucky fellow, got Arctic cloudberry."

Loki put the jelly bean into his mouth, and chewed. Then, nodded appreciatively. "Very good, these. This one is like fine rakfisk. Delicious! So what do the revolting ones taste like?"

It was all a question of what you were used to and had been brought up with, Liz supposed. But she decided it would be wise to avoid answering Loki's question. "Well, we have bribes aplenty. I think I probably have provisions for an army."

A little later Jerry sat with Liz, on the cliff top, their fingers entwined.

"I need to work on Sigyn," said Jerry.

"Why?"

"Well, Sigyn and Odin are similar in a way."

Liz snorted. "What? Is one of her eyes false?"

Jerry grinned. "No, Odin would destroy everything rather than give up power and accept punishment. And Sigyn is just as implacable in her quest for revenge. She would destroy the entire universe rather than let Odin go unpunished. Loki wants vengeance. But if all the people in the world begged him . . . well, he might compromise. Sigyn, never. Odin must die. She might compromise on Heimdall, and she was prepared to let Skadi off the hook to a large extent. But Odin is non-negotiable. If the universe must die to kill him, so be it. So: Their reasons are vastly different, but the end result will be the same."

Liz grimaced. "Classic African dictatorship dilemma. Compromise isn't possible, Jerry. Even if you could talk Sigyn into it, Odin would never agree. By the sounds of it, he's made so many enemies that if he stopped being top dog everyone would come hunting for a piece of his hide. Just like Mengistu or Mugabe or Charles Taylor, Odin either has to flee somewhere he can enjoy his ill-gotten gains in safety—or stay in absolute power. People like that will only flee if it is that or die, and they'll only go just before the absolute end with lots of dead bodies around them—*if* you manage to convince them that their precious selves will be safe and comfortable. Otherwise they'd destroy the universe rather than lose. They are the universe as far as they're concerned."

"I suppose so," Jerry chewed his lip. "Megalomania's not exactly limited to Africa, for sure. No other lives have any value to Odin at all."

"So what are you going to do?" she asked.

Jerry shrugged. "Rattle some very large sabers. And then offer him a safe out."

"You're going to find him a safe haven?" Liz shook her head. "Honey, this universe isn't big enough for him and Sigyn."

"Offer him a way out of *this* universe, is what I meant."

Home! Well, the U.S. Funny, since she'd recovered Jerry she hadn't thought much about it. Coffee, toilet paper and deodorant would be nice. But home for her was really where the heart was, and the trial by ordeal had given her a good idea just where hers was located. "Have you thought of a way?"

"No," said Jerry grimly. "But he doesn't have to know that. He just has to know we've come from outside."

"I suppose so. So now we need to raise recruits. Lots of them."

Jerry raised his eyebrows. "Well, 'raise' is the right word. We're due to leave for a visit to Loki's youngest daughter. The responsible member of the family."

Liz snorted. "Compared to Loki or Fenrir, that's not hard."

Jerry gave her a wry grin. "Jörmungand and Fenrir refuse to go along because little Hel always preaches at them."

"Jörgy is just misunderstood," said Liz defensively. "She's still very young, and having trouble with her emotions and her hormones."

"Hel is younger. But she has both of them, and Loki too, doing avoidance. Fortunately, she likes Sigyn."

"And is she a really yummy recruiting poster?" asked Liz.

"In a morbid sense, yes," answered Jerry. "She is queen of the dead that do not die in battle."

"Oh. So we're getting all the grannies armed with their zimmer frames are we? Odin, quiver in your boots."

Jerry shook his head. "Liz, you're the best proof I could ever find of the need to teach real history at schools."

She reached over and gave him a one-armed squeeze. "We only ever did SA history. And there wasn't all that much of it, so we did the Great Trek many times. All right. Tell me what obvious thing I have missed."

"That most people in history died young of things we now consider treatable. And that during wars a lot of warriors died from everything from septic wounds to diarrhea—far more than ever died in actual fighting. Hel's warriors alone outnumber those in Valhöll by five to one, at least. And Hel is a ministering angel, laboring without the advantages of Odin and Asgard. She treats as well as she can."

"I do remember someone telling me that it needs a multiple of people to the defenders' number . . . could have been three, could have been five, to take a fortified position."

"I imagine it depends on the fortifications and what you've got to throw at them," said Jerry. "Artillery, and the like, you know. And we have one thing that Odin fears most, by the way he was trying to find out."

"What? Wisdom?"

"Yes. Well, knowledge. We have knowledge that a Norse god could not have acquired."

She pulled him closer. "Balloons again?"

"Maybe. I must talk to those agent types. I wish they were as useful as Cruz and Mac were. Anyway, right now I'm finding it hard to concentrate on such distant matters." He pushed back an errant curl from her forehead.

She kissed him. "Good. Come and concentrate on something closer at hand. And don't get distracted!"

"I wouldn't dare. You might spike my food with jelly beans."

She pulled him closer, wrapping him in her cloak. "I'm not quite that cruel."

"Airborne?" Stephens shook his head. The man was looking a little sickly, probably from his vegetarian diet. How the Scandinavians hadn't died of malnutrition, let alone had the strength to go off on Viking raids was something of a puzzle to Liz. Still, this presumably was their winter diet, and the fact that they ate whole-grain cereals and a lot of fish probably helped. In spring and summer some fruit and green things must have found their way into the meals, surely? But even here in a sheltered cove next to the moderating sea, this "Fimbulwinter" was robbing people of any other harvest. It was supposed to be summer. Global warming was a problem, but global cooling like this was a much faster disaster. It was supposed to continue, from what Thor said, for three years.

"But tell us about your plans," said Bott. "We are experienced men. We can probably help."

"Yes," nodded Stephens, like a mechanical doll. "Fill us in on the details. You are the experts at all this mythology stuff."

"Unfortunately, my knowledge of Scandinavian myth is a little scanty," said Jerry. "Basically, we need to capture Odin. I wanted to find a way in past Asgard's walls. Last time we used hot air balloons as a feint. This time I thought we might just be able to do it for real."

"Do you really think you could make a balloon?" asked Bott.

Jerry nodded. "We've got a secret weapon. Lamont Jackson. He's got more practical skill and obscure knowledge than is fair to have in the possession of any one man. And we've done it before. Asgard has pretty solid walls, which are certainly high enough to hold off most siege attacks, but a balloon doesn't have to fly that high to get over them. It's silent. It's an unknown concept here."

Bott looked thoughtful. "But what are you going to do when you're on the other side of the wall? A balloon is very visible, and it can't carry many people."

"We'll do it at night. Paint it black," said Liz. "On a cloudy night, it would be easy. No one would have a clue we'd arrived."

"Yes, but what are you going to do once you have arrived?"

"I thought you were going to advise us instead of just asking questions," said Liz irritably. "What do you think we should do?"

Someone bellowed off down the passage. "That's Thor," said Liz. "We have to go, Jerry."

"That's it," said Stephens, when the door was closed. "All we have to do is get it all set up. They'll walk right into it."

Bott nodded. "Now we know what they're planning and who they're in bed with, yes."

"Do you know something I don't?" asked Stephens, for the millionth time fiddling with his helmet radio.

"Well, I know enough to know that Odin was the main god of this Norse stuff. And this Loki they've sided with was the bad guy."

Stephens nodded. "The sort that has no respect for authority."

"Now we just need to get this information through to Harkness," said Bott.

"And start arranging for a bolt-hole if this bunch gets wind of it all."

PART IV

WHEN HEL FREEZES OVER

CHAPTER 30

❀❀❀❀❀

The senior CIA official looked at the list and frowned. "Remember, Miggy, I never said this to you. But, these men . . . three of them were ours. They were . . . well, we were trying to get rid of them. They should never have made it through training. We had a bad patch a few years back."

He made a face. "The truth is the agency was furious when the PSA was formed. We were asked to second some staff." He pointed to the list. "Guess who."

Tremelo nodded. "Was Megane one of yours?"

"Sad to say, he was. There's a story—I've never tried to confirm it, but I know the agents involved swear it was true—that when he was stationed in Venezuela he got the bright idea of publicly embarrassing the Venezuelan government. We haven't had good relations with them in a long time, as you know. So, the screwball put sugar in the gas tanks of several official limousines which were to be used in an official motorcade the following day."

Miggy winced. "Oh, Lord. He got caught, I assume?"

"No. But when the motorcade got stalled in Caracas, the Venezuelan government was not amused. Neither was the special U.S. envoy who was making a semi-secret visit to see if we could iron out at least some of the controversies. Not only was he stalled in one of the vehicles himself, but the Venezuelans immediately accused *us*—the CIA, I mean—of being responsible for the affair, and broke off the talks as a result."

The official sighed. "Of course, we denied it vigorously. Even after we found out it was true. That was Megane's last overseas assignment. We were in the process of figuring out how to quietly ease him out of the company, when the PSA got set up and Garnett demanded that we provide her with some agents."

He leaned back in his chair and gave Tremelo a considering look. "You'd better know one thing, though, Miggy. Whatever else he is, Megane's not a stoolie. Even if you nail him for something, I doubt you'll be able to follow it up any further. He's the kind of person who can get the goofiest notions of what constitutes his duty, sure enough—but he also takes it dead seriously. I guess you could call it part of the syndrome. He'll clam up and take the rap himself, even if it means a long prison sentence."

"I can live with that. In a perfect world, I'd be able to get rid of Garnett and the PSA altogether. But I'm sure the best I can hope for is a much muddier conclusion. Garnett aside, there are a lot of powerful people and special interests who are backing the PSA for their own reasons."

He shrugged. "So it goes. I don't really care all that much if the PSA would simply restrict itself to gathering intelligence about the Krim pyramid, even though they'll make a royal nuisance of themselves when they try to insist on their authority to 'coordinate' all intelligence activities. It's when the stupid bastards try to *create* intelligence that they became a real threat to the nation. Intelligence, yes, so-called 'operations,' no. We simply don't know enough to be trying to conduct operational efforts. None of us—me included—much less people who are so inattentive to the intelligence they're supposed to be 'coordinating' that they send some poor schmucks into the pyramid with fancy technical equipment that won't work."

"Good luck," said his friend.

Common sense would have had PSA headquarters somewhere in Chicago. Political sense had the office exactly where it should be, in Washington. The meeting that was going on there right now was anything but cordial. Agents Reno, Schmitt and Erskine were considerably the worse for wear, still, from the prequel to their visit to the cells at Fort Campbell. Agent Supervisor Megane and his two men were less battered, perhaps because the Greek hoplite outfits had protected them to some extent.

But the only protection that would really have worked against the fury of Ms. Garnett would have been to be like Agents Sternal, Bormann, or Liber—dead.

"This has turned into a complete fiasco," she said coldly, grinding her words out between gritted teeth.

They all stood looking at her, like a bunch of dumb oxen. "Get out," she said. "I'll deal with you later."

After the agents had filed out, Garnett swiveled in the chair behind her desk and looked at Assistant Director of Operations James Horton. She was actually more furious with him than any of his subordinates, and was deeply tempted to order him out of the room also. But, at least for the moment, she still needed him.

She had one satisfaction, though. "You're coming with me, Jim. No way I'm sitting through that so-called cocktail party this evening on my own."

Horton looked alarmed. That made her feel a little better.

After the drinks were served, and the waiter withdrew from the private room in the very exclusive club in the nation's capital, Garnett looked around the table. The expressions on the faces of the four men and one woman who'd joined her and Horton for cocktails were subdued, of course. They were all long-time veterans of the Beltway, and, like experienced poker players, knew better than to wear their sentiments on their sleeves. Still, only someone a lot more obtuse than Helen could have failed to detect the anger, irritation—and apprehension. The room seemed practically saturated with those emotions, especially the latter.

Nothing for it, as much as Garnett hated doing so. She had to start with an apology. These people were beyond her control, if not her influence, and she had to stay on their good side.

"Sorry about this, everyone. But we'll get it straightened out soon enough."

The secretary of defense exchanged a glance with one of the two senators at the table, Senator Andrews from Texas. Then Secretary Antonelli said, "How soon is 'soon enough,' Helen? I warn you, you don't have much time. Tremelo's already arrived—and don't ever let that tweedy academic image he loves to cultivate fool you any. When it comes to Beltway knife-fighting, he's as tough as anyone."

"Tougher, you ask me," chimed in Senator Andrews.

Roger Delacorte, a lobbyist from the defense industry, made a face. "Yeah, he's a real shithead."

The Texas senator gave him a hard glance. "Cut it out, Roger. I *like* Miggy Tremelo personally."

His fellow senator from California chimed in. "So do I. And whether you do or don't, Mr. Delacorte, I'd advise you to remember that most congressmen who've dealt with the man like him also—and so does the public. Unfortunately, while I enjoy it in private, Miggy's got a good sense of humor—which means the talk shows love having him as a guest." Senator Martinez took a sip from her cocktail glass. "The problem isn't Miggy's personality; it's his *policy.* And since he won't budge on it—and, for the moment, has the confidence of the President—we have to do an end run around him." She used the glass to gesture at Garnett. "Hence, APSA and the PSA. But let's not lose the forest for the trees. If we could have persuaded Tremelo, I'd have had no problem at all leaving him in charge. God knows, at least he's competent."

Helen did her best not to stiffen angrily at the sideswipe. There was no love lost between Paula Martinez and her, and never had been—not since they'd first encountered each other years back in the course of a clash over environmental policy, when Helen had been on the staff of one of the senator's opponents. But she simply couldn't afford to lose Martinez's backing. The big money on their side of the dispute came from the defense industry, and no senator in the country had more clout there than the senior senator from California.

Roger Delacorte held up his hands in a placating gesture. "Fine, fine, fine. Professor Tremelo's the greatest guy in the world. He's still got his head up his ass when it comes to dealing with the alien pyramid—and let's also not forget that that's the name of the forest in the first place."

As he listened to the byplay, Melvin Steinmetz found himself wondering whether he'd backed the wrong horse in this race. Unlike everyone else at the table, Melvin didn't really have a personal stake in the outcome. True, if the policy he advocated were to be adopted by the administration in place of Tremelo's, his think tank would land a very juicy contract. So what? The Future Enterprise Institute was one of the three or four most prestigious and sought-after independent research and policy development outfits in the nation. They *already* had plenty of juicy contracts.

He was simply convinced that Tremelo was wrong, dead wrong, and the consequences of his erroneous thinking were likely to be disastrous. As bad and probably worse than any major nuclear exchange—and Steinmetz's think tank specialized in studies of nuclear war. Whether he realized it or not, Tremelo's policy with regard to the Krim pyramid amounted to a revival of the Mutual Assured Destruction policy that had governed relations between the U.S. and the USSR during the Cold War, when it came to all-out war. "You leave us alone and we'll leave you alone, because we can each destroy the other."

For all its somewhat surrealistic nature, MAD had worked pretty well during that era—but only because the "mutual destruction" part had been *true*. What Tremelo couldn't seem to grasp was that it was not true when it came to the pyramid. Who knew what the Krim could do, or not do—or would be willing to do? What Tremelo advocated amounted to . . .

"We'll leave them alone, and . . . we'll see what they do."

That wasn't good enough, not by a country mile. The United States *had* to take a proactive stance toward the pyramid. Simply waiting and watching—what Tremelo called "quarantine"—gave all the advantage to the enemy. It amounted to unilateral disarmament.

The problem, unfortunately, was that—so far, at any rate—Tremelo had all the proven and capable experts on his side of the debate. And it didn't help one damn bit that the public doted on *them* even more than they did on Tremelo himself.

One of Melvin's associates at the institute had called it the American nation's "ingrained Humphrey Bogart complex." Beneath the somewhat rueful whimsy, he had a point. No professional security force had been able to penetrate the pyramid without suffering one hundred percent casualties—all of them fatalities except for a few still listed as missing in action. Whereas the "amateurs" had come out of it unscratched. A professor whose absentmindedness was simply charming, when coupled with the rest—and with a zaftig new blond girlfriend, to boot, who exuded "outdoorswoman" rather than "bimbo." The country had gone even more gaga over her Afrikaans accent than they had over that silly Australian actor's accent a few years back. A black maintenance man. Two paratroopers, one of them Hispanic and the other a Midwestern good-ole-boy.

Racial harmony, even. It was enough to drive you mad—not because the people themselves did, but because they backed Tremelo to the hilt.

So . . .

With misgivings, Steinmetz had been persuaded to throw the considerable if very non-public influence of the Future Enterprise Institute behind the drive by the senators from Texas and California, with the open backing of the defense industry and the covert backing of the secretary of defense, to get APSA enacted and set up the PSA. The defense industry, of course, had its own completely material reasons for opposing Tremelo's policy, which came down to nothing more subtle than that Tremelo's approach didn't produce any big fat defense contracts. With a somewhat less pig-in-the-trough mentality, the secretary of defense and the senators from the nation's two biggest defense-industry states shared their views.

Melvin's misgivings had grown when Helen Garnett emerged as the front-runner for the new post. He'd had to hold his nose at some of the legal implications of APSA, to begin with, figuring you couldn't make an omelet without breaking a few eggs. But what he hadn't foreseen was that a vigorous egg-breaker like Garnett would wind up running the show. Yeah, fine, the woman was tougher than nails and was possibly the best political fundraiser in the country. And . . . this qualified her how, exactly, to oversee setting up a hands-on approach to the pyramid?

The plan she'd developed that had turned into a mare's nest was typical, he thought. Using the "need to rescue Tom Harkness"— who'd been nothing more than a second-rater on the National Security Council's staff—as an excuse to set up an "Operations Directorate" was a scheme right out of the woolliest days of the OSS in World War II. Except that Helen Garnett was no Wild Bill Donovan, and the team of operatives she'd picked bore a lot more resemblance to the Watergate plumbers than they did to OSS agents.

What a mess. Maybe if he bailed out now, he could still get Tremelo to listen to him.

Probably not, though. Miggy and he got along well enough, but Tremelo was just plain stubborn. Always had been.

While he'd been ruminating, the conversation around him had continued. Melvin had paid just enough attention not to lose track of where things were. So, he wasn't taken by surprise when Delacorte—he'd be the one, naturally; the coarse bastard—finally said it out loud.

"All right, Helen. We'll back you in the coming hearings, of course—although you *do* understand that you're going to have to let some heads roll."

That much was obvious, of course. They could only hope that Agent Supervisor Megane shared G. Gordon Liddy's stubborn sense of honor as well as his screwball cowboy attitudes. If all went well, he'd just take the fall and keep his mouth shut. If he turned out to be another John Dean, though . . .

Steinmetz couldn't help but wince a little. He didn't know any of the details of what had happened in Fort Campbell—and didn't want to know, either—but he was dead certain there'd be all hell to pay. Just from what he'd learned, he didn't doubt for a moment that the PSA's agents on the spot had grossly transgressed even the wide latitude APSA gave them. Not to mention their grasp of public relations, which made that of the devil look good. What sort of lunatic goes out of his way to infuriate officers and enlisted men in a military unit as well known and well regarded as the 101st Airborne, for God's sake?

Delacorte cleared his throat. Here it was. "As for the rest, since you have no way of getting in touch with your two agents still in the pyramid, we'll just have to hope . . ."

But he let the words trail off, the gutless prick. So Steinmetz said it for him. "We'll just have to hope that we don't wind up with the same scorecard. You're all aware, I trust, that in his talk show last night—the most widely watched in the country—Orville Trenton made the remark that, in less than three days, three out of the five PSA agents who went in came out dead. But 'the real pros'—yeah, that's what he called them—still seem to be intact."

That was good enough, he figured. He was *not* going to say out loud that the best thing that could happen now would be for the dead bodies of Jerry Lukacs and Liz De Beer—and practically the whole Jackson family, including four kids—to come plummeting out of the skies.

Melvin Steinmetz wasn't sure if he was backing the wrong horse. But he was surely backing the one that stank the most. He'd have to take a shower when he got home.

"That's it, then," said Senator Andrews, finishing his drink and starting to rise from the table. "Helen, we'll see you at the hearings."

Outside the club, while they waited for the limos, Senator Martinez leaned over and said softly to Melvin, "I still can't believe she was dumb enough to authorize such a wild-ass project."

Steinmetz shrugged. "The problem isn't her intelligence, Paula. She just still hasn't learned the same lesson that the man who was possibly England's most competent king had to learn the hard way."

Martinez frowned. "Which means . . ."

"Do *not* state, in front of drunken and stupid knights—and someone like Megane makes up for sobriety by being at least as dumb as any knight who ever lived—'will no one rid me of this troublesome priest?'"

The California senator chuckled softly. "Oh, that Thomas à Becket business. In fairness, Melvin, she didn't go that far."

Steinmetz gave her a cold eye. "I'm sure she didn't suggest anyone commit murder. But who knows what other foolishness she set in train, Paula? Who *knows* what cowboy agents will do, or try to do, if they think they're interpreting tough talk properly?" He gave Garnett a look that was colder still. She was standing out of hearing range thirty feet away, talking with the secretary of defense. "And unfortunately, that's Helen Garnett's stock in trade. Talking tough."

"The problem with Scandinavian mythology," said Dr. Gunnarsson, finishing his presentation to the Senate committee the next morning, "is that the area was thoroughly Christianized. Reading Dr. Lukacs' debriefing report of the earlier event, it seems pretty certain that we need some deity or power in the Ur-Mythology that is also worshiped in earnest here, acting as a linkage."

Miggy took it from there, to the room full of powerful people. "There is plainly more to belief than even churchmen were sincerely able to appreciate. We're also getting hints that not all 'believers' are identical. Careful measurements of the pyramid expansion indicate that although it grew slightly with all intakes, it grew at different rates with each person. Look, we know from the debriefing reports that the Krim expected the pyramid to cross some threshold relatively soon. We do not know at what point that happens. We simply cannot take a chance that through badly researched cowboy efforts, following a very private agenda, the PSA is going to put the country in jeopardy. Under military control, containment and isolation *worked*. We had zero growth and zero snatches for three weeks, Senators. We can cope with that. What we can't cope with has been the results of this foolishness. I've presented the evidence to you, and later on in the hearings you'll be able to hear the eyewitness testimony of such people as Sergeant Cruz and Corporal McKenna and their families, as well as Colonel McNamara and the Greek sphinx Throttler. There is simply no longer any question that the PSA operatives took highly unauthorized actions. I'm sure Director Garnett will insist that none of these actions were authorized by her, and that may well be true. But whether authorized or not, they were done by people on her staff, and on her watch."

By the early afternoon, as he watched from the audience, Melvin Steinmetz knew that Helen Garnett was in deep trouble.

And it only got worse after she took her seat at the witness table. Not more than two minutes after Helen finished her opening remarks, Senator Larsen picked up a piece of paper an aide had just slid in front of him. The fact that the senator didn't give it more than a glance made clear to Melvin that Larsen already knew what it contained. In fact, he was pretty sure having the aide hand it to him in front of the whole room was simply the senator's clever stage management.

Rustling the paper in front of the microphone, the senator from Montana said, "I was wondering if you could shed some light on this subject, as well, Director. I've just received a report from Director O'Hare of the Fish and Wildlife Service, who'll be testifying tomorrow or the day after. But he felt this item of information was important enough to ask me to bring it up immediately. Fish and Wildlife did blood tests on the Greek sphinx Throttler and discovered that your PSA agents had injected her with a tranquilizer after they got her on board the cargo plane." He glanced back and forth along the long hearing table, making eye contact with as many other senators as he could. "I hope I don't need to point out to the senators here that any such action is a gross violation of the law. I was wondering if you could explain to us how that criminal action came about."

Garnett stared at him, for a moment, seeming to be frozen. Like a rabbit in front of a snake. Watching her closely, Steinmetz was quite sure the information came as a complete surprise to her.

Marvelous. The captain of the ship had just found out that she had loose cannons rolling all over the deck. Melvin lifted his eyes and exchanged a glance with Senator Martinez, sitting at the long table with the other senators. After a couple of seconds, she looked away. Fortunately, she had an excellent poker face.

"Well . . . I certainly don't know anything about it, Senator," insisted Garnett. "I can assure you—"

Larsen cut her off abruptly. "Assure me of what? That you've lost control of your own subordinates? That much is obvious. Even leaving aside this latest escapade involving the sphinx, your PSA agents ran roughshod over officers and enlisted men of one of our nation's most decorated military units, even going so far as kidnapping—yes, that's what it amounts to, for all practical purposes—the families of two of its soldiers." He let that sit for a moment. Then he added grimly, "This *is* a nation of laws, Ms. Garnett. Even the Alien Pyramid Security Act—which I opposed at the time, and now intend to see repealed if I can—is a *law.* It is not a blank check."

Quietly, Melvin Steinmetz rose from his seat and made his way toward the exit at the rear of the big chamber.

Time to bail out. Miggy was partial to Italian food, if he remembered correctly. Maybe he'd be free for lunch in a day or two.

ChAPTER 31

〰〰〰〰〰

"I don't see why we have to go," said Fenrir sulkily. Liz's rule against his just gobbling huge volumes of soft meat, and insisting on him getting some bonemeal had definitely eased his aches and pains, and thereby his temper. It hadn't done a lot for his teenage demeanor, though.

"Because Lizzy asked us to," said Jörmungand. "And Papa-Loki and Step-Mama Sigyn."

"But you *know* what she's going to be like," Fenrir complained. "Holier-than-thou. 'Why don't you do something useful with your lives,'" he mimicked. "Makes me sick."

Jörmungand nodded her enormous head. "Our little sister makes me want to do something really shocking instead, but let's face it, she does mean well."

"She's a sanctimonious little cow. Not my fault Odin sent her to Niflheim, and she found it suited her. If she starts lecturing, I'm leaving. What does she expect me to do? I'm a wolf. Minister to people with my paws?"

"Probably something equally unreasonable," said Liz who had come up behind them. "Something silly like 'stop eating them.' A ridiculous idea, I know."

"Well, if they will run away, it's hard not to chase them down," said Fenrir, tongue lolling.

"So what do I need for this place?" asked Liz.

"Warm clothes. It's dark and full of freezing mists," said Jörmungand.

It was. And their reception was not a lot warmer, once the queen of Hel got the message about why they'd come. Well, Loki and Sigyn's reception was an enthusiastic hug from the piebald woman. She was literally half jet-black and half snow-white. She had obviously decided to make everything fit in with her theme colors. Liz could only be grateful that she would never have heard of zebras.

"So soon!" she said eagerly. "I knew as soon as Fimbulwinter began, but I was expecting it to be another few centuries before you broke free. We're still ready, and by the time Fimbulwinter hits the third year my troops will have swelled greatly." Then she saw Fenrir and Jörmungand. She took a deep, disapproving breath. "Family solidarity," she said. "It's a bit late for that, isn't it? I haven't forgotten last time."

"Oh shut up," said Fenrir crossly.

"You shut up! I see that you've brought your useless drinking partner with you."

"I've given it up," said Thor, affronted. "I'm an alcoholic, but I'm currently in remission. I haven't had a drink for five days. Except for rose-hip and mint tea, which has a delicate acidity to balance the cool clear flavor of the mint. It helps me to get in touch with my inner self."

Hel stared at him as if he'd just spouted a line of Japanese. "What?"

Thor looked down his nose at her. "I thought you had some sensibilities and would understand that the great warrior is also an artist, and to find his edge needs to get in touch with his creative side, which means he needs to learn to use all his senses."

"I think I understand why you brought him here," said Hel faintly. "Anyway, preparations are well afoot. We should be ready in three years."

"Uh . . . Hel, dear, we're hoping not to wait three years," said Loki.

She blinked at him. "Asgard will never fall without my full muster. And it will take *Naglfar* months to ferry them all across to Asaheim. And Surt's hosts are going to take a long time to march all that way to set the worlds aflame."

"Well," said Loki, "I have been thinking about it. And I have decided not to do that this time around."

"This time around?" Hel looked puzzled. "The end of Time comes, Papa-Loki."

"Actually, it's more like the wheel of time," said Loki. "If we just let it keep going, it never ends. It just keeps endlessly repeating the same old stuff. I had enough of it the first time around. And the more I think about it the more I remember. So I plan to break the pattern."

Hel shook her head. "You can't do that. Asgard must fall."

"Odin must fall. But Asgard I'll live with. I quite enjoy having a bunch of dimwits to play practical jokes on, and I've gotten used to the crowd in Asgard."

"Asgard must fall," repeated Hel, a little rosy flush appearing on her white cheek.

"But why, dear?" asked Sigyn. "Our fight really is with Odin. I know how you feel about your lodgers here. Fimbulwinter will bring thousands more."

"Millions," said Hel. "But if those already here are to escape, then that's the way it must be. That is the deal I made with Baldr. And he is going to rule in the new Gladheim. It is foretold."

Loki scowled. "If I ever needed a reason not to destroy Asgard, it would be to avoid having that pretty-boy on the throne."

Hel looked pained. "But he has promised that my subjects can have some of the privileges of Asgard's Einherjar and Freyja's warriors, and will not have to dwell in the cold and dark any more. I will not bend on that, Papa-Loki. It's not right as it is." There was a steely determination in her voice.

Jerry coughed. "Um. Lady Hel."

"That is a polite form of address, mortal, but not the correct one. I am the Queen of Hel."

"Pretentious baggage," said Jörmungand, not quite under her breath.

Hel drew herself up onto her toes. She still wasn't quite up to the size of Jörmungand. "This is my Kingdom and—"

"I apologize, Your Majesty," said Jerry. "What I was trying to say was wouldn't you rather be Lady Hel of Asgard than stuck down here? It seems very unfair that you were sent into exile here anyway. What had you done?"

Hel nodded. "It was unfair. But they need me."

"I think they're lucky to have you," said Jerry, trying not to feel as if he was as slimy as Odysseus. "However, I'm not au fait with the hierarchy of Asgard, but if Baldr didn't get reborn, then who would be ruler of Ás?"

There was a moment's all-round silence, broken by Thrúd. "Why . . . you would, Papa-Thor."

"I suppose that would be true," said Loki, sounding as if he didn't know whether to be horrified or amused by the idea.

Jerry nodded. "And while you may have other criticisms of Thor, he is known to be honorable and fair, to the best of his ability."

"True," said Hel, doubtfully. "But I am not sure—"

"I am," said Loki. "I'd rather pull Thor's beard than Baldr's any day. Red-beard knows how to laugh. Baldr doesn't."

Jerry wondered where his confidence was coming from. Could that time spent talking to the corpses on Yggdrasil have had some effect? "Tell me, Thor. Could you see your way clear to improving conditions down here?"

"I don't know," rumbled the thunder god. "I am a strong believer in tradition. What would there be to encourage men to die well in battle if they did not have the hope of joining the glorious ranks of the Einherjar or Freyja's warriors?"

"What about the brave warrior who dies after the battle?" asked Liz. "He gets hit on the head trying to be a hero, and takes three weeks to die."

Thor wrinkled his broad forehead. "It happens. I see your point. Not really fair, is it?"

Jerry continued. "Or a warrior who dies before the battle—that he was ready for, brave enough for, but was unlucky enough to eat some bad fish on the eve of."

Thor rubbed his forehead, as if trying to rub out the wrinkles that were threatening his brain. "Loki, help me on this one."

"You're on your own, O future Lord of the Æsir," said Loki with a crooked smile. "You will be, if you hold that position."

Thor shook his head. "Then I will have to draw the line somewhere. I understand now why Odin drew it where he did."

"What if," said Jerry, speculatively, "you judged someone's life instead of their death. That would be fairer than just choosing one moment."

"Yes," said Hel.

"It's an important moment," said Thor.

"That can be weighed too," Jerry smiled. "It is done that way in some other Mythworlds. I've seen it. And it works. You add together the good and subtract the bad."

Thor shook his head. "It's not that I don't like the idea, but, well, I'm not so good at counting, let alone addition."

"Delegate," said Liz.

"But to whom?"

"Forseti," said Thrúd. "What do you think, Hel?"

She nodded, slowly. "Baldr and Nanna's son would be a good choice. Of course, you would have to create a new hall for the dead of Hel. A great one, but unless you succeeded in getting Idun to part with her apples for them, one with good beds and comfortable chairs and easily digested food. Not all of those here are as young as they once were, you understand. Mead and fighting are very nice when you're twenty."

"Uh," said Thor.

"A bit immature and uncultured, though," put in Liz, seeing him waver. "You could have a tea house. For the more sophisticated corpse."

"And a chess room," said Thrúd.

"Chess is a battle game," agreed Thor. "And I would like to see the appreciation of fine teas spread. I could see that happening. And there'd be less fuss in Valhöll among the Einherjar that way."

"I think we could just have a deal," said Loki, looking at his youngest daughter.

Hel looked thoughtful. "Maybe."

"Come on, girl, it's better than Baldr would have offered. And more than that, you can be sure of old Thor."

Hel looked at the big red-beard. "I see that you have Mjöllnir back."

"Its twin, anyway. And I'm not letting it out of my sight again. I've taken a few hard knocks but thanks to the twelve-point plan I am my own Æsir again. We'll have to start a chapter of AA for your subjects too."

"Baldr is not going to be pleased," said Hel. "I can live with that."

She now looked at Jörmungand and Fenrir. "Neither of them are full grown this time . . ." She paused, and then stamped her foot angrily. "Now I remember last time too. Thor, you have a deal. Except that Baldr stays here. When do you want my subjects to march, Papa-Loki?"

"Soon, girl. I have some ideas to work out with my new artificer, a fellow called Lamont, and this mortal here. He's a trickster too. I owe him for freeing Sigyn and me. Now . . . two things. Can we see Narfi?"

Hel shook her head. "No. You know the rules, Papa. No visiting times."

"Oh." He sounded utterly crestfallen.

"But I will tell him that you came. And he will march with the dead . . . and hopefully face Forseti's judgment." By the smile on her face she had figured out that that would keep her father and stepmother watching over Thor. "And what is the second question?"

Loki looked at Thor, Jerry and Liz. Lamont and the children were back in Ran's watery cliff-castle. "I need to know if a soul called Marie Jackson has entered through Nágrind. If she has, I am honor-bound to tell her husband."

The wait seemed interminable.

Then Hel held up her hands. "She sits on the threshold, Papa. Only the thorn of sleep holds her from time." She paused. "She is a strong and valiant spirit. Lesser ones would have passed through."

"Stronger than a god," said Thor quietly.

chapter 32

෧෧෧෧෧෧

It was a relatively silent trip back. No one felt much like talking, not after the last revelations about Marie. "I feel," Liz said quietly to Jerry, "like we won a battle but are losing a war."

Jerry sighed. "It feels a bit like that. We're no closer to a way out of here. I still haven't solved the problem of how to attack Odin and prevent Ragnarok. Lamont says my balloon probably won't work—because of a lack of fine-weave materials that I can make airtight. I thought sail cloth . . ." He made a face. "Do you know what the sails are made of here? Wool."

Liz shook her head. "That's not possible."

"Apparently, they're made from the fleeces of special sheep. The creatures look rather different from the sheep I've seen pictures of."

"I'll look into it," promised Liz. "If necessary I'll get Thrúd to weave it. It's more useful than making me feel inferior with that purposeless embroidery of hers. That thread she uses is quite fine."

"And I'll go and talk to those two agents, Bott and Stephens. This should be their field of expertise."

"Should be. I'll come along."

They arrived back rather quietly. Without any fanfare, Liz, Jerry and Thrúd set off straightaway to the room that Ran had made available to the two agents.

Liz knocked and pushed the door open. And there were the two of them, in the act of affixing something to a raven's leg.

Startled, the first reaction of the agents was to try to hide the raven. But they must have been a bit rough about it because there was an angry squawk. Then, with Bott's hand leaking blood, a raven suddenly appeared and flew for the window. Thrúd brought the bird down with a well thrown tambour frame.

"What in the hell is going on here?" demanded Liz.

Things turned nasty, very quickly. Jerry and Liz were no match for two men trained in unarmed combat.

Thrúd was a different matter. She had her father's Ás strength, and she'd played roughhouse with her combat-trained brothers—and beaten them—for years. She also had very powerful lungs. Shrieking blue murder, she flung Stephens back against the wall, making him lose his grip on Liz. Liz knew absolutely nothing about the science of unarmed combat but she managed to grab the strap of her shoulder bag and swing it metal corner first into her attacker's cheek. Meanwhile Thrúd had advanced on Bott, who was holding Jerry. "Keep off or I'll kill him," threatened the agent.

"Do that and I'll disembowel you, attach your entrails to a horse and whip it into a gallop," said Thrúd in a matter-of-fact voice, catching the bleeding-faced Stephens as he tried to attack her from behind, and hurling him backward, crashing him into the table. Liz had taken over yelling bloody blue murder. Then the raven—perhaps because Thrúd was between it and the window—flapped off out the door and into Ran's castle. It disobeyed the first rule of flying safety and looked back as it fled—which was why it flapped into Emmitt as he ran around the corner. He fell. Thor, panting up behind him, tripped trying to avoid him and crashed into the wall just short of the agents' doorway.

Bott, hearing the commotion, threw Jerry at Thrúd, and ran for the door, hauling Stephens to his feet. He saw Thor trying to stand up, and ran the other way.

Thor bellowed, "Alarums! Seal the windows and portals. To arms! To arms!" He staggered to his feet, and then was knocked over again by Thrúd running out after them.

Thereafter followed a very confusing half hour. Thor had alerted the castle to danger, but he hadn't told the defenders what it was they were presumably being attacked by. So Lamont actually saw

Bott and Stephens, and told them to get up to the ramparts. They didn't listen to him, but that didn't stop him taking his own advice. The two agents had a close brush with Fenrir who was being petted by a frightened Ella. And that was the last anyone saw of them.

The hero of the hour proved to be Emmitt. He'd landed on the raven, and had the common sense to stay lying on it, until Thor got back to him. The raven was stunned and had a broken leg.

So they had a raven . . . and two missing agents, who were going to be dead if either Liz or Thrúd caught up with them. Jerry had a bump on his head and a bloody nose.

Having seen to his nose and done her best to examine his head, Liz was now reading the English note from the raven's leg. "We had traitors," she said grimly, looking at the bird wrapped in a shirt, with only its legs protruding.

"They're bleeding," said Fenrir. "Open the portals and I'll go a-hunting." He looked at Liz. "I promise I won't just eat their livers."

Thor nodded. "Hunt them down. Hamstring them, Fenrir. I want them able to talk."

The great wolf nodded. Liz almost felt sorry for the two agents.

She turned her attention back to the raven. "I'm going to splint this leg. And then I want some cord—thong, perhaps—to attach the other leg to this chair. We need to know what this little bird has been carrying to-and-fro. And it is going to tell us. And it better not prove to be Hugin or he'll never see a jelly bean again."

It proved instead to be Munin. "Odin will be very angry!" said the raven.

"Good," said Loki. "I must see if Ran has a cage somewhere. I always wanted something to make Odin angry with."

Fenrir returned with two small boys in tow. "I had a choice," he growled. "I promised to let the men go in exchange for these smelly objects. And hugging," he said, "is beneath my dignity."

"We'll catch up with them," said Liz, as Lamont looked in grave danger of exploding.

"They're dead men walking," said Lamont. "What the hell happened? How did they get you two?" He hugged the boys fiercely, and then, despite what Fenrir had said, hugged the wolf. "I owe you," he said thickly. "If I can do it, I will. You only have to ask."

"We were just outside the beach gate. You said we were allowed to go there," said a subdued Ty. "Doing some stuff on the sand, and they came out."

"They grabbed us. They told us you'd said that they must take us to safety."

"They were waiting for a boat. They made a signal-fire."

"And then Fenrir came."

Ty started to cry. "Bott held a knife against my neck."

"Fenrir agreed to let them go, if they let us go," said Tolly. "If my new dad catches those guys . . ."

Cruz was a long way off. But as a choice of someone's kids to take hostage, Liz would have thought that it would have been wiser for the agents to have picked on a troll. There were lots of trolls here in Jötunheim. They were less dangerous than Cruz would be.

"It's not as bad as it seems at first glance," Jerry said squeezing Liz's hand. "Look, first off, the airborne assault just wasn't practical. Second, we're better off discovering the leak now than later. And we have Munin."

"Already addicted to rakfisk jelly beans." Liz gently pushed the hair away from the large lump on his forehead.

"Good. We'll have to let him go soon, or Odin will be suspicious when he returns."

Liz snorted. "That won't delight Loki."

"Tell him to use Munin to feed disinformation to Odin. He'll like that idea."

Agents Bott and Stephens sat in conference with the man they'd been sent to rescue or kill, enjoying some of his homemade whiskey. It wasn't very good whiskey, but after their close calls and the trip in a leaky Viking boat, any whiskey was welcome. As welcome and cozy as the respect they felt they'd finally found. This was a man who knew what they did, and valued them.

The initial moments of their meeting with Harkness had been disconcerting, since he didn't look in the least like the photograph of Harkness they'd been shown by Agent Supervisor Megane. But Bott and Stephens relaxed after he explained he'd had his appearance altered by Odin's magic. By now, after all they'd seen, the two PSA agents were willing to believe that readily enough. There wasn't any question this fellow was actually Harkness, since he knew details concerning his life and position in the NSA that no scruffy Norseman could possibly have known.

"Well, sir, it's like this," Stephens explained, "we were sent on this mission to rescue you from the Krim pyramid. Unfortunately we lost most of our team members, we were betrayed by the other people with us—and we've been having severe equipment problems. But we're still here."

Harkness tugged his little beard. "Equally unfortunately, we can't get back."

"They'll send a back-up squad through," said Stephens confidently.

"Well, maybe," said Harkness. "As you must have figured out by now, that's harder than it sounds. But, in the meanwhile, well, I've established myself in a position of influence and power here. I could use some good, reliable American help. Are you boys with me?"

"Yes, sir!" they said together, glad to be back in harness.

"Good. It's a pity your cover got blown, but make some other kind of plan. Our ally here figures he can win this Ragnarok. He's gone hunting some allies of his own, after the last bit of news you sent about Surt."

The Krim hierarchies were expressed in terms which even the Krim device found confusing. Nonetheless, they knew who among them had ascendancy. Once there had been billions of Krim. Now . . . things were different. The Krim did not die, of course. Not in the conventional sense, as they had long since abandoned bodies. They . . . simply seemed to fade away.

They'd been unprepared for what they had lost with those bodies. This was what had driven them to explore millions of systems across the galaxy. The feelings and emotions were like fine wine to them, rich and rejuvenating wine. The flood of pain and rage energies in an event like Ragnarok would sustain the Krim for a long while. Long enough—if they could gather the life energies to sacrifice—to do it again. And again. There were few of the Krim left now. This planet and its Ur-worlds could sustain them until another probe found more life.

And now there was a threat against that great feast! The Krim hierarchy shifted.

Leadership came to rest instead on one who possessed a body of flames. A creature not unlike the Krim themselves, in that energy and flames have something in common.

It would happen. Ragnarok would come, no matter how myth was twisted. After all, to the inhabitants of Midgard it would make little difference as to why Surt marched on Asgard.

CHAPTER 33

꩜꩜꩜꩜꩜

"There is someone on the beach to see you, Loki." Ran had amusement written on her normally austere face. "He is very uncomfortable coming here, to my castle."

That was just about the most words Liz had ever heard her use. Loki got up and walked down, and Liz followed out of curiosity.

The man on the beach had fishing tackle with him. For Liz that was always a good sign. "Who is he?" she whispered to Ran.

"Njörd. A Vanir sea and wind god. The husband of Skadi."

That didn't sound promising.

"Njörd," said Loki. His tone was not overly friendly. "Giantesses use your mouth for a piss-pot."

The Vanir shook his head. "You always did have a foul mouth, Loki. I was angry about that. It took me a long while to work out the kenning."

Loki shrugged. "If I had left you out, the Æsir would have thought you were a friend of mine."

"If you'd left it well enough alone, it wouldn't have happened at all," said Njörd.

"Yes. Maybe. It's a bit late for wisdom now. So why are you here, sea-god?"

"The Vanir want no part in this war that Odin drags us toward,

297

not now that Öku-Thor is gone. And Frey and Freyja sent me to talk to you."

Loki raised his eyebrows. "Madam Cat-house, and your son who has swapped his good sword for a giant girlfriend."

"You're one of the giants yourself, Loki."

"I know. Most of the Ás are either giants or half-bloods. What I wanted to know was whether Frey still thought he was going to war with a stag's antler or not."

Njörd shook his head. "No. Skírnir still has it."

"And Skírnir is still trotting on errands for Odin, is he? Dangerous paths, those to the dwarves and dark elves." Loki pursed his lips. "And how is Skadi?"

"Still in the pit. Odin has been unable, or unwilling, to remove the spell of binding from her." Njörd did not seem too upset about his wife's situation, though.

Loki snorted with laughter. He clapped Njörd on the shoulder. "I'll explain that sometime. In the meanwhile . . . I need to know that I can trust you, Vanir. You've a reputation for executing hostages, if you don't mind my reminding you."

"Of course I mind," Njörd said. "But it wasn't my stupid idea to chop off Mirmir's head. I'd have chopped off Hœnir's."

"Hœnir was always too long-legged to be caught," said Loki, with a nasty grin. "Mirmir would stop to think about running or try reason."

"Sometimes running is a better option," admitted Njörd.

"Yes, it is. Let's work out how we can make you a nasty surprise for Odin."

"Oh no," said Njörd. "No, no, no. Forget your crazy schemes, Loki. Frey, Freyja and my Vanir cousins made it clear to me. They won't take up arms against Odin and the other Æsir."

"Not much good as allies, are you?" said Loki dryly.

"Maybe not. But we will fight against our hereditary enemies. Surt and the sons of Muspell are our meat."

"They're not involved, Njörd. I've been talked out of asking for that alliance. For now. Anyway, why would I want your help fighting my own side?"

"My cousins in Vanaheim say the long lines of fire-wielders are assembling in the East, Loki. They come, and not at your bidding or naysaying. Odin has made common cause with Surt—against you."

There was a long silence. "Ragnarok comes, then, whether we want it or not."

"And the Vanir cannot stand against Surt's hosts and the sons of Muspell on their own, Loki," said Njörd. "We're not coming to you to help. We're coming *for* help. Vanaheim has no walls, unlike Asgard."

CHAPTER 34

⊘⊘⊘⊘⊘⊘

The ravens still flew across the heavens bringing word to Odin about the troop build-up in Jötunheim, which was stretching even Loki's power's to exaggerate. They also, in exchange for their favorite jelly beans, brought word of what was happening in the halls of Asgard. Odin was doing his best to ready the Æsir for war. He had sent messengers to the Vanir and South and East to Surt and Muspellheim.

It was the news from there that was worrying. Surt really did have millions of minions. He also, according to Hugin—and separately confirmed by Munin—had a black, five-sided pyramid for a neck ornament.

Lamont came to Jerry and Liz's shared room. "What's happening?"

Jerry bit his lip. "It looks like the end is Surt-ain. We're still, even with all of Hel's corpse warriors, very short of troops. And this is exactly what I was trying to avoid: that apocalyptic war."

Lamont snorted. "Surt-ain! I guess we'll just have to make sure it's a dead-Surt." He sat down on the bed. "I've been thinking. I'm not finding any answers to my problem with Marie, except to leave her like that forever. And I don't think that's what she would have wished. You're supposed to have acquired knowledge too, Jerry. Have you got any ideas for me?"

Jerry sighed. "Don't get your hopes up, but in one way, yes. The thing is, it would take magic or a miracle to cure Marie. Science and medicine can't do it. At least here, well, magic can work. I can think of two possibilities. One we get this world's foremost magic-user to help. The trouble is, that's Odin—and he's a tricky, Krim-controlled bastard. Two, if we could somehow get Marie to the world of Egyptian myth, we've got contacts there. And my magical skills there are a long way ahead of what they are here."

"I didn't even know that you could do magic here at all."

"Magic isn't as big a part of this mythology as it was in the Egyptian. Magic here tended to focus quite heavily on foretelling the future. Runes were used to invoke certain powers, and symbolism is vital. It goes a bit beyond the principals of similarity and contagion, although of course those do apply."

"Don't you love it when he talks in foreign languages?" said Liz.

Jerry grinned. "It gets worse. Poetry—verse and heiti and kennings—are all part of it. So are items of power." He paused, chewed his lip and then said, "I have to point out that there are plenty of examples of Odin raising dead warriors and restoring virginity, and there are also things like one-handed Tyr, and blind Hod, and dead Baldr. But there definitely are magical aspects that ordinary humans can manage."

"And how are you getting on with learning this lot?" asked Lamont.

"Slowly. Our biggest need is time, and that seems to be what Surt and Odin have worked out too. They're rushing things on. Surt has no major barriers to his west, just Myrkvid. We have to either cross Midgard, or the sea or the great river Élivágar. And Loki's *Naglfar*-ship is big, but it is a lousy ferry."

"Lamont knows this, Jerry," said Liz tiredly. "We've been consulting with him about the pontoon bridge."

"Xerxes," said Jerry.

"What?"

"History, dear," said Jerry. "That stuff you disapprove of. Where most problems had to get solved before, and we don't learn anything from. Xerxes was supposed to have crossed the Hellespont—that's the Dardanelles—on a bridge of boats with an army of two and half plus million men. Back in 490 BC, if I recall correctly."

"So it can be done?"

"Apparently."

"Good. Because we're ready to start planking. How wide are the Dardanelles?"

"I remember less geography than history."

"A pity. The Élivágar is about a mile wide and flows strong enough to shift most anchors. Lamont showed them how to make kedges, and I finally got through to the dumb trolls that straight down is not the right place for an anchor."

"Where do you put the anchor? Straight up?"

She shook her head. "Doesn't your ancient history explain cable lengths for laying off in strong currents? About six to seven times the depth."

Lamont laughed. "You know, we make a good team. What one member of group doesn't know, the other will, and we get to insult each other too."

In Asgard, the man the PSA agents knew as "Harkness"—gullible fools, they were, just as Thjalfi's new master had foreseen—held a conference with his new two acolytes. Thjalfi had to admit he liked having them here. He was in a position of power, but the Einherjar treated him as if he was a jumped-up servant, and so did the other Ás. Some of them—Njörd for one—didn't bother to hide their contempt. And having Odin for a master instead of Thor was a lot scarier. One-eye behaved very strangely half the time, and he was alert and mean.

But he needed to concentrate on the matter at hand, so he summoned up the trapped spirit of Harkness to guide him. "Look guys, the other side appear to be managing a hell of a rate of troop build-up. And it's pretty apparent that they are too useless to do it by themselves. So it has to be that bunch of renegades over there. We need to put them out of action. They're aiding and abetting the enemy."

"There's the kids . . ." Bott fiddled with the crossbow that Thjalfi had provided him with. "But they'll probably be under tight guard now."

"Hugin and Munin say that they are," said Harkness.

"There is one other weak spot," said Stephens. "That's Lamont Jackson. His wife is missing. From what I could work out she was in a coma. Something about the thorn of sleep."

"I was there," said Thjalfi-Harkness. "She's in what you might call suspended animation. We've got her tucked away behind a fire-wall."

"Well, he's pretty worried about her," continued Bott. "She's got some kind of fast growing cancer. They reckon that she would be dead if it wasn't for this coma."

"Good thinking, guys. That's the sort of leverage we need. Let me go and have a talk with Odin about her."

"It's a good point, Thjalfi. I can see that she'd be a valuable hostage. But I have other plans for her, now that you bring it up."

"We could turn this Lamont," suggested Thjalfi slyly.

"Turn him? Is he coming toward us?"

Thjalfi shook his head. "No, I mean make him our spy."

Odin shook his head. "No. She will die too soon from what you have said, and he knows that. I have a better idea. The device," he touched the pyramid pendant, "says we need more reenactments, with belief. I will make her into the vector for turning their cause into a doomed Völsung-saga. Get me Sleipnir saddled. I will send Sigurd, both to his doom and to hers. Let the Andvari curse deal with them. It is strong enough. I just hope she is strong enough to survive for long enough to hand it on."

The smile was cruel. "It has blighted even my most powerful foe before this."

Sigurd the Dragon-slayer traversed a land abandoned to war and kinslaying. He thought nothing much of it. Thus it was due to be when Fimbulwinter came. And he had a good hoard of treasure and was better at killing than almost anyone else, thanks to the sword Gram. He even indulged in a sacrifice or two himself. Keeping the Æsir sweet was a reasonably wise idea, seeing as Odin had helped his cause so much so far.

He wasn't that surprised to see the old man with one eye, a broad hat and his blue cloak, waiting for him. He bowed respectfully. "Hail, Allfather."

"Hail, Sigurd Dragon-slayer. You must follow the green paths up onto Hindafjall, to a great hall fenced in flame. There find a Valkyrie maid stabbed with Ygg's thorn. She slew men that He had not wished dead. Find her, if you can gain her. She is like no other there, her skin the color of copper, and her hair dark. Give her your ring, the ring you took from Fafnir's hoard, and take her into the lands of Midgard to the northwest. There is great battle and much honor to be gained there."

CHAPTER 35

ⓔⓔⓔⓔⓔⓔ

"Ur-Greece," said Throttler, "is nothing like it used to be. The vineyards are taking the place over. Little Pan and Bacchus have been very busy. Anyway. It's a negative. I went and checked with Circe first, Medea. She sends her love by the way, and says she could use some more fish and a visit from your cooking Americans. She thanks you very much for the shampoo. And if possible she would like another one of those Landrace pigs. Your John Salinas did improve her stock, but he disappeared after the Krim did."

She looked cross, for a moment. "I had to fly all over to find Prometheus, but the same story. There were a rash of disappearances just after we attacked and conquered Olympus. Then we went to Ur-Egypt."

Bes took over. "Harmakhis was very cooperative. He confirmed the same thing."

"Bes dear," said Throttler, patting her breasts. "Do you think I should get one of those boob-jobs?"

Bes looked at his hands, at her frontage, at his hands. "They say that more than a handful is a waste." He looked at his large hands again. "So, maybe. If you want one."

"Well, I'd look carefully at fur-lined bras if you do," said Cruz. "Because from what we can work out this Norse Ur-Mythworld is as cold as ice, and then some. It's having some kind of three-year winter."

Throttler looked disapproving. "I don't like hiding my assets, and I don't like snow. Has the professor located a 'carrier' for us?"

"Yes," said Cruz. "One of the PSA operatives arrested by Fish and Wildlife. He's agreed in exchange for immunity from prosecution." He started rubbing down a dragon with a lifeboat oar acquired especially for the purpose. "Their scales are looking magnificent, eh?"

He was very proud of the way the two dragons were looking. It had been a tough interview with the officials and zoologists from Fish and Wildlife. But the fact that the two dragons were positively gleaming with a new metallic sheen and good health, and so obviously affectionate and happy, had won the biologists over. Eventually. The park might want them back, but the health and welfare of such irreplaceable creatures had to come first. It was a real tragedy that they could never be bred. Anibal Cruz was just glad that the Fish and Wildlife boys didn't know that Bitar and Smitar were planning on going along with the sphinx on her next venture. He was also planning to go. He had a stepson to fetch home.

His new commanding officer, Lieutenant Evans, put his foot down. "No, Sergeant. You can't. Not this first trip.

"With respect, sir. I can see Mac staying put. But we need a reliable, and uh, experienced soldier along. Throttler and Bes are not used to American military methods, sir. And we can't trust that PSA shit as far as we can throw him."

"I take your point, Sergeant. Also the point about the dragons. Dr. Gunnarsson has pointed out that they'll automatically have respect in a Norse environment whereas Throttler and Bes will have to establish it. But I think they'll do that quite fast. Let them go through. If they succeed in planting the Sphinx image . . . You can go on the next trip. My word on it."

As Cruz had seen Bes in his new down-padded jacket swatting a dragon that fancied his new epaulettes, he had no doubt about that. Bes looked like a short, squat Michelin man on steroids in that outfit. No sane Viking was going to give him too much trouble. And it did make sense. That way the pyramid got a minimum amount of energy. It didn't appear to register Throttler's flights in and out.

So Cruz had to wait, with the rest of the team, while Throttler and Bes went alone with the PSA agent.

"Some man with fake wings and hamstrung legs," said Throttler when they returned.

"Ah. Völund. Or as you might say Wayland," said Dr. Gunnarsson eagerly.

"Wrong way to land, you mean," said Bes. "I need thicker boots, by the way, Cruz. Wrong way to land shouldn't have argued about sky space with us."

Bes hefted Agent Schmitt off Throttler's broad back. Cruz caught the bundle of a man who hung limply in his arms. He was breathing. "He seems to have lost his wits. I had to subdue him, or he'd have had us out of the sky too. This Norse place is full of snow and people with no manners." Bes seemed to relish the idea of teaching them some. "Anyway. It's all set up. Throtsy needs a rest, though, before we fly again."

Throttler nodded. "At least four hours. And I need lots of food."

Three hours and fifty-eight minutes later, Bes and Throttler were ready to go again. Cruz was waiting, with his pack, a composite bow and a jungle knife, being hugged by a crying little boy and a woman with pride and tears on her face.

"I'll bring him back, Medea," said Bes indulgently.

"And my big brother," said Priones.

"Do my best," said Cruz, getting up on Smitar's back.

"Don't you dare chew," said Throttler to Bitar, as the creatures formed a daisy chain, preparing for flight.

"You sure you don't want me along?" asked Mac, looking up at him.

"Yeah. Someone has to keep the army going," said Cruz, knowing what the offer meant, and knowing just how little his buddy wanted to go into the Mythworlds again. "Okay, let's move out."

Cruz found himself airborne above the island of Sævarstad where the newly erected military issue kit-sphinx now stood.

"Hello. What's that?"

It was a dragon in the water, a huge dragon, at least twice the size of Bitar or Smitar. The last time these two had seen a dragon—which had proved to be a shape-shifter and not the real thing—they'd plunged headlong. Now both of them coughed nervously, almost in unison. "Uh, Cruz."

"Yeah?"

"What do we say?" demanded the dragons.

"We don't know how to talk to lady dragons," said Smitar.

"Yeah, you haven't told us about those birds and bees yet," complained Bitar.

"Should we . . . er, go and ask her if she's doing anything Saturday night?" suggested Smitar. "We could go clubbing . . ."

Bitar wrinkled his nose. "But I don't like them after they've been clubbed. Too tender. Maybe we could just give her a florist?"

"Offer to buy her a drink?" asked Smitar. "Candy is dandy but liquor is . . ."

"Let's just fly down and see what happens," said Cruz who really had no idea what pick-up lines worked on dragons. "How do you know she's female? You might want to say 'hello sailor.'"

"She's swimming. Females are aquatic," explained Bitar.

"It figures. Beach romances. Do they wear bikinis?" asked Cruz bemusedly.

"Not as far as I know. Is my crest straight?" asked Smitar nervously.

They were skimming the wave tops in aerobatic elegance now. The female dragon put her head up from the water. "Bitar and Smitar?" she said.

The two dragons ended up crashing into each other and splashing down into the waves, both puce with embarrassment and too tongue-tied to speak.

Cruz stood on Smitar's back. "That's them," he said. "Can I introduce my two suave dragon buddies to you, lovely lady?"

She answered him in Norse.

Beneath him Smitar quivered. "What a voice," he said faintly. "And a Swedish accent too."

"Sweetish? She's pure sugar." Bitar seemed completely besotted by the huge dragon. "I wonder how good my dragonish is?"

"Do you mind taking me to the beach before you start trying?" asked Cruz. He'd have got more response out of a brick wall.

CHAPTER 36

⊚⊚⊚⊚⊚⊚

Marie Jackson lay within the ring of fire, unbreathing and yet not dead, walking through dreams of her youth with an older man she loved. A man with a quick retentive mind, just out of the Marine Corps, hopeful of a bright future. She was not alone and afraid in those dreams.

She was not alone in the ring of fire either.

When Sigurd rode up on his great battle-steed Grani, having jumped the wall of fire and kicked open the great brass-bound door, he found the hall was so full of Valkyries that the walls were close to bulging. He had his instructions from Odin, though. Find the copper-skinned one, the one he'd fancied after killing Fafnir, wake her, give her Andvari's ring, and the usual courtesies to seal their betrothal.

He had to leave Grani outside and wander around the hall a bit, pausing for a serious drink at the end of each row. My, but there was quite a selection here! He found the woman at the end of the third row, if she'd been another five rows on, he'd have found two of her. Like dragonslaying, it was dry work, keeping his attention on their faces.

To save time later, he arranged her skirts. She had good legs. He took off his sword belt because it was in the way. Then, kneeling down between those legs he leaned forward and pulled out the thorn of sleep. He had a thorn of his own to put in instead.

⊘⊘   ⊘⊘   ⊘⊘

Marie blurred out of the sweet dream to find someone leaning over her, his lips pursed for a kiss.

And it wasn't the person she'd been dreaming of, either. He was holding her shoulders, but her legs were free, and so were her hands. The slaps he got were so fast and had all her strength in them that they must have almost popped his eardrums. Then, when he sat back, she kicked him with both feet. Hard.

He was big muscular man. But she had strong legs and he really hadn't expected it.

Sitting up and pulling her skirts down, the first thing that Marie noticed was the sword lying next to her. Seeing as the muscle-bound lover-boy was getting to his feet looking ugly, Marie pulled it out of its scabbard. She expected it to be so heavy she could barely lift it.

Instead it was as light as . . . well, a feather duster. A very big feather duster.

She'd never used a sword before, but she knew how to wield a feather duster. And was this guy ever a big cobweb!

"Be careful with that sword, Brynhild!" said the lover-boy. He backed off, and tripped over a girl in a steel breastplate. He knocked the thorn out of her neck and she groaned.

"Now look what you've made me go and do. Where is it?" He scrabbled around looking for the thorn, and pushed it back into her neck as she sat up. The girl promptly collapsed again.

"I'm not Brynhild, and take that thing out of her neck," said Marie trying another swing with the sword.

"But then she'll wake up. And it's you I am supposed to give my ring to." Marie recognized the overmuscled lover-boy. The dragon-killer. He was holding out a broad gold ring. "I am the mighty Sigurd, the Dragon-slayer, Valkyrie. I have come to make you mine."

"I got the only ring I want, thanks," said Marie, showing him her wedding band. "And that means hands off, see. I'm taken. Or I'll use this thing to make your plans genuinely unworkable. No tools left, so to speak. Now take that thing out of her neck, before I take your fool head off."

With this odd sword she felt as if she could almost do it. She looked around and realized that it wasn't just the one girl with a thorn in her neck. There were hundreds of them. Well, they probably didn't want to be in this enchanted sleep any more than she did.

She noticed that, instead of doing as he was told, the mighty Sigurd was attempting to edge around her. She took a wild swing at him, not expecting to hit him—or even really intending to.

The sword had its own ideas though. Sigurd leaped backwards, falling over yet another blond woman with a mailshirt and a thorn in her neck. He yowled and held the pieces of his chainmail vest. "That was kobold-weave, you silly bitch!"

You didn't talk to Marie Jackson like that. Not now. Not ever. And certainly not in the mood she was in. Ten seconds later, Sigurd the hero had retreated out of the door and was scrambling to mount his horse. Marie was alone in a hall of full of armored women who lay like corpses around her. She rested on the sword for a bit, looking at the scene. Well. She had a husband and kids to get back to, while she could. She stepped toward the fire-wall.

And realized that right now she wasn't going anywhere.

She took a deep breath. It hurt. Then, pinching her lips with determination, she walked back to where Sigurd's scabbard and belt lay. She put on the belt and put the sword back into its scabbard. Then she turned to the nearest woman and pulled the thorn out of her neck. And then she worked her way down the line, doing the same.

Five minutes later and she was surrounded by some three hundred puzzled looking women. "Where is the Hero?" demanded several.

"Why have we been woken?" demanded several more, looking around in the milling mob. It looked like a Macy's mailshirt sale, and sounded worse. Like an opera chorus.

"Who woke us from our enchanted sleep?" demanded yet more. They didn't sound too pleased about it either.

A lot of fingers were pointing at her. This could just get ugly, and she had nowhere to run.

"Where is the hero? Where is Sigurd? Where is Beowulf? Where is Gunnar . . ." they chorused around her, packing ever closer.

She pulled the sword out. And suddenly they backed off, silent. Then one said, "That is the sword Gram."

Then a silence. "Are you Sigurd in a woman's body?" asked one, incredulously. The rest giggled.

"Shut up!" Marie was suddenly tired, and very cross. She

pointed to one statuesque blonde. "I don't know what I'm doing here. So, maybe if you tell me what you are doing here, I'll have a better idea."

The blonde looked puzzled, a thing that was probably not hard for her. "I am the Valkyrie Sigfrida. I angered Odin and was cast out of Asgard, trapped by the thorn of sleep, doomed to lie in the hall on the hilltop behind the wall of flame until a great hero and warrior was courageous enough to leap the fire-wall and free me, and take me to be his bride." She looked inquisitorially at Marie. "So where is he, if you have his sword?"

Marie felt vaguely guilty. "Look honey, you're better off without him. It wasn't you he came to fetch anyway. And he's gone."

"But what do we do now?" wailed the blonde. "I *will not* go back to Valhöll."

"No," agreed another.

"Not a chance," said a third.

"Enough is enough . . ."

Marie held the sword up. "All right!" she yelled. "Enough, already. I heard you. Though why you want a pumpkin-head like Sigurd is beyond me. He's got no brains. And he needs a bath . . ."

"At least there is only one of him," said Sigfrida.

"Yes, even Freyja's girls get nights off."

Bit by bit, the details of a Valkyrie's life in Valhöll became clear. No wonder a life with a single hero, and handmaidens, seemed a good deal.

"I thought the South Side Cafe was bad," said Marie ruefully. At least there you could elbow off any over-familiar customers and you got tips for waitressing. "It's time someone told you girls about emancipation. Because you sure are in slavery."

"Oh, no. Slaves have it worse."

"Things have to change," said Marie.

Morgue duty—and picking out the ones that Odin wanted dead, waitressing and being a joy-girl to corpses. No wonder the place was so full.

CHAPTER 37

Jerry put his head in his hands. "I wish I knew just what we should do next."

Liz had just come in from the pontoon bridge. She sat down next to him, in front of a desk littered with bits of parchment. "You'll figure it out, Jerry. You always do."

"I just seem a bit short of inspiration this time. I need some kind of feint. Some kind of distraction."

"And unfortunately," said Liz, "I don't think you mean me."

"I have had enough of you distracting them," said Jerry.

"Well, I got a nice horn out of it last time . . ." She stopped. "What about that horn?"

"What horn?"

"Heimdall's. I stole it. We brought it with us out of Asgard. It's in that big pot full of black stuff. I know Thrúd tied a cover over it. Let me go and ask her what she's done with it."

"Heimdall's horn might do the trick," said Jerry, brightening. "It was supposed to be loud enough to be heard everywhere."

"You might need as much wind as he has to blow it, though," said Liz dryly. "I'll go and find Thrúd."

"I'll come with you. I could use a little exercise."

So they walked off in search of Thrúd. They found her and Thor together trying to teach Emmitt how to wield a sword.

313

When Liz explained, Thrúd nodded guiltily. "I had Ran put it in her treasure-room. It's mead. I . . . didn't want to leave it too close to Papa-Thor."

"I'm stronger now," said Thor stoutly. "I can resist, even if alcohol still has mastery over me. Let us go and find the horn."

They found the kettle, still sealed with a rope and oilcloth. Thrúd cut the cord and revealed the black liquor underneath. "Very dark mead," said Thor. "I've only seen one other this dark and it was made with the wise Kvasir's blood mixed with the honey."

"Ugh," said Liz.

"It's magical mead," explained Thor.

"It'd have to be, and with an added antiemetic." Liz rolled up her sleeve and stuck her hand into the liquid. She pulled up Heimdall's enormous horn, and held it above the kettle to drip. "I should have brought a towel. We'd better take it and wash it."

Thor produced a piece of linen. "Here. I was just polishing Mjöllnir when you came along."

"Thanks," said Liz, gratefully taking it and putting the horn onto it. She sniffed her fingers and then tasted one. Licked her lips. "You know, of all the mead, this is the best, indeed. Hey. I'm a poet and I didn't know it."

Thor put his hand over his eyes. At first Liz thought it was a reaction to her feeble poetry. She was about to persecute him with some more, when he turned to Thrúd. "Just where did you find this mead?" he demanded.

"In the same storeroom we found Loki," said Thrúd. "It was not one I'd seen before. Very cobwebbed."

"Call Loki," said Thor in a strangled voice. "Let us find out how he came to be in that place. Quickly, girl!"

Thrúd ran off, and returned with an out of breath Loki. "Fire? Disaster?" he said, as he tried to catch his breath.

"How did you get into that storeroom that you and Sigyn hid in?" said Thor.

Loki chuckled. "Odin's cleverness backfired on him. Back when we were still on reasonable terms he asked me devise a hiding-spell for him. I did. I'm better at that sort of trickery than he could ever be. But I recognize my own work. When we came down from the gallery, looking for a place to hide, I saw it at once. It was easy enough to break the spell on my own work. I was just reconstructing it when these two bundled in."

"Loki," said Thor slowly. "I know that you sometimes think that I am a bit slow. Sometimes I think it myself. But this time it was you who was a fool. Why would Odin use one of your cunning spells to hide a storeroom?"

Loki narrowed his eyes. Clicked his tongue. "It was a treasure-room, wasn't it? What a fine opportunity I missed to loot it. Ah, well. Too late now."

"I doubt if you would have got a chance to steal a more valuable treasure than the one you took by accident to hide Heimdall's horn in," said Thor dryly. He pointed at the kettle of black liquid. "That is Kvasir's mead of inspiration."

Loki's mouth opened wide . . . and he sat down with a thump on the floor. He started to laugh, and laugh, until the tears ran down his face. And Liz looked like she was going to throw up.

"Oh, Helblindi! If I tried for a century I could not have tweaked your beard so well," said Loki, wiping his eyes. "I wonder how I get to best taunt him with this?"

Liz took a deep breath. "Not taunt. Use it, Loki. You and him." She pointed to Jerry. "We need inspiration, genius and fine persuasive words, and yes, poetry too. We need them now. We go to war. Never was our need so great, never was the hour so late."

They all looked at her. "Kvasir talking," said Loki in a choked voice.

"I know," said Liz. "I feel sick, but it does seem to work."

She looked at Thor. "We'll boil some. Boil the alcohol off. We'll need all the inspired leadership we can get, and the warriors all look up to you."

"Skírnir rides fast and far to the caves of the black dwarves on Aurvangar to beg them for a new horn for Heimdall," said Munin, as Liz held the rakfisk jelly bean for him.

"Other than that," said Hugin, "Ull and his archers line the walls of Asgard. The Einherjar train and marshall. Freyja has donned her falcon mantle and flies across the Vrigid plain. Her warriors and Frey's band march behind his chariot drawn by the great boar Gullinborsti, out of the gates of Asgard. They lead Freyja's cat-drawn chariot too. They will give you challenge there."

Loki smiled and said nothing. Down in the workshop Lamont was building a new chariot for Thor. For some reason the artificer to new Ás (as Loki had named them) was calling it the SUV. Loki was impressed by it. It might even survive Thor's driving. Thor's huge goats Tanngnjóst and Tanngrisnir had been summoned.

He handed over the jelly bean and stood up.

A few moments later he and a party of mountain-giants were heading down the trail to Aurvangar.

Skírnir was surprised to see a black dwarf outside the caves. Normally he had to go from cave to cave, hunting them. They drove a hard bargain too.

He dismounted and bowed respectfully. "Greetings, Sindri."

The dwarf smiled at him. "And what do you want here, Skírnir?"

"I have been sent by the great Odin of the Æsir to crave a boon from the smith-artificer sons of Ivaldi. I offer the same generous payment as last time, Sindri."

Loki was interested to discover that Skírnir had had dealings with Sindri before, even if Skírnir wasn't actually having dealings with him this time. Loki hadn't known that Helblindi had had business with the dwarf-smith in the past. Like most things that Odin had a hand in, this smelled. Had Odin set him up when he'd come here to get Sif's golden hair? He began to suspect so. "And what would you need me to do this time?" Loki-in-Sindri-guise asked. "The same again?"

Skírnir shook his head. "Loki will not come here again. No, we have need of a replacement for Heimdall's horn."

Loki the shape-changer tugged his chin. "I could do it. But it is near the Time. It would cost you dearly. More dearly than just leading Loki into a stupid wager."

"Odin has said that he will be very generous. I have a full score of the apples of Idun, and a treasure in jewels."

"It is nearly the Time. What use are the apples of youth to us this close to the Time?"

"What would you have, then?" asked Skírnir.

Loki pointed. "That sword."

Skírnir clutched the handle protectively. "It is a magic sword, given me by Lord Frey."

"I know," said Loki. "I can make lesser swords. But that one is special. Give it to me and I will have a gjallarhorn at the gates of Asgard for you." *Outside the gates, but still there,* thought Loki. "A horn that will be heard across the nine worlds, as good as the one Heimdall lost. And to seal the bargain I will throw in a weapon that Odin could use. I have made a beast that will burrow under whole armies. Surely Odin will reward, generously, a loyal servant who brings him such a gift."

Reluctantly, Skírnir unbuckled the sword, and handed it to him. "Where is this mole?"

"It is in my cave," said Loki pointing. "You may try it out. How did you think we made these caves? By digging?"

So Skírnir followed Loki into the cave, and Loki took down a cage with a mole in it, from a shelf.

"It looks rather small," said Skírnir doubtfully.

"But you do know the power of such a thing? Here. You can try it. You see, it is blind and will not dig when it is in the light. I'll go out and close up the cave. You let it loose and point it where you wish it to go. Simple, really."

"But . . ."

Before he got any further, Loki and Frey's sword were outside, pushing, with a mountain giant's help, a large rock over the entrance.

"Time to ride," said Loki grinning wickedly. "And the joy of it all is that everything I told him was true."

CHAPTER 38

⊘⊘⊘⊘⊘

"Do you think you can give me a lift to the beach?" asked Cruz of Throttler. "I don't think that either of these dragons is receiving me."

Smitar shook his head, but didn't take his eyes off the huge dragon in the water below. "Sorry, Cruz. Uh . . . any advice on chatting up foreign women?"

The only intelligible words Bitar and Smitar had managed to exchange thus far with the female water dragon were their own names and one explanatory name: Liz. She must have met Nessie's big sister somewhere and told her about Bitar and Smitar.

"What about a serenade?" said Bitar. "Old Henri once said that music is a language that transcends all barriers. Except German, he said."

"Okay. You lead."

Smitar cleared his throat. "*Like a mounting in spring-time!*" he bellowed.

Bitar continued, "*Like a knight and a florist . . .*"

Wildlife exploded and fled from the woodland on the coastal headland. So did an armored horseman, clinging to his runaway steed. He didn't cling well enough though. A few seconds later he landed with a ringing clatter on the beach.

"Let's go and ask him some questions," said Cruz, knowing full well that he would have a language problem, but thinking it had to be better than the singing.

"Sure," said Bitar. "He's pre-gift-wrapped so we could give him to this lovely lady."

Smitar nodded. "We have a knight. Now all we need is a florist."

They swam toward the beach, followed by the lady-dragon. The stunned knight had already had a visit from Bes and Throttler.

Bes was sitting on his chest.

Throttler leaned over and said, "Why does the chicken cross the road?"

Cruz was close enough to hear him say, "I don't know."

"Throttler! Don't eat him!" yelled Cruz. "He speaks English!"

"No, he speaks Thracian," said Throttler.

"Puntish," said Bes.

Cruz took a deep breath. You had to get used to magic eventually. "We just got ourselves a translator. Ask him his name."

"Sigurd Dragon-slayer," said the knight.

Three large dragonish faces stared down at him from a distance of a few yards.

"Might be time for a name-change, dude," said Cruz.

Bes got off his chest and Sigurd stood up. He was a tall, muscular man. He looked down his nose at Cruz. "Do not think I fear your monsters, magician. They are illusions. I have already slain the last dragon."

Bes grappled Sigurd and threw him back down to the ground, and then jumped onto his chest. "You're irritating," he growled.

"They're imports," explained Cruz. "But the lady is local and she looks mighty pissed with you. Now I need to know. Where is Liz? And how come you understand and speak our language?"

"I have no knowledge of this Liz," protested Sigurd. "I went to rescue the Valkyrie Brynhild from the wall of flame. But she spurned me. Now I go in search of Odin or glorious war. And as for your accursed tongue, I speak and understand it by virtue of having eaten the heart of Fafnir the dragon. I can understand and speak to all the birds of the air and beasts of the field. Even these."

This guy had the ultimate in short life expectancies. Still, he was the only translator they had, for now. Cruz stopped him from becoming a three-way snack. Instead he fished out some parachute cord that had become rope in the way of the Mythworlds. While Bes kept Sigurd pinned, Cruz tied him up.

"Ask the big dragon how we find Liz," said Cruz. "And no trouble or I'll let Bes educate you properly."

Sigurd the once-dragonslayer and the now trussed-up dragon take-out did as he was told.

The female dragon replied melodiously, but in a foreign language. Sigurd translated. "She says, at the castle of Ran. She will show us the way."

Loki and his soldiers returned, laughing, with a sword. "With this, Frey can stand against Muspellheim," said Loki. "And is Surt going to be surprised . . . Hello." He pointed out to sea. "Look. Here is trouble. To arms!"

Liz looked, cheered and hugged the first person available, who happened to be Loki.

"Hold yourself back, wench," he said cheerfully. "Sigyn doesn't like it."

"She'll like this. We just got allies. Our friends."

Cruz was prepared for the cheering. What he wasn't ready for was the small dark tousle-haired boy running into him so hard that he nearly knocked him off his feet, while yelling "Papa!" and hugging as much of him as he could hold.

"I said you'd come," said Tolly thickly, from the shelter of Cruz's arms.

"Yep. I've come to take you all home."

Jerry and Lamont looked at each other.

Jerry shook his head. So did Lamont. "The kids go home. But we can't."

Lamont nodded. "You can't take me, Lord, because I can't go. I owe my soul to the company store. Come, let's explain this, while we feed everyone."

"Oh, good," said Bitar. He prodded the trussed Sigurd with his tail. "Can we start with him?"

Liz looked at the trussed victim. "Sigurd," she said. Then she turned to the two dragons. "Boys, I have a girl that wants to meet you. Only she's a bit shy so you must promise that you'll be nice to her. Her name is Jörmungand, and she's sweet."

"We met her. She's gorgeous," said Bitar, eagerly.

"But we can't talk to her," said Smitar.

"Don't be so shy," said Liz, amused. "She's dying to make your acquaintance properly. Just relax."

"She just doesn't speak our language," explained Bitar.

"And what do we talk to her about?" asked Smitar. "Is she interested in sports?"

"She's into literature," said Liz and had the rare joy of seeing two dragons say "Oh, help," simultaneously.

In the meanwhile Loki had wandered over to Sigurd. "And how is Fafnir's hoard?" he asked. "You know I won it originally from a river just near here. In those days it belonged to Andvari the dwarf." He looked at Sigurd's hand. "It seems that one part of it just came back to me."

The mead of inspiration, for all its unpleasant origins and its tendency to make one speak in verse, had one upside. It helped one link things together. Jerry turned to Sigyn as Loki bent over the unfortunate Sigurd. "Lady Sigyn, you said that you've known Loki forever."

"Close to," she said with a smile. "Of course we have only been married for a small part of that time."

"Did Loki's luck ever seem to change dramatically?"

Sigyn raised her eyebrows. "I suppose so. He was always lucky. But in the early days, if he threw a stone in a pool he'd hit a salmon. He was fun in those days. He laughs less now than he did."

"Lamont," said Jerry urgently. "Do you remember hearing in any of those sagas and skaldic verses you got Jörmungand to read for you, any mention of Andvari's ring?"

Lamont blinked. "Sure. Reginsmál. When Andvari had to hand over the ring because Loki insisted, he cursed it."

"He said 'No one wins joy with my wealth,'" said Thrúd.

Jerry cleared his throat. "Loki. Leave it." Loki was in the act of taking the ring from Sigurd's hand.

"But it is a fine piece of work," said Loki. "And it was mine once before, before we had to pay it over as part of the blood-price for Otr, that I killed in error."

"It is cursed. And in this Ur-universe the curse works—and it doesn't go away, just because the ring passed from your hands."

"But Odin bade me take it from Andvari . . . oh."

Loki stood as if frozen. Then he started to swear. He swore for a full three minutes.

At last he stopped, took a deep breath, leaned over and took the ring. "I might as well have it. Since I have the curse anyway."

"I think I might just have an answer," said Jerry.

"What? It won't help to destroy it, although doing that will stop the curse being passed on."

"You could give it back," said Jerry. "Give it to Andvari. Then he would either have to lift the curse, or be cursed himself. And while undoing the magic of another is difficult, undoing your own is easy."

Loki grinned wickedly. "Let's give him back his curse, then. Ran dear, can I borrow your net again?"

"Millions of people on Earth will thank you, Loki. You've just spared them from the dreaded Nibelungenlied."

Jerry felt that it was a good thing that he had the Mead of Inspiration that enabled him to speak so persuasively that no one could resist. Getting Bes, Throttler and Cruz to go home was taking all the skill that he could muster.

The dragons were a lost cause. Bitar and Smitar were bitten and smitten with love. Or lust, at least, and now they were armed with a translation spell. They were badly enough bitten to be trying their claws at poetry. And, to prove that love is blind, or at least severely shortsighted, Jörmungand, who poured scorn on most of the finest skaldic verse, was encouraging them.

So Cruz and Tolly, Ty and Ella were headed home.

"I'll be back with reinforcements. We're searching for snatchees, actually. But we can't do that properly if there's a war that will destroy everything and everyone."

Jerry refrained from pointing out that, from what he could establish, Norse Ur-Mythworld time ran at least five times as fast as it did back in the U.S. By the time the reinforcements arrived they'd be inside Asgard, if the plan he had kept close to his chest worked.

Lamont had had—and lost—a fight with Emmitt about going home. "Marie is not here to keep him on the rails," said the boy, stubbornly. "And we need Thor to win."

It was impossible to deny either of those points, or that Emmitt spending his time with Thor was anything but good for both of them. The boy was becoming very knowledgeable about tea, and how to split your enemy's skull with a two-handed axe.

The Krim device detected the loss in life-energy, again. It had a better grasp on what was happening now. It had not known that it was possible to manipulate the vibrations and energy of Ur-universe like that. For now it would seal off the energy level. Later . . . the mathematics was complex, but it might have a way to use Ur-myth creatures as footsoldiers back in their world.

chapter 39

Hugin cocked his head at the prisoner Sigurd. They had no reason to hold Sigurd now, but one might say that he was in protective custody. The dragons had all threatened to eat him on sight. Hugin poked his beak at him. "I thought Odin had sent you to fetch Brynhild?"

"I did," said Sigurd morosely. "I passed through the ring of fire on the mountaintop and woke the black-skinned Brynhild from her enchanted sleep."

"You did *what*?" said Lamont, scattering jelly beans.

"Bitar and Smitar will take you to this flame-walled place. They'll have to stay high up to keep off the fire, but I should be able to lower you safely," said Liz.

It was a measure of Lamont's state of mind that he did not even question the strength of Liz's homemade mountaineering equipment. Jerry thought the link and plate arrangement very frail.

"Getting you out without a winch is going to be a bit trickier, but if you get a bit of height . . ."

"I'll work it out," said Lamont. "Let's go."

So off they went, as the equipment for the attack on Asgard was loaded into *Naglfar*.

"Thor," said Marie.

"Thor?" said Brynhild.

"Thor?" said Sigfrida.

Marie wished like hell that they wouldn't repeat everything she said. But the blond bimbos from Asgard weren't exactly original thinkers.

"Yes. Thor. He's a better bet than some so-called hero. He needs people in that place of his. And he's a decent enough man. Or god, I suppose."

"Well, yes. Except when he's drinking," said Brynhild.

"He's given it up," said Marie, crossing her fingers behind her back. "So that's where we need to go." It also happened to be where her man and children were, but she didn't see any reason to get into that with the Valkyries. "Now we just need some way to put out a piece of the fire."

"The fire is magical," said Sigfrida. "It cannot be extinguished."

"But we could call our horses and go over the top," said Gudrun. "If you are sure Thor would have a place for us?"

"Honey, trust me on this. Thor will have a place for you because I will throw him out of there on his fat ass otherwise," said Marie. The Valkyries gawked at her.

"Call these horses of yours," she commanded. "Time's a-wasting and I haven't got much."

She adjusted her sword and then bent over and picked up a thorn. She wouldn't mind giving it back to the son of a bitch. She had a good idea of a great place to push it up, too.

Hel's troops had been crossing the pontoon bridge for three days now, and more were still coming. But Loki was not going to wait. He knew that he could not.

He walked beside the great wolf, and behind him followed the legions of the dead, the files of frost giants, and the huge mountain giants.

Thor's new chariot rumbled beside them as they moved across the thin snow of the Vrigid plain. As the walls of Asgard came in sight, the chunky boy beside Thor picked up a huge horn, with a silver chased mouthpiece. That Emmitt could play the trumpet—without much expertise, true—was something of a bonus.

Emmitt put the horn to lips and blew.

Emmitt blew his heart and soul into that horn, fully expecting a noise like a sick fart.

What came out the other end was the roaring of many trumpets, so loud he nearly dropped it. There was no way he could finger any notes, but somehow he was playing the "Battle Hymn of the Republic." And behind them the dead began to beat their shields like some vast heartbeat, loud and strong.

Thor raised his hammer and thunder spoke. It rolled across the plain, and echoed off the white walls. Loki and the great wolf stalked ever closer to Frey and Freyja, assembled with the Vanir on the plain.

Now the wolves howled and the great dog Garm gave tongue.

Ever closer.

No order to charge was given.

In the distance they could see the lines of fire, of Surt's minions pouring out of Myrkvid.

"If they're not all watching now . . . they never will be."

A flight of Valkyries turned above the battlefield.

"Let there be fire and smoke," said Loki.

And there was.

"Look," Jerry had said, pointing at the map that Liz had created with Thor, Thrúd, Sigyn and Loki. "This." He pointed to the river that ran through Asgard.

"It disappears around here. The bit where the fenlands are."

"Ah. The Gjalar. Yes, it disappears into the ground there."

"It comes out here," said Jörmungand pointing with her tongue. "To the north of the Vrigid plain. It is how I got into Asgard to drink with Thor. But it is no use to anyone but me. It is at least a league long and there is no air in most of it." She brightened. "I could go in and cause a distraction, if you like. The boys say I'm very distracting."

"Vain, more-like," said Fenrir.

Jerry tugged his goatee. Sigyn told brother and sister to hush. "The distraction," said Jerry, "will be on the Vrigid plain. Loki, I know you would like to conduct your battle with Odin in person, but the truth is, the Vanir will need you. They will need Frey's sword, and they will need Hel's host, to defeat Surt and the sons of Muspell. Otherwise fire will consume Asgard, Midgard and even Jötunheim. I am right, aren't I? You are the trickster, but also *Logi*, the fire-god, both the friend and foe of mankind. You can warm, or destroy. Your nature is mercurial, just like fire itself. Fire always has a place in every pantheon, just as the trickster does. I just hadn't thought it through."

Loki nodded. "And Sigyn is the hearth-goddess. She who shapes fire into something to warm and nurture."

"I should have guessed that earlier," said Jerry. "Frey is a fertility god. The maker of green things, which is why he and he alone is effective against Surt, because Surt is fire uncontained."

Loki nodded. "Surt is fire the destroyer. That is his power. Frey can stand against him, but not without huge hurt. The others are powerless."

"But you can deal with Surt. Njörd said as much."

Loki nodded.

"And just who can deal with Odin?"

Loki shrugged. "Me. Or Fenrir." He looked at the great wolf and said, apologetically, "Fenrir fully grown, that is."

"And Jörmungand? If I recall correctly she was supposed to be Thor's adversary, not his drinking buddy. Norse myth was always very balanced. This against that."

"Possibly Jörmungand. Thor would prevail against Odin," said Loki.

"If Odin didn't out-think me," said Thor.

"To keep it simple, I want a feint—a noisy feint—on the battle-field. And then I want you, Loki, to attack and deal with Surt. Do you think the Vanir will honor their bargain?"

Loki nodded. "The Vanir are old enemies of Surt and the sons of Muspell. When Odin allied with them, he lost much of the support and loyalty of the Vanir. Odin has let his vanity about his power as chief of the Æsir go to his head." He smiled wryly. "It always did. So: we deal with Surt. And Odin attacks us in the rear."

Jerry shook his head. "He'll have his own problems. What if the wall is breached?"

Loki raised his eyebrow. "If that were possible, the giants would have attacked and destroyed Asgard these ages past."

"But if it *were* possible?"

"He'd have to hold the breach, of course. Odin is as cunning as a snake. He'd assume we'd made the breach to charge through."

"That's what I thought," said Jerry. "I talked to Lamont about this, and it is basically his idea. I'm going to let him explain."

Lamont stood up. "Water weighs. It's heavy stuff. The fenland down there," he pointed, "is the lowest land in Asgard. It's a pretty narrow valley, and the river is a mighty big one since it drains all of Asgard. We estimate one hundred thousand gallons a second. If we were able to stop it flowing through its underground channel, even for an hour or two, it will build up against that wall."

Loki laughed. "The wall is magically proof against the frost and mountain giants—as well as just being high and large. But it is not proof against water. I like it. The softest will bring down the hardest." He looked at Thor. "And maybe we can even organize a bit of extra rain."

"I suppose so," said Thor. "Though it feels wrong to bring down Asgard's wall. Anyway, how would you block the river?"

"With a cork," said Lamont.

"By magic," said Jerry, more cooperatively. "We tried it out on a stream. But we'll have to get there first, and we'll have to hope it works as fast and well as we think it will."

"And how will you get there?" asked Loki skeptically. "Even with Freyja's falcon-cloak, out-flying the arrows of Ull's archers is not likely. You could go by night, but my informants tell me that great fires burn on the walls."

"Thanks to our traitors, they will be looking for an attack from above—but not from below."

Loki shook his head. "Tunneling is not an option, and there are no cave-paths that go under the walls."

"The river does. And Jörmungand swims it."

"There is a difference between her swimming it and you swimming it," said Thor. "Just a little, of course," he said, looking warily at Liz. It was funny how she had that effect on people.

"We've built a craft, what we would call a submarine, which, with a little magic, will carry us and our paraphernalia underwater. We can take several people, and Jörmungand can tow it. And we've used the principals of Ran's net to make a magical net that can hold anything. Even Loki."

Loki looked startled and then laughed again. "I was too smart for my own good."

"More than once," said Sigyn.

☯   ☯   ☯

That had been a week ago. And then, on the morning they were due to leave, had come the news of Sigurd having woken Marie the day before. Jerry had unhesitatingly modified his plans, but he felt the absence of Lamont in the enclosed space of the "submarine" very keenly.

Still, it was his project. He would have to go through with it, even on his own.

The dragons flew in tandem high over the ring of flames. The enclosed area was about two acres in extent. The dragons might be able to set down, but the convection from the fire-wall made it difficult. Even fifty meters up, the dragons were struggling not to rise. Liz checked the homemade harness and the link and plate belay device she'd organized for belaying Lamont down. Really, the sensible thing would have been for her to rappel in, but it was his wife.

He wasn't showing any of the normal signs of nerves a person ought to before this sort of thing. Just barely concealed impatience. The rope was the best she'd been able to find, hawser-laid, made of sort of some fiber—probably flax—and not too even in diameter. Not exactly a perlon braided rope, but they'd practiced on the cliff top and it didn't jam up in the belay plate, even if it did twist terribly.

"Okay," said Liz. "Take a hold on the rope and go. When you're down, untie the link. We can't keep position. We'll have to drop a rope in for you two. You've got the spare harness?"

Lamont nodded and, giving her a thumbs up, walked off the side of the dragon.

The hall inside the wall of flames was large, Lamont realized, as Liz lowered him jerkily toward it. He managed to avoid getting impaled on the sharp end of the gable. And then he was down, fingers clumsy with haste, trying to untie, yelling for Marie.

He was met with silence.

He pushed hastily in through the half open doors. It was just one big room with nothing but row upon row of empty biers.

He went back outside and set about the tricky task of getting up onto the roof, waving to Liz and the dragons. On the third try he managed to grab the rope without falling off the roof. Liz took up the slack and the dragon-lift hauled him off his feet.

Then, with horror, Lamont realized the hole in their plan. A dragon wasn't a helicopter or a fixed platform. It was a biological balloon full of biogas and hydrogen, and his extra weight brought Bitar lower. As the dragon turned to regain height, Lamont swung perilously close to the twelve-foot-high flames, like a pendulum. Just as he though he was going to be crisped, he jerked higher, and passed just above the flames. He dropped again, suddenly enough to make him scream. But his fall was arrested a few feet above the ground, and then he was lowered down. He hit the ground running. The dragons circled in and landed a safe distance from the flame-wall. Lamont was limping over when Liz bailed and ran to see if he was all right.

"She's not there!" he panted.

Liz was actually relieved. She'd been half convinced that Lamont's Marie must be dead in that building when he came out alone. "Are you all right?"

"Other than nearly being cremated, fine. My hair was pretty frizzy anyway," said Lamont with a touch of his familiar dry humor. But his pressing concern did not leave him for long. "But where is Marie? There must have been hundreds of them in there. Now they've all gone."

Liz looked at the fire-wall. "Somehow they must have got over the fire. Funny-face did it on a horse, so it is possible. Let's look for tracks."

They did, but the only tracks they could find were those of a single horse, presumably that of Sigurd. And it was a steep little mountain-hill, too, with not many places a horse could walk without leaving a trail.

"It's as if they grew wings," said Liz. "Do these Valkyrie have wings under their mailshirts?"

Lamont pursed his lips. "I've seen a picture of two Valkyrie 'choosing the slain' in a book somewhere. I think they had winged horses." He sighed. "And tracks in the air are few and far between."

"Well, where would you have gone if you managed to get out here?" asked Liz. Lamont was too distraught for clear thinking. "Back to where you left us, I would think. So let's go back to the dragons and mount up. We're on our way to Asgard."

"There is a war happening there," he said despondently.

They'd reached the dragons by then. "Can we go to look for Jörmy?" asked Bitar in a mournful tone. "I worry about her." Smitar sniffed. "Me too."

Having persuaded Sigfrida that allowing Marie to sit behind her would really be a better way to fly than hanging her over the saddlebow like a corpse, Marie was now wondering if she'd made a mistake. At least lying over the saddle she'd feel it was okay to be sick. And maybe because horses were really not designed to fly, the motion could even make a corpse queasy. But they were free and, hopefully, she was heading back to her children and her husband.

The horse was complaining. Understanding the tongues of all the animals was not always pleasant or very useful.

When they got closer to white walls of Asgard, she realized that finding her family might not be that simple. There was a huge army on the plains. The snowy landscape was black with men, and even from here she could hear the noise. The walls of Asgard were prickled with spear-points.

"What's happening?" she asked Sigfrida.

"Ragnarok. We are too late, I think. The end has come."

"Ragnarok?"

"The great and final war. Where do we go now?"

"Thor's place, I think." Where else could they go?

The current tugged at the "submarine," flinging it and the occupants around. Jerry knew the first submarine to ever make an attack on another ship—the *Turtle*—had been little more than a converted hogshead. Knowing that and being in one were two completely different things. It was bad enough to be suddenly thinking of issues such as pressure and how long the air would last, without landing on top of Thrúd. Thrúd dressed for war, to boot—which meant spiky armor.

Jerry suddenly realized he was outnumbered by women in this craft and they appeared to be keeping their calm better than he was. Sigyn had yet to say a word. They bumped against the walls and Jerry wondered if the timbers of the barrel would hold. After what seemed like an eternity, Jerry felt the wood scrape on gravel. And then a blessed sound: Jörmungand's sibilant voice. "Do you want me to tear it open?"

"Please."

A minute later they were out, blinking, standing on the beach next to the maw into which the river Gjalar poured. Jerry realized he'd misinterpreted Sigyn's silence. She was crying.

"What's wrong, Sigi? Are you hurt?" asked Jörmungand anxiously. Sigyn might be the serpent-dragon's stepmother but the stepchildren were genuinely fond of her.

"I wonder if I haven't been stupid," said Sigyn. "I have sent Loki off to war on his own, and I am parted from him for the first time in hundreds of years, for my revenge." She took a deep breath. "I suppose it is too late to just let it all go."

Thrúd shrugged. "You know my grandfather. Odin would never have left it alone, because he never would have believed you could."

"True. Come, then, master magician. Loki believes you will bring down the wall, although he does not believe we'll catch Odin."

"He doesn't?" asked Thrúd.

Sigyn shook her head. "He would never have left us to come alone if he did. He is far too clever at protecting those he loves. That was why he and Thor made no objection to us coming with Jerry. They believe that behind the wall of Asgard we will be in the safest possible position. The war out there will be bitter."

Jerry blinked. It *had* seemed that Loki was easily persuaded to let them come along, now that he thought about it.

"Uncle Fox!" said Thrúd.

Sigyn nodded. "Yes, dear. He's like that. It is an aspect of caring, I suppose. I'll bet he told Jörmungand to take care of us. Probably to take us somewhere safe."

"Hurry up, Jerry," said Thrúd. "Draw those runes and let's go and prove my father and uncle wrong."

Jerry clambered around the cave-mouth, making the symbol for ice, the symbol for sea—drawn in salt, because salty ice is much colder—and, of course, Ansuz, nine times.

Why did they have such a fixation on nine?

He then got out his funnel-shaped piece of paraphernalia, already suitably inscribed with runes, and took the stopper-piece of ice from the insulated bag. The problem, as Lamont had seen it, was that ice floated. It had to be a very rough edged hole for it to jam well enough to stay there.

It was apparent that Jörmungand had her own ideas too. As

Jerry finished his chant, and dropped the ice-plug, she swung her tail at the rocky bluff, and tumbled a thirty-ton lump of rock into the churning water.

Ice formed around the rim of the hole, and then Jörmungand's rock tumbled into the hole so hard that the ground shook. Ice grew around it.

"Run," said Thrúd, sensibly grabbing Jerry's arm and hauling him back from the edge of the river.

As it was he got his boots wet. But millions of gallons of water were already starting to back up.

"Time to go Odin hunting," said Jerry.

Frey rode forward in his chariot, drawn by his golden-bristled boars. Thor looked down on him, rather disdainfully, from the Æsir-SUV.

Frey swallowed. "Some wheels, Öku-Thor."

It was a fair comment. The wheels were large, to cope with stones, and they had spokes—weighing less than a quarter of what Thor's old solid wheels had weighed—and they had metal rims. They had leaf-springs too, and independent axles. "And with me driving it does no gallons per mile, now that I've stopped drinking. My artificer says that's better than any vehicle in America."

"Where is America?" asked Frey.

"Don't know. A place they drink a lot, but make great chariots."

"And the dog with the nodding head on the back of the chariot?"

Thor threw out his palms. "It's one of the magical mysteries, like the go-faster stripes and the sides of the wheel being painted white. But Garm says that he likes to travel by chariot. Loki asked me to give you your sword back."

He handed the weapon over. "Now, do we attack Surt?"

Frey nodded. "I never really believed it, when Ratatosk brought us word. But my father trusts him."

Loki came trotting out of the smoke. "Frey, I want you to take the east flank. Öku-Thor will take the west. And I am going to meet them in the middle. That's where they'll least expect me. And brace yourselves. We're going to be fighting in the rain."

"Rain?"

"Our Thor is a thunder-god. He can do rain if he wants to. He's drawing it now from the west. It would be better from the north, but it's too cold up there."

Loki turned to Emmitt. "Give Frey the slow count to thirty and sound the advance."

"I don't know how to play that," said Emmitt uncertainly.

Loki grinned. "The horn does. And you're a better player than Gold-teeth."

Frey turned his boar-drawn chariot. Thor looked at the mess on the thin snow. "He needs better emission control on that thing."

Among the Vanir, horns sounded. And then Emmitt raised Gjallarhorn and blew.

Even the smoke seemed to shiver.

Öku-Thor urged Tanngnjóst and Tanngrisnir into a trot and then into a gallop. Emmitt saw how he drew his hammer and gripped it in one metal-gauntleted hand while he handled the chariot with the other. All of a sudden, he didn't look at all like a fat recovering alcoholic. He looked like . . .

Well. Thor. *The* Thor. He was really pretty scary.

Lightning cracked and the thunder roared and echoed. Ahead, like a huge red wall, were the fire giants out of Muspellheim. Their swords flamed.

And hissed and spluttered a lot, as the rain suddenly came in from behind them.

"Hold tight and keep blowing!" bellowed Thor.

Emmitt would remember the next half an hour vividly for the rest of his life. Partly he would remember it as total confusion, and thunder, and blowing the great horn, but mostly for the vivid little snatches of Thor, radiating lightning, and smashing giant heads like watermelons. There were a lot of giant heads, but without their fire they were fairly feeble swordsmen.

Still, there seemed an endless supply of them. And even through the rain Emmitt caught glimpses of occasional fires. Something was still burning.

Burning hot.

CHAPTER 40

⊚⊚⊚⊚⊚⊚

The task of finding Odin was temporarily delayed by two things. The first was the need to avoid the rising water. The second was that the heavens seemed to have opened. In the rain it was hard to find their own way, let alone locate anyone else.

They fought their way uphill. There was lightning about, but it all seemed to be to the east somewhere. "Papa," said Thrúd proudly. "Look at that!"

Sheets of lightning lit up the sky. "I feel almost sorry for the fire giants," she added, not sounding sorry at all.

The rain did seem to be slackening off by the time they got up the rise. They could see a short distance now, far enough to see that the Gjallar river had already filled its gorge and was spilling out onto the fenlands next to the wall.

"Well, at least I know where we are now," said Thrúd. "Odin's Valhöll lies over that ridge."

"He's not likely to be there, though," said Jörmungand, peering through the rain.

"Two of the life-sources from outside this Ur-world have penetrated your walls," said the Krim device. "And you need to intervene in the battle on the plain. It goes badly for Surt."

"I am Lord of Battles, Thing. Don't try to tell me what to do."

337

Odin had long since banished the Krim persona and taken complete charge of himself. "Even if Surt falls, the walls of Asgard cannot be taken by frost or mountain giants. They are stuck outside."

"Except that two of your enemies are inside, I told you."

"Mortals?"

That was what Odin termed life-sources. "Yes."

Odin took Gungnir and stood up. "Thjalfi, bring those retainers of yours. You've got some of your own kind to deal with."

Odin-Krim did not seem to understand. What had been done so far, raising the old altars, reenacting the old myths with believers had reanimated this Mythworld. It would inevitably start to slowly fade without non-Ur-Mythworld believers importing energy into the system. Such a construct was energy expensive. It might be stable enough for a few hundred years, but real stability, the kind the Krim liked, took far more energy. A lot more belief and a lot more lives, both within and from outside.

Dripping wet, Marie led her Valkyrie troop into Bilskríner, Thor's home.

Nobody was at home, except for the stable thrall, Lodin. He swallowed hard at the sight of her.

"The master is away." Lodin rose hastily from in front of a fire he probably wasn't supposed to be sitting at, looked at her guiltily and put down a foaming horn. "It was so cold and wet, and with even the goats gone, and Ragnarok here I thought . . ."

Marie waved him to sit. "We've brought three hundred and eleven horses for you to look after. And I reckon you deserve a raise and some decent living quarters. And we're all starving. Any food in the place?" The truth was, she wasn't starving. But maybe food would help her with the light-headedness.

"Lots of smoked salmon. And some flattbrød."

"Excellent," said Marie, vaguely wondering what flattbrød was. "Let's get the horses in and eat. Brynhild will organize food and some more fires. Lodin, drink up and come and open the stables, and you can tell me where that husband of mine has got to."

The ravens were up, flying across a rain-drenched Asgard, and Odin was riding Sleipnir followed by a pack of Einherjar. Trailing behind them were Thjalfi-Harkness and Bott and Stephens, struggling to ride.

The sun broke through as they crested a ridge . . . and stopped. Relieved, Agent Bott managed to catch up, in time to see the entire group staring out across a lovely lake. It was a pretty sight, even if you could see the mirrored reflection of two dragons in it.

"*Loki!*" screamed Odin. "*Curse you, trickster!*" He turned on his Einherjar. "Get down there and unblock it!"

Bott looked at the lake, lapping against the wall. Must be some sort of drain that was blocked. It looked quite deep.

A raven dropped onto Jerry's shoulder. "Odin is looking for you," said Hugin. "Got any jelly beans?"

Jerry didn't. But Thrúd did. "Where is he?"

"Back along that trail," said the raven. "Good war going on down there. Plenty of fresh corpses. Waste of time to be flying around here."

"Why don't you go and fly there and tell Loki we're in and the Gjallar river is blocked and rising."

"Has he got more jelly beans?"

Thrúd nodded. "And lots of dead fire giants. I think you'll like them."

Hugin took flight and the party of four took the trail that the raven had pointed a wing at. It was narrow and steep, leading up a spur, and hard going for Jörmungand.

"I wonder if we wouldn't be wise to wait in ambush," said Jerry.

"Too late," said Sigyn.

Sure enough, there was Odin on the neck of the trail. He couldn't have chosen a better spot for self-defense either. There were a series of steep curving rock steps zigging into the little gully and then zagging out again, so that if they came up to attack him they could be neatly speared from above. It was also such a narrow gully that Jörmungand would have to skirt around rather than go up it.

Behind Odin were the traitorous Bott and Stephens and Thor's man Thjalfi. Odin started to lower his spear and then spotted Jörmungand. "*Einherjar!*" he bellowed.

Odin didn't have Thor's voice, but he obviously thought he had backup coming.

Jerry studied the situation, and didn't like what he saw. If the

Einherjar came up behind them, they could attack Jörmungand before she could turn. And if she did turn, then Odin, on horseback and with a spear, would surely kill some of them. Sigyn had a knife and Jerry a sword he really didn't know how to use, and a net that he could see no way to use at all. Thrúd could certainly use her battle-axe, but one-eyed Odin was the lord of battles, for all his faults. He probably was the second most powerful warrior of all the Æsir, and he had cunning on his side.

Cunning that led him to turn to Thjalfi. "Go down."

Thjalfi paled, and turned to his foot-soldiers. "Get them."

Nervously, they began to advance.

Jörmungand spat venom at them. It fell short, but where it landed, it actually ate into the rock, hissing.

The two PSA agents stopped. Both began unlimbering what looked suspiciously like crossbows.

Jerry decided to try to beat Odin at his own game. He concentrated on speaking English. He had no idea if his words were being translated or not.

"Why are you doing this? I'm a fellow American!" he shouted.

"We've got a job to do. And we're as stuck here as you are!" That came from Stephens, putting a quarrel in the groove. He jerked his head at Thjalfi. "And we figure Mr. Harkness here is the boss, in this situation—and those are his orders."

"Think very carefully about what you are doing. We have found a way back. The sphinx and Bes and Cruz made it through. They've taken Ella and Ty and Tolly back. Cruz is coming with reenforcements and soon we should all be able to head home to America. That applies to you too, if you take that bastard down."

The agent stopped in the act of cocking the crossbow.

His fellow agent put a hand on Stephens' weapon, pushing it down. "We can go home," said Bott, with huge relief. "Stephens, we'll have succeeded in our mission. We've got Mister Harkness, after all." He, too, nodded at Thjalfi.

Suddenly, a lot of things made sense to Jerry. "Harkness is in his fifties and overweight and bald. I know. I was shown pictures at the debriefing. You must have seen pictures too. This guy is not Harkness. Anyway, I don't care who he is. Right now we have one Æsir against us. Help us, and we'll help you."

Stephens blinked. "But he knows all the codes..."

Bott blinked also. "He said he was magically disguised..."

"Apples of youth," snarled Thjalfi. "And I am telling you that it is in the national interest that you kill that man. He's anti-American."

"Do that and you lose all chance of going home," said Jerry with a confidence he didn't feel. "Odin—"

The wavering Bott turned, and at that moment, Thjalfi-Harkness cut him down from behind, with a vicious stroke through his spine and heart. Stephens, beginning to turn, realized that Odin's spear was leveled at him. His companion's body abruptly disappeared.

"You killed him," said Stephens incredulously.

"Shoot them," said Thjalfi-Harkness, his voice harsh. "I haven't got this far to be stopped by some longhaired university left-wing asshole. Get the dragon first."

Just then a bat-winged spiky shadow passed overhead.

"Down there! That's Jerry!" yelled Liz, looking at the scene.

"And that's our darling," said Bitar, almost throwing Liz off with his delighted wriggle. "Jörgy! Roses are red, and violets are blue, and they both stink compared to you!"

Lamont was also having to cling, desperately, as Smitar did an aerial dance for Jörmungand too. "My darling, how I hunger for your touch and your lunch, let's get a bunch to munch!" he caroled.

"Set us down before you drop us. And spare us any more Vogon poetry!" said Liz.

Hastily the dragons swooped down on the ridge, and Liz and Lamont bailed onto the rocks above the stand-off. It was a dangerous maneuver, but it beat more poetry.

Looking down, Liz could see Stephens raising his crossbow, and Jörmungand fluttering her eyelashes at her suitors.

"Stephens, I'll shove that thing up your ass sideways unless you drop it!" yelled Liz.

Lamont, ever practical, was lifting a large rock.

Jörmungand looked up at the aerial acrobatics. "Boys," she said, "I hear some knights coming to attack our rear. Could you . . . "

Marie had come out to get a bit of fresh air. The smell of food was appetizing, but maybe the cancer had advanced more rapidly than she'd expected or she'd been asleep longer than she realized. Lodin, poor thrall, had retreated from a house full of females too. He was about to run into the stables, when Marie looked up at the ridge. And screamed.

"What's wrong?"

"I know those two dragons! And I'll bet that's my husband! I can tell by the way he moves. Lodin, please—help me up onto one of these damn winged nags."

Marie Jackson had never ridden a horse on her own in her life before, let alone been in control of one with wings. But she wasn't going to let that stop her.

She nearly fell off as the horse reared aerially at the sound of a great roar . . . as the weight of the water burst through the wall of Asgard. But she kept her seat somehow, and forced the horse on to the drama unfolding below.

She heard yells behind her, and realized that the better part of her three-hundred-odd Valkyries were also following. They were much better riders. Her horse had gained more height than she'd intended—but that let her see Odin's Einherjar charging upward from the broken wall to answer their master's summons.

Somehow Marie had drawn the sword Gram without cutting herself or the horse. "Get them!" she yelled, pointing. And then, suddenly realizing that she could in fact talk to this stupid animal, she leaned forward. "Get me down there or I'll chop your head off."

Out on Vrigid plain, Loki felt an itch between his shoulder blades that said "Gungnir," and waited for the sally and the attack to his vulnerable rear. He and Fafnir and Hel's corpse-army had cut deep into Surt's demon-troops. The rain had dealt a severe blow to the fire giants, but their flames did not die. So Loki had found he could turn the flames against them. They burned hot and he made them hotter, until they burst, destroying themselves and those around them.

And then came . . . not the sound of Einherjar horns that he'd feared, but a far sweeter sound. A raven caw. It said, "Gjallar is blocked and rising."

"The Einherjar are trying to fix it," said Munin, joining his brother.

"Got any jelly beans?" they demanded in chorus.

It was a good thing that he was fond of the magical beans himself and had brought a few with him. He turned to Fenrir. "Howl! Let the others know that we must press forward hard now."

Fenrir howled. The wolves and Hel's dead took up the sound. It would echo across Asgard. Let Odin know fear, now. From close, far closer than he'd realized, came the answer of the Vanir horns, and then the deep-throated terrible song of Gjallarhorn.

And almost as a reply came the distant roar of water and stone.

"*Charge!*" shouted Loki. His wolf-steed son needed no urging. Surt's remaining fire giants fled. Thunder roared from the west. On the East, Frey's sword sang.

And then there was space. In front of them stood Surt the fire demon of the East, burning so hot that nothing could stand close. Loki dismounted from Fenrir, and walked forward. Fenrir followed. "Go back, son," said Loki. "Your fur will burn."

"And you?" asked Fenrir.

Loki laughed. "One cannot burn a flame." In the periphery of his vision he saw Thor fling a thunderbolt at Surt. It was ineffectual, as Loki knew it would be. Surt was a creature of flames himself.

Frey and Freyja had halted their chariots. They could come no closer.

So it was up to him.

Again.

He always got the Æsir into messes. This one too had its roots in his deeds and laughter, he knew. And in the end they always wanted him to get them out.

Again.

Well, he was one of the oldest. Not the greatest, but certainly the trickiest.

Surt stood like a tower of flame fifty feet high and as unstoppable as an inferno. The only point that was not flaming was the pyramid pendant around his vast neck. Loki knew that they could still lose here. Surt didn't really need an army.

Loki made him burn hotter.

Surt grew. And laughed, a sound like fire-splintering forest. "No use against me. I feed on that."

Loki smiled. "Then try this." He drew on his frost giant kin. He drew on the cold of Fimbulwinter. He drew the fire down.

Surt shrank visibly. He lashed out with a tongue of flame at Loki—but he might as well have beaten at a fire with a feather. Loki, at the core, was fire. He knew that briefly all those around the circle would see him as he truly was, no matter what form he took. That was unimportant now. He concentrated his will on Surt.

Surt shrank visibly. Now he was barely twenty feet high. Loki drew breath, preparing for the final destruction of the wild flame.

"Enough," said a voice, atonal and quite unlike that of Surt, though it seemed to issue from him. "I am Krim. Stop and I will make you powerful. I will make you the Lord of the Æsir. We should have offered the power of mastery of this Ur-universe to you rather than Odin. He has rebelled and stolen our device's powers. You can have power and mastery over all. We have the power to make you irresistible."

Loki laughed. "I may be quite wicked, but never evil. There is a difference, even if you don't understand it. And unlike Odin, I have no desire to rule. It would bore me to tears to have to be responsible."

"Power means that you are above responsibility," said the Krim.

Loki shook the flames that were his head. "Power without responsibility *is* evil," he said. He reached out his hands and drew the cold out of Fimbulwinter, the only cold that was strong enough to balance the heat of Surt. Norse myth was a place of balances. "Die, Surt—or Krim. This world doesn't need you."

Loki's exercise of his will drew him down too. But he had his hearth, Sigyn. Her love and that of his children. It gave him something that wildfire could never have.

There was an abrupt purple flash, and Surt fell into a pile of ash.

"Ah," said Odin, as the shadows of the Valkyries passed over-head. "A rescue."

And then a lot of things happened in such close succession that it was hard to tell what happened first.

A rock probably. A three pound rock flung by Lamont, which missed its target—Stephens—but knocked Thjalfi-Harkness off the trail and down onto the rocks below.

Thrúd's axe did not miss. And neither did the explosive deto-nation of ball-lightning with it.

Odin's eyes widened. So did the trail where Stephens had stood. All that was left of him was an ozone reek.

૭૭   ૭૭   ૭૭

"Surt is destroyed and the Krim has fled," said the Krim device. *"The wall of your fortress has been breached. Flee this world. I will take you to another Mythworld."*

Odin clutched at the pendant around his neck. "No! You will do my bidding! I am Odin, the master."

Liz and Lamont spilled down onto the trail behind him.

He turned Sleipnir and lowered his spear. The Einherjar were being aerially harassed by dragons. He would deal with that. He still had Gungnir and his Æsir allies. Thor's daughter wielded a power he feared, but two mortals were no barrier.

Marie saw what was happening and screamed, "Dive!"

Flying horses do not do that well. But she did—right over its neck. She cannoned into Odin. He was kicking his horse into a gallop when he met her coming the other way—fast. Odin was a great horseman, and Sleipnir the greatest horse, but a hundred and forty pound human missile knocked him sideways off the horse.

If the sword in her hand had hit him he would have been a kebab.

Instead it hit the shaft of the spear Gungnir. She lost her hold on the sword but the deadly spear lost its head.

Marie and Odin lay sprawled against the wall, as Sleipnir thundered on, knocking Liz sideways off the trail, and Lamont into the wall.

Jerry had, to his amazement, beaten both Sigyn and Thrúd up the trail. Odin and a gasping Marie fought.

Odin grabbed the sword that Marie had dropped. Jerry knew that neither he nor Lamont was ever going to get there in time. So he threw what he had in his left hand.

Jerry could no more throw a net than he could toss a caber. But this was a magical net, using the same spells that had been used to hold the trickster, Loki. Nothing could escape it. Like Sigurd's magical sword, Gram, in Marie's hands, it took will for the deed, and spread and enveloped and entangled.

Unfortunately, the sword in Odin's hand was Gram, wrought with rune magic and all the skill of the dwarf Reginn. It could cut a shred of wool borne by the stream-flow. It could cut this net too. Not easily, but the net couldn't stop Odin's stroke from wounding Marie, even if it did stop Odin from killing her outright. And now he fought to cut his way free of the tangling mesh.

Marie felt the pain and the blood, and saw the red brightness of the sword. Saw Lamont running closer. Heard him scream.

Well, this bastard might have killed her—but she was dying anyway. He wasn't going to get her man too.

She took the thorn of sleep from her pocket, and pushed it deeply into Odin's butt.

Lamont held her to his chest, crying, as the others arrived. Liz, scratched and bruised, swung her handbag at Odin's head. Twice. He was down and staying that way. Thrúd made doubly sure. She had recovered her axe, and sat down on him.

"Guess it's the end, honey," said Marie weakly. "I love you so much. Take care of the kids."

"You can't die," said Lamont, as if his sheer fierce will could hold her back.

"Hold me, love."

And then Sigyn ran up, took one look and shouted up at the Valkyrie circling above: "Find Idun and bring her here!"

The Valkyrie blinked in surprise. "Idun? I came to ask what you want us to do with the rest of Einherjar."

"*Idun*. Now! Or I will curse you with a cold hearth for always and always."

The Valkyrie clapped her heels to her horse, as Jerry and Liz tried to staunch the blood from Marie's wound. They were successful in that, but it didn't look as if it was going to make any difference. She was slipping away.

And then, much sooner that they would have thought possible, the Valkyrie returned and dropped an angry Idun next to them.

"Sister, I will not help you," said the Lady of Spring, the rejuvenator, the custodian of the apples of youth. She sounded very cross. "Loki can die, for all I care. He got me kidnapped. And then he turned me into a nut."

Thrúd looked up from her seat on Odin before Sigyn had a chance to reply. "Idun, see who I am sitting on. And understand what this means. Thor is now Lord of the Æsir. If you don't help this woman he's not going to be just angry. We owe her more than we can repay."

"It's not for Loki?" asked Idun, startled.

"Loki has won on the plain," said Sigyn. "Ragnarok will not come. Look—already Fimbulwinter is past and the sun is shining. Your spring comes. Anyway, the flame does not ever need your apples. This woman does."

"She helped Thor to beat his drinking problem," said Thrúd. "And we need her to keep him that way."

Idun nodded. "That we do." She opened her golden casket and took out an apple.

Jerry used the first blade to hand—that was Gram—to cut a sliver off the apple, and insert it between Marie's lips. "Chew if you can. Even the juice helps."

She did, weakly.

Jerry, Liz and the rest of them watched. And then Idun shook her head. "It is not the wound. She must eat the entire apple now. There is much within that needs it. The wound is a slight thing. The other, well . . ."

She looked at Lamont, tears still wet on his cheeks, a look of incredulous hope on his face. "You are her husband?"

He nodded.

Smiling, she took out another apple. "Then you'd better eat this one. A young woman, as she will need to become to take her body back to before it was affected by this disease, would be too much for you otherwise. You'll need your stamina."

CHAPTER 41

◎◎◎◎◎◎

Miggy Tremelo was amused by Melvin Steinmetz's sangfroid. The head of one of the nation's premier think tanks—an academic on steroids, so to speak—was handling the discussion with a Greek sphinx and an Egyptian dwarf-god as if he were sitting around a conference table in the Future Enterprise Institute or participating in a university seminar—instead of being perched on a mechanic's stool in the maintenance garage attached to Miggy's headquarters. They were having the meeting in the cavernous garage, of course, because Throttler wouldn't fit anywhere else.

"If I understand this correctly, what this lady,"—Steinmetz nodded at the sphinx—"has just proved is that it is possible to travel though the Ur-Mythworlds *without* going through the pyramid."

"Some of them, it would be better to say," cautioned Miggy.

"But if I also have this correctly, the pyramid showed no growth as a result."

Tremelo nodded. "That's right, Melvin. That could be because the Krim is no longer active in those Mythworlds as a result of Dr. Lukacs and the rest of his group's efforts."

"But—" Steinmetz looked almost cross-eyed, for a moment. The thinktank president shook his head. "Miggy . . . have you considered the implications?"

349

Tremelo chuckled. "I'd make a wisecrack here about people teaching their grandmothers to suck eggs, except I'm way too polite."

Melvin winced, but half-smiled also, acknowledging the hit. "All right, point taken. You don't need to rub salt into my wounds. Obviously you have considered them"—he cocked his head a little—"and may I presume you came to the same conclusions I'm coming to?"

"That the Mythworlds have an independent existence? That they are—in some sense, at least—real and not simply virtual constructs of the Krim?"

"Or Krim constructs that have taken on a life of their own," Steinmetz said. "That strikes me as the most likely possibility."

Miggy nodded. "Me, too." He jabbed a thumb at one of the university maintenance vans parked alongside a wall of the garage. "The fact that that vehicle was made by human beings doesn't mean that it's simply a figment of our imagination. It was *before* it was made, sure enough. Just a gleam in an automobile designer's eye, so to speak. But now it's as real as—"

Grinning, Bes slapped his chest. "Me! I can prove it, too. You want me to crumple up the van?"

A bit hastily, Tremelo said, "That won't be necessary, I think."

Steinmetz was studying Bes a lot more intently than Miggy was comfortable with. As often as he and Melvin had clashed over policy issues in times past, Miggy was well aware that the man had a very keen mind. Until he was sure that Steinmetz was actually switching sides in the current dispute with the PSA, Tremelo really didn't want him probing too deeply into some of the other mysteries and conundrums that surrounded the pyramid and the Mythworlds.

Right at the top of that list was the problem that Miggy himself had been wrestling with since the day after Jerry Lukacs and the others returned from the Greek Mythworld, bringing with them Bes and Athena.

Why had Bes retained his powers—and Athena *hadn't?* The Greek goddess was still in police custody in Las Vegas, since no one had been able to figure out what else to do with her. Former goddess, rather, it would seem. If she had any divine powers they were not evident at all. She just seemed to be a spiteful, nasty middle-aged woman.

There were a number of possible answers to that question. All of them were uncomfortable, and some were downright scary.

Steinmetz now turned that sharp, considering gaze on Throttler. "So . . . she can operate from any sphinx image where there is even a modicum of belief in that universe. What that would seem to imply is that the sphinx, yes, and Bes, have acquired at least demi-god status in our universe. We're still in the realm of guesswork here but belief seems to be very powerful stuff, not constrained by the terms of ordinary logic."

Miggy hesitated. Melvin had seized upon the most obvious of the possible explanations, and one that was unsettling but not nearly as disturbing as some others. Tremelo was tempted to leave it at that. But his innate honesty rebelled a little. Clash as they might, from time to time, he and Steinmetz were basically colleagues. You didn't leave colleagues needlessly groping in the dark.

"I don't think that theory holds up, Melvin. Yes, you might be able to explain Bes' continued powers as being due to the fervor of wrestling fans. Just as you could explain Athena's lack of such being due to the fact that she has no equivalent . . . let's call it 'fan base.' The problem is Lamont Jackson."

Steinmetz narrowed his eyes. "Explain, please. I'm not following you."

"It's simple. Why did Lamont Jackson keep his Tyche-bestowed luck for a time—but *only* for a time? That he still had it when he came out of the pyramid was blindingly obvious by the wealth he piled up so rapidly. Within two days, he'd been banned from every casino in Las Vegas; within a week, any in the world; within two weeks, every state lottery in the U.S. had done the same. By then, of course, Lamont was a multimillionaire several times over. But then that same luck vanished overnight, when his wife Marie turned out to be dying from a particularly virulent form of cancer. And if that didn't prove the luck had gone, having himself and most of his family snatched back into the pyramid surely did."

Miggy made a groping motion with his hand, in midair. "How do you explain *that*, Melvin? It certainly can't be from any lack of faith in the country—the whole world over—in luck."

"Maybe . . ." Steinmetz ran fingers through his thick gray hair. "Argh. I swear, Miggy, a particle physicist like you may be used to it. But this stuff makes even a hard-bitten old nuclear war theorist like me feel like a fish out of water—and you know how screwball most of our theories were."

"Still are," grunted Tremelo humorously. "But if it makes you feel any better, this hard-bitten old particle physicist feels the same way."

Steinmetz sat up a little straighter. "All right. But no matter what theories you lean toward, the thing that now seems very apparent—"

Tremelo cut him off. "—is that directly intervening in the pyramid is at least possible, because there has got to be some basis for reality in there that doesn't depend on the Krim. Yes, I understand that, Melvin. And I'm willing, for the first time, to start considering the matter. But I've got one condition, and it's absolute."

"You run the show. Not the PSA."

"Yes. If you agree to that, we can keep talking."

"Agreed," came Steinmetz's immediate reply. "You understand, I can only speak for myself. Well, and the institute. I sided with the defense industry and their political spokesmen, but I never had their vested interest in the answer. They did and still do—and they don't call them 'vested interests' for nothing. They're not going to let up, Miggy."

Tremelo shrugged. "No—but they just took a bad hammering in Congress, too. Senator Larsen tells me he doesn't think he can get APSA repealed outright, but he's dead sure he can get the worst provisions altered. And he also thinks he's got a very good chance of getting all operational efforts involving the pyramid placed clearly and unequivocally under the authority of the Pyramid Scientific Research Group."

It was his turn to bestow a sharp, considering gaze—on Steinmetz. "It would help . . ."

"If the Future Enterprise Institute weighed in publicly in support of that. I'll point out to you that it would give us still more weight if one of us—that'd be me—were formally added to the Pyramid Scientific Research Group's board of directors."

"Agreed," said Miggy, without hesitating. Leaving aside the fact that it would be a shrewd political move, having Melvin Steinmetz on the board probably *would* be helpful. The man's way of looking at everything, from that incredibly dark perspective that came with being a nuclear war strategist, rubbed Miggy the wrong way. But there was no denying that Steinmetz was as shrewd as they come—and the truth was, Miggy himself was scared by all the possible implications of the pyramid. Having Steinmetz with them was probably a good idea, now that he'd broken from the PSA crowd.

"In that case, your newest board member will give you his first piece of advice. Change the damn name. I'd recommend the Pyramid Control Agency."

Miggy scowled. "Don't you think there are enough 'agencies' floating around already?"

"It's the way it is, Miggy," said Melvin, shrugging. "'Research Group' is a title that has elbow patches on it. You might as well hang a sign around your neck that says 'kick me, I'm a professor.' There's no way most people—and nobody at all in the so-called 'intelligence community'—is going to believe that an outfit that calls itself a 'research group' is capable of doing serious operational work."

"Well . . . yes. You're probably right."

Melvin's mouth twisted into a wry smile. "I presume you intend to use the dragons as part of your . . . can I call it a 'commando unit'?"

"I suppose it's as good a term as any. Yes, Bitar and Smitar—and Bes has agreed. So have Sergeant Cruz and Corporal McKenna. And their wives, for that matter."

"You realize the 'pros' are going to have a fit, I hope."

Tremelo snorted. "You mean the 'real experts' on commando operations like the SEALs and Delta Force and whatever cowboys the spook outfits round up? I will point out two things. First, the scorecard still stands."

Steinmetz's wry smile became a grimace. "Yes, I know. The remaining two members of the PSA, Bott and Stephens, finally came out dead. What little was left of Stephens, anyway—but there was enough to identify his DNA. And none of your people have. The talk shows are having a field day with it. Sometime I'll explain to you my theory—well, not mine, but I subscribe to it—of America's Humphrey Bogart syndrome. What's the second point?"

"Any 'real pro' who gets too obstreperous will simply be required to prove their superior skills at unarmed combat against Bes here."

Bes grinned.

Steinmetz looked a bit disconcerted. Tremelo chuckled. "I'm

throwing the security establishment a big bone, though. I've talked it over with the military and they've agreed—seeing as how Cruz and McKenna are already in the unit anyway—that the 101st will be officially designated as the force assigned to provide whatever military personnel are needed for pyramid operations. There's a Lieutenant Rich Evans who seems quite promising. Cruz and McKenna tell me that Evans won't have any trouble understanding that everything has to be done differently in the Mythworlds. And he's got a Private Henderson that Cruz and McKenna think highly of, as well."

"Tough soldier, I take it."

"No, it's not that. He got arrested for pizza."

Melvin frowned. "I don't get it."

Tremelo shrugged. "Neither do I. But Cruz and Mac figure anybody who can get arrested for pizza will probably manage just fine in the weirdness of the pyramid. And if there's one thing I've learned, it's to trust the instincts of the only people in the world who can really claim to be 'pyramid pros.'"

"Fair enough," said Steinmetz. "I'll back you up on that point, for sure, after watching Garnett's fiasco." He took a long, slow breath. "I just wish we knew what was happening now with your people in the Norse Mythworld."

"We'll find out soon enough. But there's one thing we already know for sure. This isn't over yet. In fact, I think the . . ."

Steinmetz chuckled. "Call it a 'war,' why don't you, Miggy? That's what it is, you know."

"Yes," sighed Tremelo. "The first skirmishes are over. The Krim pyramid war is just starting."

CHAPTER 42

@@@@@@

Standing on the hillside, Jerry had his arm linked with Liz as they watched Loki and Thor entering Asgard's gates. Lamont and Marie stood with them.

With the wall breached, and the forces of Vanir arrayed with those of Loki, and the dragons and the Valkyries having harried the now leaderless Einherjar into retreat, Thrúd had had no trouble in getting Idun to offer terms to the remaining Æsir. Only Heimdall had wanted to fight on. Tyr sat on him, and reminded him exactly why he'd had to get gold teeth.

The only other possible serious objector, Thjalfi-Harkness, had disappeared. Not died. Just vanished while in custody.

Liz squeezed Jerry's hand. "It's just occurred to me why the Norns were so sour and uncooperative when I asked them to tell our futures. Loki said they only ever tell you things that make matters worse. They also apparently don't lie. So, the fact that they wouldn't tell us anything meant that the future was looking far too rosy for their liking."

Jerry kissed her.

She grinned. "See what I mean?"

"Something else occurred to me, Lamont," said Jerry, looking at his now much younger friend and wife, standing next to them, unable to stop hugging each other. "You were lamenting about your luck no longer following you, because Marie was dying. But actually you've never stopped being lucky. In fact, I think we've been seeing your luck at work. From what the doctors said, Marie's condition must have preexisted your blessing by Tyche. The only way that she could be cured—or at least treated—was by magic. So luck brought you to where you could get a reprieve for her. I don't know if it's a cure, but you've either reversed it or at least put it off."

Lamont pursed his lips thoughtfully. "So now we go home and pick it up before it starts . . ."

Jerry shook his head. "Some magics seem to continue to work in our world. But Athena's didn't. I don't know what would happen."

"Then somehow I'm going to get all my kids over here," said Lamont. "The fishing looks good," he added with a huge smile.

"And we have the Krim device's controller. This pyramid pendant off Odin. I imagine Miggy is going to be more than a little excited once we can get back in touch with him. It looks like Odin actually took control of it, not the other way around. That's an interesting concept. It implies that the pyramid is something that possibly *we* could control, not just the Krim. If other Myth-worlds exist . . ."

Liz chuckled. "It might just make a degree in comparative mythology rather desirable in the employment market, outside of esoteric academia."

"No!" exclaimed Jerry, horrified by the idea.

"A mythtake," agreed Lamont.

appendix

〇〇〇〇〇〇

Myth is by its very nature a fragile thing, viewed through a murky glass of time and poor record-keeping, subject to much distortion and various regional interpretations. Neither of the authors claim to be experts in the field and the definitions and explanations in this appendix undoubtably contain much that reflects their own biases. This is a novel, not a research tome, and we often had to choose one of several versions of events (as well as spellings of names). However, for the purposes of following this story it may be useful. Or funny. Or even accidentally informative.

Ás: the singular of Æsir, although it may occasionally be tempting to think of it as another way of writing "donkey."

Asgard: The great walled home of the Æsir. The original gated community where the upper-crust have their homes. Complete with backyard mountain and all other modern tenth-century conveniences for the discerning Ás.

Ægir: A sea giant. Sometimes indicated as the husband of Ran, at whose home the flyting of Loki (the Lokasenna) is supposed to have taken place.

Æsir: Norse Gods—strictly speaking, the ones that live in Asgard, and not the Vanir . . . Except that some of the Vanir came to be hostages, and live in Asgard and intermarry with Ás, or with giants. (Njörd married the giantess Skadi and Frey married the giantess Gerd.) It's a little difficult for a mere biologist to tell the difference between an Ás and a giant as they appear to have sprung from the same origins, and cheerfully interbreed with each other and with Vanir. However, as the Æsir are associated with war, death, and power—unlike the Vanir, associated with growth and fertility—if they say they're different, you'd better believe them, at least in public.

Andvari: The shape-changing dwarf whose hoard of gold Odin, Hœnir, and Loki take as a ransom for his freedom. The gods need this to pay a blood price for Loki's accidental killing of another shape-changing dwarf, Otr. Andvari attempts to hold back one ring, and when it is spotted, tries to persuade them to let him keep it. When they refuse, he curses the ring, thereby giving rise to the long and horrible and doom-filled Völsung saga, which Wagner used as the basis for the Ring of the Nibelung operas.

Angbroda: "Harm-bidder." A giantess upon whom Loki is supposed to have fathered Fenrir the wolf. Later, in his thirteenth-century version, Snorri Sturluson also gave her credit for being the mother of Hel and Jörmungand. Personally, we suspect Jörmy was adopted.

Aurvangar: "Wet gravel plains" where the dwarves live. The guys who actually made all the weapons and treasures of the gods get to live on the wet gravel plains. Some things are eternally true.

Baldr: The beautiful god with white brow and fair hair. A child of Odin and Frigg, he was troubled with dreams of his own death. So Mummy extracted solemn promises from fire, water, metal, stones, plants, beasts, birds etc. etc. not to harm Baldr. She just happened to miss out mistletoe. Loki is supposed to have found this out (in disguise, naturally) and then talked blind Hod (Baldr's brother) into flinging a dart of mistletoe, as the gods were having a little game of throwing things at Baldr, to see how they wouldn't hurt him. Baldr drops dead and is duly consigned to Nifelheim. At Hermód's entreaty Hel agrees to relent and let Baldr go if all the things in world (fire, water, stones etc.) wept for Baldr. A giantess called Thökk (supposedly Loki in disguise) refused, so Baldr stayed in Hel's hall. It is foretold that after Ragnarok, Baldr will return to rule after the death of Odin.

Bilskríner: "Lightning crack." The home of the God Thor, with 540 doors. Very drafty, probably.

Disir: Supernatural female figures. Not ghosts, although sometimes referred to as "dead women."

Dragon: Dragons are one of the most common motifs in Norse myth, and are of course widely portrayed, not least as the sculpted prows on Viking longships. It's a pity they couldn't have had a big dragon artists and sculptors conference and agreed what they were supposed to look like. Flying dragons are mentioned in some sagas, whereas others appear to be nothing more than mighty serpents. The two are so often conflated that we decided on this being a case of sexual dimorphism.

Einherjar: "Lone fighter." The dead who are chosen by the Valkyries on the field of battle to come and occupy the halls of Odin. Despite the fact that they are not actually "lone," the theory that it was a misspelling and that these were "loan" fighters has been almost entirely discredited. Half of the dead warriors go to Odin's halls where they spend their day in fighting and their night in feasting on the ever-renewed boar-flesh and abundant mead, and sport with the Valkyries. Their livers are praying for Ragnarok.

Élivágar: The river that separates Jötunheim from Midgard.

Fenrir: The translation "fen dweller" is a rather obscure name for the wolf that will devour Odin and possibly the sun and the moon. Fathered by Loki on the giantess Angbroda, and therefore the brother of Hel and the Midgard-serpent, the growing Fenrir frightened the Æsir so badly that they tricked him into being bound by successive chains—which he snapped in turn, until he was bound by the chain Gleipnir. The giant wolf is supposed to wait, bound, with an upright sword holding his jaws open until Ragnarok. This is a popular and foolish choice of name for miniature daschunds, as it makes them even more aggressive than they would be anyway.

Fimbulwinter: "Terrible winter." A three-year winter, which precedes Ragnarok.

Flyting: A contest of abuse, usually focused on charming pointed comments about the sexual habits and courage of the protagonists. Usually in verse. The Lokasenna in which Loki abuses each of the Æsir in turn is the prime example.

Freki: One of Odin's two wolves. Not in the same league as Fenrir.

Frey: "Lord" Chief of the Vanir, a fertility god, portrayed with a big beard and an even bigger phallus. Sitting on Odin's lookout point, he spotted the beautiful giantess Gerd, and fell in love with her. He sent his servant Skírnir to press his suit, but had to bribe him to do so, with his magical sword. Frey drives about in a chariot drawn by the golden boar Gullinborsti.

Freyja: The Vanir goddess of love and sex. Famed for having acquired her most precious possession, the Brísingamen, in payment for her services to four dwarves. It was Loki who led to the betrayal of this escapade, with his usual shape-changing tricks. She has a chariot drawn by cats and a falcon cloak which enables her to assume that shape and fly, which she has on occasion lent to Loki.

Gambanteinn: A wand, whose touch causes certain conditions—wandering madness for example.

Garm: The mighty dog which guards the Nágrind (corpse gate), the entry to Hel's kingdom.

Ginnungagap: "Beguiling void."

Gjallarhorn: "Yelling horn." The great horn with which the god Heimdall will call all of the Æsir's allies to war at Ragnarok. Also indicated in the eddic poem "Grímnismál" as Heimdall's drinking horn.

Góin: One of the snakes who creep around Yggdrasil.

Gram: "Wrath." The sword of the hero Sigurd, supposedly so strong it could split an anvil, yet so sharp it could split a hank of wool drifting against the blade in the river current. Supposedly forged with all the skill and magic that the dwarf Reginn could impart, from the remains of Sigurd's father's legendary sword.

Grid: "Greed." A friendly giantess, who got really friendly with Odin, and also lent Thor a belt of strength, iron gauntlets and "Grid's rod," a staff of iron that had various magical properties.

Grotti: The magical handmill (powered by two giantesses) which ground out whatever you ordered it to.

Gungnir: "Swaying one." Odin's magical spear, supposed never to miss its target, which was made for him by the dwarves—the sons of Ivaldi—and given as a gift to the Æsir when Loki went to see them for new hair for Thor's wife Sif.

Heimdall: The gate-guard of Asgard, Heimdall has gold teeth and a historical feud with Loki. He is supposed to have immensely keen vision, and a horn that can be heard across the nine worlds. In the Norse myth way of balancing things, he is Loki's counterpart, and the two are supposed to kill each other at Ragnarok. Heimdall is given the credit for setting up the order of men, determining (by birth) if they should be noblemen, farmers, or slaves. It seemed a good reason to make him a villain.

Hel: The name applies to both the kingdom and the queen-goddess of the dead. Hel is supposed to be a daughter of Loki and

Angbroda. She is half black and half white, and gets all the dead who do not die in combat.

Helblindi: "Helblind." One of the many names for Odin. Also listed in one source as a brother of Loki.

Hœnir: The one-time companion of Odin, who is supposed to have actually been the one to give life to the first humans, Ask and Embla, who were tree-trunks before that. One of the two hostages sent by the Æsir to dwell among the Vanir. His fellow hostage Mirmir got his head chopped off because Hœnir couldn't say a word without asking Mirmir first.

Hrímner: "Frosty." A giant.

Hugin: "Thought." One of Odin's two ravens, who fly around spying for the boss.

Idun: A goddess. The wife of the god of poetry, Bragi. The custodian of the apple of youth and supposedly as fair as spring. Her apples are purported to restore youth and health. In return for his freedom, Loki once lured her outside of Asgard and into the clutches of the giant Thjazi (the father of Skadi). Eventually Loki is prevailed upon to rescue her, which he does in falcon form, transforming Idun into a nut and carrying her in his claws. The pursuing Thjazi is killed. In the Lokasenna, Loki accuses Idun of having sex with her brother's killer.

Jörmungand: The Midgard Serpent. A dragon, supposedly the child of Loki and Angbroda, whom Odin cast into the sea, where it grew so large that it encircled the world.

Jötunheim: The home of giants in Utgard.

Kvasir's mead: Also called the mead of inspiration, brewed with honey mixed with the blood of the vastly wise Kvasir—a man created by the mixed spittle of the Æsir and Vanir, who was murdered by two dwarves. The brew thus created gave such cunning to the tongues of the dwarves that they were able to trick a giant and his wife into being murdered too. There their luck ran out because the giant's son, Suttung, came along and marooned them on a rock. In exchange for their liberty and survival, the mead changed hands. Suttung kept it under tight guard by his daughter, in a locked cave, but Odin gained entry to the place, seduced the daughter and stole the mead. (You don't want to know the details. It's too gross for modern tastes. The mead would be too.)

Loki: Loki is one of the most confusing figures in all of Norse myth. It is apparent that both his role and popularity changed with the passage of time, with his final demonization occurring in the thirteenth century when Snorri Sturluson in his collation of myth (in which he did some sterling work—and also took some large liberties) used Loki as the chief bad guy to blame for everything. Snorri was collecting myths in Iceland, where Christianity had been the religion for a few centuries.

Some things are certain about Loki. First, he was a trickster. Second, he was as much at home among the giants as among the Æsir. Third, although his frequently thoughtless mischief plunged him and the Æsir into trouble, he never failed to extricate them from it. He got precious little thanks for the latter, despite his role in saving Freyja (twice) and his role in recovering Thor's hammer, or the treasures of the Æsir.

Loki differs from the bulk of the Æsir in a couple of notable ways. For one, he is one of the giants and never claimed to be anything else. For a second he is referred to in matrilineal terms as "Son of Laufey" (Laufey = leafy, his mother's name) which is in direct contrast to normal Norse tradition. Third, it appears that Norse society (in contrast to the Ancient Greeks of *Pyramid Scheme*) was homophobic. Loki, by being the mare that lured the giant builder's stallion away (so that the Æsir did not have to pay the giant) "played a woman's part" and gave birth to the horse Sleipnir, whom Odin seems to have had no moral qualms about appropriating. The origins of his name have been associated with both fire (logi) and air (loft).

Minni-toast: The toast to the dead. The last toast drunk in the evening.

Mjöllnir: "Lightning." Thor's hammer, created by the dwarf Sindri, one of the sons of Ivaldi. It would never miss and never fail to find its way back to his hand.

Munin: "Memory." Odin's other raven spy.

Myrkvid: Mirkwood. A lot of Tolkien is drawn from Norse sources. The forest that borders Muspellheim dividing it from Midgard.

Naglfar: The corpse-ship. Made from the nails of the dead, it will carry the dead from Hel to Ragnarok.

Nágrind: "Corpse-gate." The entry to Hel's kingdom.

Njörd: One of the Vanir hostages. Chosen as a bridegroom (on the basis of his feet) by the giantess Skadi, in recompense for the Æsir killing her father. He is a sea divinity, which makes the kenning from Loki's flyting make sense. "The daughters of the giant Hymir use his mouth as a pisspot." Hymir being a mountain giant, his "daughters" are the rivers off that mountain, which then empty into the sea. His relationship with Skadi produced Frey and Freyja, but considerable marital discord, as Skadi wanted to live in the mountains in her father's castle, and Njörd wanted to live in his seaside home. In theory they settled for a week in each, but the relations frayed and they went back to separate lives. Skadi is later cited as one of Odin's bits of fluff on the side.

Norns: Three women—Urd (past), Verdani (present), and Skuld (future, or literally "debt")—who chart the destiny of all of mankind. Found hanging out at Urd's well, at the foot of the world tree.

Odin: Generally considered the top god in Norse mythology. He is also a serial adulterer, oathbreaker, thief, liar and self-serving creep. Sometimes known as "evil-worker." Odin's character can scarcely be described as reliable. He is obsessed with the collection of knowledge, which to the biased observer looks like "how do I preserve number one?" If this incidentally involves the safekeeping of Asgard, that's a good reason to do very nearly anything. Known for traveling among men in his wide hat and blue cloak, the one-eyed wanderer has misled many to their doom, and helped others whom, as Loki points out in the Lokasenna, one can see no justification for helping. Odin claims the reasons for his lies, adultery and murderous "help" are beyond the understanding of ordinary gods. It's for their benefit, really. Among Odin's varied deeds include his spending nine days hanging from Yggdrasil with the dead sacrifices, to learn the runes, giving one eye for a drink from Mirmir's well (supposed to confer wisdom), and also seducing the giantess Gunnlöd to get the mead of poetry. He is accompanied by two ravens and keeps two wolves to feed on his table scraps.

Öku-Thor: "Charioteer Thor."

Ragnarok: "Fate of the Gods." The final battle that will destroy the world.

Ran: A sea giantess in charge of the drowning department. It was she who helped Loki with the net that the Æsir used to capture Andvari to pay the blood-price for accidentally killing Otr.

Ratatosk: The squirrel that lives in the world-tree Yggdrasil, and carries little messages of spite and hatred between the eagle at the top and the serpent at the bottom. As he says: it's a job.

Roskva: The sister to Thjalfi and serving maid to Thor.

Seid: A kind of magic, not very savory but very powerful, which only women and Odin are allowed to practice.

Sif: Thor's wife. Shorn one night of her blond hair by Loki in an act that looks very suspiciously like payback for sexual coquetry (Sif also played the field a bit), Thor then forced Loki to do something about it. He went to the Sons of Ivaldi (dwarf artificers) and had real gold made into hair that actually grew on her head.

Sigfrida: A Valkyrie trapped behind the ring of fire for angering Odin and not choosing for death those he wanted ... in part of a Norse saga. The next bit is lost and then the name seems to be Brynhild. It's all very confusing. Maybe there was a selection of Valkyries.

Sigurd: A hero who at the instigation of the dwarf Reginn killed Reginn's shape-changing brother, the dragon Fafnir. From the hoard of the dragon, Sigurd took various treasures, among them the cursed ring of Andvari. It was Sigurd's horse that jumped the ring of flames protecting the Valkyrie Brynhild/ Sigfrida sleeping within. Sigurd is supposed to have woken her before going off to make a complete mess of his life and hers, thanks to the cursed ring.

Sigyn: "Victorious girlfriend." The wife of Loki and a goddess in her own right. Mother of two children by Loki, both abused by Odin to punish Loki. Váli was turned into a rabid wolf to kill his brother Narfi, whose entrails were then used to bind Loki. The epitome of loyalty in a mythology not known for it, Sigyn shields her husband from the venom of Skadi's snake.

Skadi: Giantess daughter of Thjazi, estranged wife of Njörd. She is a patron of hunters and also seems to have slept with Loki and later Odin. It is she who hangs the snake that spits at the captive Loki.

Skírnir: The rather shifty and unpleasant servant of the god Frey who acts as a threatening go-between for the light of Frey's fancy, the giantess Gerd. He also ran errands for Odin, notably fetching Gleipnir, the chain that eventually bound Fenrir.

Sleipnir: Odin's eight-legged horse. The offspring of Loki in the form of a mare.

Surt: "Black." The fire demon from the flaming South.

Svarthöfdi: "Black head." The father of all sorcerers.

Tanngnjóst: "Tooth gnasher." Thor's magical goat that draws his chariot. He can slaughter them and eat them at night, and reanimate them from the bones.

Tanngrisnir: "Tooth gritter." The other goat.

Thjalfi: Thor's bondsman, taken in exchange for cracking one of the goat's bones at the evening goat barbeque. This was absolutely forbidden as the goat was then reanimated with a broken limb.

Thor: The thunder-god was the son of Odin and the giantess Jörd. He was the mightiest warrior and strongest of the Æsir. He has a belt of strength, Megingjörd, that doubles his already formidable strength, iron gauntlets and the famous thunderbolt hammer. Very popular among warriors, less so among nobles; rival armies would often dedicate themselves to one or the other god. Not subtle or of any great intelligence, Thor was still the second greatest of the Æsir. Married to Sif of the golden hair and the father of three children: Modi, Magni, and Thrúd.

Thrúd: "Power." Thor's daughter.

Thrúdvangar: The power plains; lands belonging to the god Thor.

Ull: The archer god.

Valhöll: "The hall of the fallen." More commonly known in its English spelling of Valhalla. Odin's hall where fully half of the warriors slain in battle feast and fight and wait to serve Odin in the final conflict.

Vidólf : The mother all witches.

Vrigid Plain: The plain on which the great battle of Ragnarok will take place.

Yggdrasil: The world tree, an ash, whose branches extend over the whole world and whose roots go down to the deepest part. It is big enough for stags to feed on its branches.

೮೦   ೮೦   ೮೦

From *Pyramid Scheme*:

Arachne: Daughter of Idmon of Colophon (a city in Lydia), a weaver of great renown, who had a run-in with Athena. In the weaving competition between them, Arachne wove as her theme the philandering and sordid tricks of the gods. Her weaving was flawless. Athena with the justice, generosity, and nobility of spirit which was characteristic of the Olympians tore the work in shreds, destroyed the loom and turned Arachne into a spider, doomed to weave forever, and draw her thread from her own body. A good loser, Athena.

Bes: A dwarf-god, the protector of man against evil spirits and dangerous beasts. He is always portrayed grinning and bearded, with a topknot adorned with ostrich plumes and a leopard-skin cloak. Fond of fighting and dancing, his symbol was used to protect against dangerous beasts, and evil spirits that haunted dreams. He presided over marriages, and the make-up and adornment of women, as well as protecting pregnant mothers. Revered in Punt and Carthage as well as Egypt, the little hell-raiser was definitely one of the good guys.

Bitar and Smitar: Two winged dragons from Colchis.

Circe: The sorceress from the Odyssey. The daughter of Helios and sister to Aeëtes, and aunt to Medea. She lived on the island of Aeaea, attended by four nymphs, in a house or castle of well-built stone. In the glades around the castle roamed wild beasts, boar, wolves, leopards and lions—all apparently tame.

Medea: One of the most villainous characters described in Greek mythology. Medea the sorceress was a princess and priestess of Hecate, living in the kingdom of Colchis (on the Black Sea, present day Georgia). She fell in love with Jason, leader of the Argonauts and it was only with her help that Jason was able to accomplish the "impossible" tasks set by Aeëtes,

King of Colchis, and gain the golden fleece. In return Jason promised to marry her. In their flight from Colchis, Medea and Jason were trapped by Absyrtus, Medea's stepbrother. Under the flag of truce Medea and Jason murdered Absyrtus, and in their subsequent flight delayed Aeëtes by casting the pieces behind them for the king to gather up for burial. On their route back to Hellas, Medea and Jason stop at Aeaea, the isle of the enchantress Circe, who is Medea's aunt and sister to king Aeëtes. Circe gives them forgiveness for the blood-debt. On their return, Medea is supposed to have contrived the murder of King Pelias by his daughters (by convincing them that the aging king could be restored to youth by chopping him up and boiling him with certain herbs). After living for some time with Jason at Ephyra, and bearing him two children, she is told by Jason that he is going to set her aside and marry Glauce, the daughter of the king of Corinth. This is perfectly permissible as she is a non-Hellene and has no rights. Medea is then supposed to have contrived the death of Glauce (with a dress of gold cloth and a coronet), accidentally killing her father too. Medea is then supposed to have killed her children and fled Corinth in a winged chariot drawn by dragons.

Throttler: The name of the Theban sphinx.

Tyche: The goddess of chance. Her attribute is abundance, and she is the daughter of Oceanus and Tethys. One is prompted to wonder if this is why fishing and luck should go hand-in-hand.